18 Lies
and 3 Truths

NARRATIVE LIBRARY

18 Lies
and 3 Truths

GREAT AMERICAN FICTION AND NONFICTION

THE 2007 STORYQUARTERLY
ANNUAL EDITED BY TOM JENKS,
WITH CAROL EDGARIAN AND M. M. M. HAYES

The *Narrative* Magazine 2007 StoryQuarterly Annual
December 2007

A first edition from Narrative Press

Copyright 2007 *Narrative* Magazine, Inc.

ISBN 978-0-9798727-1-6

Narrative Magazine, Inc. is a registered 501 (c)(3) nonprofit organization.
WWW.NARRATIVEMAGAZINE.COM

Please direct any questions or comments to
LiteraryEditor@NarrativeMagazine.com.

CONTENTS

Introduction

THIS YEAR'S *STORYQUARTERLY ANNUAL* features stories by an all-star cast of great contemporary authors who have appeared in *SQ* across its three-decade history, as well as stories by some of today's best up-and-coming authors. For our readers who are also writers, we have included a special nonfiction section with pieces about the art of writing and the writing life by three of our longtime favorite authors, known for their teaching as well as their writing. The book in your hand thus represents both a remarkable summation of *SQ*'s heritage and an illustrious new beginning for the magazine.

Long recognized for its dedication to new writers, *SQ* recently transformed itself from a prodigious once-a-year publication with a small audience to an online magazine updated throughout the year with new works, available worldwide 24/7, now enjoyed by tens of thousands of readers. As a result of this shift to Internet publishing, we decided to make the 2007 *Annual* a somewhat slimmer volume than it's been in past years and to offer it as a companion to *SQ* online rather than as a reproduction of it. Traditionally the *Annual* contained new stories selected from thousands of manuscripts received earlier in the year during a submission period that was several months long. This year *SQ* opened its submission period year-round and began publishing issues online, so instead of simply repeating what *SQ* has already published this year, the 2007 *Annual* features a strong mix of previously unpublished works and of carefully chosen reprints drawn from *SQ* and other quality publications. Indeed, no other annual currently offers the range and depth of literary art, complete with an insider's view, that we've provided here.

The 2007 *Annual* contains a selection of best stories by well-known writers published in past issues of *SQ*, including Jhumpa Lahiri's first published short story, Lorrie Moore's second published story, and early stories—all excellent—by Richard Bausch, T. Coraghessan Boyle, Janet Burroway, Robert Olen Butler, Joyce Carol Oates, and Lore Segal. Widely esteemed authors Alice Hoffman, Charles Johnson, X. J. Kennedy, and *SQ* founding editor Pamela Painter headline our lineup of new works, which also features stories by a roster of talented, must-read newer writers: Kevin Brockmeier, Elea Carey, Tessa Mellas, Hannah Pittard, Hasanthika Sirisena, and Don Waters. Additionally, three contemporary greats, Rick Bass, Robert Olen Butler, and Gail Godwin, have contributed new nonfiction pieces that offer inspiration and insights to the writers in our audience.

Twenty-one wonderful pieces are gathered here by the grace of the writers who sent their works to *SQ;* by the unstinting efforts of the magazine's editors and staff, past and present; by the support of the friends and patrons of both *SQ* and its publisher, *Narrative* Magazine; and finally by the interest and enthusiasm of readers like you, who believe in the value of good writing and stories, in all times and in all places.

We dedicate the 2007 *SQ Annual* to the future of literature in the digital age.

Oh, and about the title: It's a commonly acknowledged truth that sometimes you have to lie to get to the truth. Enjoy!

—CAROL EDGARIAN AND TOM JENKS

FICTION

Byron the Lyron

A STORY

by Richard Bausch

Richard Bausch's ten novels and six collections of stories include *Take Me Back, The Stories of Richard Bausch,* and *Thanksgiving Night.* His work has been included in O. Henry Award's *Best American Short Stories* and *New Stories from the South.* He was awarded the 2005 PEN/Bernard Malamud Award for Excellence in the Short Story and has also received the Academy of Arts and Letters Award in Literature. A devoted teacher, Bausch is a chaired professor of English at the University of Memphis.

SHE WAS EIGHTY-FOUR and had lived a long, rich life, and she told her one son, Byron, that she was ready. Byron Mailley wept, putting his head down on her shoulder. Georgia's shoulder.

They were in her hospital room—the hospital wing of Brighton Creek Farm, the assisted living facility she had resided in over the last decade. She patted the back of his head. That had always been her most charming gesture of affection toward him—since he was nine or ten and learning the complications of being a bookish boy on a street full of rough characters. Her name for them. She had a way of setting all his problems in terms of the books they read together in the evenings, because he couldn't sleep. The books were all adventure: Hardy Boys, and Nancy Drew, Robert Louis Stevenson, Theodore J. Waldek's book *Lions on the Hunt,* written from the point of view of the young lion. Byron the lyron, Georgia called him. It was their little joke, just between them. Byron the lyron had night terrors, panic attacks.

Fears of cancer, fears of madness, split personality, delusions, polio, tuberculosis, the atomic bomb, the death of parents. His father gone—first with the military, flying jets, then just gone. Remarried far away. Far away was good, actually, because Father had wanted Byron to be tough, and had worked to accomplish it: a drill-like discipline early; its looming displeased powerful presence early. Byron tried hard, and couldn't make the grade, as Father put it. There were fights between Georgia and the old man about the boy. The old man was gone but the panics started not long after he left.

Night was a terrible prospect. He'd sit crying, nine years old, and she, pregnant with the child she would lose, her husband gone away, sat up with Byron, patiently holding him, humming to him, patting the back of his head; then, on into the next year, the terrors recurring, and it was really just the two of them for good (her words). And she'd read other things to him: Dickens, the Bible—laughing and making fun of all the begots, and scoffing at the heavy seriousness. Language is fun, she told him. Play.

Let's play.

He had always felt that she was more friend than mother.

N OW HE WEPT, and she patted his head and murmured, "Stop. Stop."

So he stopped. Brave girl, he thought. But kept still.

"Tell me what happened," she said.

She meant this about Reese. "I'm not crying about Reese," he told her. But partly he was. The look in his own eyes, he knew, admitted it. She patted the side of his face.

"Just tell me."

He kissed her hand, and held it. "Georgia," he murmured. "What will I do?"

"Tell me about Reese."

Last week, after twelve years, Reese had announced tearfully that he was leaving—this just two days past a big surprise party, Byron's forty-fifth birthday. He'd invited everyone Byron knew, going back to his school days. Even Ms. Evelyn Wasson, his seventh-grade teacher showed up to read a wonderful tribute she had written about her certainty that Byron Mailley would make something of himself. Such a bright, look-right-at-you little boy, she said, with her endearing habit of using hyphenated expressions in her talk. She went on about Byron, talking about his work as a magazine photographer, his time in Rome, in his twenties, sending her postcards and pictures he had taken of the magnificent places and the wonderful people he had come to know. Reese stood there proudly, smiling during it all. He'd arranged everything. He led the applause and offered a toast to Byron for his generosity and his goodness. Nobody more kindly than Byron, taking Reese in at such a time in his life, offering love, nurture, tolerating his nightmares, his neuroses, his failures of love and sensibility. A true artist, Byron. Not Reese—who was in fact a fairly successful painter. But about whom, indeed, the flat statement he uttered next happened to be true: "My work is bunk," Reese, who couldn't really believe that, said. One lie leads to another. Reese said uncharacteristically self-deprecating things all night, praising Byron. He had put together an elegant panel show of some of Byron's photographs; and during the celebration several people rose to read from Byron's poems. They were political verses, clever, funny. Light verse. Byron liked the sensibility of the original, Lord Byron, with his insistence that poetry was just something occupational and fun.

His mother, ill, failing, already in the hospital wing, couldn't be there, but Reese made a tape, and took it over there the next morning and played it for her. She was listening to it when Byron came to see her that evening, not twenty minutes past the revelation, delivered in the upstairs hallway of the house, in a weepy sorrowful voice by Reese, that he must find his way alone for a time, and was leaving. Byron had been an emotional nursemaid all these years, surely Byron could see this, and Reese would never reach any kind of autonomy if he stayed any longer. "We can be friends," Reese said. "I so want that, Byron."

Byron suspected there must be someone else for Reese, now, though it was true that Byron had done plenty of nurse-maiding from the beginning. Reese had been Georgia's physical therapist; that was how they had met—Reese, a young artist, working for Blue Ridge Orthopedic Clinic to make enough money to put food on the table, had worked with Georgia after her knee replacement surgery, and Georgia had introduced him to Byron. Reese came over to see Georgia and to work with her, and then it was just visiting. They made each other laugh. Reese was sad a lot of the time and had other troubles, mostly having to do with confidence in his work, and confidence in general. There was a neediness in him, about which he often teased. It was charming, though like most teasing it hinted at the truth. Byron and Reese began going to see Georgia together, and everything went quite naturally to the next stage. They had lived together quite happily, it seemed to Byron, but then Reese had begun to do well enough with his painting to quit the physio-therapy, and there were, Byron had to admit, subtle changes.

The kindest way of seeing this now was that Reese was being honest in his own self-deluding way; he had depended on Byron so long, and now wanted to strike out on his own. Byron chose to look at it this way, suffering with quiet dignity through the whole thing, while also going through the anguish of his mother's last illness. He was by nature kindly, and this is not to say that kindness came easily to him: as we all know, kindliness is work. It was in all the details of his lived life. Perhaps Reese felt the necessity of the big surprise party and the tributes to salve his conscience for what he knew he was already in the process of doing. But the hundred-twenty townspeople who came to the party wanted to honor Byron. They all loved him, and for good reason.

Georgia reminded him of this, looking at him now, her still-dark hair spread so lovely on the pillow. "You know you could never hide anything from me. It hurts when someone leaves you. I felt it too, you know."

"I don't want to talk about Reese anymore," Byron said. "Let's talk about something else.

"Reese was here, earlier."

"Well, he's moving out."

"He wants to come see me tomorrow."

Byron shrugged. "I guess that's between the two of you."

"Tell me about your party," she said. "The good parts."

But she was drugged, and the drowse began to work in her. And he felt uncomfortably sullen, because she had talked so casually about Reese coming to see her. He spoke half-heartedly about Mrs. Wasson and her memory of him, writing to her from Rome. Try as she might—and she did try—Georgia's lids grew heavy; they closed and opened in that sluggish way, the eyes glazing over. Feeling the pressure to bring it up anyway, Byron went on to say that Reese had planned the party and seemed very happy doing that—deciding on the guest list, on the way it would all go. He drove a hundred miles west and south, to the Tennessee line, and bought five hundred dollars' worth of fireworks, using his own savings account. Byron, seeing how much he apparently needed this, let him have his way about it. It was not in Byron's makeup to seek this kind of thing. He liked a party; he was gregarious, and—people talked about it—he had wonderful ability as a raconteur and storyteller, could do any accent in the world, and would do so, telling a joke, so that the experience of it was positively dramatic. But in truth, he was also rather self-effacing. He had known so many punk jerks parading themselves during his time in Rome, and New York. All those years hustling photographs. His strongest sense of how life ought to be lived had always involved the old idea that one didn't let the right hand know what the left was doing. One was generous without considerations about who might know it. No telling how much can be accomplished if we don't care who gets the credit. Byron had performed all sorts of kindnesses, the source of which the recipients of those kindnesses never knew. No one ever knew. Not even Georgia, who knew most everything else.

SHE SLEPT NOW. He adjusted the blanket across her slowly rising-and-falling chest, kissed her cheek softly, and stood there weeping silently for a time. Then he moved to the door and out. It would be soon, the doctors all said. A week, two weeks. The heart was so tired; it was giving out slowly. Byron went to the nurse's station and reiterated that he wished to be called if there was the slightest change. Each of the last five nights, he had left Georgia sleeping peacefully. She claimed no night-mares, no frights. It was all right. He held her hand and she went in and out of sleep, and when they talked it was nearly as it always had been—her interest in the world hadn't flagged a bit.

Outside, in the chill of early March, he walked to the car and got in. The street was windy; the traffic light wavered and threw its red light on the walls of the buildings at the first intersection. Byron drove there and waited for the light to change. The street looked empty, and the emptiness of it seemed itself a kind of anguish coming at him, not for himself, but for Georgia, lying alone in that room in the coming night. He turned around in the middle of the intersection, drove back to the parking lot, and hurried into the building. At the nurse's station the woman gave him a look. A past-visiting-hours look. He nodded at her and went on to Georgia's room, and took his chair.

THE NIGHT OF THE PARTY the fireworks went off into the trees, and there were hurrahs and shouts of excitement, and everyone had such a good time. Byron talked to Georgia from the bedroom telephone, and she sounded so chipper, so happy for him. He heard the weakness, and the slight breathlessness, but she had her wits about her, in spite of the medicine, thinking to ask if his next-door neighbor, Mrs. Ewing, had brought her dog with her to the party—Mrs. Ewing being one of those people who treated her dogs and cats better than she ever treated any human being, including her own daughter, Marvina, who was a good friend of Georgia's, and Byron's.

Eight years ago, the three of them had gone to Rome on one of Georgia's whims. She had lived there briefly when she went to Europe before the war, and she said she wanted to be in the city with Byron, to see where he had lived and walked and been happy. One of her dearest friends was an opera singer who lived near the Pantheon. They all sat out on the Piazza Navona, drinking Campari and soda, and the opera singer, whom she called Umberto, broke into an aria, drunk and happy, leaning toward Georgia as if to serenade her. He was a big, florid man, who kept say-ing when will you come live here with me. It was all joking, because Umberto already had a companion, named Pietro, who had lost a leg in the war, and served as his personal secretary. Georgia kept saying that she wished Reese had been able to make the journey—but Reese was recovering from shoulder surgery.

Over the years, Byron often thought of returning to the ancient city, and he would trouble Georgia about it, believing that she was settling too well at Brighton Creek Farm. She knew this of course, and she would say "I'm happy. Really. I can go anywhere, just closing my eyes."

Marvina also talked about Rome, and she had done so more often recently, because her mother had shown up to take over her house, wresting it from the daughter in an act of pretended salvage, telling everyone that it was necessary because of Marvina's lack of practical skills. Marvina had been quite funny about all this to Georgia, and they both imparted some of it to Byron. There had been times when they all talked about Mrs. Ewing. Even Reese, who hated gossip—even the positive kind, and in fact seldom talked very interestedly about anyone but himself. It was something people tolerated because he could be funny, and at times his very vanity was comical.

He could be appallingly self-absorbed, and he had a way of supposing that, because he was an artist, people would understand. Perhaps for a Picasso, people would. But Reese was no Picasso—his paintings were all of boating scenes, harbors in sunset light, sailboats on a lake, reflections on the surface, houses at lakesides with little docks at the ends of the lawns, beach houses and white sand and fishing trawlers off ocean shores. About Mrs. Ewing, Reese was cruel, in fact. There wasn't anything funny or catty in it. It was serious and rather brutal. Mrs. Ewing represented all the evils of respectability, Reese said. He reserved this part of his opinion of her for Byron, who tried to argue that she was a product of her time and place, a little dull, perhaps, and even someone about whom one could make a joke, but she wasn't evil—certainly not deserving of the invective with which Reese spoke of her. Byron wondered, sitting in the chair by his mother's hospital bed, what, in other circumstances, Reese might have found to say about Georgia, who had come from her time and place. But Reese had been devoted to her, all these years, and she was one of the few people who could bring him out of himself. Byron recognized the thought as unworthy: his erstwhile companion would never criticize her for anything.

HE STAYED IN HER ROOM until well past midnight. She slept, breathing easily, perfectly still, no slightest stress in her features. He nodded off, and shook himself awake; it happened several times. When he went home at last, he couldn't sleep. Reese had come in and taken most of his things. A row of his paintings leaned against the downstairs wall, with a note attached: he'd be by to pick this up in the morning. There were a few items of furniture, a few books, some bric-a-brac. It had always been Byron who did most of the collecting of things. Reese never kept many books; yet the empty places in the shelves showed.

The lights were on next door at the Ewings's, so Byron went out and walked the sidewalk in front of the two houses. A clear, cold night, with a moon and moon-shadows everywhere. If Marvina wanted company, she would see him and come to the door. This was how they had navigated socializing since Mrs. Ewing had moved into the house. Marvina had never been one to keep regular hours and was often awake all night. She liked to sleep in, and often took naps in the middle of the after-noons. Alma had attempted to put a stop to all that. Like most people concerned heavily with morality in others, Alma believed that early to bed early to rise was the most healthy way of living. Tonight Marvina was up—he could hear music—but she didn't come to the door, and finally he went back into his own house, and into bed. He could still hear her music—the Rolling Stones, and she was probably playing it loud to annoy her mother. Perhaps it was partly the music that kept him awake.

EARLY NEXT MORNING, he heard Reese downstairs, collecting the last of the paintings, and realized that there were two voices. Byron buried his face in his pillows and tried not to hear anything, his heart hurting so badly he wondered if he were not having a coronary: how physical heartbreak was! He would never have believed it. He thought he had felt it before; but this was completely and awfully new. The rattling downstairs took a very long, bad time, but at last it ended. He took the pillow away, got up, slowly, rubbing his chest, and walked downstairs. Paintings gone. The house to himself. He sat at the kitchen table, with a cup of coffee, and wept quietly.

Marvina walked over perhaps an hour later to ask if there was anything she could do. He'd showered, shaved, and dressed, and he felt slightly better. It was just itself, the same pure pressure under the heart, the same band of deep aching. He had gathered some of the cards and letters that had come from Georgia's far-flung friendships—many of these people were bedridden themselves, or housebound. They ranged as far away as India, and as close as next door (Marvina).

She wanted to bring something for Georgia to read. She was also contemplating a basket of fruit—Georgia had always loved Bosque pears, and they were particularly good now. But then she also had no appetite to speak of.

"What do you think?" Marvina asked.

"How late were you up last night?" Byron asked her.

She thought a moment. "1 took a pill and went to sleep."

"Your music was on late."

"Did it keep you up? I meant it to keep Alma up."

Byron smiled. "Did it?"

"Alma's sleeping late," Marvina said.

They smiled. He was astonished that he could smile. It rose up in him like a breath, and he could feel it traveling along his nerves.

THEY WENT TOGETHER to the small grocery store down the street. Marvina drove. They bought several pears, some apples and Clementines. She found a small straw basket in the little boutique next to the grocery. She bought it, and a linen cloth which she folded over the fruit. It looked enough like a gift basket. Georgia liked things homemade, this way. For her, always, something that took time to make was much more valuable and fine as a gift. Every year in early fall she began fashioning the things she would give for Christmas: knitted mittens and scarves, calendars she had made out of old photographs, cards with cutout trees on them, decorated frames, corkboards. Every gift had something of the person it was intended for— a theme or a special flavor reflecting her feeling for that person.

"She'll like the smell of the Clementines," Byron said.

"Some flowers?" Marvina frowned. "No."

They said little for the drive over. It was bright, chilly, windless; the little puffs of scattered cloud seemed utterly motionless in the wide, pure blue. At the hospital she got out first. Byron carried the basket of fruit. In the room, they found Reese sitting with Georgia, who was asleep.

"She hasn't waked yet," Reese said. His eyes were rounded with shadow. He didn't look at Byron, or at Marvina. Byron moved around Georgia's bed and took her hand. It was warm. He squeezed it. There was the slightest squeezing back. Perhaps he had imagined it.

"Tell her I was here?" Reese said, looking sorrowful.

Byron nodded at him. Marvina and Reese went out, then, and he was alone with Georgia, and the basket of fruit, in this room that was so institutional and clean, with its dull art and its cheerful paint and its television. He went around to the chair and sat down, but the chair was still warm from Reese. He stood again, reached over and took his mother's other hand, and she opened her eyes.

"It's hard on poor Reese," she said. "I think he's confused."

"You were awake."

"For some of it. Some. He didn't know." She squeezed his hand. "He just sits there looking at me and trying not to cry. I didn't let him know I saw."

"I think he has someone else," Byron said.

She squeezed his hand again. "Maybe not."

Byron told her about the two voices he had heard.

"Could be a friend."

"I don't understand him," Byron said. "Does he not know I'd tell you he left me?"

She shook her head, but didn't speak. A moment passed, in which he thought she might have gone back to sleep. Then: "I'm so tired, son."

He sat down again, still holding her hand. "Marvina drove me over here. We brought you some fruit."

The little squeeze, again. He began to have to fight tears. He had so wanted to be cheerful, to get Marvina talking and gossiping about her mother. Georgia would like the idea of Alma Ewing sleeping late, having been kept up with Hot Rocks playing at volume. The dogs and cats would feel neglected. But Alma Ewing would never give the satisfaction, as she saw it, of ever letting Marvina know that Marvina was getting to her. Alma Ewing was too proud for anger, or any display of temper.

After a time, when it was clear that Georgia was sleeping again, very gently he took his hand away and went to the door of the room. At the far end of the hall, two nurses stood talking. There was no sign of Marvina or Reese. He went back into the room and sat down, and took Georgia's hand once more. Just in time. She turned slightly, and looked at him.

"I smell Clementines," she said, and smiled.

He reached for the basket, but when he turned back around, she had gone back to sleep. He ate a pear, and waited, and began quietly to cry again, the tears running down his cheeks. When he heard Marvina talking to one of the nurses, he slipped into Georgia's little bathroom and ran water over his face, wiped his eyes, dried himself with one of those brown paper towels. His nose was running, like a kid's, with crying.

In the room, Marvina had opened the curtains wider to let in more sun. Georgia was still asleep.

"Reese is a mess," Marvina said.

"I don't want to talk about him," Byron said. "Really, Marvina." He offered her the chair, and she declined, standing there looking over the fruit, picking up a pear and setting it back, finally settling on a Clementine. When she opened it, the fragrance went all over the room. A nurse brought another chair, Marvina having apparently asked for it earlier. Byron thought of these humble practical arrangements in a kind of nightmarish light, as if their very ordinariness were a flaunting of the awful facts, the plain objective world brandishing itself at him, while his mother slipped away forever.

GEORGIA SUSAN MICHAEL Townsend Mailley. The Michael was there at her father's insistence, after his younger brother, who was killed at the Marne River in 1918. A picture of this young soldier hung on the wall in her parents' house all their lives. Soft features, round eyes, small straight mouth—an innocent, intelligent face. Hard to imagine him being shot in the neck, bleeding to death on a barbed-wire fence in the rain and sludge of a terrible May morning all those years ago. Georgia had kept the picture on the foyer wall of her own house for most of Byron's growing up. It had lain in a box of her things for the years she lived at Brighton Creek Farm. Byron, according to his grandfather, favored the long-dead uncle. Georgia had resisted the name for him, incurring her father's wrath. As she had often done. Headstrong, willful, stubborn—all these terms her father used to describe his one daughter. He would talk about how she had confounded him at every turn—in fact, he had taken it upon himself to warn others about the difficulties of raising a daughter. He would call friends when their wives had children, to congratulate them if they had sons, and to commiserate with them if they had daughters.

Georgia married young, and then left that marriage after only a period of weeks; the fellow reminded her too much, she said, of her father—it was her father, though, who had it annulled. And in fact his frustrations with her over the years were tinged with admiration, no matter how dismayed he seemed. Georgia had done more in the world than all the sons of his friends and associates. After the marriage episode, which took place her last year of high school, she went on to Radcliffe, graduated early, then traveled to live in Europe. She didn't return until just before the out-break of hostilities in 1939. One of her favorite stories was how, in June of 1938, working for a foreign press service as a secretary and occasional feature writer, she had climbed partway up a lamppost to set eyes upon Adolf Hitler himself, a ridiculous-looking little Chaplinesque man standing in the back of a big black automobile with one hand up in that farcical salute. She was later ejected from a café for imitating the Führer's stance. She would laugh, telling the story. "I was young, you know. Only twenty or so."

Byron got his storytelling ability from her. He'd gotten the adventuresome, generous spirit, too—though he would never attribute this kind of thing to himself. Others, who knew them both, did. Georgia was her own country, some said, meaning it as the highest praise. An empire, was Georgia, with her several careers, her loves and tumultuous friendships and loyalties. No one ever left her willingly except one—the second husband. The military man. He had flown for the Air Corps over Germany, and after the war he flew for the airlines, three years of that before re-enlisting. He was a retired Colonel somewhere out west, the last Byron heard, with a fourth wife and a pair of young twins. Probably ramrod straight, those twins, Georgia would say. She had outlived so many of her friends and companions, most of whom were older than she had been. There was something about her that drew people to her, from her earliest life. Who could imagine a girl nineteen years old traveling alone, employed by a wire service, to write about conditions in the new Germany? But she had done that. She had also been in plays off-Broadway, and written a memoir that was published, about life in England just after the war—the rebuilding of London. And when she had Byron, from the Air Corps chap, as she called him, she settled in this little Virginia town to raise her son, her family. She thought she would have more children—hoped for half a dozen, anyway. But things changed rapidly: hostilities in Korea—and at home—caused her husband to go away, and she lost the second child unexpectedly, at almost eight months. Byron had memories of the long night when that happened, pacing in the too-brightly lit waiting room with his grandfather and several friends from the library where she had gone to work. He would never forget the look of fright on his grandfather's face. "I'm afraid we're going to lose her," the old man said.

H OW STRANGE TO THINK of that now. He held her hand, and wept a little more, trying to keep it from Marvina, who ate another pear and then called her mother to wake her. That was the announced purpose of the call, and she said it to please Georgia, who had opened her eyes long enough to nod and smile.

"No answer," Marvina said.

"Poor woman," said Georgia.

A little later, she asked Byron for a piece of paper. It hurt to talk. She signaled that her throat was sore and dry. Marvina got her some water, and she sipped it carefully, seemed to hold it a long time in her mouth. Byron was afraid she might pass out with it still there, and choke. But she swallowed it, and then wrote on the paper: Byron, I'm dying. He looked at it, and then at her face, with that strange peaceful smile. She wrote again: For a Clementine.

Marvina, reading over his shoulder, sobbed and said, "Oh, God. Georgia—if that isn't typical of you." She was laughing and crying at the same time.

"I'm sorry," Georgia said, rasping. "That was mean."

Byron shook his head and helped calm Marvina down. Georgia wrote another note, asking for some music—she had brought with her a complete set of the Sinatra-Dorsey recordings, and Byron put it on for her. She had two songs she especially liked from these years: "I'll Never Smile Again," and "Everything Happens To Me."

They put the music on, and sat listening to it. A nurse came in and worked on the I.V. lines for a time, then asked Byron and Marvina to leave so she could help Georgia go to the bathroom and take a sprits bath. They went together down to the cafeteria and had a cup of coffee. There were several other people there, all looking tired and worried, clearly wishing they could be anywhere else. At one table a pair of young girls sat with an older brother, and they had balloons announcing the birth of a sister. The balloons were tied to the chair in which one of the girls sat. They were eating pastries and ignoring each other.

"Guess I'll call Alma again," Marvina said. "Poor woman."

"Tell me about Reese," said Byron.

She shrugged. "He's confused. Sick at heart. You know how he feels about Georgia. And you."

"He's seeing someone else, Marvina."

"I think he was feeling smothered by everyone's love of you, Byron. No kidding. That's what it sounded like this morning, talking to him. He kept saying he didn't want to compete. He felt awful that we got there while he was visiting Georgia."

"How could he think we wouldn't come to see her?"

"He was leaving—you know."

"I don't want to talk about him."

Again, she shrugged. Then she reached into her purse, brought out her cell phone, and dialed Alma, who answered this time. Alma claimed she'd been up and around, had gone out to the store to buy groceries. She asked how Georgia was.

Marvina told her about the Clementine incident, winking at Byron. The Clementine incident would profoundly disturb Alma, who considered that the occasion called for somber music and long faces. Marvina said this, after disconnecting with Alma, and then seemed to catch herself. "God almighty, what the hell am I saying?" And she began to cry.

They returned upstairs, to find that Georgia was still being attended to. The door was closed. They waited at the nurse's station in the garish light, while people moved around them and past them. An old, old man walked by, slow, pulling his own I.V. apparatus with him. His slippers made a whispery noise, and Byron noted that he could hear the faintest strains of Georgia's music coming from the closed door.

When they were let in at last by the nurse, Georgia was falling asleep again. Movement of any kind, the nurse said, was exhausting for her. She had been a little sick.

"What a lady," the nurse whispered. "You know what she said? She apologized to me for being such a bore. Imagine it."

Byron wanted to embrace her. For a moment they all just stood there, appreciating the small, slender woman in the bed, lying so still, breathing softly, sleeping, it seemed, without dreams.

THAT AFTERNOON, Marvina had to go home for a while, and Byron told her to go on. He'd stay the night. "Oh, I'll come back," Marvina said. "I would've been here last night only—" she shrugged. Her mother, of course. Alma, for all her talk about salvaging things for her impractical daughter, needed attention. And poor Marvina had to give it without actually seeming to.

Byron accompanied her to the elevators and hugged her.

"Can I bring you something to eat?" she asked.

"I'll get something downstairs."

She kissed his cheek and got on, and she was sniffling as the doors closed on her. He went back to Georgia's room, and found her awake.

"I had a dream," she said. Her eyes were blazing. "It wasn't a good dream."

He moved to the chair and took her hand again. "Tell me."

"It's silly. I was doing a calendar for someone. But then something went wrong with it. All the pictures kept dissolving, and I couldn't pick them up. It swept over me, somehow. It was just awful. It was just a calendar I had ruined, but it was terrifying."

He reached for her other hand, and they sat there for a time. He thought she might be going back to sleep, and he felt himself hoping for it.

"I'm scared," she said suddenly. "Oh, hell. I thought I'd dealt with this."

"I'm right here," Byron said.

She held tight. She was weathering it, enduring it; it swept through her in a trembling, her hand was so tight in his that he marveled at how strong she still was. She'd shut her eyes, but was not sleeping. No, she was trying to put something away from her, inside, trying to master herself. When she opened her eyes again, they were still rounded and too bright. "Oh," she said. "Damn it all."

He put his other hand over hers, then stood and leaned over, trying to embrace her—but she wouldn't let go of his hand. "I love you," he said.

"Read something to me," she said. But she wouldn't let go of him. So they remained that way until, at last, she seemed to let down, sighing, drifting a little, then jerking awake. Each time this happened, she squeezed tight again, and looked at him out of those brilliantly lighted eyes. There was something almost supernatural in the way they shone.

After a long interval, she let go, and he sat back down. She was still awake. She stared at him as if not quite able to discern who he was. Then she patted the bed and said, "I'm sorry. Read to me?"

So he read some of the cards and letters, all expressing the hope—the faith, really—that she would come through this and be her old self. One of them was from a priest she had known in Europe before the war.

"I miss the consolations of religion," she said, interrupting him.

"Do you—would you like me to see if—"

"If someone would take me?" She smiled, then. "Funny."

He was at a loss. He went on reading the letter, but then saw that she was staring beyond him, at the door. He turned, expecting Marvina, but it was Reese. Evidently he had waited until Byron saw him. He came forward into the room, with his own little gift of soaps and lotions in a basket. "For your hands," he said to Georgia.

She raised one arm so he could come be hugged and kissed. It was always the way they had greeted each other. Byron took his clumsy embrace in turn, and then they were both sitting there while Georgia opened one of the lotion bottles and put it on her hands, being careful of the place where the I.V. went into the back of the right one. Georgia looked from one to the other of them. There was still that unsettling brightness in her eyes, as if the fear were still climbing inside her and she was choosing to pretend it wasn't there. But then the nurse came in, and it was time for changing things again, and she shooed them out into the hall. They stood there, in the fading, early-evening light from the window at that end. Across from them several people were arranged around the bed of another woman, also old, and probably also dying; this was, after all, where they brought people from the assisted living part of Brighton Creek Farm.

Out the window was the building itself, where she had come to stay ten years ago. They were both staring out at it. Byron feeling the pain in his lower chest, wanting not to show it, wanting to be far away from Reese. Perhaps he would go down now to the cafeteria for something he wouldn't eat, having no appetite now. But Reese might go with him. Or stay and be alone with Georgia.

"Remember when we brought her here to talk to them," Reese said now. "That first time?"

Byron nodded, without quite looking at him.

"Who was that guy? I can't remember his name."

"Scottish sounding," said Byron, who remembered perfectly well the name, McCutcheon. He said, "Mac-something."

"I can't recall it," Reese said.

They were quiet. Georgia had sat patiently listening to McCutcheon talk about all the advantages of assisted living, and she had abruptly interrupted him to say, "Excuse me, are you quite serious?"

The man was stunned, and silent. He stared.

Georgia turned to Reese—yes, it had been Reese—and said, "This guy's an ass, isn't he?"

Byron remembered that now, and he knew Reese was remembering it, too. He almost said something. But the nurse opened the door again and came out, and they could go back in to Georgia, who lay with eyes closed, in fresh sheets, fresh nightgown. Soon they would bring dinner. But she would probably not eat it. She had eaten a little of the Clementine. Food was the one thing that had ceased to interest her particularly; it was such an effort to chew.

She opened her eyes. "Boys," she said.

"Sister," Reese said. That was what he had always called her.

"Tell me about it," she said, looking at neither of them.

Reese began to cry. Byron lifted himself from the chair and went back out into the hall. He heard Georgia say his name, and hesitated. But when he looked back into the room he saw that Reese was bent over the bed, holding her hand, and she was saying something to him.

Byron felt a rage working in him, and he went down to the cafeteria and ordered coffee. He sensed, with a small stab of regret, his own abruptness toward the slow lady behind the counter, who handed him the coffee with a lackluster shrug and went about cleaning the grill. He went to a table alone and sat there, hands shaking, sipping the coffee, which was too hot. He couldn't believe his own anger. And he felt it at Georgia, too, for accepting Reese's affection, knowing what she knew. It hurt him, at a level for which he was unprepared. How could she, knowing what she knew? But then, he remembered with a sinking at his heart what she also knew. He couldn't decide what to do with his own emotions. He drank the coffee, which burned his tongue, and he sat there feeling childish. He actually had the child's thought, I'll go away and then they'll be sorry. "Stupid," he said, aloud. Then put his hands to his face and wept.

When he went back up to the room, he found the door open, Reese gone. Georgia was lying there staring out the window. He went to the chair and sat down. They had brought her a meal, which she hadn't touched—such meager fare: a roll, mashed potatoes, three slices of turkey, all of it looking like a frozen dinner. She'd had a little of the apple juice, which she had apparently asked for.

"You didn't eat," he said.

"Don't be mad at me, son. I'm unable to select anymore. Don't want to."

"I don't understand," he told her, because he didn't.

"I don't know what happened with you and Reese," she said.

Then she took a deep breath, so weighted with exhaustion that he thought, with alarm, that she might pass out. "I don't want to send anybody away," she said. "Not now. Do you understand?"

"Yes," he said.

"I'm not convinced."

"No," he said. "I do."

"Byron, the lyron," she murmured. "You know I always meant it, that you were brave."

"I'm not brave," Byron said.

"Yes." She raised one hand, almost as if to wave at him. "I'll be the judge of that." It was automatic now, and she was falling asleep again. He moved the tray of food away, and then sat there watching her sleep. Marvina came back in at last, with her mother. Alma wanted to say hello. Marvina had brought cards, and when Georgia woke, the two of them played a couple of slow rounds of gin rummy on Georgia's dinner tray. Later, Reese came back and stood off to one side, watching the card game. Everyone was gentle, and in the pauses when Georgia slipped off to her fitful sleep, they were quiet, and quite still, almost as if frozen that way in a photograph.

They all left at the end of the evening visiting hour. Georgia was sound asleep. Very still, breathing very easily. Reese kissed her cheek. Marvina and Alma did, too. Byron held her hand again for a time, and then kissed her himself. Outside the room, he took Reese by the arm just above the elbow. For a second, it was almost impossible to draw in air. Marvina and her mother had gone a ways down the hall. "I'll be right along," Byron said to them. They went on. Reese was looking at him with a kind of resigned alarm.

"I want you to be here for her," Byron said, low. Managing to get it out. "She wants it, and I want it. No standing to the side. No hanging back. Please."

Reese nodded, his eyes widening slightly.

"I don't want any confusion about it. Nothing is changed between you and me if you're here for her. Only don't let her see you hanging back. This is about her bravery. Not yours, or mine."

"Thank you," Reese said, with a deep sigh. "You have always been—" He didn't finish. He just looked down and repeated the phrase: "Thank you."

Byron let go, and they walked side by side down to where the other two waited.

He rode with Marvina and her mother back to the house. Reese had gone off to wherever he was staying now in the city.

When they got to the house, they saw that the Ewings's dogs and cats were setting up a ruckus. Marvina hurried her mother in, and then came back to where Byron was standing on his porch. He'd had the sense she wanted to speak with him.

"Reese is seeing someone else," she said. "I hope I'm doing the right thing telling you."

He bent slightly at the waist, from the pain. He turned from her, and looked out at the lights of his town.

"I'm sorry, Byron. And I think he's miserable."

He couldn't get enough air again. He faced her, breathless, all dark inside, a desolation—a man losing everything. Marvina walked over and put her arms around him. "I'm so sorry," she said. "Want me to stay tonight?"

He shook his head. "I told him to keep coming to see Georgia. She wants it."

Marvina shrugged; her expression seemed to say that it was hard to explain.

No, Byron thought. It wasn't really so hard to explain at all. Georgia had said to him, quite honestly and gently, what she required. It wasn't too much to ask. He could find a way to do what she wanted. He was Byron the lyron.

Georgia Susan Michael Townsend Mailley passed away in the middle of the night, almost exactly one week later. There was no warning; it happened quite suddenly and peacefully. Her son was downstairs in the cafeteria with Marvina, drinking coffee. Reese had left, with a promise of returning in the morning, first thing. Everyone had settled into a pattern of visiting with the failing woman, who seemed at the end to be growing stronger, and holding on. She was alert when awake, and herself right to the end. After her passing, the people who had stood with her at the edge of her darkness drifted to other lives, as people often do—Marvina took her mother's advice and sold her house. The two women live in a duplex in the old-town section of Charlottesville, Virginia. Reese drifted out to California with his new companion for a time, and then came back to Virginia. He took a job teaching art in the local high school, and continued to make money with his painting. Byron moved to New York again and worked for a magazine there for a year or two, then settled in a little walk-up flat on a narrow street in Rome. He still lives there, and not always alone. Now and then he walks out near sunset and takes pictures of the old part of the city, those ancient buildings, with their long history, their beauty and complication, their tragedy and sorrow. SQ

All the Wrecks I've Crawled Out Of

A STORY

by T. Coraghessan Boyle

T. Coraghessan Boyle is the author of nineteen books of fiction, including *World's End*, *The Tortilla Curtain*, and, recently, *Talk Talk*. Known for his exploration of the joys, sorrows, and misguided appetites of baby boomers, Boyle has been compared to Mark Twain for his mixture of humor and social insight. He has received many literary honors, including a National Book Award nomination for *Drop City*. He teaches in the English Department at the University of Southern California.

ALL I WANTED, really, was to attain mythic status. Along the lines, say, of James Dean, Brom Bones, Paul Bunyan, my father. My father was a giant among men, with good-sized trees for arms and fists like buckets of nails, and I was not a giant among men. I wasn't even a man, though I began to look like one as I grew into my shoulders and eventually found something to shave off my cheeks after a close and patient scrutiny, and I manfully flunked out of three colleges and worked at digging graves at the Beth-El cemetery and shoveling chicken-shit at the Shepherd Hill Egg Farm till I got smart and started bartending. That was a kind of wreckage, I suppose—flunking out—but there was much more to come, wrecks both literal and figurative, replete with flames, blood, crushed metal and broken hearts, a whole swath of destruction and self-immolation, my own personal skid marks etched into the road of my life and maybe yours too.

So. Where to start? With Helen, I suppose, Helen Kreisler. She was a cocktail waitress at the restaurant where I was mixing drinks six and a half days a week, four years older than I when I met her—that is, twenty-seven—and with a face that wasn't exactly pretty in any conventional sense, but more a field for the play of psychodrama, martyrdom and high-level neurosis. It was an old face, much older than her cheerleader's body and her still relatively tender years, a face full of worry, with lines scored around her eyes and dug deep into the corners of her mouth. She wore her hair long and parted in the middle, after the fashion of the day, and her eyes—the exact color of aluminum foil—jumped out of her tanned face from a hundred feet away. They were alien eyes, that's what I called them. And her too. *Alien,* that was my pet name for her, and I used it to urge her on when she was on top of me and my hands were on her breasts and her mouth had gone slack with the feeling of what I was doing *to* her.

It was about a month after I started working at Brennan's Steakhouse that we decided to move in together. We found a two-bedroom house dropped down in a blizzard of trees by the side of a frozen lake. This was in suburban New York, by the way, in the farthest, darkest reaches of northern Westchester, where the nights were black-dark and close. The house was cheap, so far as rent was concerned, because it was a summer house, minimally insulated, but as we were soon to discover, two hundred dollars a month would go up the chimney or stovepipe or whatever it was that was connected to the fuel-evaporating furnace in the basement. Helen was charmed, despite the water-stained exterior walls and the stink of frozen mouseshit and ancient congealed grease that hit you in the face like a two-by-four the minute you stepped in the door. We lied to the landlady (a mustachioed widow with breasts the size of New Jersey and Connecticut respectively) about our marital status, got out our wallets and put down our first and last months' rent. It was a move up for me at any rate, because to this point I'd been living in a basement apartment at my parents' house, sleeping late, as bartenders will do, and listening to the heavy stolid tread of my father's footsteps above me as he maneuvered around his coffee cup in the morning before leaving for work.

Helen fixed the place up with some cheap rugs and prints and a truckload of bric-a-brac from the local head shop—candles, incense burners, ceramic bongs, that sort of thing. We never cooked. We were very drunk and very stoned. Meals, in which we weren't especially interested, came to us out of a saucepan at the restaurant—except for breakfast, a fuzzy, woozy meal heavy on the sugars and starches and consumed languidly at the diner. Our sex was youthful, fueled by hormonal rushes, pot and amyl nitrate, and I was feeling pretty good about things—about myself, I mean—for the first time in my life.

But before I get into all that, I ought to tell you about the first of the crashes, the one from which all the others seemed to spool out like fishing line that's been on the shelf too long. It was my first night at work, at Brennan's, that is. I'd done a little bartending weekends in college, but it was strictly beer, 7&7, rum and coke, that sort of thing, and I was a little tentative about Brennan's, a big softly lit place that managed to be intimate and frenziedly public at the same time. Ski Silinski, the other bartender, gave me two shots of 151 and a Tuinal to calm me before the crush started. Well, the crush started, and I was still about as hyper as you can get without strictly requiring a staitjacket, but way up on the high end of that barely controlled hysteria there was a calm plateau of rum, Tuinal and the beer I sipped steadily all night long—and this was a place I aspired to reach eventually, once the restaurant closed down and I could haul myself up there and fade into a warm, post-conscious glow. We did something like a hundred and ten dinners that night, I met and flirted with Helen and three other cocktail waitresses and half a dozen partially lit female customers and, all things considered, acquitted myself well. Ski and I had the door locked, the glasses washed and tomorrow's fruit cut and stowed, when Jimmy Brennan walked in.

Helen and one of the other waitresses—Adele-something—were sitting at the bar, the stereo was cranked and we were having a celebratory nightcap at the time. It didn't faze Jimmy. He was the owner, only thirty-two years old, and he'd really stepped in it with this place, the first west-coast-style steak-and-salad-bar restaurant in the area. He drove a new Triumph, British racing green, and he drank martinis, straight up, with a twist. "How'd it go tonight, Lester?" he asked, settling his lean frame on a barstool, even as Ski set a martini, newborn and gleaming with condensation, before him.

I gave the waitresses a look. They were in skimpy waitress outfits, long bare perfect legs crossed at the knees, cigarettes propped between elegantly bunched knuckles that in turn propped up their weary silken heads. I was a man among men—and women—and I feared no evil and felt no pain. "Fine," I said, already amending what seemed a much-too-modest assessment. "No. Better than fine: great. Stupendous. Magnificent."

Jimmy Brennan wore glasses, the thin silver-framed discs made popular two years earlier by John Lennon. His eyes were bright behind them and I attributed that brightness to the keenness of mind and Darwinian fortitude that had made him rich at thirty-two, but I was wrong. That gleam was the gleam of alcohol, nothing more. Jimmy Brennan was, as I would discover, an alcoholic, though at the time that seemed just fine to me—anything that altered your consciousness and heightened your perceptions was cool in the extreme, as far as I was concerned.

Jimmy Brennan bought us a round, then another. Helen gave me a look out of her silver-foil eyes—a look of lust, complicity, warning?—picked up her bag and left with Adele. It was three-thirty in the morning. Ski, who at twenty-seven was married and a father, pleaded his wife. The door closed behind him and I remember vividly the sound of the latch clicking into place as he turned his key from the outside. "Well," Jimmy said, slapping my back, "I guess it's just us, huh?"

I don't remember much of the rest of it, except this: I was in my car when I woke up, there was a weak pale sun draped over everything like a crust of vomit, and it was very, very hot. And more: there was a stranger in a yellow slicker beating out the glass of the driver's side window and I was trying to fight him off, till the flames licking away at my calves began to make their point more emphatically than he could ever have. As I later reconstructed it, or as it was reconstructed for me, I'd apparently left the bar in the cold glow of dawn, fired up the engine of my car and then passed out with my foot to the floor. But as Jimmy said when he saw me behind the bar the next night, "It could have been worse—think what would've happened if the thing had been in gear."

MY FATHER SEEMED to think the whole affair was pretty idiotic, but he didn't deliver any lectures. It was idiotic, but by some convoluted way of thinking, it was manly too. And funny. Deeply, richly, skin-of-the-teeth and laughing-in-the-face-of-Mr.-D. funny. My father rubbed his balding head with his nail-bucket hands and said he guessed I could take my mother's car to work until I could find myself another heap of bolts, but he hoped I'd show a little more restraint and pour a drop or two of coffee into my brandy before trying to make it home on all that glare ice.

Helen—the new and exciting Helen with the silver-foil eyes—didn't seem particularly impressed with my first-night exploits, which had already entered the realm of legend by the time I got to work at four the following afternoon, but she didn't seem offended or put off in any way either. We worked together through the cocktail-hour rush and into the depths of a very busy evening, exchanging the thousand small quips and intimacies that pass between bartender and cocktail waitress in the course of an eight-hour shift, and then it was closing time and there was Jimmy Brennan, at the very hub of the same unfolding scenario that had played itself out so disastrously the night before. Had I learned my lesson? Had the two-paragraph story in the local paper crediting Fireman Samuel L. Calabrese with saving my sorry life had any effect? Or the loss of my car and the humiliation of having to drive my mother's? Not a whit. Jimmy Brennan bought and I poured, and he went off on a long soliloquy about beef suppliers and how they weren't competent to do a thing about the quality of the frozen lobster tails for Surf 'n' Turf, and I probably would have gone out and wrecked my mother's car if it wasn't for Helen.

She was sitting down at the end of the bar with Adele, Ski, another cocktail wait-ress and two waiters who'd stayed on to drink deep after we shut down the kitchen. What she was doing was smoking a cigarette and drinking a Black Russian and watching me out of those freakish eyes as if I were some kind of wonder of nature. I liked that look. I liked it a lot. And when she got up to whisper something in my ear, hot breath and expressive lips and an invitation that electrified me from my scalp to my groin, I cut Jimmy Brennan off in the middle of an aside about what he was paying per case for well vodka and said, "Sorry, gotta go. Helen's having car trouble and she needs a ride, isn't that right, Helen?"

She already had her coat on, a complicated thing full of pleats and buckles that drove right down to the toes of her boots, and she shook out her hair with a sideways flip of her head before clapping a knit hat over it. "Yeah," she said. "That's right."

There were no wrecks that night. We left my mother's car in the lot out front of Brennan's and Helen drove me to the apartment she and Adele shared on the second floor of an old frame house in Yorktown. It was dark—intensely, preternaturally dark (or maybe it was just the crust of salt, sand and frozen slush on the windshield that made it seem that way)—and when we swung into a narrow drive hemmed in by long-legged pines, the house suddenly loomed up out of nowhere like the prow of a boat anchored in the night. "This is it?" I said, just to hear the sound of my own voice, and she said something like "Home sweet home" as she cut the engine and the lights died.

The next thing I knew we were on the porch, bathed in the dull yellow glow of a superfluous bug light, locked out and freezing; she gave me a ghostly smile, dug through her purse, dropped her keys twice, then her gloves and compact, and finally announced that the house key was missing. In response, I drew her to me and kissed her, my mind skewed by vodka and the joint we'd shared in the car, our breath steaming, heavy winter coats keeping our bodies apart—and then, with a growing sense of urgency, I tried the door. It was locked, all right. But I was feeling heroic and reckless, and I put my shoulder to it—just once, but with real feeling—and the bolt gave and we were in.

Upstairs, at the end of the hallway, was Helen's superheated lair, a place that looked pretty much the way our mutual place would look, but which was a revela-tion to me at the time. There was order here, femininity, floors that gave back the light, books and records arranged alphabetically on brick-and-board shelves, prints on the walls, a clean sink and a clean toilet. And there was a smell connected to and interwoven with it all, sweet and astringent at the same time. It might have been patchouli, but I didn't know what patchouli was or how it was supposed to smell, just that it was exotic, and that was enough for me. There were cats—two of them, Siamese or some close approximation—but you can't have everything. I was hooked. "Nice place," I said, working at the buttons of my coat while the cats yowled for food or attention or both and Helen fluttered around the living room, lighting candles and slipping a record on the stereo.

I didn't know what to do with myself, so I eased my haunches down on the floor in a pile of pillows—there was no furniture in the usual sense—and shrugged out of my coat. It was hot as a steam bath, Helen had left the room through a set of bead curtains that were still clacking, and a beer had magically appeared in my hand. I tried to relax, but the image of what was to come and what was expected of me and how exactly to go about it without ruining everything, weighed on me so heavily even the chugging of the beer had no effect. Then Helen returned in a white terry cloth robe, her hair freshly brushed and shining. "So," she said, settling into the pillows beside me and looking suddenly as vulnerable and uncertain as I, "you want to get high?"

We smoked hash. We listened to music, very loud music—Buffalo Springfield; Blood, Sweat and Tears; The Moody Blues—and that provided an excuse for not saying much of anything beyond the occasional murmur as the pipe was passed or the lighter sprang to life. The touch of her hand as we shared the pipe set me on fire though and the music invested me with every nuance and I thought for a while I was floating about three feet above the floor. I was thinking sex, she was thinking sex, but neither of us made a move.

And then, somehow, Adele was there, compact, full-breasted Adele, with her sheenless eyes and the dark slash of her bangs obliterating her eyebrows. She was wearing a pair of black pantihose and nothing else, and she settled into the pillows on my left, languidly reaching for the pipe. She didn't say anything for a long while—none of us did—and I don't know what she was thinking, so natural and naked and warm, but I was suffering from sensory overload. Two women, I was thinking, and the image of my father and my sad dumpy mother floated up in my brain just as one of the cats climbed into Adele's lap and settled itself between her breasts.

That was when I felt Helen's hand take hold of mine. She was standing, and she pulled me to my feet with surprising force, and then she led me through the bead curtains and down a hall and into her bedroom. And the first thing she did, before I could take hold of her and let all the rest unfold, was shut the door, and lock it.

AND SO WE MOVED IN together, in the house that started off smelling of freeze-dried mouseshit and wound up taking on the scent of patchouli. I was content. For the first time I was off on my own, independent, an adult, a man. I had a woman. I had a house. Two cats. Heating bills. And I came home to all that pretty religiously for the first month or two, but then, on the nights when I was working and Helen wasn't, I started staying after closing with Jimmy Brennan and a few of the other employees. The term Quaalude speaks to me now when I think back on it, that very specific term that calls up the image of a little white pill that kicked your legs out from under you and made your voice run down like a windup motor in need of rewinding. Especially when you judiciously built your high around it with a selection of high-octane drinks, pot, hash, and anything else you could get your hands on.

There we were, sitting at the bar, the music on full, the lights down low, talking into the night, bullshitting, getting stoned and progressively more stoned, and Helen waiting for me in our little house at the end of the road by the frozen lake. That was the setting for the second wreck—or it wasn't a wreck in the fundamental, literal sense of the word, because Helen's VW bus was barely damaged, aside from some unexpected wear and tear on the left front fender and a barely noticeable little twist to the front bumper. It was four or five in the morning, the sky a big black puddle of nothing, three feet of dogshit-strewn snow piled up on either side of the road till it looked like a long snaking bobsled run. The bus fired up with a tinny rattle and I took off, but I was in a state of advanced confusion, I guess, and I went right by the turnoff for our road, the one that led to the little house by the frozen lake, and instead found myself out on the main highway, bouncing back and forth between the snow berms like a pool ball that can't decide on a pocket.

There was something in the urgency of the lights flashing behind me that got me to pull over, and then there was a cop standing there in his jackboots and wide-brimmed hat, shining a flashlight in my face. "Out of the car," he said, and I complied, or tried to, but I missed my footing and pitched face-forward into the snow. And when I awoke this time, there were no firemen present and no flames, just an ugly pale-gray concrete block room with graffiti scrawled over it and three or four hopeless-looking jerks sitting around on the floor. I got shakily to my feet, looked around me and went instinctively to the door, a heavy sliding affair with a little barred window set in the center of it at eye-level. My hands took hold of the handle and I gave the door a tug. Nothing. I tried again. Same lack of result. And then I turned round on my companions, these pathetic strangers with death masks for faces and seriously disarranged hair, and said, as if I were in a dream, "Hey, it's locked."

That was when one of the men on the floor stirred himself long enough to glance up at me out of blood-flecked eyes and a face that was exactly like a bucket of pus. "What the fuck you think, motherfucker," he said. "Your ass is in jail."

THEN IT WAS SPRING and the ice receded from the shore of the lake to reveal a black band of dead water, the driveway turned to mud and the ditches along the blacktop road began to ululate with the orgasmic cries of the nondescript little toads known as spring peepers. The heating bill began to recede too, and to celebrate that minor miracle and the rebirth of all things green and good, I took my Alien—Helen, that is—out for dinner at Capelli's, where all the waiters faked an Italian accent, whether they were Puerto Ricans or Swedes, and you couldn't pick up a cigarette without one of them rushing over to light it for you. It was dark. It smelled good. Somebody's grandmother was out in the kitchen, cooking, and we ate the usual things—cannelloni, baked ziti, pasta primavera—and paid about twice what we would have paid in the usual places. I was beginning to know a little about wine, so I ordered a bottle of the second-highest-priced red on the menu, and when we finished that, I ordered another. For dessert, my balled fist presented Helen with two little white Rorer Quaaludes.

She was looking good, silver-eyed and tanned from an early-spring ski trip to Vermont with Adele and one of the other waitresses. I watched the rings glitter on her fingers as she lifted her glass to wash down the pills, and then she set the glass down and eased back into her chair under the weight of all that food and wine. "I finally met Kurt," she said.

I was having a scotch and Drambuie as an after-dinner drink, no dessert thanks, and enjoying the scene, which was very formal and adult, old guys in suits slurping up linguine, busty wives with poodle hair and furs, people of forty and maybe beyond out here in the hinterlands living the good life. "Kurt who?" I said.

"Kurt Ramos? Adele's ex?" She leaned forward, her elbows splayed on the table-top. "He was bartending at this place in Stowe—he's a Sagittarius, very creative. Funny too. He paints and writes poetry and had one of his poems almost published in the *Hudson Review*, and of course Adele knew he was going to be there, I mean that was the whole point. He's thirty-four, I think. Or thirty-five. You think that's too much? Agewise, I mean? Adele's only twenty-four."

"Almost published?" I said.

Helen shrugged. "I don't know the details. The editor wrote him a long letter or something."

"He is pretty old. But then so are you, and you don't mind having a baby like me around, do you?"

"Four years, kiddo," she said. "Three years and nine months, actually. I'm not an old lady yet. But what do you think—is he too old for her?"

I didn't think anything. Helen was always giving these speeches about so-and-so and their sex life, who was cheating on who, the *I-Ching*, reincarnation, cat breeding,

UFOs and the way people's characters could be read like brownie recipes according to their astrological charts. I gave her a sly smile and put my hand on her leg. "Age is relative," I said. "Isn't it?"

And then the strangest thing happened, by way of coincidence, that is. There was a flurry of activity in the foyer, the bowing and scraping of waiters, the little tap dance of leather soles as coats were removed, and suddenly the *maître d'* was leading Adele and the very same Kurt Ramos past our table.

Helen saw them first. "Adele!" she chirped, already rising up out of the chair with a big stoned grin on her face, and then I glanced up and saw Adele there in a sweater so tight she must have been born in it (but no, no, I had vivid proof to the contrary). Beside her, loping along with an athletic stride, was Kurt Ramos, half-German, half-Puerto Rican, with crazily staring eyes and slick black hair that hung to his shoulders. He was wearing a tan trench coat, bell bottoms and a pair of red bowling shoes he'd borrowed from a bowling alley one night. There were exclamations of surprise all around, the girls embraced as if they hadn't seen each other in twelve years and I found myself wrapping my hand round Kurt Ramos's in a complicated soul shake. "Good to meet you, man," I said in my best imitation of a very hip adult, but he just stared right through me.

IN MAY, Ski Silinski quit to move up to Maine and live among goats and liberated women on a commune, leaving his wife and kid behind, and I found myself elevated to head bartender at the ripe age of twenty-three. I was making good money, getting at least a modicum of exercise rowing Helen around the defrosted lake every afternoon, and aside from the minorest of scrapes, I hadn't really wrecked anything or anybody in a whole long string of weeks. Plus, I was ascending to the legendary status I'd sought all along, stoked by the Fireman Calabrese incident and the high drama of my unconscious dive into the hands of the state police. I'd begun dealing Quaaludes in a quiet way, I tripped and had revelatory visions and went to concerts with Helen, Adele and Kurt, and I pretty generally felt on top of things. The prevailing ethos was simple in those days—the more drugs you ingested, the hipper you were, and the hipper you were, the more people sought you out for praise, drugs and admiration. I even got to the point where I could match Jimmy Brennan drink for drink and still make it home alive—or at least partially so.

Anyway, Ski quit and on my recommendation we hired Kurt Ramos as second bartender. The two of us made quite a pair behind the bar, he with his shower-curtain hair and staring eyes and me with my fixed grin that was impervious to anything life or the pharmaceutical industry could throw at it. We washed glasses, cut fruit, mixed drinks, talked about everything and nothing. He told me about Hawaii and Amsterdam, drugs, women he'd known, and he showed me his poetry, which seemed pretty banal to me, but who was I to judge? When work was over, he and Adele would come over to our place for long stoned discussions and gleeful drug abuse, or we'd go to a late movie or another bar. I liked him. He had heart and style and he never tried to pull rank on me by virtue of his greater age and wisdom, as Jimmy Brennan and his drinking cronies never failed to do.

It was a month or so after Kurt started working behind the bar that my parents came in for the first time. They'd been threatening to make an appearance ever since I'd got the job—my mother wanted to check the place out because she'd heard so much about it, everybody had, and my father seemed amused by the idea of his son officially making him a drink and pushing it across the bar to him on a little napkin. "You'd have to give me a discount," he kept saying. "Wouldn't you?" And then he'd laugh his high husky laugh till the laugh became a smoker's cough and he'd cross the kitchen to the sink and drop a ball of sputum in the drain.

I was shaking a martini for a middle-aged guy at the end of the bar when I glanced up and saw my father looming there in the doorway. The sun was setting, a fat red disc on the horizon, and my father extinguished it with the spread of his shoulders as he maneuvered my mother through the door. The hostess—a terminally pretty girl by the name of Jane Nardone—went up to him with a dripping smile and asked if he'd like a table for two. "Yeah, sure," I heard him say in his rasping voice, "but only after my son makes me a vodka gimlet—or maybe two." He put his hands on his hips and looked down at the little painted doll that was Jane Nardone. "That okay with you?" Then he made his way across the room to where I stood behind the bar in white shirt and tie.

"Nice place," he grunted, helping my mother up onto a barstool and settling in beside her. My mother was heavily made-up and liquid-eyed, which meant she'd already had a couple of drinks, and she was clutching a black patent-leather purse the size of a refrigerator. "Hi, honey," she said, "working hard?"

For a minute I was frozen there at the bar, one hand on the shaker, the other on the glass. There went my cool, the legend dissolved, Lester the ultra-wild one nothing more than a boy-faced boy—and with parents, no less. It was Kurt who saved the day. He was thirty-five years old, after all, with hollow cheeks and the faintest weave of gray in his mustache, and he had nothing to prove. He was cool, genuinely cool, and I was an idiot. "Mr. Rifkin," he said, "Mrs. Rifkin. Lester's told me a lot about you"—a glowing, beautiful, scintillating lie. "What can I get you?"

"Yeah," I said, adjusting the edges of my fixed smile just a degree, "what'll it be?"

And that was fine. My father had three drinks at the bar and got very convivial with Kurt, and my mother, perched on the edge of the stool and drinking Manhattans, corralled anybody she could—Jane, Adele, Helen, random customers, even one of the busboys—and told hem all about my potty training, my elementary school triumphs and the .417 batting average I carried one year in Little League. Jimmy Brennan came in and bought everybody a round. We were very busy. I was glowing. My father was glowing. Jane showed him and my mother to the best table in the house and they kept Helen and two waiters schmoozing over a long, lingering, three-course dinner with dessert, after-dinner drinks and coffee. Which I paid for. Happily.

THE SUMMER THAT YEAR was typical—heat, mosquitoes, fat green flies droning aimlessly round the kitchen, the air so dense with moisture even the frogs were sweating. Helen and I put off going to bed later and later each night, hoping it would cool off so we could actually sleep instead of sweating reservoirs on each other, and we saw dawn more times than I'd like to remember. Half the time, I wound up passed out on the couch, and I would wake at one or two in the afternoon in a state of advanced dehydration. Iced coffee would help, especially with a shot or two of Kahlua in it, and maybe a Seconal to kill some of the pain of the previous night's afflictions, but by the time we got around to the deli for a sandwich to go, it was four and we were on our way to work. That became a real grind, especially when I only got Monday nights off. But then, right in the middle of a heat wave, Jimmy Brennan's mother died and the restaurant closed down for three days. It was a tragedy for Jimmy, and worse for his mother, but for us—Helen, Kurt, Adele and me—it was like Christmas in July. Three whole days off. I couldn't believe it.

Jimmy flew back to California, somebody pinned a notice to the front door of the restaurant, and we took advantage of the fact that Kurt had recently come into twenty hits of blotter acid to plan a day around some pastoral activities. We filled a cooler with sangria and sandwiches and hiked into the back end of Wicopee Reservoir, deep in Fahnestock Park, a place where swimming was prohibited and trespassing forbidden. Our purpose? To swim. And trespass. We could have spent the day on our own muddy little lake, but there were houses, cabins, people, cars, boats and dogs everywhere, and we wanted privacy, not to mention adventure. What we wanted, specifically, was to be nude, because we were very hip and the puritanical mores of the false and decrepit society our parents had so totteringly constructed didn't apply to us.

We parked off the Taconic Parkway—far off, behind a thick screen of trees where the police wouldn't discover the car and become overly curious as to the where-abouts of its former occupants—shouldered our day packs, hefted the cooler, and started off through the woods. As soon as we were out of sight of the road, Kurt paused to strip off his T-shirt and shorts, and it was immediately evident that he'd done this before—and often—because he had no tan line whatever. Adele was next. She threw down her pack, dropped her shorts, and in a slow tease unbuttoned her shirt, watching me all the time. The woods were streaked with sun, deerflies nagged at us, I was sweating. I set down the cooler, and though I'd begun to put on weight and was feeling self-conscious about it, I tried to be casual as I rolled the sweaty T-shirt up over my gut and chest and then kicked free of my shorts. Helen was watching me too, and Kurt—all three of them were—and I clapped on my sunglasses to mask my eyes. Then it was Helen's turn. She gave me a look out of her silver-foil eyes, then laughed—a long musical girlish laugh—before pulling the shirt over her head and dropping her shorts and panties in a single motion. *"Voilà!"* she said, and laughed again.

And what was I thinking? "How about a hit of that acid, Kurt?" I said, locked away behind my shades.

He looked dubious. Lean, naked and suntanned and caught between two impulses. "Sure," he said, shrugging, the green mottled arena of the untrodden woods opening up around him, "why not? But the lake's maybe a mile off and I can still hear the parkway, for christ's sake, but yeah, sure, it's going to take a while to kick in anyway."

It was a sacramental moment. We lined up naked under the trees and Kurt tore off a hit for each of us and laid it on our tongues, and then we hoisted our packs, I picked up the cooler, and we started off down the path. Kurt, who'd been here before, was in front, leading the way; the two girls were next, Adele and then Helen; and I brought up the rear, seeing nothing of the sky, the trees, the ferns or the myriad wonders of nature. No, I saw only the naked buttocks of the naked women as they eased themselves down the path or climbed over a downed tree or a spike of granite, and it was all I could do to keep cool in a vigilantly hip and matter-of-fact way, and fight down an erection.

After a while, the lake began to peek through the trees, a silver sheen cut up in segments, now shining in a gap over here, now over there. We came down to it like pilgrims, the acid already starting to kick in and alter the colors and texture ever so subtly, and the first thing we did was drop our packs and the cooler and cannonade into the water in an explosion of hoots and shouts that echoed out over the lake like rolling thunder. There was splashing and frolicking and plenty of incidental and not-so-incidental contact. We bobbed like seals. The sun hung fat in the sky. There was no finer moment. And then, at some point, we found ourselves sitting cross-legged on a blanket and passing round the bota bag of sangria and a joint, before falling to the sandwiches. After that, we lay back and stared up into the shifting shapes of the trees, letting the natural world sink slowly in.

What happened next, I don't remember exactly—maybe I was seeing things, maybe I was dozing—but when I came back to the world, what I saw was no hallucination. Kurt was having sex with Helen, my Helen, my Alien, and Adele was deeply involved too, very busy with her hands and tongue. I was thoroughly stoned—tripping, and so were they—but I wasn't shocked or surprised or jealous, or not that I would admit to myself. I was hip. I was a man. And if Kurt could fuck Helen, then I could fuck Adele. A *quid pro quo,* right? That was only fair.

Helen was making certain small noises, whispery rasping intimate noises that I knew better than anyone in the world, and those noises provoked me to get up off the blanket and move over to where Adele was lying at the periphery of all that passionate action as if she were somehow controlling it. I put one hand on her shoulder and the other between her legs, and she turned to me with her black eyes and the black slash of her bangs caught in the depths of them, and she smiled and pulled me down.

WHAT HAPPENED NEXT, of course, is just another kind of wreckage. It wasn't as immediate maybe as turning over a car or driving it into the trees, but it cut just as wide a swath and it hurt, ultimately, beyond the capacity of any wound that can be closed with stitches. Bang up your head, it's no problem—you're a man, you'll grow another one. Broken leg, crushed ribs—you're impervious. But if there's one thing I've learned, it's that the emotional wrecks are the worst. You can't see the scars, but they're there, and they're a long time healing.

Anyway, later that day, sunburned and sated, we all came back to our house at the end of the lane on the muddy lake, showered—individually—and ordered up takeout Chinese, which we washed down with frozen margaritas while huddling on the floor and watching a truly hilarious old black-and-white horror film on the tube. Then there came a moment when we all looked at one another—consenting adults, armored in hip—and before we knew it we were reprising the afternoon's scenario. Finally, very late, I found my way to bed, and it was Adele, not Helen, who joined me there. To sleep.

I was stupid. I was inadequate. I was a boy playing at being a man. But the whole thing thrilled me—two women, two women at my disposal—and I never even heard

Helen when she told me she wanted to break it off. "I don't trust myself," she said. "I don't love him, I love you. You're my man. This is our house." The aluminum eyes fell away into her head and she looked older than ever, older than the mummy's ghost, older than my mother. We were in the kitchen, staring into cups of coffee. It was a week after the restaurant had opened up again, four in the morning, impossibly hot, the night alive with the shriek of every disturbed and horny insect, and we'd just got done entertaining Kurt and Adele in the way that had become usual and I didn't want to hear her, not a word.

"Listen," I said, half-stoned and rubbed raw between the legs, "listen, Alien, it's okay, there's nothing wrong with it—you don't want to get yourself buried in all that bourgeois shit. I mean, that's what started the War. That's what our parents are like. We're above that. We are."

The house was still. Her voice was very quiet. "No," she said, shaking her head slowly and definitively, "no we're not."

A MONTH WENT BY, and nothing changed. Then another. The days began to grow shorter, the nights took on a chill and the monster in the basement clanked and rumbled into action, devouring fuel oil once again. I was tending bar one night at the end of September, maybe twenty customers sitting there staring at me, Jimmy Brennan and a few of his buddies at the end of the bar, couples lingering over the tables, when the phone rang. It had been a slow night—we'd only done maybe fifty dinners—but the bar had filled up after we shut the kitchen down, and everybody seemed unnaturally thirsty. Helen had gone home early, as had Adele and Kurt, and I was getting drinks at the bar and taking orders at the tables too. I picked the phone up on the second ring. "Brennan's," I said, "how can I help you?"

It was Helen. Her voice was thick, gritty, full of something I hadn't heard in it before. "That you, Les?" she said.

"Yeah, what's up?" I pinned the phone to one shoulder with my chin to keep my hands free, and began dipping glasses in the rinse water and stacking them to dry. I kept my eyes on the customers.

"I just wanted to tell you I'm moving out."

I watched Jimmy Brennan light a cigarette and lean out over the bar to fetch himself an ashtray. I caught his eye and signaled "just a minute," then turned my back to the bar. "What do you mean?" I said, and I had to whisper. "What are you saying?"

"What am I saying? You want to know what I'm saying, Les—do you really?" There it was, the grit in her voice, and more than that—anger, hostility. "What I'm saying is I'm moving in with Kurt and Adele because I'm in love with Kurt. You understand that? You understand what I'm saying? It's over. Totally. Adioski."

"Sure," I whispered, and I was numb, no more capable of thought or feeling than the empty beer mug I was turning over in my hands, "—if that's what you want. But when, I mean, when are you—?"

There was a pause, and I thought I heard her catch her breath, as if she were fighting back the kind of emotion I couldn't begin to express. "I won't be there when you get home," she said.

Somebody was calling me—"Hey, bartender!"—and I swung round on a big stupid-looking guy with a Fu Manchu mustache who came in every night for two or three drinks and never left more than a quarter tip. "Another round here, huh?"

"And Les," she was saying through that cold aperture molded to my ear like a compress, "the rent's only paid through the thirtieth, so I don't know what you're going to do—"

"Hey, bartender!"

"—and you know what, Les? I don't care. I really don't."

I stayed late that night. The bar was alive, roaring, seething with camaraderie, chaos, every kind of possibility. My friends were there, my employer, customers I saw every night and wanted to embrace. I drank everything that came my way. I went out to the kitchen and smoked a joint with the busboys. Muddy Waters thumped through the speakers with his mojo workin'—

All you womens, stand in line,
I'll make love to you, babe,
In five minutes' time,
Ain't that a man?

I talked to a couple of people, comatose, smoked a whole pack of cigarettes. Then came the moment I'd been dreading since I'd hung up the phone—Jimmy Brennan got up off his barstool and shut down the lights and it was time to go home.

Outside, the sky seemed to rise up out of itself and pull the stars taut like separate strands of hair till everything blurred and there was no more fire, just ice. It was cold. My breath steamed in the sick yellow glow of the streetlights. I must have stood in the empty parking lot for a full five minutes before I realized Helen had the van—her van—and I had no way to get home and nobody to call. But then I heard a noise behind me, the rattle of keys, a slurred curse, and there was Jimmy Brennan, locking up, and I shouted, "Jimmy, hey, Jimmy, how about a ride?" He looked puzzled, as if the pavement had begun to speak, but the light caught the discs of his glasses and something like recognition slowly transformed his face. "Sure," he said, unsteady on his feet, "sure, no problem."

He drove like a zombie, staring straight ahead, the radio tuned so low all I could hear was the dull muted snarl of the bass. We didn't say much, maybe nothing at all. He had his problems, and I had mine. He let me off at the end of the dark lane and I fumbled my way into the dark house and fled away to unconsciousness before I could think to turn the lights on.

Two days later I put down five hundred dollars on a used Dodge the color of dried blood and moved in with Phil Cherniske, one of the waiters at Brennan's, who by a cruel stroke of fate happened to live on the next street over from the one I'd just vacated, right on the shore of the same muddy lake. Phil's place stank of mouseshit too, and of course it lacked the feminine touches I'd grown accustomed to and cleanliness wasn't all that high on the list of priorities, but who was I to complain? It was a place to breathe, sleep, shit, brood and get stoned.

In the meanwhile, I tried to get hold of Helen. She'd quit Brennan's the day after our phone conversation and when I called Kurt and Adele's, she refused to talk to me. Adele wouldn't say a word the next day at work and it was awkward in the extreme going through an eight-hour shift behind the bar with Kurt, no matter how hip and impervious I tried to be. We dodged round each other a hundred times, made the smallest of small talk, gave elaborate consideration to customers at the far end of the bar. I wanted to kill him, that's what I wanted to do, and I probably would have too, except that violence was so unhip and immature. Helen's name never passed my lips. I froze Kurt out. And Adele too. And to everybody else I was a combination of Mahatma Gandhi and Santa Claus, my frozen smile opening up into a big slobbering insincere grin. "Hey, man," I said to the cheapoid with the mustache, "how you doin'?"

On my break and after work, I called Kurt and Adele's number over and over, but Helen wasn't answering. Twice I drove my Dodge down the street past their house, but nobody was home the first time and then all three of them were there the next, and I couldn't face going up those steps. For a while I entertained a fantasy of butting down the door, kicking Kurt in the crotch and dragging Helen out to the car by her hair, but it faded away in a pharmaceutical haze. I didn't run through a check-list of emotions, like one of those phony Ph.D.s in the women's magazines Helen stacked up on the coffee table like miniature Bibles and Korans—that wasn't my way at all. I didn't even tell my parents we weren't together anymore. I just got high. And higher.

That was what brought about the culminating wreck—of that series, anyway. I was feeling bad one day, bad in every sense of the word, and since it was my day off I spent the afternoon chasing down drugs in every house and apartment I could think of in Westchester and Putnam counties, hitting up friends, acquaintances and acquaintances of acquaintances. Phil Cherniske was with me for part of the time, but then he had to go to work, and I found myself driving around the back roads, stoned on a whole smorgasbord of things, a bottle of vodka propped between my legs. I was looking at leaves, flaming leaves, and I was holding a conversation with myself and letting the car take me wherever it wanted. I think I must have pulled over and nodded out for a while, because all of a sudden (I'd say "magically," but this was more like treachery) the leaves were gone and it was dark. There was nothing to do but head for the restaurant.

I came through the door in an envelope of refrigerated air and the place opened up to me, warm and frank and smelling of cigarettes, steak on the grill, fresh-cut lime. I wasn't hungry myself, not even close to it, so I settled in at the bar and watched people eat dinner. Kurt was bartending and at first he tried to be chummy and unctuous, as if nothing had happened, but the look on my face drove him to the far end of the bar, where he tried to keep himself urgently occupied. It was good sitting there with a cigarette and a pocketful of pills, lifting a finger to summon him when my drink needed refreshing. Once I even made him light my cigarette and all the while I stared hate into his eyes. Adele was waitressing, along with Jane Nardone, recently elevated from hostess. I never even looked at Adele, but at some point it seemed I tried to get overly friendly with Jane in the corner and Phil had to come out of the kitchen and put a hand on my arm. "Brennan'll be in soon, you know," Phil said, his hand like a clamp on the meat of my arm. "They'll eighty-six you. They will."

I gave him a leer and shook him off. "Hey, barkeep," I shouted so that the whole place heard me—all the Surf 'n' Turf gnashers and their dates and the idiots lined up at the bar—"give me another cocktail down here, will you? What do you want me, to die of thirst?"

Dinner was over and the kitchen closed by the time things got ugly. I was out of line, and I knew it, and I deserved what was coming to me—that's not to say it didn't hurt, though, getting tossed out of my own restaurant, my sanctuary, my place of employ, recreation and release, the place where the flame was kept and the legend accruing. But tossed I was, cut off, eighty-sixed, banned. I don't know what precipitated it exactly, something with Kurt, something I said that he didn't like after a whole long night of things he didn't like, and it got physical. Next thing I knew, Phil, Kurt, Jimmy Brennan and two of the busboys had ten arms around me and we were all heaving and banging into the walls until the door flew open and I was out on the pavement where some bleached-out overweight woman and her two kids stepped over me as if I were a leper. I tried to get back in—uncool, unhip, raging with every kind of resentment and hurt—but they'd locked the door against me, and the last thing I remember seeing was Kurt Ramos's puffed-up face peering out at me through the little window in the door.

I climbed into my car and fired it up with a roar that gave testimony to a seriously compromised exhaust system. When the smoke cleared—and I hoped they were all watching—I hit the gas, jammed the lever into gear and shot out onto the highway on screaming tires. Where was I headed? I didn't know. Home, I guessed. There was no place else to go.

Now, to set this up properly, I should tell you that there was one wicked turn on the long dark blacktop road that led to that dark lane on the muddy lake, a ninety-degree hairpin turn the Alien had christened "Lester's Corner" because of the inevitability of the forces gathered there, and that was part of the legend too. I knew that corner was there, I was supremely conscious of it, and though I can't say I always coasted smoothly through it without some last-minute wheel-jerking and tire-squealing, it hadn't really been a problem. Up to this point.

At any rate, I wasn't really paying attention that night and my reaction time must have been somewhere in the range of the Alzheimer's patient on medication—in fact, for those few seconds I was an Alzheimer's patient on medication—and I didn't even know where I was until I felt the car slip out from under me. Or no, that isn't right. It was the road—the road slipped out from under me, and it felt just as if I were on a roller coaster, released from the pull of gravity. The car ricocheted off a tree that would have swatted me down like a fly if I'd hit it head-on, blasted down an embankment and wound up on its roof in a stew of skunk cabbage and muck. I wasn't wearing a seat belt, of course—I don't even know if they'd been invented yet, and if they had there wouldn't have been one in that car—and I found myself puddled up in the well of the roof like an egg inside a crushed shell.

There was no sense in staying there, underneath two tons of crumpled and drooling machinery—that wasn't the way things were supposed to be, even I could see that—so I poked my hands through the gap where the driver's side window had formerly been and felt them sink into the cold ooze. There was a smell of gasoline, but it was overpowered by the reek of deconstructed skunk cabbage, and I didn't give the situation any more thought or calculation than a groundhog does when he pulls himself out of his burrow, and the next thing I knew I was standing up to my ankles in cold muck, looking up in the direction of the road. There were lights there, and a shadowy figure in a long winter coat. "You all right?" a voice called down to me.

"Yeah, sure," I said, "no problem," and then I was lurching up the embankment on splayed feet, oozing muck. When I got to the top, a guy my age was standing there. He looked a little bit like Kurt—same hair, same slope to the shoulders—but he wasn't Kurt, and that was a good thing. "What happened?" he said. "You lose control?"

It was a ridiculous question, but I answered it. "Something like that," I said, my voice thick with alcohol and methaqualone.

"Sure you're not hurt? You want to go to the hospital or anything?"

I took a minute to pat myself down, the night air like the breath of some expiring beast. "No," I said, slowly shaking my head in the glare of the headlights, "I'm not hurt. Not that I know of, anyway."

We stood there in silence a moment, contemplating the overturned hulk of the car. One wheel, persistent to the point of absurdity, kept spinning at the center of a gulf of shadow. "Listen," I said finally, "can you give me a lift?"

"A lift? But what about—?"

"Tomorrow," I said, and I let one hand rise and then drop.

There was another silence, and he was thinking it over, I could see that. From his point of view, this was no happy occasion. I wasn't bleeding, but I stank like a corpse and I was leaving the scene of an accident and he was a witness and all the rest of it. But he was a good man, and he surprised me. "Yeah, sure," he said, after a minute. "Climb in."

That was when things got very strange, because as I directed him to my house at the end of the lane by the side of the soon-to-be-refrozen lake, a curtain fell over my mind. It was a dense curtain, weighted at the ends, and it admitted no glimmer of light. "Here," I said, "stop here," and the curtain fell over that part of my life that played itself out at Phil Cherniske's house.

A moment later, I found myself alone in the night, the taillights of the good samaritan's car winking once at the corner and then vanishing. I walked down the dark lane thinking of Helen, Helen with her silver-foil eyes and smooth sweet smile, and I mounted the steps and turned the handle of the door thinking of her, but it wouldn't turn, because it was locked. I knocked then, knocked at my own door, knocked until my knuckles bled, but there was no one home. **SQ**

The Lives of Philosophers

A STORY

by Kevin Brockmeier

Kevin Brockmeier lives in Little Rock and is the author of two novels, *The Brief History of the Dead* and *The Truth about Celia*, as well as two story collections, *Things That Fall from the Sky* and *The View from the Seventh Layer* (2008). His stories have appeared in *Best American Short Stories* and an anthology of *O. Henry Prize Stories*, a prize he has received three times. Brockmeier was recently named one of the Best Young American Novelists and is a recipient of a Guggenheim Fellowship, as well as a grant from the National Endowment for the Arts.

THERE MUST HAVE BEEN a window of seconds, after he was seized by his vision of the unknown but before he was awed into silence, when Thomas Aquinas would have been capable of describing what he had seen. He was working alone in his cell when it happened—drafting a sermon on the four cardinal virtues, maybe, or a commentary on the *Metaphysics* of Aristotle. A tallow candle was burning on his desk. The candles at the friary were not perfumed, so the odor of animal fat must have lingered in the air, but Aquinas would not have noticed that. He paused to blot the ink from his quill. Perhaps he heard the wind filtering through a crack in the shutters. Then he turned his head to follow the quivering motion of a cobweb and was filled with the white light of revelation.

Jacob can envision the scene down to the smallest detail. He can picture Aquinas hunched over in his wooden chair, his giant's body locked into its writing posture, his oxlike eyes absorbed in concentration. The sleeves of his robe were gathered at his elbows. A grain of sand, caught in the wick of the candle, gave off a tiny spark. He can see it all so clearly, but he cannot cross the threshold of the image and slip inside. He cannot guess what Aquinas was thinking. It is the one surpassing mystery of the great man's life, a mystery that has occupied the attention of the philosophical community for more than seven hundred years. What happened that night in his cell to make him lay aside his pen? What did he understand in that one brief moment before he lost the will or the ability to express himself?

Aquinas was not yet fifty at the time, though he would die just a few months later. When Friar Reginald asked him why he had abandoned his work, he answered, "I can write no more. I have seen things which make all my writings like straw."

I can write no more. I have seen things which make all my writings like straw.

Jacob has printed the words on the back of an envelope which he has tacked to the bulletin board above his desk. He shares his office, a converted classroom on the top level of the humanities building, with half a dozen other graduate students, but Bertram College is such a small institution, and the philosophy department so lackadaisical, that he often has the space entirely to himself. Sometimes, when he is trying to think through a rough spot in his thesis, he can stay at his desk staring at the words on the envelope until long after midnight, leaving only when he hears the custodian's cart rumbling down the hall, reverberating over the pebbled floor like an oncoming train. There is nothing waiting for him at home and no reason for him to hurry. His girlfriend, Audrey, works the late shift at the college health clinic. Even on her nights off the two of them no longer know what to say to each other.

It is a Thursday evening in early March when Jacob meets the woman he will later come to think of as the gypsy. He is supposed to be grading student midterms, but instead he has spent the last few hours bookmarking passages in Aquinas's *Summa Theologica*—searching for clues, as he thinks of it. He has become so engrossed in the project that when a knock comes at the door, he twists around in his chair as though someone has dropped an ice cube down the small of his back.

It takes a moment for his heart to settle. "The door's unlocked," he calls out.

The woman who comes edging into the room looks to be maybe nineteen or twenty. She is wearing a long, loose skirt, a sweater with a neck that reveals the collars of several smaller sweaters, and dreadlocks that are trussed up in a bright red scarf. "Sorry, man, you were the only light I could find on."

Jacob looks at the clock and sees that it is almost midnight. "That's okay. What can I do for you?"

"I'm having problems with the change machine."

She gives the words an unusual emphasis, hovering over them with her voice like a flyswatter before falling dramatically on the final syllable. The change machine? Jacob pictures something straight out of a science fiction novel, an immense apparatus of hatches, levers, and conveyor belts that allows you to step in as one human being and step out as another, in which atheists change into Christians, stock car drivers change into politicians, great beauties change into wallflowers.

"You know, the one over by the elevators," she says. "It ate my dollar."

"Oh—the *change* machine. Well, I'm not sure what I can do to help you out there. You'll have to talk to somebody in maintenance, I imagine."

"Yeah, I would, but that's the problem. I can't find anybody. And I need that money if I'm going to catch the bus. Is there some sort of refund button I can press, do you think?"

"I doubt it. But look, here—" He fishes a couple of dollars' worth of change out of his pocket, maneuvering his fingers past his keys, his handkerchief, and a tattered roll of breath mints. "Will this be enough?"

The woman's manner as she walks across the room, without hesitation, skimming the floor in her long brown skirt, reminds him of a tree in the late days of autumn. It is in the thinness of her limbs, he thinks, and the way that everything about her seems to rustle: her hair, her clothing, even her voice.

"That's *so* cool," she says as she takes the change. "Let me pay you back, man. Here. I know. Are you right-handed or left-handed?"

"Left-handed."

Thomas Aquinas was left-handed, too. He had to hold his pen at a crook, writing from below the line to avoid smearing his letters across the page. The few surviving examples of his penmanship are barely legible.

The gypsy takes a chair out from under the desk next to Jacob's, sits down, and turns his hands palms up. "Okay, that means that your left hand is your active hand and your right hand is your passive one. Most people are right-handed, so for them it's the opposite. Basically how it works is that your passive hand shows you the character you were born with, and your active hand shows you the changes you make to yourself. The passive hand is heredity. The active hand is choice."

She leans in to peer at his hands like a jeweler examining a gem for flaws. Her lips are so close that he can feel her breath on his palms. For a moment he imagines that she is going to kiss him. The tips of his fingers give an involuntary twitch.

"Huh. That's weird. In your case, though, the lines are exactly the same."

"What do you mean?"

She traces each line slowly with the nail of her index finger. "Well, you've got your heart line here at the top. In your case it's got a sharp upward curve to it and a lot of little breaks, which means that you're affectionate but you're going to experience periods of sorrow in love. Then you've got your head line in the middle—

a good, sharp line, you see? That means you're intelligent. But there's this bit here at the beginning, which shows me you're also kind of cautious. You're a teacher, right? That makes sense. And then this curved line at the bottom is your life line. There's a lot of space between the life line and the thumb in your case, which is good, but you've also got this strange gap here in the middle—not so good. At any rate, the line has a nice fluid curve to it, so all in all what I'm looking at is a pretty decent life. The weird thing, though, and this is what I was telling you, is that the lines on the passive hand and the lines on the active hand are absolutely, one hundred percent identical. I've never seen that before."

"Is it significant?"

She folds his hands together and gives them a motherly pat. "What it means is—no change. You were born to be a certain kind of person, and you're going to die a certain kind of person. Sorry, man." She is standing in the doorway again before he can decide what to say to her. "Thanks for the bus money, though. I hope your next life is a little more spiritually dynamic."

And with that, she is gone. He listens for the sound of her footsteps as she walks away, but there is only the crisp, irregular rustling of her skirt and then, from out of nowhere, the clatter of the custodian's cart.

Absurdly, Jacob finds that he is flustered. He can feel his palms gathering sweat. Everything the woman has told him about himself is true, he realizes. Every last detail. But then wouldn't most people describe themselves as affectionate and intelligent? And who hasn't experienced periods of sorrow in love? It occurs to him that he ought to have asked her a test question, one with an answer he could either verify or falsify. Something about Audrey and the baby, maybe, or something about his dissertation. He rushes down the hall to see if he can catch her, but the elevator has already descended into the floor. He goes to the window that gazes down on the parking lot. The streetlights pick out a single abandoned car with an hourglass-shaped patch of rust on the hood.

He will continue to look for the woman over the next few weeks, searching for her face in the campus's flowing river of students, but he will never see her again.

Audrey is waiting for him at the kitchen counter when he gets home, using the ball of her index finger to cull the toast crumbs out of a tub of butter. There is a certain look she wears when she is too brittle or hopeless or beaten down by the demands of the world to sustain her disappointment in him any longer, a kind of bruised slackness concentrated mostly around her eyes and lips. He never knows whether it is his job at such times to put his hand on her arm and console her or to disappoint her so radically that the old passion takes spark in her again.

"Where have you been? I've been waiting for you," she says.

"I'm sorry. I thought you were on at the clinic tonight."

"I was. They sent me home early."

He has to be careful here and he knows it, so he flattens his voice, stripping it of even the slightest trace of emotion. "Is there something wrong with the baby?"

She shakes her head no, concentrating on the butter again, and for a moment he is almost able to believe that he has gotten away with it. She says, "I had a touch of vertigo, that's all. But after the spotting last week, Dr. Phillips told me I should take the rest of the night off just to be on the safe side." Then she gives him a little poison dart of a smile. "Not the answer you were hoping for, is it, Jacob?"

"Now, that's not true. You know it isn't. I want only the best for you."

She sniffs dismissively. "You know, maybe you really mean that. But listen to the way you say it. 'I want only the best for you.' For *you*, second person singular. Never *us*, first person plural."

He can tell that he is making a false step before the words have even left his mouth, but still he asks her, "'Us' meaning you and me, or 'us' meaning you and the baby?"

He is not trying to lay the ground for a debate, only raising a question, but for the past five months, ever since Audrey felt the first intimations of the baby growing inside her, slowly spinning around on itself like a dandelion seed, it seems as though the two of them have been doomed to misunderstand each other. Her face tightens with indignation. She says, "*Us* meaning this family—all three of us." She wipes her finger clean on a paper towel and replaces the cap on the tub of butter, then thinks better of it, pries the cap back off, and flings it at him. It bounces ineffectually off his chest.

"Whatever you're waiting to figure out, you need to go ahead and figure it out, Jacob. Put the butter away for me," she says. And she storms off to the bedroom, slamming the door behind her.

Jacob has never wanted to raise a child. He has always thought of parenthood as something like those sand mandalas that Buddhist monks create grain by grain over a period of months, then sweep away in a matter of seconds—the sort of noble yet exhausting activity that, no matter how beautiful or enriching it might be, he can only imagine himself observing from a distance. Audrey used to tell him that she felt exactly the same way. It was one of the things that had bound them together through seven years and four apartments and all the changes life had brought them. But when she found out she was pregnant, a transformation took place inside her, as profound in its way as the transformation that turned all the accomplishments of

Thomas Aquinas's life to straw in his eyes. She realized that she wanted to keep the baby and start a family. The fact that Jacob did not share this wish was at first a mystery to her, and later an annoyance, and finally, he had come to see, a humiliation, as though he were gazing through an open door at her deepest instincts, her most intimate desires, and refusing to step inside.

Which in a way, he supposed, he was.

It has become clear to both of them that if he does not experience a change of heart soon, they are going to split cleanly apart down the center, falling away from each other like the two halves of a plastic Easter egg.

He takes a bottle of water into the living room and sits down on the couch. Because of the hot spells Audrey has been having, she has left the apartment's windows cracked open an inch or two, and a small, soft wind flows through the air. He finds himself thinking of the mystery of Aquinas again—how the story of his final days was both like and unlike a fairy tale, since in the traditional fairy tale straw was transformed into gold, whereas in the case of Aquinas gold was transformed into straw.

He listens to Audrey washing her face on the other side of the bedroom door.

He does not know what he is going to do.

The light from the kitchen has turned the clock on the mantel into an expressionless white disk. Jacob glances at his wristwatch to check the time. But something is wrong. For some while now, he has been aware of a strange feeling of floatiness in his hand, the slight tingle of cool air on his skin, but not until this moment has he really given the sensations his proper attention.

He looks in his lap, on the carpet, and in the crevice behind the couch cushions. He gets up to check the inside of his satchel and the pockets of his coat. He even goes outside with a flashlight to search the sidewalk and the grass along the curb. It is no good, though. He must have lost his watch somewhere.

ON THE MORNING of January 3, 1889, Friedrich Nietzsche was walking through the Piazza Carlo Alberto in Turin when he experienced an insight that would cripple him for the rest of his days. It was a bright, brisk morning. The sun was spreading a glossy light over the pavements of black granite. Nietzsche must have been reasoning out some minor difficulty in his philosophy—the antagonism between the evolution of man and the persistence of the moral imagination, perhaps, or the problem of memory in the doctrine of the eternal recurrence. He was often incapacitated by headaches and nausea in those days, symptoms of his midstage syphilis, yet his boldest ideas always occurred to him while he was walking. He struggled against his illness for the sake of his work.

He was stepping into the lane when he saw a coachman thrashing his horse. The driver whipped the animal three, six, seven times. The horse locked its withers and lowered its head. It was the sort of sight one could witness on the streets of Turin every day, but something had been waiting for Nietzsche at the highest corner of his thinking, some desperate revelation, and at that moment, like a jumper perched on the edge of a building, it tilted forward and tumbled into space.

Nietzsche staggered into the square and flung his arms around the neck of the horse. He buried his head in the dark hair of its mane and wept. All around him people stood and stared.

"Someone should help that man," he heard one of them say.

When at last he lifted his face, the dust on his eyeglasses shone like a cluster of stars.

That night he wrote a few last letters, signing himself "Dionysus," "Nietzsche Caesar," and "The Crucified." After which, like Thomas Aquinas, Nietzsche, too, fell silent. He spent the final years of his life as a mental paralytic, barely aware of himself or his surroundings. He never explained—and Jacob imagines he was incapable of explaining—what it was that he understood that morning in the piazza.

It is late April now, six weeks since the gypsy stepped into Jacob's office and saw the contours of his life marked out on his hands, six weeks since Audrey told him he needed to figure out whatever it was he was waiting to figure out. The elms and the poplars have finished leafing out, and the students of Bertram College spend hours every day loafing around on the courtyard, tossing footballs and Frisbees to one another and spreading out in the sun and the clover. Jacob can see them from the window of his office. He has given himself until the end of the semester to come to a decision about Audrey and the baby. He loves Audrey, or at least he loves the Audrey he can still see glimpses of occasionally, the Audrey who has not yet lost the last of her faith in him. He cannot imagine the shape his life would take without her. But— and this is the problem—he cannot imagine the shape his life would take with a baby, either. Again and again he has tried to envision himself as a father, tending his child through thousands of late-night sicknesses and crying jags, but the picture will never come clear.

Maybe what he is really suffering from is a failure of the imagination. It certainly seems that way. But there is something inside him that resists thinking about it, and he is no closer to making up his mind now than he was before. He finds it easier just to prepare his lectures, grade his students' essays, and attempt to sort through the never-ending puzzle of his dissertation, which he has been putting together word by torturous word, a page or so every week, for almost two years now. He often feels as though he is making no real progress at all. It is not that he is unwilling to engage with the work or unable to tease out the implications of his ideas. It has simply become obvious to him that he is writing around the edges of his subject rather than directly into the center of it. He has all the right ingredients for a thesis—an interesting premise, a set of unusual propositions, and an important question in need of an answer. And yet, somehow, no actual thesis.

Here is where he stands: the two figures at the center of his project, Thomas Aquinas and Friedrich Nietzsche, were polar opposites in their roles as icons and thinkers, one the father of Christian philosophy and the other the father of anti-Christian philosophy. Yet both of them underwent mysterious, deeply interior ordeals of thought that fundamentally reshaped their visions of the world. They were the two most articulate minds of their day, capable of expressing even the finest and most elusive distinctions, yet after they had their revelations—Aquinas in the darkness of the friary and Nietzsche in the cold morning light of the piazza— they ceased writing altogether.

The question Jacob has is, Why? What did they realize at the final stage of their lives? What was it that came apart or locked together inside them? And, more important, were the revelations they experienced one and the same? No matter how much consideration he gives the questions, he cannot seem to come to an answer.

The problem is never far from his mind. He thinks about it while he is exercising and shopping for groceries, while he is walking across campus and preparing his notes for class. Sometimes, in the middle of a lecture, he will pause for a moment, pursuing the bright flash of an idea, but as soon as he goes to his desk to jot it down, he will find that it has been extinguished. Countless times he has fallen asleep thinking of Aquinas and Nietzsche, Nietzsche and Aquinas. He has even dreamed about them—dreamed that Aquinas was looking out over the Bay of Naples, watching the birds dive like white scythes into the ocean; dreamed that Nietzsche was dangling a pocket watch from his fingers and feeling its weight shift as it swayed back and forth; dreamed that Nietzsche was dining with Lou Salomé when he looked across the restaurant and saw Aquinas sitting alone beneath a yellow lamp, and he tore at his hair and held up his copy of Aquinas's *Summa Contra Gentiles*, and he dropped it in despair, saying, "He *knows* me, Audrey. He *contains* me." Jacob finds himself thinking about the men as if they are two old friends of his from whom he has been waiting to receive a letter: *Dear Jacob, I must offer my apologies for not writing sooner. I have been changed by the events of the last few weeks. Here is what happened. . . .* Sometimes, when he and Audrey are alone in the house together, he will listen to her filing her nails with an emery board or watch her passing through the kitchen in her quilted blue robe, and though he is watching and listening to her, and it would seem that she should fill his senses, he will be unable to separate her from the great rolling mill wheel of his speculations. *Aquinas and Nietzsche and Audrey. Nietzsche and Audrey and Aquinas.* She no longer asks him what he is thinking about. She no longer wants to know.

One day, shortly after his morning office hours have ended, he goes to the cafeteria for a sandwich and some coffee and overhears a couple of his students talking about one of his classes. "I mean, you would think that a course like Introduction to Ethics would at least teach you something about the difference between right and wrong, wouldn't you? Isn't that, like, the whole point? But I don't understand anything more about the difference between right and wrong than I did back in January."

"The professors always cover their tails pretty well on that one. It's the standard first-day-of-class lecture: Philosophy Is About Asking Questions, Not Getting Answers."

"Yeah, but." It is a finished statement: *Yeah, but.* "Here's what I think: I think we should treat philosophers the same way we treat job applicants. Have them put down their name, their employment history, and their answer to every important philosophical dilemma of the last two thousand years. You can't get away with that kind of wishy-washy the-questions-are-what-really-matters crap if you want somebody to hire you for their marketing team."

Jacob puts his hand to his mouth to cover his grin. The boy who is speaking is one of his least motivated students, someone who spends most of the class hour taking his baseball cap off, limbering up the brim, and replacing it on his head. Nevertheless, there is a part of him that can't help but agree with the kid.

Later that day, after he has finished teaching his Wednesday afternoon aesthetics seminar, he heads over to the humanities office to check his mailbox. He finds a note from the department chair:

> *J.—*
> *Please stop by when you have a moment.*
> *—H.*

The fluorescent lamp at the end of the hall has burned out, which makes all the offices there look deserted, as if that one small wing of the building has been abandoned for demolition. Jacob can see a thin rectangle of white light filtering out from around the edges of one of the doors, though, and he walks down the hall and gives a few raps on the scuffed blond wood beneath the nameplate: HART MOSER, PHILOSOPHY CHAIR.

He waits for an answer.

"Come on in."

Jacob opens the door. Hart Moser is sitting behind an electric typewriter, his hands poised over the keyboard, a blank sheet of paper curled around the roller. Friedrich Nietzsche owned a Malling-Hansen Writing Ball, a typewriter whose circular arrangement of keys prevented him from seeing his words as they struck the page. He was, like Jacob and Thomas Aquinas, left-handed.

"You wanted to see me?" Jacob asks.

"I did." Hart switches his typewriter off, and the humming noise of its machinery slowly dwindles away. He turns and sifts through the stack of material on his desk. "Ah, here it is," he says. He peers over his glasses at a sheet of paper, silently reading a few lines. "Yes, this is it," and he holds the paper out to Jacob. "Here you go, tell me what you think."

Jacob takes it from him. It contains a description of a summer course for upper-level undergraduates contrasting the religious philosophy of the medieval Scholastics with that of the existentialists—the kind of class he has been requesting from the department for years. "Are you asking me if I want to teach this?"

"Are you interested?"

"Definitely."

Hart takes a pencil from behind his ear. "I thought you would be. The class meets Tuesdays and Thursdays from three to five. It's a ten-weeker, beginning June the second. Should I put you down?"

"Yes, yes, absolutely."

"Good." He scrawls Jacob's name on a piece of correspondence paper, punctuating it with an emphatic period. "All right then. I'll have Theresa give this to Academic Affairs first thing in the morning. So how is your dissertation coming along, may I ask?"

Jacob can tell by the tightening in his cheeks that something is happening to his face. It must be something amusing, because Hart chuckles and says, "That bad, huh?"

"No, no, it's not so bad really. I just feel a bit overwhelmed by it all. For the amount of time I spend thinking about the damn thing, I should have a magnum opus by now."

Hart says, "It's like that for everybody. Do you want to hear how long it took me to finish my dissertation after my committee gave me the go-ahead? Eight years. You know that old chestnut about what ABD stands for, don't you? All But Dead." He punches the joke with a vaudevillian cock of his eyebrows. Then he swivels back around to his typewriter. "Well, listen, Jacob, I have to get some work done before I head home to the wife and kids. Oh, and by the way—your pen is busted."

"What's that?"

"Your pen." He motions toward Jacob's hand. "It's busted."

Sure enough, the ballpoint pen Jacob has been carrying has left a gummy black stain on his palm, so thick that it crackles when he flexes his fingers. He notices an ugly black streak at the belt line of his pants, and another on his satchel, and, as he makes his way to the bathroom to clean himself off, another on the door of the mail room. He is like a character in a comic strip, he thinks, leaving a dotted line of filth behind him. With a little soap and water he is able to wash most of the ink off his skin, but a bruiselike trace of gray remains on his palm, thickening to black where it has collected inside the lines. It will be another full week before the mark fades away entirely.

Jacob takes the elevator up to his office and checks his voice mail. There are three messages waiting for him. The first is from Audrey: "Jacob, listen, I'm not feeling so well. If you get this message, I need you to come home and give me a ride to the clinic. The sooner the better. Please hurry."

The second, also from Audrey, says, "Jacob, where are you, Jacob? I'm not kidding, I need you to—" She lets out a gasp. "Jesus, it's like a goddamn soldering iron. All right, I'm going to try to make it to the clinic on my own. I want you to meet me there as soon as you get this message. Do you hear me? *As soon as you get this message.*"

The third message is from Dr. Phillips at the college health clinic: "Jacob, this is Nate Phillips—um—over at Health Services. Listen, we need you to come in right away. Don't worry, Audrey is going to be okay. But I'm afraid there's been an accident with the baby."

When did Jacob's baby first notice the heartbeat that enveloped him, the seawatery amniotic fluid in which he floated? Was there a moment when his consciousness began to stir and he knew he was alive? Sometime in the months following his conception, he must have undergone the transformation from a simple collection of cells and enzymes to an individual human being, from a process of assembly to the person being assembled. Jacob almost believes that he can imagine what it was like. His baby lay in the warmth and buoyancy of the darkness, immersed in a sound so engulfing that it seemed like just another kind of silence. He listened to the roar of his own blood, to the roar of the blood that surrounded him. There was the occasional tick of something settling into place. He noticed a mild gurgling sound that rose up from out of nowhere and he could not be sure whether the sound was something he heard or something he was.

Now and then the baby felt a soft elastic pressure against his skin—it was Audrey pushing down on her stomach with her hand, though he could not have known that—and he threw his head back and over to the side in order to roll. Audrey stacked three quick breaths on top of each other and sneezed. The baby dove and turned like a fish. He liked to move when Audrey was still, and to rest when she was moving. Her footsteps reverberated through his body like an incantation.

His thumb was tiny, the size of a cherry pit, and sometimes, without trying, he would find that he had fit it into his mouth. He could taste a salty, coppery flavor that seemed infinitely familiar to him. The gentleness of the sensation was everything he knew. And because he did not yet exist in synchronicity with time, with no memory of the past, and no expectation of the future, he was able to believe that it had been there forever.

Did he realize what was happening when his heart stopped beating and his muscles went limp?

What did he apprehend in that one brief instant before the light filled his head?

If the baby had lived, he would have been a boy named Nicholas.

Jacob repeats the name to himself as he goes sprinting across the campus. *Nicholas*, he thinks. *Nicholas and Audrey. Nicholas and Jacob and Audrey.* Though he leaves his office as soon as the doctor's message finishes playing, taking a shortcut across the glass atrium of the fine arts building, then cutting through the alley behind the cafeteria, he can tell by the dwindling number of cars in the parking lot that a large portion of the afternoon has passed.

The early evening patient lag has commenced at the health clinic, and the waiting room is nearly empty. A man Jacob has never seen before is staffing the admissions desk where Audrey usually works. Nobody has to tell Jacob what has happened. He knows in his gut that Audrey has suffered a miscarriage. But there is still a part of him that has yet to accept the situation as fact, a part of him that is waiting for someone to utter the words out loud.

He gives the desk clerk a few seconds to finish slotting a patient file onto its shelf. Then he interrupts him with, "Excuse me, I got a call from Dr. Phillips a while ago. My girlfriend, Audrey, is—"

"Ah. Which would make you Jacob, right? Audrey's Jacob. Yes, the doctor called you, but that was two and a half hours ago. Don't you realize what time it is?"

Though Jacob has yet to replace his missing watch, he continues to check his wrist for the time once or twice every day. He feels like a fool whenever he catches himself doing it. To the average person, he supposes, it must look as though he is bowing his head in embarrassment—as though he is only barely managing to keep himself from covering his face with his hand. "I'm sorry, I'm afraid I don't."

"Well." It might be the first time he has ever actually heard a man tut. "Audrey was transferred to St. Vincent's at four o'clock this afternoon. I presume you're on foot. Would you like me to phone a cab to take you to the hospital?"

"Yes, I would appreciate that—" He pauses to let the clerk fill in his name.

"Monty."

"I would appreciate that, Monty. Listen, can you tell me what's wrong with Audrey?"

The clerk shakes his head. "No, I think you'd better wait for one of the doctors to give you that information. It's not my place. I'm not qualified."

By the time Jacob arrives at the hospital, the sun has fallen into the treetops, and the sky has taken on the motionless quality of a peaceful midspring evening—a pale blue, just beginning to darken to red, and stitched together by the condensation trails of half a dozen airplanes. Jacob pays the cabdriver and then finds his way to the reception area, where a nurse directs him to the obstetrics ward on the third floor. The waiting room is almost deserted, just like the one at the health clinic. The glowing panel of a vending machine flickers on and off with a barely audible ticking noise. An old man in hard-soled shoes and a fedora sits paging through a tattered magazine. A custodian walks by carrying a push broom over his shoulder.

It takes Jacob a few minutes to find a doctor who can tell him what has happened to Audrey. "Placental abruption": those are the words the doctor uses, and he says that although most women go into delivery within fourteen days of termination, the hospital might need to induce labor "if it looks like your wife isn't cooperating. Look, I'm sorry for your loss," he tells Jacob, placing a meaty red hand on his shoulder. "But all the indications are that Audrey—it is Audrey?"

Jacob nods.

"That Audrey is going to come through this just fine. There's no reason why the two of you won't be able to try again."

A great tidal flood of relief spreads through Jacob: relief that he knows what has happened; relief that Audrey is out of danger; even, to his surprise, relief at the prospect that the two of them might still have a child together. It seems that, without his awareness, something has locked together inside him, tumbling to one side by the very slightest of degrees. He has figured out whatever it was he was waiting to figure out. He feels an overwhelming tenderness for Audrey, an irresistible desire to comfort her. "Can you show me which room she's in?" he asks the doctor.

"She's right down the hall—go past the swinging doors, and it's the first room on your left."

"Thank you so much."

Jacob finds her lying down along the exact center of her bed, entirely hidden beneath the immaculate white sheets—except for her head, which is propped up on two thick pillows. She reminds him of an overturned dressmaker's model he once saw: heavy with the weight of its body, fixed in its own curves. The skin of her face is colorless and slack. Her hair is damp, and she has tucked it behind her ears.

She tracks him with her eyes as he crosses the room, but does not say anything until he pulls a chair up to the bed and brushes her cheek with the backs of his fingers. "Oh, Jacob," she whispers, and before she can go on, her face crumples and she begins to cry.

His first instinct is to hush her and hold her close to him, to pat her back as a parent would a child, but Audrey has always hated being hushed, so he stops himself and continues brushing her cheek. "It's all right," he says. "Everything is going to be okay."

"It's not going to be okay. It's not. I lost the baby. Where have you been all day?"

"I was in class this afternoon, and then I had a meeting with Professor Moser. I didn't have my phone on me, Audrey. I'm sorry."

"Dr. Phillips had to drive me here from the clinic."

"I know." He watches her take a deep breath, then clench her jaw as though a fist has gripped her stomach. He says to her, "You're not still in pain, are you?"

"No. The doctors said that that part was over."

"Have they told you what's going to happen next?"

She nods and shuts her eyes. Then she brings her hands to her face to massage her forehead. The sheets rise up in a pair of slowly moving finlike ridges that subside back into place as soon as she has worked her elbows free. She is the only woman Jacob has ever loved.

"Here, let me do that for you," he says.

She lets her hands fall to her chest, and he begins rubbing the soft notches of her temples with his fingers, tracing endless tiny circles over the stray wisps of brown hair.

After a while she asks, "Have you been in a fistfight with somebody?"

It is such an unusual question that he has to laugh. "Of course not. What do you mean?"

"Your hand," she asks. "What happened to your hand?"

"Oh, that. I broke a pen. I got ink all over myself."

She nods, satisfied. A patient walks down the hallway wheeling an infusion bottle on a tall metal stand, his loose clothing rustling in the draft from the overhead vents. Audrey lifts her head to watch him shuffle past the door. Then she falls back onto her pillow, giving a long exhalation through her nostrils. Jacob can feel it blowing against the side of his face. She begins to cry again. "I really wanted this baby," she says.

"I know you did."

"I'm so exhausted."

"Then you should let yourself rest. Don't worry. I talked to the doctor, and he says we can try again whenever we're ready."

He sees Audrey's shoulders go tense, hears the mattress creak as her body bears down against it. At first he imagines it must be some spontaneous expression of gratification, the final tightening of the spring before the watch begins to tick.

But then she grits her teeth and says, "We can try again?"

"That's what the doctor told me."

Her answer is slow and quiet. "It's been six months, and *finally*, after all this time, you tell me *we can try again. Now* you say that? I absolutely cannot believe you." She grips his hands, which are still reflexively massaging her temples, and sets them aside like a couple of broken toys. "Please leave, Jacob."

"No, you don't understand. I—"

"Get out," she tells him, and then she says it louder: "Get out!" And she must find it satisfying to repeat the words, because she keeps yelling them even as he stands up and backs away—"Get out! Get out! Get out!"—the venom rising in her voice as he passes through the door and out of sight.

As he stands in the hallway trying to decide what to do—should he leave Audrey to her grief and anger, or should he go back in and begin the long work of explaining himself?—the answer to his other dilemma, the one he has been considering for the past two years, comes to him in an instant. It is like the concussive burst of a camera flash. He knows, or believes he knows, what Thomas Aquinas comprehended that night in his cell, what Friedrich Nietzsche perceived as he watched the horse trembling beneath the blows of the whip. He knows why the two men laid aside their pens.

Both of them had spent their lives as thinkers and writers attempting to repair the material of the past. How could the past be salvaged? How could it be used to prepare the way for the future? Aquinas joined the philosophy of Aristotle with the teachings of the Church, showing how the mechanisms of logic might open up a pathway to God. Nietzsche concluded that the traditions of Christianity were a burden that must be cast aside so that the human race could achieve the nobility that was its true inheritance. They both had such hope for the dawning era, such confidence in mankind's ability to transform itself. And then, Jacob believes, they were given a glimpse of the future. They observed the brutality in whose service their ideas would be employed, the cruelty and the barbarism. They witnessed the centuries of suffering that lay ahead. They saw how the writings of Aquinas would lead directly to the horrors of the Inquisition and how those of Nietzsche would lead to the savagery of the Second World War.

Aquinas received his vision in a candle that burned like a stake.

Nietzsche received his vision in a whip that fell like a thousand bombs.

And after their visions were disclosed to them, they folded their hands and never wrote another word. They wished their ideas had never been set to paper.

Jacob waits in the stillness of the obstetrics ward, where the only sound he can hear is a hoarse voice telling him to get out, get out. There is no change machine, he thinks. The past is irreparable and so is the future. He presses his palms to the wall and listens to Audrey weeping for the child they have lost. **SQ**

Extra Days

A STORY

by Janet Burroway

Janet Burroway is the author of seven novels, including the Pulitzer Prize nominee *The Buzzards* and *Raw Silk*, a National Book Award runner-up. Her work includes a volume of poetry, numerous plays, a collection of essays, two books for children, as well as *Writing Fiction*, the most widely used creative writing text in America. Burroway was educated at Barnard College, Cambridge University, and Yale and is the Lawton Distinguished Professor Emerita at Florida State University.

EVENTUALLY, HIS BREATHING slowed and she could free her arm. She knew he was overtired and had had too much sun and that in the morning he'd go on about nothing but whether she'd got the new Alligator Point patch sewed on his patch jacket and he couldn't find any socks and was there crackerjacks for his break; she knew all that. The fundamental source of sanity is the knowledge that grief won't last. If that gives you your suspicions about joy, too bad for you. It's the price of sanity; you don't expect the price of anything to go down, do you? Nevertheless, she thought ten years was young to have an actual suicide plan.

She shook the sand off his things into the shower and picked up the conch, the plastic bag of clam shells and periwinkles, and the horseshoe crab. (A find, that— amber, translucent, only an inch-and-a-half across— usually the little ones broke as they washed up.) Still smaller, the fiddler crab crouched in the sand pail and, when her shadow fell across it, put up its claws like a boxer in mismatched gloves. Come'n get me. How do you convey your kind intentions to minor crustacea?

She picked up the pail as well, in the crook of her little finger, and juggling his wet things and the fruits of their scavenging, watched Michael for a moment to make sure. Salt over salt, the tears had left streaks in the fine-powdered seacrust around his ears. His freckles hid in the fever flush; the new-bleached hair was scattered from his thrashing and a shock of it fell across his lashes. He was beautiful, all right. Which was a fact to take out and acknowledge only incidentally, in the moments, say, between shaking sand into the shower and setting a belligerent fiddler crab outside. Because there's nothing special about the beauty of a sleeping child. Because she would not give him a memory, not one, to drag on into adulthood, like the memories she dragged, ruffled and smothered and cooed over, "Booful dolly! Baby girl!" Also, because she wanted to live in Garth's perspective, and to Garth, Michael must be just another boy, unchosen, set more or less by chance in continuing proximity. Yes, and because apart from that, out of some letter or other from her erstwhile husband, was a phrase her anger still snagged over: *You owe it to the beauty that is Michael.* What it was she owed she couldn't now recall. Something to do with money, probably, or preserving the family, or keeping him in the True Church. *The beauty that is Michael.* You don't love a child unless you'll wipe its nose.

She closed the door as quietly as she could with her few free fingers and went to make space on the living room shelves among the driftwood, shells, skulls, and stones already crowded there. She passed Garth cleaning snapper at the sink as she headed for the back porch.

"He asleep?"

"Mn-hmmm."

"I heard you. You were terrific with him."

"Was I? Thanks."

She spread his things on the line between the old pillars and turned to the fiddler crab. Alarmed, no doubt, from its roller coaster ride, it huddled now against the piece of moss, claws clenched back into its body and the body minutely jerking back and forth with watchfulness. The sand was dry, but they'd found it on dry sand. She didn't know whether she should wet the sand. She didn't know whether she should set it in the shade or where the morning sun would hit it. She didn't know what it ate. So she did nothing except reach to stroke its back with her index finger, and because she knew perfectly well this wouldn't be allowed, scarcely flinched when it took a grab of the toughened skin beside her nail. She lifted her hand and the crab clung, held, persisted till it was tipped up on the edge of its shell, then lunged for a better hold and fell, scurrying bellicose around the rim. Come'n get me. Okay, now *you* go to sleep.

In the kitchen, she poured the Clorox out of the butter tubs and rinsed the three bleached sand dollars they'd chosen of their bucketful. At the Point this time of year they were so plentiful that anywhere you dug your fingers half-an-inch below the sea bottom you'd encounter one, little hairs waving like a round brown meadow and the mouth at the center of its star slowly pulsing. It was as if the sea was paved with them, Garth said, and said every inch of the water was invisibly alive like that.

And said, "Is there room in the freezer? We've got snapper for a month."

"We can take some to Merri and Doug."

He was nearly done, and into his rhythm: the point of the fishknife at the anus, a single clean slit through the white belly flesh, his thumb pushing up from the bottom while the knife arched toward the spine, and the guts plopped out in a lump on the slimy newsprint. He tossed it aside and took another. Point, slit, push, plop. The offhand competence of Garth's gestures always stirred her. Shifting gears, or building a fire. As if the idea of work itself was caught in his easy hands, though you do not tell a man you love him because he can tie his shoes, or that watching him gut a fish makes you want to go to bed. And yet when it came to that it was not necessarily more grotesque than the fact that, now, she was going to light a candle and a stick of incense to sit by while she hemstitched a souvenir on a jacket. It doesn't do to focus too hard on your incongruities, because that leads to selfweariness, which leads to depression, which leads . . .

"You look upset." Although he'd scarcely broken his rhythm to glance between fish and fish.

"Of course I'm upset. You said you heard."

"Just part of it."

She turned off the tap and dried the sand dollars in paper towels, thumbing off the hardened hairs that clung underneath.

"He says he sits in school feeling as if his insides were being scraped, and if he knew how to go on scraping he'd kill himself that way. He said he tried to drown himself this afternoon."

"That's bullshit. He was having a great time till we got ready to go."

"It doesn't matter if it's true, Garth. It's true to the way he was feeling then."

"He'll be over it in the morning."

She took the sand dollars to the living room and lit the incense angrily. Why is it that being told what you know amounts to accusation? And why, being accused, do you seem to deny the thing you know? She was pinning the alligator on Michael's cuff when he followed her in, wiping his hands.

"I just think," he said, "it's about time he ought to be able to see me put my hand on your ass without pulling the Hamlet routine."

"Okay, I agree with you. So what am I supposed to do, since I'm so terrific?"

Carefully, he wiped a few flecks of fish dirt from his tee shirt, his belt, his jeans. "Do you want to get married?" He flipped the hair out of his eyes, new-bleached, if not as blond as Michael's then blond enough to be Michael's father's. Come'n get me.

"I don't see what good that would do. He doesn't believe in second marriages."

"Believe! Did he tell you that?"

"He told me that a week or two ago. He thinks marriage is a sacred rite, and you only get one chance. If you flunk it, that's it."

"Where does he get that stuff?"

"God knows. Maybe Catholicism is hereditary."

"Well, to tell you the truth I don't feel bound to live by his moral code."

She shoved the needle through a section of alligator tail and caught it through the loop, pulling it tight before she asked, "What about you? D'you want to get married?"

"I'm perfectly satisfied the way things are."

"Well, so am I." Conscious of her mother's voice in her own—why is triumph *prim*?—"So to tell you the truth, I don't feel bound to get married just to spite him."

At which he laughed and went to get his book; as easy as shifting gears.

Whereas she, as usual after one of Michael's overarticulate tantrums, sat ragged in the yellow light from the old globe, jumpy as the candle flame, not done with it. You couldn't say Michael didn't come by his tendencies honestly. His paternal grandfather had damned himself in the old style, shotgun in the mouth, on the 28th floor of an office building in Stamford, Connecticut, on a Friday night. And his father had called hysterical once a week for six months after they left, fifteen-hundred miles down the eastern seaboard, to say the gas was on, the pills were in his hand, if they found him at the bottom of a cliff it'd be her fault, until finally her fist-clenched nights and haggard mornings erupted in the right phrase, "Well, for God's sake, do it then, so I can get some sleep!" And he'd stopped calling and bought himself an MGB and married an editorial assistant out of Boston. And she herself, twice before she was thirty, had gone so far . . .

She knew that Garth was deep in Cambodia with Malraux, and that reading brought a fishing weekend to closure for him, like coffee after dinner or a cigarette after sex. She knew that if she brought it up again he'd have no choice but to turn sensible and soothing on her, as she had with Michael. He reads too many war comics. Television. It's the way kids are. And that she would then have no choice but to thrash out, like Michael: I won't be soothed! Having reasoned this through, she said, "All the same, ten years old seems early to have an actual plan."

He looked up, leaving a finger on his sentence. "He's got a plan?"

"A beauty. You know those Vietnamese spear traps you told him about?"

"Pungee sticks."

"That's it. He's saving up for a boy scout knife, and he's going to whittle a stick to a point and smear it with dog shit, then plant it in the ground and fall on it. If the spear doesn't kill him, the poison will. He told me it was 'very inventive' of the Vietnamese."

He let his finger slide from the page and leaned back to look at her. "You blame me?"

"Oh, Garth, don't be dim. He'd've picked up some other idea somewhere else. I just think it's a pretty ugly obsession for a ten-year-old."

He granted, "Pretty heavy." And then, almost visibly shouldering the role she'd cast him in, "But, you know, when he gets his boy scout knife he's going to take up soap carving."

"I know."

"I always liked the ant-torture myself when I was a kid. You know, where the Indians tie you down and smear honey in your eyes and ears?"

"I know, Garth."

"Hey." He laid the book aside and made as if to come to her, and then—maybe she looked more stubborn than distressed—set his mouth and leaned back again. "You told me you stole sleeping pills yourself a time or two. And here you are. Just waiting for me to finish this chapter so I can take you in there and throw ya' every-whichway."

"Actually, I'm sewing."

He went back to his book. She sewed, eyes sun-sore in the inadequate light, but not wanting any more light. Such sounds as there were attested to absolute domesticity—a tap somewhere, his page turning, the old beams sighing from the temperature drop. It was not that she thought Michael was going to kill himself, or at least not on a pungee stick, and not for forty or fifty years. It was precisely that she, herself, was still here, and knew what it had cost her, in mistakes and hate and self-contempt, before the night she reached up into Myrtle Clifford's gilt medicine cabinet and pocketed two amber plastic vials of Nembutal; and then before the night she finally, keening and rocking on the bathroom rug, flushed them down the toilet with her vomit. She wished her son survival, but she couldn't easily wish it at such a price. It hurt her, tired her, to foresee what years he was going to go through, and that she had no more weapon against it than "being terrific with him."

"It's not as if death isn't real!" she blurted, not to be answered, and was not. Just because he's a child and I've turned childish; there's evidence enough, God knows . . .

And looking around the dim room for it, found, suddenly, more evidence than she bargained for. The dog skull's sockets flickered. The parched driftwood was hung with seahorse skeletons and dried crabs. Her own chair was a felled tree, the floors and walls dozens of others. Bound and hung with jute, skins, hide. She wasn't sentimental about causing death—slitting fish or bleaching sand dollars. But we *decorate* with corpses. Peacock feathers. Cattails. Grass. The candle is consuming tallow melted out of animal flesh. There are jars and jars of shells that are the bodies of creatures once alive; the jars themselves are melted sand, which is nothing but crushed shells, which are the bodies of dead sea things. The life cycle is not the point; the point is that death *accumulates*. If matter stays, and the earth re-creates out of the dead, then every atom carries in every incarnation another death upon its back, and every live and dead thing in this room has died over and over again. Pollution is only a cosmic joke to lay the blame on us; in any case, everything would eventually be so dragged down by death that the cells would fail to hold, the hair would slide from its follicles, sap would puddle at the roots, the sea would go sluggish with the weight of it while we sat ignorant with oysters in our ears, stupefied with alligators on our feet, staring at pulp logs consumed in oozing flame in the center of the grate.

Perversely—she know she was perverse—this terror partly stilled her. When he clapped the book shut at the same instant she bit her thread, they laughed at the felicity of their timing and became more or less mutually aware—that their muscles were comfortably overextended and the skin burn-stretched no more than they could take, this time of year. In bed they came together, easily, smelling the sea again.

Which would have brought them out of another weekend in the black if he had not, as if to illustrate her point, to make the briefest possible interlude of fecundity, fallen asleep just as she turned to tell him what she'd seen, and so left her alone awake, damp with however many million poisoned sperm and fingering the blanket binding, which was in fact acrylic (crushed and burned from coal; nothing is synthetic, it's only dead), but had been deliberately devised to resemble the unwound cocoons of a Japanese vat's worth of steamed worms.

When she finally slept, she found herself at the butcher counter of the old Cochran Grocery on Seventh Street, where she had brought her mother's body to be trussed. It was already skinned, and had so little flesh on it that she did not know what animal she could say it was that Mr. Cochran would find credible. The teeth, particularly, stripped of the softening skin, protruded forward like a rodent's jaw. Also, her handbag was overflowing with capsules of Nembutal, which squirmed out through the orifices and dropped to the floor, where they crawled away. She kicked sawdust over them, as inconspicuously as possible. The black-haired woman beside her said pleasantly, "How do you fix that? With garlic plugs?" "Yes, I do," she said. I take the point of a fishknife and make however many million slits . . . "I use tarragon," she said. "Rosemary." Mr. Cochran put an apple in the corpse's mouth.

So that, by morning, she was caught in the ineluctable superiority of the neurotic. She could not eat, but cooked an elaborate breakfast, to make this the more evident. The bacon bubbling made her nauseous and the nausea panicked her; the last time she had stood for an hour at a time at the supermarket meat counter, unable to choose, unable to remember what it was she did to meat. Michael knelt on the back porch in his pyjamas dragging a twig in front of the fiddler crab, laughing when it lunged. She said he was not to tease it. He said he wasn't teasing it, it was his. She said that was lousy logic and to get himself dressed right now, he'd be late to school. Which he didn't until she yelled like a fishwife: This minute! So when she showed him the jacket he grumbled a begrudging "Ummph," and when Garth asked was he feeling better this morning, Michael defied him, "No!" and, sly-eyed, threatened to buy a boy scout knife. To which Garth replied that he'd better make sure it had a nail file because he badly needed one. To which she said, "For Christ's sweet sake," and they left by various doors in settled mutual hostility.

Day chastened her. Indulging her vision, she had worn it out by noon. Pig's feet and lettuce leaves in the supermarket, tomatoes she picked herself, newspapers she burned, ammonia with which she expunged the overripe germs on the sink drain, spray against aphis, fake sponge, real chamois, bleach . . . once aware of the omnipresence of death and her steady domestic murders, it became so obvious that it lost any saving dimension of discovery. But like someone condemned to see the road passing under the car all night, she registered this food, that cloth, the other disinfectant, until she was shaking with the boredom particular to anguish, ready to repent, as if she might stand before the interrogator, pigeon-toed, pleading, "I *will* be normal."

Or maybe day chastened all of them, or simply rounded to its balance. When she went to pick Michael up, he came swinging his lunch pail down the hill, stopping to engage in intense negotiation with a pale girl in a scarlet undershirt and the boneless stance of incipient sexuality. Merchandise changed hands. He crashed and slopped himself into the front seat crowing, "That dumbhead traded me four motorcycle cards for a crackerjack ring!"

She mother-feigned interest in his motorcycle cards. But he caught, perhaps, something controlled about her, because he studied her sideways, looked away and mumbled, "I'm sorry about last night."

"That's okay, Mike. Sometimes it's good to get it out." This minimal absolution left him uneasily shuffling his cards. Thinking perhaps it was the wrong thing to do—she didn't want to reward him for a tantrum—but reasoning recklessly that if she took it for a gesture of trust then he would, too, she drove to the shopping center and advanced him a dollar-and-a-half on his allowance toward the knife. Then she bought him a dozen blocks of blunt balsa wood and sat on the back porch steps with him, assuring herself that he knew how to hold it. He had never owned a knife, but he knew perfectly well. He notched and whittled skillfully which—had he been Garth's son it would have come as no surprise—startled and delighted her; the delight registered as genuine, and it was all right. Half-an-hour later he was raking flat the sand in a sandbox he hadn't bothered with for years, and she, relieved and wry, supposed he wouldn't even get around to soap.

But she misjudged his attention span. The next time she looked, he had upturned the fiddler crab's pail into the sandbox, and by the time Garth got home he had constructed a whole subdivision of balsa buildings, bungalows and towers, with a lake in the middle and a faintly oriental bridge of whittled popsicle sticks.

"Right. Now," said Garth. He hadn't got his jacket off. They went to the woods and, with the biggest blade, sliced out plugs of damp earth around pine sprouts three or four inches high. They dug holes in the sandbox and banked wet sod around them. Michael found a cypress sapling which they planted by the bridge so it over-hung the lake. The balsa buildings were solid, fake, so they made a mutual decision to sacrifice the sand pail and sliced a door in it, over which they hung a wood sign: CRAB. They disagreed about the fence, but Garth stood firm on his superior experience in favor of palm bark over popsicle sticks, and he carved the chips while Michael poked them in a square around the pail. Their air of solemn enterprise left her very much on the sidelines until it occurred to her to go in for a jar of shells. She edged a path with periwinkles from the sand pail to the break in the fence.

"That's it. And around the lake," Michael said.

The object of these attentions cowered for the most part in the shade of the corner brace, and though they talked to it (praising the lake view, the solid construction, the high tone of the neighborhood) only twitched occasionally—a fat client, suspicious of a hard sell. When they returned from the woods with a taller pine sprout for the front yard, it had disappeared. Mike cried out in disappointment, but Garth searched around the box, pointing—"There"—to a little mound of sifted sand; and within a few minutes the crab emerged on the other side of a balsa hut, scuttling upward big-claw-first and racing a foot or so sideways before stopping to take up its pugnacious stance again. "Digging the cellar," Garth explained. After that, out of some obscure amphibian instinct impossible not to take for enthusiasm, it stayed on the surface dashing in short spurts back and forth, streaking a maze of paths around its property.

They left Michael weaving string between the fence posts, brought out the snapper and lit the grill. While it burned down they lay in the grass, using his jacket for a pillow. He'd shrugged it off on the ground at some point and it was so stained she'd have to take it to the cleaner's anyway, where they'd remove the evidence of crushed grass and sterilize out such invisible organisms as it had picked up off the ground. . . .

Okay. Day was dying too, and the sky decorated with it, blue-black behind them and yellow in the west, the pines shifting, soughing in the air and throwing thin shadows over them, over the one sharp point of light where the coals died down. Mike humming absently. She hoped Garth wouldn't find it necessary to say I told you so.

"You had a bad day over him," he said.

"And a night. It's strange to me to think . . . that sometime or other he'll dream about my corpse."

He took a heavy handful of her hair and pulled her toward him. "I close up because I don't know how to help."

"You do all right."

He stretched against her and leaned up on one elbow, tracing the hump of her hip with his palm. She let herself roll into him and gave in altogether to gravity, sagging into the corner formed by his body and the grass, feeling the unstable gusts, the surer cadence of his hand, the individual blades of grass against shoulder and thigh where her body didn't fit the ground.

Michael's shriek split them apart. She stumbled up guiltily, caught only a glance of him by the sandbox before her hair, trapped under Garth's elbow, jerked her back. Garth moved, she pushed up to one knee and stood awkwardly, already taking up the weight of it, collecting the slim resources for another day. Two nights in a row is hardly fair, it's about time he ought to be able to see me put my hand on your ass, it's not as if death isn't oysters in our ears, however many million poisoned I'm sorry about last night . . .

"I killed him!" Michael shrieked. He stood by the sandbox shaking, one hand extended, splayed. It took her a moment to understand because, teeth bare and eyebrows meeting, his face so clearly seemed to fling out accusation.

"He pinched me and I broke him! I killed him!"

The hand hysterically fended them off. If they touched him he would fight. The crushed crab lay against the sandbox where he had flung it, bloodless, instantly inert, a piece of trash.

"I didn't mean to!" Michael screamed, and began to howl. The hand went limp and he ran toward her, she put her arms out, no, past her, to throw himself on Garth.

"I didn't mean to . . . he pinched me and I just . . . !"

In one motion Garth swung him up and sat down with him, huddled him on his lap where he clutched at Garth's back and butted his head into the collarbone.

"I didn't *mean*!"

"Of course yon didn't, of course you didn't," Garth repeated again and again against the rhythm of the butting head until it subsided into mere rocking and the howls diminished to sobs.

"Look, he'd've been dead on the road by last night if we hadn't found him, Mike. you probably gave him an extra day."

Garth sat holding him like a child of two, stroking his back and the hair out of his eyes, forming the sentences whose meaning is in their tone, while Michael cried, insisting now and again, "I killed him," but meaning by it, "Hold me," and clutching up for reassurance with his arms, his eyes, to Garth.

To Garth, because Garth was the fixer, the doer, the one for whom the sea was alive. She, herself, was not at all reassured; not reconciled. She was only, standing at a little distance from their private enterprise, flooded with unabashed pity for her son, because he was her son and her son, for whom the longest thing to learn and the hardest to remember, for whom the decision of every day, never finally made nor wholly understood, would be how willing he was, after all, to live. SQ

Mother in the Trenches

A S T O R Y

by Robert Olen Butler

Robert Olen Butler was born in Illinois, and his experiences in Vietnam inform much of his fiction. He is the author of ten novels and five short story collections, including *A Good Scent from a Strange Mountain,* which won the 1993 Pulitzer Prize. Butler's stories have appeared in *Best American Short Stories,* and he is the recipient of several literary prizes. He currently holds the Michael Shaara Chair in Creative Writing at Florida State University.

WITH A WORLD full of foolishly dangerous men, what's a mother to do? Like all the mothers of the world I am stuck with the barbarian Kaiser Wilhelm, a man full of himself but as hollow as a soufflé, and that well-meaning fool of a schoolmaster, Woodrow Wilson—I have known men like this all my life, being around preachers and teachers and also around my father, rest his soul, who was himself a bit of both, men who are certain they grasp things that no man can grasp for certain—and Black Jack Pershing, another kind of man, like the one I married, a man with quick, sure hands, I'd wager, and a single-minded bond with other men under whatever flag it may be—American, for General Jack and my own Jack—and there's nothing in the world to weaken that bond or soften those hands. My son is a man, too, according to the Selective Service Act, but God help me if I'll let him be a man yet without a fight.

This is something I know like any mother knows. The boy is not fully a man if I can remember so clearly lifting his wee body up and placing it on a rectangle of cotton clean from the boiling pot and warm from the sun and I swaddle him up and hold him against me and he is gentle and he is quiet and I carry him away, carry him through the world, and all the while he is taking in the things I know as his mother, as a woman, but cannot say, cannot even put into words except to hold him close and whisper softly to him that he is a good boy and I love him.

They eat rats. I have heard people speak of this. They live in foul water so their feet swell and rot away. They cannot sleep for fear of the guns. They kill each other. My son was taken away to this kind of life. And so I packed a bag because my husband Jack was dead of influenza now and could not stop me and I boarded a ship and went to Paris and I hired a man who had already paid for all this madness of other men—one of his arms was merely a stump, from the early days of this war—and he drove me in a cart into the countryside and we slept in the fields along the way and it was June and there was no rain and he spoke a little English, and on one of the nights, as we neared the front he said, from the dark a-ways off, behind some other tree, "Madame. You look at your son, yes?"

I knew what he meant. "Yes," I said. "Oui."

There was a long silence, and then he said, "You are mother of me also, yes?"

"I have my hands full," I said, which I'm not sure he understood. But he said no more.

I could hear a very faint thumping on the horizon down the road.

The next day there was a thin stream of civilians passing us. Most of them had already left this place up ahead, I assumed. These refugees had no sense of urgency, as one might expect, but moved with a terrible weariness about them. A mother on foot, carrying her infant, lifted her face as we passed, and her eyes seemed very old, though she was quite young. She was perhaps as young as my son. I could have been the infant's grandmother. I glanced over my shoulder as we passed and she, too, had turned her head.

I looked before me again. Edward was my only living child, Private Edward Marcus Gaines of the 108th Infantry, 27th Division, Company such and such. I had it written down in his letter. In a trench in a place in France. He had no infant child. He and I faced something together here in this foreign place. The end of our blood. I thought of the young woman we'd passed and of holding her child, just for a moment. Stopping the cart and she would have stopped, too, and I would climb down and she would come to me and she would say, perhaps in her own language but I would know what she meant, *Here,* she would say. *Hold him.* And so I would and then I'd give him to his mother and I'd say, *Carry him off now. Quickly.*

There was a smell of burning in the air. The cart creaked in the ruts of the road. With each turn of the wheel there was a sound as if it would break. This one-armed man next to me muttered under his breath, I assumed to his horse. The explosions had ceased up ahead. I drifted into sleep and for a time I was in Yonkers, tending my roses, and the morning was bright and quiet and it was hot already. It was summer. The air hung heavily about my shoulders. In the dream it was only me and the roses and I was clipping the faded heads. I worked steadily but the garden was full of dead roses. The scissors chinked and chinked with a sound like a turning wheel.

And I awoke to tents passing and the rumble nearby of motorized vehicles with armor plating upon them and I got down from the cart and found my way through a trail of foolish men who were astonished to see me but compliantly helpful, and at last I was with an officer who had the authority to deal with my needs. We sat on reed chairs in a tent that smelled of grass and earth.

My son had written, *Mother the men suffer here greatly, those who have been here a long while. These are the French and the British and the Australians, mostly, where I am. I am filthy already, though it is all right because I feel like one of them.* This colonel before me was not filthy at all. He was quite properly clean and starched and his uniform rustled with gentility as he leaned forward and offered me tea.

"You've found the right place," he said, sitting back and holding his own cup with a steady hand before his face. "But I must ask you why. What is it that you wish to do here for your son?"

I had not put the question to myself with this sort of bluntness. The colonel reminded me of my husband. I had learned long ago, with Jack, to be prepared for the direct question. But he would ask for answers that were rarely as simple as he wanted them to be. I had not prepared myself for this similar moment with a stranger.

I sipped my tea.

The colonel waited, lifting his own cup to his lips. After both our cups settled back in their saucers and I kept silent for a moment more, he asked, "Are you opposed to our entry into the war?"

"I am an American," I said. "I am a patriot, as is my son."

"I'm sure you are," the colonel said. He nodded very faintly to me. His face was long and heavily jowled, the face of a man with grandchildren.

I was still trying to find an answer to his question. For myself, as well. *I know there are things that need to be done,* my son wrote to me, *and I'm glad to be the one to do them instead of another fellow. But I have always spoken the truth to you, Mama. I am afraid.*

"My son did not ask me to come," I said. "He is a brave boy."

"He has a brave mother," the colonel said.

"I want to see him, is all." I could think of nothing to add to this.

The colonel seemed to consider taking another sip of his tea, but I knew men like him. He didn't actually like tea. He didn't like sitting in this delicate way with another person. He didn't like having to deal with emotions he could not understand. The colonel put the cup of tea on the table beside him. He squared around to me. It was time to get down to the business of a decision. "I cannot guarantee your safety," he said.

"I understand that," I said.

"How can I in good conscience put a civilian—a woman, no less—in harm's way?"

"It is a choice I have made for myself," I said. "I simply want to see him, to encourage him. And his friends, as well." This last came to me all at once. I knew that military officers cared greatly for the morale of their men. "It will make them do better," I said, wandering even farther from some true answer to his question.

The colonel pursed his lips and lifted his chin. He looked away from me, out of the tent. Many men were moving around out there. I could hear their footsteps. And the hard whine of vehicle engines. But I kept my eyes on this man's face.

A long moment passed and finally the colonel said, "The trenches here are well established. There are three lines of them. One at the front. You can't go there, of course. Even if your son has been rotated forward already, which may be the case. You can't go to the support line, either. The German guns reach there quite easily, though it's not impossible for even this tent to receive a hit. I'll let you pass as far as the reserve line. You can return before dusk and the bombardments."

And so I was put in an automobile and a young officer drove me forward and we bounced hard in the rutted earth and there were large tents and the sign of the Red Cross and there were cries—muffled, but clearly men crying out—and I closed my eyes and put my hand on my chest to calm the fluttering inside me. And I thought of my son. Not Edward. It was the summer before he came into this world, when I lost my firstborn George. I lost him in his second summer. So very many mothers lost a child in its second summer. It was the killing time for children. I should have given him a different name, or at least called him Georgie when I had the chance. He never had a child's name. He was named for my husband's father and Jack called him his *little man*.

And then at last I approached a vast wilderness of earth, dead to the near horizon and a distant line of trees, and the earth was full of narrow pits stretching off as far as I could see and they were all broken and angled and ragged, never going for more than a dozen yards before breaking off briefly in some other direction. The young officer led me from the automobile and I insisted on carrying my own bag and he brought me to a set of rough wooden steps and I descended into the earth, as if we'd gotten it wrong all this time, the preachers and their followers: this thin man with bad teeth, dressed in a drab uniform, was all there was of angels, and you packed your bag and you followed him down some log steps into the earth and it was suddenly over, your life, you could not draw a breath, the air was thick with the stink of bodies and decay and the shadows were heavy on your eyes and the strip of blue sky above was just a faded memory of the life that was gone from you. I staggered a little bit and put the bag down.

"Are you okay?" the lieutenant asked, laying his hand on my arm.

"It comes to all of us," I said.

"Pardon me?"

I waved his concern away.

We moved along the trench, which was lined on its sides and under foot with wooden planks. I watched where I put my feet, with puddled water all about, black shiny water, and there were little pockets of men huddled down together, a few sleeping in a lump, another group playing cards—a face lifted there and a man with a British accent said, "Mum," half in acknowledgment and half in wonder, and the other three faces lifted and they all watched me, startled but in an oddly muted way—and I moved on and another group of men were smoking and chatting softly and they too looked up and nodded at me. A solitary man lifted his hand, black with grime, and crossed himself—forehead, chest, left shoulder, right.

We turned a corner and immediately ahead were some men gathered around a great ugly black pot at full boil. They looked up and gaped at me and the lieutenant went ahead to guide me to the side of the pot but I stopped and said to these young men, "Do you know my son? I've come to encourage him. And you too. He's Private Edward Marcus Gaines, l08th Infantry, 27th Division."

"Eddie Gaines," one of them said. "I know him."

"Can you encourage our slumgum?" another boy said.

"Is that your stew you mean?"

"Our stew."

I peered into the pot and it was the color of the Hudson River on a stormy day. "Do I want to know what's in here?" I asked.

"No," came a chorus of voices.

"Mrs. Gaines," said the first one, who knew Eddie. I looked up through a column of steam from the pot, and the boy had a camera and the others retreated and he took my photo.

We all stood in silence over the stew, and for a brief, odd moment they were just a bunch of boys, my son's friends, and they'd dropped by for lunch. Eddie'd invited them and hadn't told me, and there we all stood, awkward like that in my kitchen.

Then I thought of my son and where, in fact, he was, and I moved around the pot and it smelled like the corner of a cellar and the boys were helmeted and dark from grime and this was another country and I moved up beside my lieutenant and we went along the trench until he touched my elbow and said, "Here."

We turned to the left, and walked into a dark slash in the wall of the trench and he said, "Watch your step," and my eyes were rubbed hard by the dark, but I saw the dim downwardness of steps and I descended into a sharp cold smell of earth. I went down, as if this tattered angel had been from hell all along and hell was simply cold and dark, not fire at all.

But we came into a large dugout room and there was a pallet and a hurricane lamp and another thin man who rose from a small table with papers before him. The two men exchanged a greeting, though there was no snapping-to, no saluting, and the lieutenant gave this new officer my letter from the colonel and the officer angled it to the lamp and read it.

"This is Captain Morgan," the lieutenant said, and he went away. The captain glanced up only briefly at this and gave a faint nod and he studied the letter and I could see his hands trembling slightly. His face was strange in the lamp light. I could not tell if he was very young or very old. Young, I decided, from his skin, jaundiced by the lamp but smooth still, though there was something else, perhaps in his eyes, like the eyes of the young mother I'd passed on the road. Who can say what that is? Another contradictory thing. Deadness, from what they'd already seen, but a faint, forced animation as well, knowing that there was more to come.

Finally he said, "I've read this twice."

He paused, as if trying to find more words. I waited. He opened his mouth, closed it, twitched a little at the shoulders. "Yes?" I finally said.

"I'll see if he's not forward," the captain said.

He left me without another word.

I stood waiting there for what felt like a long while. I did not think to sit down. This place was the captain's and he'd not said to have a seat or make myself comfortable, he'd just gone up the steps and left me inside the earth. His desk was covered with papers and a map spread out, and a pistol lay there beside them as well. His bed was a pallet on a dugout's step of dirt. There was a table with a few books, some newspapers. A few photos were pinned to the earthen wall. I took a step toward them. The light was dim and the figures were small, standing on a porch on a wood frame house with dormers and a maple tree.

Then I felt something in this place. I turned. No one had entered. But still I felt it. Then my gaze fell to the floor and there in the spill of kerosene light was a rat as big as a squirrel. He was sitting on his haunches and calmly licking his paw and then wiping at his face, like a cat. He was grooming himself, this rat that would go out later tonight and dine on sewage and corpses. I am not a squeamish woman. I did not cry out at this sight. But I touched my chest, held myself hard there to stop the fluttering. Then the rat paused and looked over his shoulder and lowered himself to all fours and scurried into the shadows.

A moment later, my son appeared. I took a step toward him as he descended.

"Mother," he said, his voice terribly flat.

This represented a change in him. I had always been *Mama.*

I was prepared to take him in my arms. But I stopped, as he had stopped at the foot of the stairs.

I found myself looking about for small talk. "Your captain," I said. "He seemed . . . burdened."

Edward furrowed his brow, not wanting to talk small and not knowing how to stop it. Finally he said, "He's been here nine months now. The officers are good for about six and then they start to fall apart."

I should have felt bad for Captain Morgan, but the sadness that dragged itself into my chest at that moment was for my son, for his having this knowledge of how it is that men fall apart. And for his calling me "Mother."

"What have you done?" he asked.

"You're not happy to see me," I said.

"I'm a soldier," he said. "I'm in France. The front line is a thousand yards away. I may die there tonight."

"This is why I've come," I said, though I hadn't thought of it in these terms, that my child, my one remaining child, was thinking of dying. But of course he was.

"I'm rotating forward in a few hours," he said.

For a moment I thought of taking him up and carrying him away. There was a surge in me and I felt as if I was suddenly strong enough to sling this overgrown boy over my shoulder and carry him away. We should all do that, all the mothers of the world, I thought. Just pack a bag and come out here and carry these children home. The German mothers too. It would take all of us doing this at once. But instead, of course, we kissed them good-bye and told them we were proud and we packed a knit sweater in the bag they carried.

"Do you have your sweater?" I asked him.

"Mother," he said again, sharply, looking away.

I'd helped him pack his bag. I'd waved a flag at the train station. They'd given flags to all the mothers and fathers and sisters and brothers and wives and sweethearts and we waved them—with all the forty-eight stars now—and a brass band played and we shouted *hooray* for the war, We'd cleaned their faces and sent them away.

"I shouldn't have come," I said.

Edward shrugged.

"Can I have a hug and a kiss good-bye then?"

"Sure," he said, and he crossed the space in two steps and his arms were around me, this grown child, this soldier, this man. We hugged and I kissed him on both cheeks and he kissed me on mine and he smelled bad, my son. He needed a bath, and then he was gone, up the steps, and I thought of lifting him dripping from his bath and wrapping him in a towel and I stopped this memory at once. That was a long time ago.

I sat down on the edge of the captain's bed. I could not stand. I looked at my bag where I'd left it in the middle of the room. I sat that way for a long while and I watched the circle of light on the floor, waiting for the rat to return, but he did not.

Then there was a sound at the top of the stairs. It was the captain. "Is it all right?" he asked.

"Yes," I said.

He came down as quiet as the rat and he stood before me. I found that I wanted to cry and I worked on that, holding back the tears, before I looked up at him. Finally I did.

The captain's face was dark, with the lamp behind him, but I could see his eyes, darker than the shadows, and he said, "He hasn't been here long enough."

I didn't understand. He sensed it.

"To appreciate your gesture," he said.

I clenched back the tears for a final time. Captain Morgan jittered before me, trying to hold still, obviously, but he shifted ever so slightly from foot to foot, and his hands were shoved hard into his pockets, perhaps to keep them from trembling.

"Where is your mother today?" I asked.

"Omaha," he said.

I patted the pallet next to me, and for a moment he hesitated. "Please," I said. He sat down. I lifted my arm and put it around him. I could feel him trembling. Then he laid his head on my shoulder. Softly, very softly, I said, "You're a good boy. Your mother loves you." SQ

First Love, Last Love

A S T O R Y

by Elea Carey

Elea Carey was born and raised in Memphis, Tennessee. A graduate of the Creative Writing Program at San Francisco State University, she is currently working on an MFA in the Rainer Writing Workshop at Pacific Lutheran University. Her many skills include announcing for a Puerto Rican radio station. She lives in rural Washington with her husband and their two children.

N O W I A M A L I V E , she thinks.

He's across the room, something's opened up between them, a path that goes into the unforeseeable future. She's been avoiding his look for weeks, knowing who he was, a lawyer, a lot older, someone with a thing for young girls. She'd already heard all that and knew without saying it that she'd wait until the look was about her and only her. I'll make him see me, she thought, while one party after another his glance came to her out of the corner of his eye. Now he's across the room and turns all the way, and it opens up between them. I'm alive, Sarah thinks, the slam of his look going all the way in.

There are parties like this, lots of them, events at the edge of the regular world. A fund-raiser for the community radio station, say, or a theater party, where she has friends in the play. Her mom drops her off because her mom has somewhere else she wants to be on a Friday after a long week at work, or on a Saturday, because she and her mom are sick of being with each other all the do-nothing day, and now the days of just the two of them together are over. Sarah longs—she doesn't often admit it to herself, but she longs to be just the two of them on the sofa in front of a movie and bedtime at ten o'clock.

But those days are over, and something is forcing her, demanding that she enter the world. Her mom drops her off, saying she'll pick Sarah up at ten, and seeing her mom's last-minute worried, guilty, relieved face, Sarah goes into the party, where there are friends from school and some older guys, and that's how it happens.

"He really likes you." Laura's yelling over the band. She's a senior, jangling her car keys, no pockets, no purse, narrow and sharp, swooping black eyeliner and everything in place. Sarah has always felt large and lumpy next to her, but tonight there's not so much of that, as if she's growing out of something. A little taller tonight, a cross between will and hope.

"Where is he?"

"By the bar. Reaching into his pocket. Don't look, don't look, okay, look." Same as she's seen him before, russet hair and a halfway smile. Broad shoulders confident under the linen shirt.

"He thinks he can trust you, because it would be illegal and all, because of the statutory rape, but he says he thinks he can trust you."

Sarah watches as he hands some bills to the bartender and then hands him some more. "What's his name again?" She already knows, but she likes asking. Say his name again.

"Rick. He's not a bad guy. He works for the clinic for free sometimes."

It's a party for Planned Parenthood, Laura's mother works there. Sarah and Laura don't approach the bar, they drink from cups people have left behind. "He really likes you. He says he'd like to meet you sometime." Then Laura stands back, and Rick is looking at Sarah and the time is now.

You're fifteen, fifteen. The insides of your thighs tell you as he starts across the room. The backs of your knees say it, they'll rely on your ankles to hold you up. He's smiling, he's coming. You're irrevocably pointed at each other.

"This is for you." He hands Sarah a glass, yellow wine licking at the rim. "You look thirsty."

The band had announced a break, some other people are leaving, Rick tilts his head toward the door and raises an eyebrow, and Sarah walks out. They walk out not exactly together, but at the same time. Sarah stares ahead, waiting to feel him come up beside her.

The interior of the car is like an airplane, a spaceship, glittering and intelligent with blue lights, sleek surfaces. The door closes with a hush, the gentle warning someone would make in a church. "It's quiet in here," he says. "Away from all those people. Do you like Nick Lowe?"

He touches a button on the dash, then the rich sound—breath, guitars, voices—as if someone's in the backseat but it's all around. She loves Nick Lowe, but this is like meeting Nick Lowe, like shaking his hand. The streetlights peer in, curious, craning their necks. Don't let it stop, not yet, Sarah thinks. The clock assures her. Not ten, not yet.

They sit, turned a little toward each other. The blue light of the car makes his white shirt glow, his tie is loosed around his neck. She's been in cars with boys before, they never cease their motion, like a thousand moving things are alive under the surface of their skin, hands like dizzy bats flying at her in the dark. Was she drunk when those things happened, or did they make her feel drunk? What is it about Rick that feels solid? He knows what's unfolding.

"Can I put my hand here?" he says as he does it anyway. He palms her open thigh. With the boys before she always thought about something else, but this hand, how this hand turns the skin of her thigh, how that skin pulls at the skin farther up her leg, that's just gold, a feeling of liquid gold going everywhere. It runs up her throat, comes out of her deepest throat in a moan she didn't know she had.

"That's it," he says. "That's right."

FOR A FEW WEEKS, they only see each other at parties. Rick is near the bar, Sarah sees him, and the space between them closes. "Hello." "Hello, again." A circle of heat rising up around them. She goes outside without looking to see who is looking, waits for him, and they go to the car. Then they make a plan. It turns out he lives close to her school, close enough to walk. One day during lunch period she walks out the front door of the school, goes down the long steps, and keeps going. She walks out the way she's learned to leave the parties, with intention, defiance, she doesn't look back, and he's there to meet her like he said he would be. He opens his door, and she steps inside. After that, she does it as often as she can, she disappears, and at night she lets her mother drop her off somewhere, and he's waiting nearby, or she walks, her head up, against the glare of traffic, to find him home.

They sit on the sofa. It sighs in complaint as they shift and kiss, Sarah's hands moving over his chest, his rocky shoulders. Rick kisses with muscle and restraint. He's never lost in her. Always, after a while, he pushes her back, broad hand against the flat of her sternum, he lifts her skirt, takes down her underpants, parts her skins with his tongue. Naming her, speaking to her, until the gold comes up from her throat, rapt and flowing.

One night he says, "Will you touch me with *your* mouth?" He's beside her as they sit on the sofa, his large hands over hers. His whole being, its crisp shirt, the snake of his belt, the slowly corroding athletic bend of his hips, all is very still except for his thumbs, which are rubbing the backs of her hands, not so hard that it hurts right away, but over and over until it feels like the skin will come off, worn down to the pink, unready skin below. The cars are hissing by, Sarah's supposed to be at the movies with Laura and another girl. She has to be home by eleven. Rick is tilting his head, that appealing way he has. He's really pretty handsome. Not young anymore, and it's weird to have a boyfriend who isn't a boy, who's going bald, but his high forehead makes him look intelligent. He smells like things that get old in a good way, leather and linen. He had a hard day, he said. Nothing was going right. The case . . . Sarah didn't know what it meant, but she knew how to make her face look like she was listening. Now he's saying this: "Will you touch me with *your* mouth?" It's like great music coming back to the chorus. She can't get it out of her head.

"Of course." Yes. Of course. Why didn't she think of it before? "Tell me what to do."

He takes his hands away from her and pulls at his cuffs. His eyes are smiling, bright at the corners. He can't seem to say anything. Sarah's hands go up to his chest, she pulls him to her by his shirtfront, she's avid, thirsty, she brings him in close. "Tell me what to do," she says, and he tells her and she kneels.

STILL, HE WON'T GO further. She doesn't know the right way to ask. What is this they're having if it isn't sex? Finally what she says is, "I want you to do more to me."

They're in his kitchen, early afternoon. He's noosing his tie, getting ready to go back to work. He holds his chin up, watches his reflection in the window, the hands busy with the automatic motions.

"I don't want a virgin." Businesslike, the chin kept high. "Too much responsibility. You'll have to find someone else to pop your cherry." That's it. He takes her back to school, drops her at the nearest corner. He's already looking toward downtown when she gets out of the car.

So she doesn't come around one night when he's expecting her. It's not a plan, it just happens. That week in the hallway at school, a boy she's known since they were kids, Mark, he mentions that his parents are out of town. There's going to be a party. "Where you been keeping yourself lately?" he asks. His father knew her mother a long time ago. Now he looks at her, Mark looks at Sarah.

It's a Friday. Her mother drops her off. Sarah thinks, this is the first time she's really known where I'm going in weeks.

On the back porch there's a watermelon filled with vodka. Mark hands her a cup. Queen is singing, "We will we will rock you" from speakers wedged in the upstairs windows. She and Mark spin in a hammock. Freshmen and sophomores, juniors and seniors are jumping up and down on the fiberglass pool cover, the watermelon drink dancing up from plastic cups in rosy arcs. Later she doesn't know how they got from the hammock to the floor of a bedroom, where there's a drink spilled under her. It glues her gauzy shirt to the floor and sugars her back when she presses into it. Mark takes off his jeans, balances his weight over her, and pokes between her legs with something that feels like a large thumb. I could be anybody, she thinks. It touches her three or four times. I could be somewhere else all together, she thinks. Mark's hand pins her shoulder to the hardwood, he moves against her in a way that makes her shift her hips—where is it supposed to hurt?—until he arches and sighs, falling on top of her.

She calls Rick the next day from the pay phone near the gym.

"I'm not a virgin anymore."

"Well, good for him," says Rick.

In the gym, the coaches are shouting "Baseline! Hustle!"

"Good for him," says Rick.

A week later, skipping algebra, she goes over and lies down on the cool sheets for the first time. He rises over her. She doesn't know what to do with her legs, and they lie straight out to the sides. "Is that all right?" he says. His teeth are tight together, gating him in. Something breaks inside her, but she swallows her gasp. Tiny cuts all around where he is, it's supposed to be a connection, but everything feels frayed. This must be right. It's right, it's right, it must be right. "It's all right," she says. "It's good." Later, at school in the bathroom, what comes out of her is tinged with pink. She touches it, rubs it dry in her palms, and cups her hands to her face to smell the two of them together. "New. This is new." Checking the mirror to see how she's changed.

HER MOTHER DECIDES she should see a therapist, a guy her mom used to date. "He's a good guy. He's helped a lot of people." She says it with her head up, eyes straight forward, the way she does when she's talking about a new job. "Something's going on with you, Sarah. It's not just the typical teenage moodiness." They're driving to school. Rick's apartment is a few blocks away. He likes to stand on the terrace in the morning with his shirt off, he's told her this, given her this image of himself alone. Sometimes Sarah sits on the floor of her closet in the dark and thinks about him. "I made you an appointment for after school tomorrow."

The name of the therapist is George. Sarah sees him on Tuesdays. When she comes in she says, "Hello, George," like someone entering a room in a television show. He looks like he's in perpetual recovery from some wasting sickness. Hair yellowed by smoke, hollowed-out cheeks. I don't believe in you, she thinks. Using the one ashtray between them, they sit on opposite sides of a high desk. They talk for fifty minutes, although because he's still friends with her mother, he often gives her a little more time. She tells him everything, but in a way that makes it clear that she has it all under control. He tells Sarah's mom that he cries after she leaves: "Because there's nothing I can do." Her mom tells her this one morning on the way to school. Sarah doesn't know what to say. When she's sixteen, she'll drive herself to school.

"What are you telling him to make him cry?" says her mother.

Sarah follows the line of the curb. People walking, waiting for the bus, and the dust swirling when the bus goes by. The gray stone corner of Rick's building catches the sun. For as long as she can remember, she wanted just this: a small room, no one else in it but herself and him. Outside, the busy world, whirling and twisting with its dust and noise and, inside, something bright and solid. At first there wasn't a bed with its ropy sheets, there wasn't the surprise of skin on skin, there wasn't the searching when he rolled away and left her cool and lonely afterward, but she'd been right, right about how strong and bright this something.

Turning around to look at her mother, Sarah makes her face go soft and kind. "There's nothing you don't know about my life, Mom." She puts a hand over her mother's on the gearshift. She says it quietly: "It's okay, Mom. There's nothing you don't know."

AFTER SOME MONTHS, they become a fact in the dark world. She sees him at his apartment, leaves a part of herself on the sheets, and they go out, too, parties and bars where no one bothers to ask her for ID. "You're with him?" people ask. She carries this news wherever she goes.

In public he doesn't touch her often, but Sarah notices other people watching, how the men come close with their curious eyes, how sour the women are, looking over their shoulders.

"You better be careful, little girl," says someone she almost knows, a blond woman her mother's age, a secretary or a clerk. Cheap draft beer is swinging in her cup, she comes so near that Sarah can see the bled-out lines of lipstick trickling off her lips. Everything about her is being sucked toward the earth, the tributary lines run down to her cleavage. Jealous, thinks Sarah. There are no lines on me like that. "You don't know what you're getting yourself into." The woman slights Sarah's foot with her spiky heel. Rick's across the room, women near him in small clusters.

"What are you, fifteen? Sixteen? It doesn't matter." A hushed snort. "No, ma'am, it doesn't matter. You'll be all used up by the time you're twenty."

I'm more than that to him, thinks Sarah. When Rick opens the car door for her, he puts his hand on the small of her back. I'm more than that.

AND BESIDES, there's nothing he can't have. That's what she thinks while he wrestles between her legs. All of me, every spot and bend. But something's wrong lately. When he's on top of her, he pushes harder, sweats longer. The bowl between her hips is full of liquid, she's sodden on seeing him, and it doesn't hurt anymore, everything's silk and velvet when he goes in. It's an afternoon, a Saturday. She's supposed to be at the library. She wraps her legs around him, pulling him all the way up to her heart, she could swallow him that way. But the look on his face is almost like anger, and he rolls off without the final, quick victory, sits up and lights a cigarette.

"Here," she says, turning onto her stomach. Her breasts are twisted against the mattress, she pulls a pillow under her and angles her back. She hasn't heard of it, but surely people do it. There's traffic outside, voices. Right through those curtains everything else spins by.

"No," he says. He's turned away, sitting on the side of the bed. "Not yet," he says. His hand rests on her as if his whole life and everything about him is in it. She feels the lines of his palm, his fingerprints like little hurricanes. And it's almost like she can see right through him, right through his solid body and through the apartment walls, out to the lurching world and beyond.

YEARS LATER, long after Rick, after others, she'll get pregnant, get married, and give birth to a daughter. When her labor starts, she remembers what it was like to be fifteen and what it was like to think, This is what I'm made to do.

There will be a divorce before the daughter is two, and Sarah ends up raising her daughter mostly by herself, going to night school, taking one job after another, sometimes two jobs at once. Her body becomes a formless, waddling joke. There are parts of it she doesn't see or know for years, parts that surprise her in moments before a dressing-room mirror, like seeing friends she thought had moved away, left town years ago. But there's the person she loves beyond any other, the one, final, true love of her life, her daughter, who looks like her, and is so often near her, and to whom she shows the last, worst parts of herself, almost every day.

At night, when the world and all its need have left her drained and dry, Sarah stands at the edge of her bed as if it were a gateway to a vastness where she's doomed to float without orbit or reason. There's never anyone in the bed but her.

When her daughter begins high school and starts going out with her friends, Sarah is alone. And instead of staring down into the doomed bed, she sits up and waits. She sits at the kitchen table with a newspaper, or in a chair by the window with her feet pulled under her, or in the dining room with its brassy fixture of cheapest glass, and she waits until long after the appointed hour for her daughter to come in the door, flushed, alive, and talking lies. And while she waits, she says a prayer that begins: O brave, ambitious human.... SQ

Listen Up

A STORY

by Alice Hoffman

Alice Hoffman was born in New York City in 1952 and published her first novel, *Property Of*, when she was twenty-one and still a student in the writing program at Stanford University. Since then she has become a prolific writer, the author of sixteen novels, including *Practical Magic*, *At Risk*, and *Here on Earth*, an Oprah Book Club selection. She is also the author of two collections of short fiction, eight books for children and young adults, and several screenplays. Hoffman lives in Boston and New York.

WHEN SHELBY RICHMOND was called into her supervisor's office, she assumed she was being fired. Frankly, if she'd been in charge, she would have fired herself. She'd been at the pet store for three months, time enough, she was sure, for people to see she was a fake and a phony and a black hole and a malcontent. She smoked weed in the ladies' room. She wore her smock inside out, seams showing, as a small act of rebellion. If she thought someone was shady, she wouldn't sell him a parakeet, let alone a puppy. She gave herself a 50 percent discount when she bought kibble for the two dogs she'd liberated from a homeless person's scam. If you were downscaling, Shelby would be the perfect person to get rid of. Instead, she was made the manager. One more mark on the checklist of how unfair life was.

"I don't deserve it," Shelby said.

She may have been a black hole, but she was honest. Shelby had been shaving her head for eight years and couldn't even remember how she had looked with hair. She knew she scared some people; she had big eyes, the better to see right through a person. She had sharp little teeth. Ever since she'd moved to New York with Ben

Mink, she'd had a recurring dream about werewolves climbing up the fire escape. They were not bad dreams; in fact, Shelby looked forward to them. She was always somewhat disappointed when she woke up and saw her two little white dogs, Blinkie and General Gao, on their doggy bed, another item she'd marked down for herself at the Pet Shop.

The manager's job paid a hundred dollars more a week. Shelby would have to do more office work, meaning less time with the customers, a definite plus. Shelby was good at math, even though she hated it. She could figure things in her head, and she didn't know how she did it. The problem was that Maravelle, who'd been working at the store for two years and supported three children, should have been the one to be promoted. In a fair and just world, Maravelle would have gotten the raise and Shelby would have been fired.

"Maravelle should have the job," Shelby said.

"Do you know how much time she took off last month?"

"Her kid had the chicken pox." Maravelle had twin seven-year-old boys and a twelve-year-old girl named Jasmine. She had pictures up everywhere.

"Hey, this is not the Red Cross. Maravelle's absent too much. If you don't take it, I'll hire from outside."

So Shelby accepted. She was self-destructive, not stupid. Word got around fast. When Shelby took her break and went to have a cigarette in front of the bookstore, Maravelle came outside.

"I can't believe you screwed me like this. I've been here two years!"

"They were going to hire from the outside if I didn't take it. I'll give you half the money."

"I don't want half the money!"

"Fuck it. I'll give you all of it!"

"You just don't get it, Shelby."

Maravelle went back to the pet store, clearly pissed, if not with Shelby, then with the universe. Shelby threw her cigarette on the ground and stomped it out. She was wearing her red sweatshirt and faded jeans and a pair of Frye boots that she had to wad up with newspapers. She could afford new boots, but she didn't like to spend money on herself. Maravelle was the closest thing she had to a friend, not that they actually were. All the same, she knew Maravelle's kids' names: Jasmine, Teddy, Dorian.

That night Ben and Shelby went to the Half King. There were tables out on the street, so they could bring along Blinkie and the General, who were actually pretty well-behaved for ex-homeless mutts. Blinkie, the flopsy dog, was completely blind and had to be carried across the street. The General, a terrier type with shaggy eyebrows, always sat closer to Ben, who was messy, and therefore more likely to drop food, even though the General was 100 percent attached to Shelby. She didn't even have to use a leash with him. Shelby felt that if she gave Ben and the General identical intelligence tests, the General would win. If the General had been a man, Shelby would probably run away with him, even though he had an annoying habit of licking his feet. Ben had some pretty annoying habits, too.

"If you want to make things right with Maravelle, get her something she'd never get for herself," Ben said. Leave it to Shelby to be depressed about a raise. Ben had gone from being a weed salesman who lived in one room over a quick market to a pharmaceutical student who seemed to have an answer for everything.

"You think bribery is morally correct?" Shelby asked. Lately Ben had been bringing her things. Bunches of tulips, a new pillow, a gray scarf.

"Sometimes. What does she want more than anything in the world?"

"I can't offer her that! I'm not God. I can't make her stay young and beautiful for life."

"Is she beautiful?"

Shelby liked to keep the separate parts of her life separate. Ben had never met anyone she worked with. Shelby believed that the people who survived were the ones who compartmentalized their lives. If she thought about her own past, for instance, a total disaster of a life, she wouldn't be sitting at a bar in Chelsea drinking a Magic Hat beer and watching Ben devour a burger. She'd be in her parents' basement, slitting her wrists.

"She looks like Mariah Carey. Actually, she sounds like her, too. She has an amazing voice."

"Mariah's going to be at the Garden, and a guy I know at school can get cheap tickets to anything."

It sounded like a good idea, but when Ben came home the following night he had bought two tickets for three hundred dollars.

"Maravelle can't afford to buy new clothes for her kids, and you paid three hundred dollars for these?"

"I thought you wanted them. You said it was a good idea."

Shelby went to the night table and got out the weed. She hated reality. The General trotted over. "Good boy," Shelby said.

"You get stoned every time you get pissed," Ben said.

"You should talk," Shelby said. "You do it every day."

"I don't do it because I'm pissed off, I do it to improve my quality of life."

"Hah." Shelby knew about Ben's past drug usage. He had basically tried every-thing. If you strung out all the drugs he'd ever used in a line, they'd probably reach across the river to New Jersey.

Ben lay down on the bed. He was tall and skinny. He always wore a white shirt and black jeans to school. He'd changed from his old, grungy self, but not com-pletely. He watched Shelby roll a joint and light it, then took a hit himself. Shelby patted the bed so that the General knew it was all right to jump up. He was such a smart dog. When Shelby was upset, the General always lay down right next to her with his nose against her thigh. If only Ben Mink knew enough to be quiet.

"Three hundred dollars for the experience of a lifetime," Ben said. "Isn't it worth it? Think of how much people pay to have weddings."

"Weddings? Who's talking about weddings?"

"No one. It's just that people pay a fortune for so much excess and crap like two-story-tall cakes that taste like white bread when they could easily elope and spend the money on a trip to Mexico."

"Are you planning a trip to Mexico?" Shelby was wearing underpants and a T-shirt. She was pale and bald, and her feet were thin and long. She hoped to God Ben Mink wasn't thinking of asking her to marry him.

"It's a what-if situation."

"Oh, yeah?" Shelby liked to test Ben. "OK. What if a werewolf climbed up the fire escape?"

"Timber werewolf or New York werewolf?"

"New York."

Shelby grabbed Blinkie off the floor and held him on her chest. She had no idea how old either dog was or how long Blinkie had been blind. When Blinkie fell asleep he rumbled. Shelby wondered if he'd seen so many horrible things he just decided to go blind. He had scars around his neck and on his belly. She had once tried to bathe him in the kitchen sink, but he'd cried. He'd sounded so much like a person, so grief-stricken and panicky, Shelby had lifted him up, toweled him dry, and had never tried to bathe him again. He was pretty filthy, but Shelby didn't care. Blinkie had a weird reaction to rain, too. When he heard it, he climbed into the bathtub and stood there shuddering. Sometimes, when Shelby came home from work on a rainy day, she'd find the General posted next to the bathtub, standing guard over Blinkie.

"A New York werewolf couldn't cross to the east side of Tenth Avenue, so it's a moot point."

"Yeah. Right. Moot." Shelby laughed. She so rarely laughed it was always a surprise that she could.

"I mean it. New York werewolves can only go as far as the yellow line in the center of the Avenue. Everybody knows that." Ben grinned. He was better-looking when he let his guard down. "They can go to the Half King for a beer, but they can't go any farther."

"This concert better be good," Shelby said. "It better make Maravelle happy."

She gave Maravelle the tickets the next day out in front of the bookstore. Maravelle was having a cigarette, even though she had given up smoking for the sake of her voice.

"You are fucking kidding me," Maravelle said. She never cursed, so this was either a very bad or a very good sign. "You little crazy ET." Maravelle threw her arms around Shelby.

It was good. Maravelle hopped up and down praising Jesus, even though Ben was the one who'd gotten the tickets and Shelby had paid for them.

"Shelby, I do think you have a good heart," Maravelle said. "I always knew it."

"Well, you're wrong." All the same Shelby felt OK about the price of the tickets now that she saw Maravelle's reaction. What the hell.

"I want you to come with me," Maravelle said. "We'll go together, and we'll always remember it. It will be like number one or two or three in our most treasured memories."

"I don't go to concerts," Shelby said.

"What if I can't get a babysitter?" Maravelle worried. Her mother lived in Delaware and her little sister had moved to Texas and she was pretty much on her own.

Ben was the only choice. Maravelle's place wasn't far from St. John's out in Queens, and Ben was pretty good with kids. He liked TV. He'd probably have them all watching CSI and eating marshmallows toasted over a match, but he'd take good care of them. Ben didn't even complain. He took down Maravelle's address when he left for class and he told Shelby not to worry.

"Who said I was worried?"

"There's nothing to taking care of kids," Ben assured her.

"They better be alive when Maravelle gets home, or she'll crucify me."

On the night of the concert Ben phoned as Shelby was getting ready to go. She was wearing her same old jeans and her red sweatshirt.

"You're not dressing up?" Ben said. "Wait till you see Maravelle. You didn't tell me she was gorgeous."

"Is she?" Shelby gazed at herself in the mirror. What big eyes she had. Little Miss Riding Hood.

"She's wearing a flowy green blouse and white jeans and huge hoop earrings with coral-colored things on them."

"What was I wearing this morning?" Shelby suddenly asked.

Shelby stood in the middle of their bedroom in her jeans and her sweatshirt looking at herself in the mirror. The General looked up at her and wagged his tail. It had started to thunder, and Blinkie took off for the bathroom and the safety of the tub.

"You always look beautiful," Ben said.

Narrow escape, Shelby thought.

"What are her kids like?"

"They're kids. They all sleep in the bedroom, and Maravelle sleeps on the couch in the living room."

When she got off the phone with Ben, Shelby took off her clothes and pulled on a pair of black slacks and one of Ben's white shirts. She looked at herself again. She looked like a waiter. She took off the white shirt and found a pale-gray cashmere sweater her mother had sent her. She'd never worn it, and had to rip off the tags. By now it was raining like crazy. Shelby threw on Ben's denim jacket. Just as she about to leave, she peered into the bathroom. There was the General standing guard as Blinkie shivered. Blinkie was making a low howling sound. Blinkie sounded more like a person than any dog Shelby had ever heard. He was scrawny and filthy and blind, and now he was crying.

"Oh, God," Shelby said. She went to the tub and knelt down. "It won't rain for long."

Blinkie had begun picking up his feet as though he was standing on coals. His crying sounded like a woman having a panic attack. Shelby went back to the closet and got the canvas tote she used to take the dogs to the vet. She picked up Blinkie and set him inside, then she set the bag down and let the General climb in.

"Don't say a word," she told them.

Now she was late, so as soon as she went out, she hailed a cab. There was traffic and rain, and the tote bag was heavy on her shoulder. Maravelle was waiting on the corner of Eighth and Thirty-fourth when Shelby got there.

"At last." Maravelle had a green umbrella that matched her blouse. Ben had been right; she looked gorgeous.

Shelby felt self-conscious. A rarity for her. "The rain held me up."

"What have you got in there?" Maravelle eyed the big tote bag.

"Nothing," Shelby said.

They were walking down to the garden entrance. The place was packed with security.

"You've got those damn dirty white dogs! Shelby, are you crazy?"

"Blinkie's afraid of storms, and I couldn't leave the General by himself."

"My children are afraid of storms and I left them, you crazy girl. I left them with your boyfriend, who told me he has never babysat in his whole life! Now security won't let us in. Did you ever think of that?"

"They'll let us in."

There was a crush of people going inside the Garden. All bags were being checked by security.

"I told you!" Maravelle said. "Why couldn't you leave them home?"

"They're my babies," Shelby said.

It was such a stupid, pathetic statement she couldn't believe she'd said it aloud.

"Well, I know that. You think I didn't know that, Shelby?"

Shelby noticed a crush of official-looking people wearing tags over by the far entrance. Inside the tote bag the dogs were asleep; Shelby could hear Blinkie's familiar rumbling. They had to move fast or they wouldn't get in. Shelby grabbed Maravelle, and they went along to that entrance and glided inside with the official crowd, flashing their tickets. Shelby overheard the woman in front of them, shouting into her cell phone. The woman worked for Mariah's manager, and she was having a meltdown. One of the backup singers had been coming up from Atlanta and her plane couldn't land.

"You know when something happens and you have a chance at something and you'll never have that chance again?" Shelby said. She was a fast thinker. She'd always been that way. She could see the *before* and the *after*, although sometimes she could also see the *here and now*.

"I think we go up to the mezzanine," Maravelle said as she examined her ticket.

Shelby grabbed her friend. "When I was sixteen my best friend wanted to drive past her ex-boyfriend's house. We were stoned and it was snowing and I knew I shouldn't have done it, but I did."

Maravelle was listening. "OK."

"This is the opposite of that."

"If you say so," Maravelle said.

"Wait here."

Shelby followed the woman with the phone. "Hey," Shelby called. When the woman didn't respond, Shelby tugged on her raincoat. It was Burberry. Shelby hated fashion, but she had always liked Burberry.

The manager's assistant turned as though she were under attack. "What?"

"I've got a backup singer for you," Shelby said.

"Do you?" The woman's name was Lila Hannagan, and she'd heard all sorts of bullshit stories. She figured she'd be fired later in the day. The backup singer from Atlanta was supposed to fly up the night before, but Lila had told her it was OK to come on the day of the concert. "Where is she? In that bag?"

The tote bag was moving along with the rumbling breathing of Blinkie and the rhythmic snoring of General. Lila peered in and laughed. She had a Maltese herself.

"They're so ugly they're cute." She looked at Shelby more carefully. "Where's the girl?"

Shelby signaled Maravelle, who made her way over.

"We've got to go to the mezzanine," Maravelle told Shelby. "What is wrong with you?"

"Sing something," Shelby said.

Maravelle laughed.

"No, really. Sing 'Butterfly,'" Lila told her. "The harmony."

Maravelle shrugged and started to sing. The same thing that always happened happened. People around them grew silent. Maravelle had an amazing and perfect voice. Maybe she wasn't as good as Mariah, but she was good enough to make everyone shut up.

"Holy shit," Lila said.

"That's a good holy shit, right?" Shelby asked. She had trouble reading people. She often couldn't tell good from bad.

"I can't promise you anything more than tonight," Lila said to Maravelle. "And I don't have time to talk money right now."

Maravelle had a dazed look.

"We'll discuss all that later," Lila assured her.

Shelby thought about the night when she'd had the accident with her high school friend. The way the snow had been coming down, how they'd been laughing before they went into the skid.

"Is this for real?" Maravelle said.

Lila called to someone who would show Maravelle backstage, where she would quickly be fitted into the old backup singer's costumes. If the clothes didn't fit they'd be pinned onto her or the seams would be opened up.

"Tell me the truth," Maravelle said to Shelby. "Am I dreaming?"

Right after the accident Shelby couldn't stop thinking *Life is but a dream*. The possible seemed impossible; the impossible was an everyday occurrence. No wonder poor Blinkie was afraid of rain. No wonder Maravelle was standing there, frozen.

"Go on," Shelby said to Maravelle. "Hurry."

Shelby had never gone to a concert in her life, but she wasn't about to miss this one. All the same she had to call Ben first. She got her phone out and leaned up against the wall. That Lila woman had said Shelby could watch the show from back-stage. She'd looped a pass on a string around Shelby's neck.

"Just don't let those freaking dogs bark," Lila said as Shelby was making her call.

"They're half basenji. They don't bark."

"Right. I recognize a Maltese when I see one. I've got to say, your friend is actually good. I didn't think she was going to be, but she is."

"Guess what?" Shelby said when Ben finally picked up the phone. Maravelle's kids were all watching TV, and Ben had fallen asleep on the floor.

"You miss me," Ben guessed.

"You were right. This really is an extraordinary night."

"Are you saying something positive? Did I enter an alternate reality?"

Shelby laughed. Since Ben probably wouldn't believe what had happened, Shelby said the first thing that came to her.

"I want a Burberry raincoat."

She really did. Shelby Richmond, who'd been wearing the same pair of boots for five years, wanted something.

"That can probably be arranged," Ben said. "Am I supposed to give these kids dinner?"

People were passing Shelby in the hallway, paying no attention to her or her tote bag full of dogs.

"Definitely," Shelby said. "Give them whatever they want." SQ

Night Watch, 500 BCE

A STORY

by Charles Johnson

Dr. Charles Johnson received the National Book Award in 1990 for his novel *Middle Passage* and is a 2002 recipient of the Academy Award for Literature from the American Academy of Arts and Letters. He is the author of three other novels and three story collections. Literary critic, biographer, screenwriter, philosopher, international lecturer, and cartoonist, with more than one thousand drawings published, he was awarded a Lifetime Achievement Award from the Corporate Council for the Arts. Dr. Johnson is the S. Wilson and Grace M. Pollock Endowed Professor of English at the University of Washington in Seattle.

ONCE UPON A TIME, my companions and I lived in the forest near the village of Uruvela on the banks of the Nairanjana River. We were known far and wide as five men who had forsaken worldly affairs in order to devote ourselves completely to the life of the spirit. For thousands of years in our country, this has been the accepted way for the Four Stages of Life. First, to spend the spring of one's youth as a dedicated student; the summer as a busy householder using whatever wealth he has acquired to help others; the fall as an ascetic who renounces all duties at age fifty and retires into the forest; and the goal of the winter season is to experience the peace and wisdom found only in the Atma (or Self), which permeates all parts of the world as moisture seeps through sand. My brothers in this noble Fourth Stage of tranquillity, which we had just entered, were Kodananna, Bhadiya, Vappa, and Assajii. We had once been family men, members of the Vaishya (trader) caste, but now owned no possessions. We lived, as was right, in poverty and detachment. We wore simple yellow robes and fasted often. Wheresoever we walked, always in single file, Vappa, a small man with a snoutlike nose, took the lead, sweeping the ground before us with a twig-broom so we would not crush any living creatures too small to see. When we did not leave our ashram to make alms-rounds for food in Uruvela, we satisfied our hunger with fruit, but not taken off trees; rather, we gathered whatever had fallen to the ground. Each day we wrote the Sanskrit word *ahum,* or "I," on the backs of our hands so that we rarely went but a few moments without seeing it and remembering to inquire into the Self as the source of all things. People throughout the kingdom of Magadha affectionately called us *Bapu* (or father) because they knew that we had just begun the difficult path described in the Vedas and Upanishads. The scriptures say that a fast mind is a sick mind. But we, my brothers and I, were slowly taming the wild horses of our thoughts, learning the four kinds of yoga, banishing the ego, that toadstool that grows out of consciousness, and freeing ourselves from the twin illusions of pleasure and pain.

But one day it came to pass that as we made our monthly rounds in the summer-gilded village, begging for alms, the merchants and women all looked the other way when we arrived. When Assajii asked them what was wrong, they apologized. With their palms upturned, each explained how he had already given his monthly offering to a stunning young swami, a mahatma, a powerful sadhu who was only twenty-nine years old and had recently crossed the River Anoma, which divided our kingdom from the land of the Shakya tribe. They said that just being in his presence for a few moments brought immeasurable peace and joy. And if that were not shocking enough, some were calling him *Munisha*, "Prince of the Ascetics."

"How can this be?" My heart gave a slight thump. "Surely you don't mean that."

A portly merchant, Dakma was his name, who was shaped like a pigeon, with bright rings on his fingers, puffed at me, "Oh, but he *is* such. We have never seen his like before. You—*all* of you—can learn a thing or two from him. I tell you, Mahanama, if you are not careful, he will put you five lazybones out of business."

"Lazybones? You call *us* lazybones?"

"As your friend, I tell you, this young man gives new meaning to the words *sacrifice* and *self-control.*"

Needless to say, none of this rested happily on my ears. Let it be understood that I, Mahanama, am not the sort of man who is easily swayed, but whatever serenity I had felt after my morning meditation was now gone, and suddenly my mind was capricious, like a restless monkey stung by a scorpion, drunk, and possessed by a demon all at the same time.

"This sadhu," I asked, helplessly, "where might we find him?"

Sujata, the unmarried daughter of a householder, with kind, moonlike eyes, stepped forward. "He lives at the edge of the forest by the river where the banyan trees grow. I have never seen *any* man so beautiful. Everyone loves him. I feel I could follow him anywhere. . . ."

Now I was in a mental fog. There was a dull pounding in my right temple as we trekked forthwith at a fast pace back into the forest. Vappa was sweeping his twig-broom so furiously—he was as angry and upset as I was—that billowing clouds of dust rose up around us, and we must have looked, for all the world, like a herd of enraged, stampeding elephants. Soon enough we tracked down the brash young man responsible for our alms bowls being empty.

To my surprise, and yet somehow not to my surprise, the villagers had not lied. We found him meditating naked, except for a garland of beads, in a diagonal shaft of leaf-filtered light from the banyan tree above him. Straightaway, I saw that his posture in meditation was perfect, his head tilted down just so, leaving only enough space that an egg could be inserted between his chin and throat. He was twenty years younger than I, no older than one of my sons, his body gaunt and defined, his face angular, framed by a bell of black hair. He looked up when we approached, introduced ourselves, and pressed him to explain how he could have the nerve to install himself in *our* forest. In a sad, heavy way he exhaled, holding me with eyes that seemed melancholy, and said, "I seek a refuge from suffering."

"Who," asked Bhadiya, cocking his head to one side, "are your teachers? What credentials do you have?"

"I have studied briefly with the hermit Bhagava. Then with Ālākara Kālāma and Udraka Rāmaputra, who taught me mastery of the third and fourth stages of medi-tation. But," he sighed, "neither intellectual knowledge nor yogic skills has yet led me to the liberation I am seeking."

I felt humbled right down to my heels. Those two venerated teachers were among the greatest sages in all India. Compared to *them*, my own guru long ago was but a neophyte on the path.

Twilight was coming on as he spoke, the blue air darkening to purple the four corners of the sky. A whiff of twilight even tinctured the shadows as he unfurled what I surmised was a bald-faced lie, a fairy tale, a bedtime story so fantastic only a child could believe it. Until a year ago, he said, he had been a prince whose loving father, Shuddodana, had sheltered him from the painful, hard, and ugly things of the world. The palace in which he was raised, with its parks, lakes, and perfectly tended gardens, gave you a glimpse of what the homes of the gods must look like. He was raised to be a warrior of the Shakya tribe, had a hundred raven-haired concubines of almost catastrophic beauty, and ate food so fine and sumptuous even its rich aroma was enough to sate a man's hunger.

He said he would have continued this voluptuous life of pleasure and privilege, for he had all that this world could offer, but one day while he and his charioteer, Channa, were out riding, he saw a man old and decrepit. On a different day he saw a man severely stricken with illness. On the third day he saw a corpse being carried away for cremation. And when he recognized that this fate awaited *him*, he could not be consoled. All satisfaction with the fleeting pleasures of his cloistered life in the palace left him. But then, on a fourth trip, he saw a wandering holy man whose equanimity in the face of the instability and impermanence of all things told him that *this* was the life he must pursue. And so he left home, abandoning his beautiful wife, Yoshodhara, and their newborn son, Rahula, and found his lonely way to our forest.

Once he had breathed these words, my companions begged to become his disciples. Kodanannna even went as far as to proclaim that if all the scriptures for a holy life were lost, we could reconstruct them from just this one devoted ascetic's daily life. He had seduced them with his sincerity for truth-seeking. I, Mahanama, decided to remain with my brothers, but, to be frank, I had great misgivings about this man. He came from the Kshatriya caste of royalty. Therefore he was, socially, one *varna* (or caste) above us, and I had never met a member of royalty who wasn't smug and insensitive to others. Could only *I* see his imperfections and personal failures? How could he justify leaving his wife and son? I mean, he was not yet fifty, but he had forsaken his responsibilities as a householder. True enough, his family was well taken care of during his absence because he was a pampered, upper-caste rich boy, someone who'd never missed a meal in his life but now was slumming among the poor, who could shave his waist-long beard, his wild hair, take a bath, and return to his father's palace if one day the pain and rigor of our discipline became disagreeable. I, Mahanama, have never had an easy life. To achieve even the simplest things, I had to undergo a thousand troubles, to struggle and know disappointment. I think it was then, God help me, that I began to hate *every* little thing about him: the way he walked and talked and smiled, his polished, courtly gestures, his refined habits, his honeyed tongue, his upper-caste education, none of which he could hide. The long and short of it was that I was no longer myself. Although I consented to study with him, just to see what he knew, I longed, so help me, to see him fail. To slip or make a mistake. Just *once*, that's all I was asking for.

And I did get my wish, though not exactly as I'd expected.

To do him justice, I must say our new teacher was dedicated, and more danger-ous than anyone knew. He was determined to surpass all previous ascetics. I guess he was still a warrior of the Shakya tribe, but instead of vanquishing others, all his efforts were aimed at conquering himself. Day after day he practiced burning thoughts of desire from his mind and tried to empty himself of all sensations. Night after night he prayed for a freedom that had no name, touching the eighty-six sandalwood beads on his *mala* for each mantra he whispered in the cold of night, or in rough, pouring rain. Seldom did he talk to us, believing that speech was the great-grandson of truth. Nevertheless, I spied on him, because at my age I was not sure any teacher could be trusted. None could meet our every expectation. None I had known was whole or perfect.

Accordingly, I critically scrutinized everything he did and did not do. And what struck me most was this: it was as if he saw his body, which he had indulged with all the pleasures known to man, as an enemy, an obstacle to his realization of the highest truth, and so it must be punished and deprived. He slept on a bed of thorns. Often he held his breath for a great long time until the pain was so severe he fainted. Week after week he practiced these fanatical austerities, reducing himself to skin, bone, and fixed idea. My companions and I frequently collapsed from exhaustion and fell behind. But he kept on. Perhaps he was trying to achieve great merit, or atone for leaving his family, or for being a fool who threw away a tangible kingdom he could touch and see for an intangible fantasy of perfection that no one had ever seen. Many times we thought he was suicidal, particularly on the night he made us all sleep among the dead in the charnel grounds, where the air shook with insects, just outside Uruvela. During our first years with him he would eat a single jujube fruit, sesame seeds, and take a little rice on banana leaves. But as the years wore on, he—being radical, a revolutionary—rejected even that, sustaining himself on water and one grain of rice a day. Then he ate nothing at all.

By the morning of December seventh, in our sixth year with him, he had fallen on evil days, made so weakened, so frail, so wretched he could barely walk without placing one skeletal hand on Bhadiya's shoulder and the other on mine. At age thirty-five, his eyes resembled burnt holes in a blanket. Like a dog was how he smelled. His bones creaked, and his head looked chewed up by rats, the obsidian hair that once pooled round his face falling from his scalp in brittle patches.

"Mahanama," he said. There were tears standing in his eyes. "You and the others should not have followed me. Or believed so faithfully in what I was doing. My life in the palace was wrong. This is wrong too."

The hot blast of his death breath, rancid because his teeth had begun to decay, made me twist my head to one side. "There must be. . ." he closed his eyes to help his words along, "some Way between the extremes I have experienced."

I kept silent. He sounded vague, vaporish.

And then he said, more to himself than to me, "Wisdom is caught, not taught."

Before I could answer he hobbled away, like an old, old man, to bathe, then sit by himself under a banyan tree. I believe he went that far away so we could not hear him weep. This tree, I should point out, was one the superstitious villagers believed possessed a deity. As luck would have it, the lovely Sujata, with her servant girl, came there often to pray that she would one day find a husband belonging to her caste and have a son by him. From where we stood, my brothers and I could see her approaching, stepping gingerly to avoid deer pellets and bird droppings, and, if my eyes did not deceive me, she, not recognizing him in his fallen state, thought our teacher was the tree's deity. Sujata placed before him a golden bowl of milk-porridge. To my great delight, he hungrily ate it.

I felt buoyant, and thought, *Gotcha*.

Vappa's mouth hung open in disbelief. Bhadiya's mouth snapped shut. Kodananna rubbed his knuckles in his eyes. They all knew moral authority rested on moral consistency. Assajii shook his head and cried out, "This woman's beauty, the delights of food, and the sensual cravings tormenting his heart are just too much for him to resist. Soon he will be drinking, lying, stealing, gambling, killing animals to satisfy his appetite, and sleeping with other men's wives. Agh, he can teach us nothing."

Disgusted, we left, moving a short distance away from him in the forest, our intention being to travel the hundred miles to the spiritual center of Sarnath in search of a better guru. My brothers talked about him like he had a tail. And while I cackled and gloated for a time over the grand failure of our golden boy, saying, "See, I *told* you so," that night I could not sleep for thinking about him. He was alone again, his flesh wasted away, his mind most likely splintered by madness. I pitied him. I pitied all of us, for now it was clear that no man or woman would ever truly be free from selfishness, anger, hatred, greed, and the chronic hypnosis that is the human condition. Shortly after midnight, beneath a day-old moon in a dark sky, I rose while the others slept and crept back to where we had left him.

He was gone, no longer by the banyan tree. Up above, a thin, rain-threaded breeze loosed a whirlwind of dead leaves. It felt as if a storm was on its way, the sky swollen with pressure. And then, as I turned to leave, seeking shelter, I saw faintly a liminal figure seated on kusha grass at the eastern side of a bodhi tree, strengthened by the bowl of rice-milk he had taken, and apparently determined not to rise ever again if freedom still eluded him. I felt my face stretch. I wondered if I had gone without food so long that I was hallucinating, for I sensed a peculiar density in the darkness, and the numinous air around him seemed to swirl with wispy phantoms. I heard a devilish voice—perhaps his own, disguised—demanding that he stop, which he would not do. Was he totally mad and talking to himself? I could not say. But for three watches of the night he sat, wind wheeling round his head, its sound in the trees like rushing water, and once I heard him murmur, "At last I have found and defeated you, *ahumkara*, I-Maker."

At daybreak everything in the forest was quiet, the tree bark bloated by rain, and he sat, as if he'd just come from a chrysalis, in muted, early-morning light, the air full of moisture. Cautiously, I approached him, the twenty-fifth Buddha, knowing that something new and marvelous had happened in the forest that night. Instead of going where the path might lead, he had gone where there was no path and left a trail for all of us. I asked him, "Are you a god now?"

Quietly, he made answer. "No."

"Well, are you an angel?"

"No."

"Then what are you?"

"Awake."*

That much I could see. He had discovered his middle way. It made me laugh. These rich kids had all the luck. I knew my brothers and I would again become his disciples, but this time, after six long years, we'd finally be able to eat a decent meal. SQ

These six lines of dialogue are from the spiritual teachings of the late, great Eknath Easwaran.

Grinder

A STORY

by X. J. Kennedy

X. J. Kennedy began publishing his own science fiction magazine, *Terrifying Test-tube Tales*, at age twelve. *Nude Descending a Staircase*, his first collection of poems, won the Lamont Award in 1961. Kennedy is the author of many books for children and has coedited several textbooks and anthologies. In September 2007 Johns Hopkins University Press published *In a Prominent Bar in Secaucus: New & Selected Poems*; and BOA Editions, *Peeping Tom's Cabin: Comic Verse.* Kennedy lives in Lexington, Massachusetts, with writer Dorothy M. Kennedy.

For Sale

Orgen Grinder Orgen & Monky. — Apt. 2

The hand-lettered sign stopped Brod in his tracks.

It had jumped out at him from a window in a triple-decker house whose picket fence enclosed a postage-stamp-sized lawn with a statue of the Virgin, her eyes rolled toward heaven. He had been walking aimlessly through the North End, a part of the city he hadn't known, wondering what to do with his time now that he wasn't going to be an account manager anymore.

An irresistible impulse swept over him. He entered the house, went down the hallway, and knocked on the door of Apartment 2. A woman on the other side of the door said, "Yes? Who is it?"

"I've come about the organ."

"That's my husband," she cried, throwing the door open and revealing herself: a bleached blond, short, plump, in an apron, her hands white with flour. "Glauco! Glauco, you got somebody!"

A potbellied man, about seventy, appeared in his undershirt, clutching an Italian newspaper. He was a walking cliché of an organ-grinder. His long white moustache curled up at both ends.

hold it in her long slim fingers, as if ready to take dictation. "See? She like you," the old grinder said. "A she-monkey always like men."

"And don't like women," put in his wife. She made a chittering noise at the monkey, and the monkey chittered back.

Brod felt the warm weight of the seven-pound animal in his arms, nuzzling his breast. "Does she bite?"

The grinder laughed. "C'mere," he said to the monkey, and sat Gina down in his lap. He forced the monkey's jaws apart and said to Brod, "Put you finger in her mouth. Feel all around."

Hesitantly, Brod did as he was told. He ran a finger over the monkey's lower gums. They were smooth and hard, like rubber.

"That's right," the grinder said. "Took 'em all out, so she no can bite anybody. Hey, this time you give her her food."

Obediently, Brod dumped Purina Monkey Chow out of a twenty-pound sack into the monkey's bowl. Guido showed him how to mash up the pellets and stir in apple juice till they were soft and gummable. Gina sniffed the bowl disdainfully at first but in a few minutes began gobbling.

"Monkey eat all the time," the old man explained. "Nine, ten bowls a day. When you out grinding, you gotta carry some food with you. Maybe a box of Shredded Wheat. Sometimes you give her a treat. Mix her chow with whip cream."

The next day Brod brought along a can of Reddi-wip and moistened the dry food with squirts. After she ate, Gina bounded into his lap and clung to him, surrounding his neck with her thin, hairy arms, showering him with small wet kisses.

Guido beamed. "You two gonna get along fine." He taught Brod how to file the monkey's fingernails ("so she don't scratch nobody").

On the fifth of Brod's visits, the old grinder showed his apprentice how to diaper Gina ("Pampers—newborn size"), how to persuade her into her purple suit trimmed with gold braid and fasten her red pillbox hat under her chin. He told Brod to say *Go!* and the monkey picked up her pewter begging cup and circled the room, collecting coins from invisible spectators.

On the sixth day Brod came in his Mercedes coupe to take away Gina and her cage. "You ready," the old man said. "Start in Fennel Hall Market. That's the easiest crowd. Lot of room to work. First, you go look up Sullivan. That's the cop stands around alla time in the square. You tell him you take over for Glauco. Oh, and you gotta get a moustache. Gotta have a moustache when you grind."

Brod drove straight to the marketplace and parked in the public garage. A tall slim black man in police uniform stood next to a newspaper and candy

"You want to be a grinder?" he said, looking Brod up and down. "Can you stand in the street cranking all day in the rain?"

"I guess so," Brod said.

"You like monkeys? They get along with you?"

"I don't know. I don't know any monkeys personally."

Without a word, the man waved Brod into a sitting room cluttered with glass-domed clocks, where a tiny gray monkey with a red collar sat on a swing in a six-foot-high cage. In the corner stood a massive handle-powered hurdy-gurdy mounted on a post, a thing of glittering brass embossed with scrolls, cupids, and flowers. It had a worn leather strap for mooring the organ to the waist of its operator.

The grinder opened the cage and stuck out a fist, and the monkey leaped onto it, chattering. He held the monkey out to Brod. "This Gina," the man said. "Good monkey. Young, six-year-old. A capuchin. Had her only a year. I train her good."

The monkey looked at Brod with its large brown eyes, and he looked at the monkey in return.

"Good monkey like this," the man went on, "you never go broke. She hold a cup, see? Go around to people, tip her hat, get plenty money. Don't scare off anybody."

"And the organ?"

"Been in my family a hundred year. My father, he was a grinder too. Brought it over from Montecassino."

"Why do you want to sell?"

"Stiff hands. You out in all kinda weather, no good. My son, he don' want to grind. He stamps the purple on the meat for the government."

The man opened the hurdy-gurdy and showed Brod how to insert wooden cylinders. Each cylinder held two tunes. It was studded with metal pins that struck keys when you cranked the handle. "You gotta change your tune every day," the man said, "so people don't get tire of you."

The woman brought coffee in small white porcelain cups, and the two men talked price. Only last week Brod had quit his job and collected severance pay. He wrote a check and signed it with a flourish.

The old man seemed disappointed that negotiations hadn't gone on longer. He said, "It take maybe two, three weeks for the monkey get used to you. You come here every day, so she get to know you. And I see your check clear."

Every day Brod went to the apartment for instruction. In the beginning he felt uneasy, and the monkey knew it, but gradually she would come over to him, fuss with his shoelaces, climb into his lap, chitter, take the pen out of his shirt pocket and stand, finishing off a Butterfinger. A small gold crucifix hung on a chain around his throat.

"Yeah," he said when asked if he were Officer Sullivan. "What you want?"

"I'm replacing Glauco."

The patrolman grunted. "Shee-it. I thought I was gonna get some peace and quiet when that old bastit retired. Man, I can hear 'Come Back to Sorrento' in my sleep. Well, you gotta get a street musician's license, mister. Stop by City Hall. And another thing. No monkey poop on my square, or you clean it up yourself."

At the office of the city clerk, a stern-faced woman insisted that a street organ had to be in tune, so Brod had to haul the massive instrument out of his car and up three flights of stairs to audition for her. Cranking slowly, he ground out "O Sole Mio" and "Over the Waves" while she sat behind her desk, listening critically.

"I think you need to crank more steadily," she said. "You were a little wavery there, but you'll pass. That'll be eighty dollars."

When Brod wrote down his address on the application card, she glared at him. "Harbor Towers? What kind of organ-grinder are you, living in a fancy place like that?"

"It's temporary. Just till I run out of money."

The next day at noon, in new blue jeans and checkered shirt with a red bandanna around his neck and a handlebar moustache stuck on with spirit gum, Brod took his station in Faneuil Hall marketplace. The sun blazed, and the area filled with office workers out for lunch. He started to crank. It was harder than he'd expected. The cylinders had some broken pins, resulting in skipped notes, and every once in a while he'd have to crank fast to get over the bad patches. Gina, in red cap and purple suit, skittered about on a long leash tied to his wrist. When a crowd had collected, Brod would say "Trick," and the monkey would turn a somersault. There was laughter and a patter of applause. In a minute Brod said, "Go," and Gina made a circle of the crowd, bowing, doffing her hat, and thrusting out her cup. In two hours they had made twenty-eight dollars and thirty cents and a fifty-peso coin.

The crowd's reactions varied wildly. One middle-aged woman, when the monkey approached her, cried, "Eek! Does it bite?" A young woman said, "Isn't he the cutest thing you ever saw?"

"Naw," her date replied, "looks like a rickety squirrel." One man shooed the monkey away, muttering, "I'll bet it's trained to pick pockets." There was one complaint that using a helpless animal to make money was inhumane, but Brod argued in his own defense. Gina worked only two hours a day, no more, with a twenty-minute break to drink a can of coconut milk and eat some chow and have her belly rubbed.

"Isn't that Brod Dempster?" a woman from the ad agency asked her companion. "The guy that just chucked everything?" Brod gave them a debonair wave and went on grinding.

The next day, equally sunny, brought still more success. Brod tried other plazas in the city, so as not to wear out the marketplace. He was enjoying his work as he hadn't enjoyed it for years. It was great to watch facial expressions—those of children, especially. Some would crowd too close to Gina, smothering her with attention, and then Brod would become worried and rein the little monkey in. But most of the time, life was calm and satisfying.

He thought back over his past. When he'd written copy for radio commercials, he had found himself longing to be the announcer. To get up in front of people and perform—he had been starving for that satisfaction. Grinding, he soon realized, was an art. You could alter the tone of a song depending on how fast you cranked. The songs became one with your feelings. A slow "O Sole Mio" was enough to fill him with wistfulness, while a fast rendition lifted his spirits to the skies. He imagined himself a medieval bard performing songs in a banquet hall, strumming his lute while courtiers quaffed mead and tossed gold pieces.

An occasional rainy day was a vacation. All day long Brod gave Gina the run of the penthouse. The spare bedroom would be hers, he decided, but the little monkey preferred the sunlit living room. It was dangerous to leave the sugar bowl on the kitchen table. Gina would pick it up, dump it over her head, and sit there licking her fur while Brod swept up after her. She could open the fridge, as Brod learned when he found all the apples in the fruit drawer with bites taken out of them.

But the monkey proved unexpectedly helpful. Brod showed her how to pop a tape into the stereo, and with a little practice she was able to sustain him with music without his having to get up. Soon she learned to fetch objects from the far end of the room—a book, his cigarettes. She carried things with her tail as easily as if it were a hand.

Moreover, the little beast was good company. Her face shone with sensitive intelligence. She appeared to listen when he spoke, cocking her head to one side. She grew more and more affectionate, cradling herself in his lap, giving him hugs.

"Gina," he sighed, "you're spoiling me."

So what if he wasn't earning enough to make ends meet. Who cared? For years he had saved his money and invested shrewdly. Now he would live the life of a dedicated artist.

One day in the marketplace, Brod beheld a new face in the crowd—a delicate, Botticellian face, surrounded by a sleek black waterfall of hair. A slender woman in her late twenties, wearing a rough linen jumper over a black body stocking. The jumper was open in front, and the nubs of her small breasts protruded, nipples faintly discernable. She was back the next day, and the next, always at his quitting time, two in the afternoon. When she struck up a conversation, asking about the monkey, Brod invited her to a latte in a café. Moored to a table leg by her long leash, Gina chattered and sulked.

His new friend, Marcella, had been a Wellesley philosophy major. She worked an early-morning shift in a brokerage, but she was really a dancer.

"I could dance for you," she said brightly. "As part of your act."

"Would you?" he said, managing by a tremendous exertion of willpower not to stare at her boobs.

"Sure. I have an Oriental costume. Maybe it would help draw a crowd." She extended a long slender leg across the black plastic seat of the booth and cupped her chin with a tapering white hand. She had a habit of striking poses without meaning to. Brod was enchanted.

"You're on," he said. They toasted their agreement in new lattes.

"You don't talk like an organ-grinder," Marcella said.

"How's an organ-grinder supposed to talk?"

"Not like somebody who's been to Yale."

"Stanford."

"So what are you doing performing in the street?"

"Used to write ad copy for Dunn and Fitzgammon till I wore out. God, it just killed me. All that top-speed searching for clever lines. One day I woke up and felt brain-dead. So I quit. Quit cold."

"Then why this?"

"It's great. I don't have to think at all, just crank. Besides, all my life I've had this yearning to be a performer, face a crowd, make people happy, be appreciated. Sometimes I wish I'd been born a bard in the Middle Ages. Might have composed the *Nibelungenlied* or *Beowulf.*"

Marcella swept back her hair with an easy hand and smiled a smile that dissolved his heart. Gina, who had been surrounded by a group of kindergarteners, returned to the café table. She glared at Marcella, showed her missing teeth, chittered abuse, and with her tail picked up a half-full cup from the table and raised it threateningly. Brod stopped her before she could fling the latte in Marcella's face.

The very next day, Marcella joined the act. She showed up in the flowing pants suit of a Turkish harem dancer, a blaze of crimson with silver threads, a veil, slippers with upturned points. Brod stocked the organ with a slower tune that sounded vaguely Oriental. Marcella danced a slithering dance while he cranked soulfully.

The crowd swelled to twice its usual size. Gina danced in a circle around Marcella, and the spectators clapped lustily. Coins showered the street, and the monkey picked them up.

After work, Brod would take Gina home and cage her, so that he and Marcella could spend the day's profits on beer in a microbrewery with a perfumed miniature waterfall. Brod's pent-up feelings flowed. He found himself making up impromptu poems for his new love and, with every beer, the poems seemed to him better and better.

Soon it became a sensible economy for Marcella to move into Brod's apartment. Gina, who hadn't much cared for the dark bedroom Brod had given her, now grew possessive of it. When Marcella arrived with her suitcase and began bringing her things into the room, the monkey squealed in rage, leaped atop the dresser, and flung cosmetics in all directions.

Marcella bit her lip. "I don't think she likes me."

"That's the way female monkeys always are," Brod said. "They prefer men. Don't feel bad. It's nothing personal."

He collared Gina and bundled her into her cage, where she threw a tantrum, hurling her body against the bars.

Luckily, that very night Marcella moved out of the room and into Brod's king-sized bed.

"Who are you, anyhow?" Brod asked one Saturday morning as they lay in bed nibbling a caviar omelet delivered hot by messenger.

"I don't know. That's what I'm trying to find out."

"Do I help?"

"God, yes. You've shown me how to live like an artist, all the way. I'm going to quit the brokerage."

Their life was an idyll. Every day, late in the morning, the three of them would locate a promising square and do their two-hour stint. Then for the rest of the day Brod and Marcella would wander by the river, or make love, while Gina sulked in her cage.

It was the juggler who ended their idyll. He stationed himself at the opposite side of the marketplace and balanced balls on his head, stacking them higher and higher. At the close of his act he'd balance a firebrand on his nose. The crowd once loyal to Brod and Marcella drifted away. Even their most generous patron, the white-bearded Hasidic Jew, went off to watch the juggler instead.

That night in their favorite Thai restaurant, Brod fumed. "The nerve of the bastard, muscling in on our territory. Him and his damned torches. What suckers people are. He ought to be arrested for smoke pollution."

"Maybe our act needs revving," Marcella said. "A new gimmick or something."

"You will absolutely not do a striptease. We will not shoot Gina out of a cannon. Don't worry—I'll think of some damn thing. I'm an idea man. Or used to be."

Marcella continued to dance, but the coins showered down more sparingly.

Brod's head still hadn't delivered any inspiration. For one terrible night, he thought of flinging his hurdy-gurdy out of the penthouse window, like that medieval Gaelic bard who protested the indifference of his listeners by slashing the strings of his harp.

But in the morning, quite by accident, he found his inspiration. In the window of a costume shop, he beheld an ape suit, lightweight, with a rubber head-mask of a stupidly grinning chimp. Brod tried the outfit on, and it fit perfectly.

The next day in Faneuil Hall Marketplace, Brod appeared in his new outfit. An organ-grinder who himself was a monkey—that was a novelty. People came over to watch. But when at the end of the day he and Marcella counted the take, it was still just petty cash. They retreated to the café and had more drinks than usual.

"I hate to tell you this," Marcella said, "but I don't like dancing with an ape. It kind of brings the act down. Lacks dignity."

"Dignity!" Brod snorted. "I suppose it's dignified to dance on the sidewalk in a Turk suit, with a monkey begging for change? Get off that artistic high horse, will you?"

"Don't be brutal. Why shouldn't I have an artistic horse, if you do? Doesn't my art mean anything to you?"

"Your art? Your art?" Then Bart blurted words that he came to regret. "With your art, you could do lap dances."

Marcella's tears welled. She stood up. "For two cents I'd—I'd—" Her lower lip trembled.

"Marcella, wait. I didn't mean it. I'm sorry. Please, let's go home."

Back in the penthouse, Gina sensed an opportunity to win the upper hand. She flung herself at Marcella in a frenzy of chitters, tweaking her nose, pulling her hair, trying to rip her blouse. Brod was thankful the little monkey was toothless.

"That settles it!" said Marcella, between sobs. "Either that little horror goes, or I'm going!"

"Are you out of your mind?" Brod protested. "What's an organ-grinder without a monkey?"

"That monkey means more to you than I do."

"No way. It's just that the two of you mean—well, different things to me."

"You want Gina for your lover? Well, I won't stand in your way."

In bed, they didn't face each other.

"And another thing," Marcella said to the wall. "You want to be a troubadour, but what do you create? Nothing. You make that little monkey dance for the people, and you—all you do is crank."

"That's a lie!" said Brod, with the fury of one who feels the sting of truth. "It's my show! Gina is only my monkey, that's all."

In the morning Brod woke to find Marcella gone, along with her costume, toothbrush, and body stocking. Gina was bouncing about in her cage, chittering merrily.

All day long Brod made the rounds, searching for Marcella in places they'd frequented—bars, coffee shops, the Mongol and Afghan restaurants, the parks and squares, the bush-lined riverbank where so often they had strolled. He inquired, but no one had seen her. By midnight his hopes had dwindled. It was as if she had vanished from the earth.

He woke to overcast skies and a hangover. He sat up and stared at the clock—eleven already! He had to get to the marketplace. Maybe Marcella would be there. Maybe she'd had a change of heart. He'd forgotten to turn off the coffeemaker the night before, and the glass pot had cracked. Gina was bounding up and down wildly. Brod opened the cage door. The monkey leaped into his arms. She circled his neck and kissed his cheek passionately, with little snickers of triumph. For a moment her embrace seemed comforting.

Then a terrible realization hit him.

"So!" he cried. "Is that your game? You think you can win me for yourself?"

With a curse, he shook off the monkey. Gina hit the floor with a squeak of surprise. She scampered under a bookshelf and sat there, peering out at him with sad eyes.

It was past noon when man and monkey finally showed up in the marketplace. The juggler had cornered the crowd. Swearing under his breath, Brod planted his hurdy-gurdy on the pavement beside the café and began to crank out "Funiculi, Funiculà." Tense, anxious, worried sick, he scanned the square. There wasn't a sign of Marcella. And Gina was misbehaving. She didn't want to frisk on her leash today, but huddled in a little clump on the pavement, inert.

Hey Baby, gimme a taste of yo' kiss—
You got that sweet gravy too hot for me to miss—

The song lyric exploded from a portable boom box not six yards away. A lanky white teenager with a close-clipped haircut sat on the pavement twisting the volume high. Two friends, a shorter boy with slicked-down hair and a girl in a halter, short skirt, and high heels leaned against a building beside him, covertly sharing a joint.

Brod felt a wave roll over him, a wave of blind cold rage. His hand froze on the crank of the hurdy-gurdy.

"Turn that thing down, will you?" he bawled. "This is my turf!"

In response, the sound rose louder. The lanky kid just glared.

"I said turn it down, you son of a bitch!" Brod shouted. "You're killing my business!"

"Ain't none of my business," the kid said. "You want to turn down my box, you come do it yourself, you fucking fake *Eyetalian*."

Brod unstrapped his hurdy-gurdy, laid it down on the sidewalk, and tied Gina's leash to it. He felt himself shoved to the frontier of violence. He strode confidently toward the boom box and the three adolescents. Spindly, undernourished punks, that's all they were.

"I'm asking you nicely one last time," Brod said evenly.

The kid got slowly to his feet. He was surprisingly tall. "And I'm tellin' you go jizzy yourself. Me and my friends here, we don't like your shit-sucking kind of music."

Brod aimed a kick at the boom box and set it spinning on the pavement like a top. The two boys made a grab for Brod. They were strong for their size. The lanky kid twisted Brod's arm behind his back, while the short kid punched his nose. Helpless, Brod tried to writhe free, but he couldn't duck a second blow. His nose spurted blood. The kid with the wrestler's hold on his arm twisted harder and forced him to the pavement. Brod felt the impact of the girl's spiked heel on the back of his neck. The lanky kid grabbed Brod's hurdy-gurdy, swung it high above his head, and slammed it to the pavement with a sickening crunch. There was a hail of splinters. The wooden cylinder with the little pins came flying out, and the kid stomped on it. The pavement was strewn with decorative angels and roses.

The kid stood over him, looking down. "That's for kickin' my box, you puddle o' puke." Brod felt too sick even to groan.

Tied to the hurdy-gurdy post, Gina had been hurled into the air. Her leash had come unsnapped, and she had landed on the lanky kid's back. Now she was chewing his left ear. He yelped and shook the monkey loose.

A crowd had gathered—a larger crowd than Brod had drawn in weeks. Officer Sullivan came charging through them. The three kids took to their heels, leaving Brod still kneeling in the street, puddling the pavement with red splashes.

"You still alive, bro?" Sullivan asked, helping him to his feet. "Get some water, somebody, let's clean this man up. Couldn't nab them kids, grinder man. Too bad about your organ. Looks like they did you a job on it."

Sullivan handed Brod a glass of water and a paper napkin snatched from a café table, and Brod swabbed blood from his nose. People in the crowd murmured sympathy.

From nearby came a shrill quavering scream. In horror, Brod beheld his former patron, the bearded Hasidic Jew. The old man lay prone, with Gina sitting on his chest nibbling a banana.

"It was the monkey!" a woman cried. "It bit that gentleman, because it wanted his piece of fruit! *EEE-EE-EEK!*—look out! It's gone crazy!"

"King Kong!" said somebody in the crowd.

Gina had sprung away from her victim. Now, holding the stolen banana, she was dancing up and down on the pavement, chittering insanely, keeping the old man's rescuers at bay.

Sullivan said, "That thing's gone ape." He was reaching for his gun.

"No, no!" said Brod. "Let me get her and rub her belly! I can calm her down!"

"Stand back!" Sullivan shouted to the crowd, at the same time waving off Brod. Pistol in hand, three yards from the monkey, he was drawing a bead. . . .

"Stop, you idiot!" Brod screamed. "That little animal can't hurt anybody! She can't bite—she hasn't any teeth!" Saving Gina—that was all that mattered now. Brod charged Sullivan and aimed a kick at the policeman's gun hand. The hand jerked up, and the gun exploded with a roar. Brod felt the bullet slam into his right thigh, heard toenails scratch pavement as Gina scampered off through a gap in the crowd. Then both his legs went useless, and he slumped to the street. Sullivan was standing over him, looking down, holding the smoking gun, saying, "You dumb bastit."

When Brod regained consciousness he was lying on a stretcher. Two attendants were lifting him through the back doors of an ambulance. Someone had taken off a T-shirt and made a tourniquet for his leg.

"Where's my monkey?" Brod groaned to the paramedic. "I've got to find her. Please!"

"Don't worry, pal. I saw Sister Bartholomea going off carrying it. Your monkey couldn't be in better hands. If you want it back, try Angels of Saint Aloysius Orphanage."

"Damned thieving nun!" Brod tried to sit up, but tight straps bound him.

"Mister, don't even think about walking right now. Lie back and relax. Don't worry about anything."

Brod's leg felt all on fire. A dizzy lassitude stole over him. He would lay his burden down, a burden too heavy to bear. Marcella had been right. He was no bard. He'd only been a monkey's appendage. Let the orphans have Gina. His harp hung mute. The harp that once through Tara's halls the soul of music shed. The paramedic was applying a compress.

Brod said, "I thirst, doctor. Pray, have you a cup of mead?"

"Mead? Did you say mead? You must be kidding, mister." He wound adhesive tape around and around Brod's leg. "Mead, for chrissake. Nobody's drunk that stuff in a thousand years. Want some nice cold water?"

Brod shook his head, fell back on the stretcher, closed his eyes. The ambulance began to move, gathering speed, emitting a high-pitched wail. Jolting and swerving, it sped down the potholed streets, playing the same three-note tune over and over as though someone with an inexhaustible arm were steadily turning a crank. **SQ**

The Treatment of Bibi Haldar

A STORY

by Jhumpa Lahiri

Jhumpa Lahiri was born in 1967 in London and grew up in Rhode Island. Her debut collection of stories, *Interpreter of Maladies*, received the O. Henry Award, a Pen/Hemingway Award, and the Pulitzer Prize for Fiction. Her second book and first novel, *The Namesake*, was published in 2003, and a movie based on the book was released in 2007. Lahiri lives in Brooklyn with her husband and two children.

FOR THE GREATER NUMBER of her twenty-nine years, Bibi Haldar suffered from an ailment that baffled family, friends, priests, palmists, spinsters, gem therapists, prophets, and fools. In efforts to cure her, concerned members of our town brought her holy water from seven holy rivers. When we heard her screams and throes in the night, when her wrists were bound with ropes and stinging poultices pressed upon her, we named her in our prayers. Wise men had massaged eucalyptus balm into her temples, steamed her skin with herbal infusions. At the suggestion of a blind Christian, she was once taken by train to kiss the tombs of saints and martyrs. Amulets warding against the evil eye girded her arms and neck. Auspicious stones adorned her fingers.

Treatments offered by doctors only made matters worse. Allopaths, homeopaths, ayurvedics—over time, all branches of the medical arts had been consulted. Their advice was endless. After X-rays, probes, auscultations, and injections, some merely advised Bibi to gain weight, others to lose it. If one forbade her to sleep beyond dawn, another insisted she remain in bed till noon. This one told her to perform headstands, that one to chant Vedic verses at specified intervals throughout the day. "Take her to Calcutta for hypnosis," was a suggestion still others would offer. Shuttled from one specialist to the next, the girl had been prescribed to shun garlic, consume disproportionate quantities of bitters, meditate, drink green coconut water, and swallow raw duck's eggs beaten in milk. In short, Bibi's life was an encounter with one fruitless antidote after another.

The nature of her illness, which struck without warning, confined her world to the unpainted four-story building in which her only local family, an elder cousin and his wife, rented an apartment on the second floor. Liable to fall unconscious and enter, at any moment, into a shameless delirium, Bibi could be trusted neither to cross a street nor board a tram without supervision. Her daily occupation consisted of sitting in the storage room on the roof of our building, a space in which one could not comfortably stand, featuring an adjoining latrine, a curtained entrance, one window without a grill, and shelves made from the panels of old doors. There, cross-legged on a square of jute, she recorded inventory for the cosmetics shop which her cousin, Haldar, owned and managed at the mouth of our courtyard. For her services Bibi received no income, but was given meals, provisions, and sufficient meters of cotton at every October holiday. At night she slept on a folding camp cot in the cousin's place downstairs.

In the mornings, Bibi arrived in the storage room wearing cracked plastic slippers and a diagonally patterned housecoat whose hem, stopping some inches short of bloated ankles, exposed shins sprayed with a generous number of pallid freckles. She bemoaned her fate and challenged her stars as we hung our laundry or scrubbed scales from our fish. She was not pretty. Her upper lip was thin, her teeth too small. Her gums protruded when she spoke. "I ask you, is it fair for a girl to sit out her years, pass neglected through her prime, listing labels and prices without promise of a future?" Her voice, louder than necessary, extended beyond the circumference of our ears, as if she were speaking to a deaf person. "Is it wrong to envy you, all brides and mothers, busy now with lives and cares? Wrong to want to shade my eyes, scent my hair? To raise a child and teach him sweet from sour, good from bad?"

Each day she unloaded her countless privations upon us, until it became unendurably apparent that Bibi wanted a man. She wanted to be spoken for, protected, placed on her path in life. Like the rest of us, she wanted to serve suppers, and scold servants, and set aside money in her *almari* to have her eyebrows shaped every three weeks at the Chinese beauty parlor. She pestered us with details of our own weddings: the jewels, the invitations, the scent of gardenias strung over the nuptial bed. When, at her insistence, we showed her our photo albums embossed with the designs of butterflies, she studied in detail the snapshots that chronicled the ceremony: butter poured in fires, herbs tied with strings, vermilion-painted fish, trays of shells and silver coins. "An impressive number of guests," Bibi observed, stroking with her finger the misplaced faces that had surrounded us. "When it happens to me, you will all be present."

Anticipation began to obsess her with such ferocity that the thought of a husband, on which all her hopes were pinned, threatened at times to send her into another attack. Amid tins of talc and boxes of bobby pins she would curl like a dried tamarind pod on the floor of the storage room, speaking with a curious word order and manipulating her knees and feet as if riding a sticky bicycle. "I will never dip my feet in milk," she whimpered. "My face will never be painted with sandalwood paste. Who will rub me with turmeric? My name will never be printed with scarlet ink on a card."

Her soliloquies mawkish, her sentiments maudlin, malaise dripped like a fever from her pores. In her most embittered moments, we wrapped her in shawls, washed her face at the cistern tap, and brought her glasses of yogurt and rose water. In moments when she was less disconsolate, we encouraged her to accompany us to the tailor and replenish her blouses and petticoats, in part to provide her with a change of scenery, and in part because we thought it might increase whatever matrimonial prospects she had. "At any rate, no man wants a woman who dresses like a dishwasher," we told her. "Do you want all that fabric of yours to go to the moths?" She sulked, pouted, protested, and sighed. "Where do I go, who would I dress for?" she demanded. "Who takes me to the cinema, the zoo-garden, buys me lime soda and cashews? Admit it, are these concerns of mine? I will never be cured, never married."

But then a new treatment was prescribed for Bibi, the most outrageous of them all. One evening on her way to dinner, she collapsed on the third-floor landing, pounding her fists, kicking her feet, sweating buckets, lost to this world. Her moans echoed through the stairwell, and we rushed out of our apartments to calm her at once, bearing palm fans and sugar cubes, and tumblers of refrigerated water to pour on her head. Our children clung to the banisters and witnessed her paroxysm; our servants were sent to summon her cousin. It was ten minutes before Haldar emerged from his shop, impassive apart from the red in his face. He told us to stop our fussing, and then with no efforts to repress his disdain, he packed her into a rickshaw bound for the polyclinic. It was there, after performing a series of blood tests, that the doctor in charge of Bibi's case, exasperated, concluded that a marriage would cure her.

News spread between our window bars, across our clotheslines, and over the pigeon droppings that plastered the parapets of our rooftops. By next morning, three separate palmists had re-examined Bibi's hand and confirmed that there was no doubt evidence of a union etched into her skin. Unsavory sorts murmured indelicacies at cutlet stands; grandmothers consulted almanacs to determine a propitious hour for the betrothal. For days afterward, as we walked our children to school, picked up our cleaning, stood in lines at the ration shop, we whispered. Apparently some activity was what the poor girl needed all along. For the first time we imagined the contours below her housecoat and attempted to appraise the pleasures she could offer a man. For the first time we noted the clarified quality of her complexion, the length and languor of her eyelashes, the undeniably elegant armature of her hands. "They say it's the only hope. A case of over-excitement. They say—" and here we paused, blushing— "relations will calm her blood."

Needless to say, Bibi was delighted by the diagnosis, and began at once to prepare for conjugal life. With some damaged merchandise from Haldar's shop, she varnished her toenails and softened her elbows. Neglecting the new shipments delivered to the storage room, she began hounding us for recipes, for vermicelli pudding and papaya stew, and inscribed them in crooked letters in the pages of her inventory ledger. She made guest lists, dessert lists, listed lands in which she intended to honeymoon. She applied glycerin to smooth her lips, resisted sweets to reduce her measurements. One day she asked one of us to accompany her to the tailor, who stitched her a new *salwar-kameez* in an umbrella cut, that season, the latest fashion. On the streets she dragged us to the counters of each and every jeweller, peering into glass cases, seeking our opinions of tiara designs and locket settings. In the windows of sari shops she pointed to a magenta *Benarasi* silk, and a turquoise one, and then one that was the exact color of marigolds. "The first part of the ceremony, I will wear this one, then this one, and this."

But Haldar and his wife thought otherwise. Immune to her fancies, indifferent to our fears, they conducted business as usual, stuffed together in that cosmetics shop no bigger than a wardrobe, whose walls were crammed on three sides with hennas, hair oils, pumice stones and fairness creams. "Pious folk have little time for indecent suggestions," replied Haldar to those who broached the subject of Bibi's health. "What won't be cured must be endured. Bibi has caused enough worry, added enough to expenses, sullied enough the family name." His wife, seated beside him behind the tiny glass counter, fanned the expansive mottled skin above her breasts and agreed. She was a heavy woman whose powder, a shade too pale for her, caked in the creases of her throat. "Besides, who would marry her? The girl knows nothing about anything, speaks backwards, is practically thirty, can't light a stove, can't boil rice, can't tell the difference between fennel and a cumin seed. Imagine her attempting a feed a man!"

They had a point. The girl had never been taught to be a woman; the illness had left her naive in most practical matters. Haldar's wife, convinced that the devil himself possessed her, kept Bibi away from fire and flame. She had not been taught to wear a sari without pinning it in four different places, nor could she embroider slip-covers or crochet shawls with any exceptional talent. She was not allowed to watch the television (Haldar assumed its electronic properties would excite her), and was thus ignorant of the events and entertainments of our world. Her formal studies had ended after the ninth standard.

For Bibi's sake, we argued in favor of finding a husband. "It's what she's wanted all along," we pointed out. But Haldar and his wife were impossible to reason with. Their rancor towards Bibi was fixed on their lips, thinner than the strings with which they tied our purchases. When we maintained that the new treatment deserved a chance, they contended, "Bibi possesses insufficient quantities of respect and self-control. She plays up her malady for the attention. The best thing is to keep her occupied, away from the trouble she invariably starts."

"Why not marry her off, then? It will get her off your hands, at least."

"And waste our profits on a wedding? Feeding guests, ordering bracelets, buying a bed, assembling a dowry?"

But Bibi's gripes persisted. Late one morning, dressed under our supervision in lavender eyelet chiffon, with a silver-threaded blouse and mirrored slippers lent to her for the occasion, she hastened in uneven steps to Haldar's shop and insisted on being taken to the photographer's studio so that her portrait, like those of other brides-in-waiting, could be circulated in the homes of eligible men. Through the shutters of our balconies we watched her press a scented square to the back of her neck, though perspiration had already left black moons beneath her armpits. "Apart from my X-rays I have never been photographed," she fretted. "Potential in-laws need to know what I look like." But Haldar refused. He retorted that anyone who wished to see her could observe her for themselves, weeping and wailing and warding off customers. She was a bane for business, he told her, a liability and a loss. Who in this town needed a photo to know that?

The next day Bibi stopped listing inventory altogether and regaled us, instead, with imprudent details about Haldar and his wife. "On Sundays, he plucks hair from her chin. They keep their money refrigerated under lock and key." For the benefit of neighboring rooftops, she strutted and shrieked; with each proclamation her audience expanded. "In the bath she applies chick-pea flour to her arms because she thinks it will make her paler. The third toe on her right foot is missing. The reason they take such long siestas is that she is impossible to please."

To get her to quiet down, Haldar placed a one-line advertisement in the town newspaper, in order to solicit a groom: "GIRL, UNSTABLE, HEIGHT 152 CENTIMETERS, SEEKS HUSBAND." The identity of the prospective bride was no secret to the parents of our young men, and no family was willing to shoulder so blatant a risk. Who could blame them? It was rumored by many that Bibi conversed with herself in a fluent but totally incomprehensible language and slept without dreams. Even the lonely four-toothed widower who repaired our handbags in the market could not be persuaded to propose. Nevertheless, to distract her, we began to coach her in wifely ways. "Frowning like a rice-pot will get you nowhere. Men require that you caress them with your expression." As practice for the event of encountering a possible suitor, we urged her to engage in small conversations with nearby men. When the water-bearer arrived, at the end of his rounds, to fill Bibi's urn in the storage room, we instructed her to say, "How do you do?" When the coal supplier unloaded his baskets on the roof, we advised her to smile and to comment on the condition of the horizon. Recalling our own experiences, we prepared her for an interview. "Most likely the groom will arrive with one parent, a grandparent, and either an uncle or aunt. They will stare, ask several questions. They will examine the bottoms of your feet, the thickness of your braid. They will ask you to name the prime minister, recite poetry, feed a dozen hungry people on half a dozen eggs."

When two months had passed without a single reply to the advertisement, Haldar and his wife were exultant. "Now do you see that she is unfit to marry? Now do you see no man of sane mind would touch her?"

Things had not been so bad for Bibi before her father died. (The mother had not survived beyond the birth of the girl.) In his final years, the old man, a teacher of mathematics in our elementary schools, had kept assiduous track of Bibi's illness in hopes of determining some logic to her condition. "To every problem there is a solution," he would reply whenever we inquired after his progress. He reassured Bibi. For a time he assured us all. He wrote letters to doctors in England, spent his evenings reading casebooks at the library, gave up eating meat on Fridays in order to appease his household god. Eventually he gave up teaching as well, tutoring only from his room, so that he could monitor Bibi at all hours. But though in his youth he had received prizes for his ability to deduce square roots from memory, he was unable to solve the mystery of his daughter's disease. For all his work, his records led him to conclude only that Bibi's attacks occurred more frequently in summer than winter, and that she had suffered approximately twenty-five major attacks in all. He created a chart of her symptoms with directions for calming her, and distributed it throughout the neighborhood, but these were eventually lost, or turned into sailboats by our children, or used to calculate grocery budgets on the reverse side.

Apart from keeping her company, apart from soothing her woes, apart from keeping an occasional eye on her, there was little we could do to improve the situation. None of us was capable of understanding such desolation. Some days, after siesta, we combed out her hair, remembering now and then to change the parting in her scalp so that it would not grow too broad. At her request we powdered the down over her lips and throat, penciled definition into her brows, and walked her to the banks of the fish pond where our children played cricket in the afternoon. She was still determined to lure a man.

"Except for my condition, I am perfectly healthy," she maintained, seating herself on a bench along the footpath where courting men and women strolled hand and hand. "My doctor told me. I have never had a cold or flu. I have never had jaundice. I have never suffered from colic or indigestion." Sometimes we bought her smoked corn on the cob sprinkled with lemon juice or two *paise* caramels. We consoled her; when she was convinced a man was giving her the eye, we indulged her and agreed. But she was not our charge, and in our private moments we were thankful for it.

IN NOVEMBER we learned that Haldar's wife was two months pregnant. That morning in the storage room, Bibi jittered and wept. "She says I'm contagious, like the pox. She says I'll spoil the baby." She was breathing heavily, her pupils fixed to a peeling spot on the wall. "What will become of me?" There was still no response to the advertisement in the newspaper. "Is it not punishment enough that I bear this curse alone? Must I also be blamed for ruining another?" Dissent within the Haldar household grew. The wife, convinced that Bibi's presence would infect the unborn child, began to wrap woolen shawls around her tumid belly. In the bathroom, Bibi was given separate soaps and towels. According to the scullery maid, Bibi's plates were not washed with the others.

And then one afternoon, without word or warning, it happened again. On the banks of the fish pond, Bibi fell to the footpath. She shook. She shuddered. She chewed at her lips. A group encircled the convulsing girl at once, eager to assist in whatever way possible. The opener of soda bottles pinned down her thrashing limbs. The vendor of sliced cucumbers attempted to unclasp her fingers. One of us doused her with water from the pond. Another wiped her mouth with a perfumed handkerchief. The seller of jackfruits was holding Bibi's head, which struggled to toss from side to side. And the man who cranked the sugarcane press gripped the palm fan, which he ordinarily used to chase away flies, agitating the air from every conceivable angle.

"Is there a doctor in the crowd?"

"Watch that she doesn't swallow her tongue."

"Has anyone informed Haldar?"

"She's hotter than coals!"

In spite of our efforts the tumult persisted. Wrestling with her adversary, wracked with anguish, she ground her teeth and twitched at the knees. Over two minutes had passed. We watched and worried. We wondered what to do.

"Leather!" a voice snapped suddenly. "She needs to smell leather." Then we remembered; the last time it had happened, a cowhide sandal held under the nostrils was what had finally freed Bibi from the clutches of her torment.

"Bibi, what happened? Tell us what happened," we asked when she opened her eyes.

"I felt hot, then hotter. Smoke passed before my eyes. The world went black. Didn't you see it?"

A group of our husbands escorted her home. Dusk thickened, conch shells were blown, and the air grew dense with the incense of prayers. Bibi muttered and staggered, but apart from this she said nothing. Her cheeks were bruised and nicked here and there. Her hair was matted, her elbows caked with dirt, and a small piece of one front tooth was missing. We followed behind, at what we assumed to be safe distances, holding our children by the hand.

She needed a blanket, a compress, a sedative tablet. She needed supervision. But when we reached the courtyard, Haldar and his wife would not have her in the flat.

"The medical risk is too great for an expectant mother to be in contact with an hysterical person," he insisted.

That night they put Bibi to sleep in the storage room.

THEIR BABY, A GIRL, was delivered by forceps at the end of June. By then Bibi was sleeping downstairs again, though they kept her camp cot in the corridor, and would not let her touch the child directly. Every day they sent her to the roof to record inventory until lunch, at which point Haldar brought her receipts from the morning's sales and a bowl of yellow split peas. At night she ate milk and bread alone in the stairwell. Another seizure, and another, went unchecked.

When we voiced our concern, Haldar said it was not our business, and flatly refused to discuss the matter. To express our indignation, we began to take our shopping elsewhere; this provided us with our only revenge. Over the weeks the products on Haldar's shelves grew dusty. Labels faded and colognes turned rank. Passing by in the evenings, we saw Haldar sitting alone, swatting moths with the sole of his slipper. We hardly saw the wife at all. According to the scullery maid, she was still keeping to bed; apparently her labor had been complicated.

Autumn came, with its promise of the October holidays, and the town grew busy shopping and planning for the season. Film songs blared from amplifiers strung through trees. Arcades and markets stayed open all hours. We bought our children balloons and colored ribbons, purchased sweetmeats by the kilo, paid calls in taxis to relations we had not seen throughout the year. The days grew shorter, the evening colder. We buttoned our sweaters and pulled up our socks. Then a chill set in that made our throats itch. We made our children gargle with warm salt water and wrapped mufflers around their necks. But it was the Haldar baby that ended up getting sick.

A doctor was summoned in the middle of the night and commanded to reduce the fever. "Cure her," the wife pleaded. Her shrill commotion had woken us all. "We can give you anything, just cure my baby girl." The doctor prescribed a glucose formula, crushed aspirins in a mortar, and told them to wrap the child with quilts and covers.

Five days later the fever had not budged.

"It's Bibi," the wife wailed. "She's done it. She's infected our child. We should never have let her back down here. We should never have let her back into this house."

And so Bibi started to spend her nights in the storage room again. At the wife's insistence Haldar even moved her camp cot up there, along with a tin trunk that contained her belongings. Her meals were left covered with a plastic colander at the top of the stairs.

"I don't mind," Bibi told us. "It's better to live apart from them, to set up house on my own." She unpacked the trunk—some housecoats, a framed portrait of her father, sewing supplies, and an assortment of fabrics—and arranged them on a few empty shelves. By the week's end the baby had recuperated, but Bibi was not asked to return downstairs. "Don't worry, it's not as if they've locked me in here," she said in order to set us at ease. "The street begins just at the bottom of the stairs. Now I am free to discover life as I please."

But in truth she stopped going out altogether. When we asked her to come with us to the fish pond, or to go see the temple decorations, she refused, claiming that she was stitching a new curtain to hang across the entrance of the storage room.

Her skin looked ashen. She needed fresh air. "What about finding your husband?" we suggested. How do you expect to charm a man sitting up here all day?"

Nothing persuaded her.

BY MID-DECEMBER Haldar cleared all the unsold merchandise off the shelves of his beauty shop and hauled them in boxes up to the storage room. We wives had succeeded in driving him more or less out of business. Before the year's end, the family moved away, leaving an envelope containing three hundred rupees under Bibi's door. There was no more news of them.

One of us had an address for a relation of Bibi's in Hyderabad and wrote explaining the situation. The letter returned unopened, address unknown. Before the coldest weeks set in, we had the shutters of the storage room repaired and attached a sheet of tin to the door frame, so that she would at least have some privacy. Someone donated a kerosene lamp; another gave some old mosquito netting and a pair of socks without heels. At every opportunity, we reminded her that we surrounded her, that she could come to us if she ever needed advice or aid of any kind. For a time we sent our children to play on the roof in the afternoons, so that they could alert us if she was having another attack. But each night we left her alone.

Some months passed. Bibi had retreated into a deep and prolonged silence. We took turns leaving her plates of rice and glasses of tea. She drank little, ate less, and began to assume an expression that no longer matched her years. At twilight she circled the parapet once or twice, but she never left the rooftop. After dark she remained behind the tin door and did not come out for any reason. We did not disturb her. Some of us began to wonder if she was dying. Others concluded that she had lost her mind.

One morning in April, when the heat had returned for drying lentil wafers on the roof, we noticed someone had vomited by the cistern tap. When we noticed this a second morning as well, we knocked on Bibi's door. When there was no answer, we opened it ourselves, as there was no lock to fasten it.

We found her lying on the camp cot. She was about four months pregnant.

She said she could not remember what had happened. She would not tell us who had done it. We prepared her semolina with hot milk and raisins; still she would not reveal the man's identity. In vain we searched for traces of the assault, some sign of the intrusion, but the room was swept and in order. On the floor beside the cot, her inventory ledger, open to a fresh page, contained a list of names.

She carried the baby to full term, and one evening in September, we delivered her son. We showed her how to feed him, and bathe him, and lull him to sleep. We bought her an oilcloth and helped her stitch clothes and pillowcases out of the fabric she had saved over the years. Within a month Bibi had recuperated from the birth, and with the money Haldar had left her, she had the storage room whitewashed and placed padlocks on the window and doors. Then she dusted the shelves and arranged the leftover potions and lotions, selling Haldar's old inventory at half price. She told us to spread word of the sale, and we did. From Bibi we purchased our soaps and our kohl, our combs and our powders, and when she had sold the last of her merchandise, she went by taxi to the wholesale market, using her profits to restock the shelves. In this manner she raised the boy and ran a business in the storage room, and we did what we could to help. For years afterward, we wondered who in our town had disgraced her. A few of our servants were questioned, and in tea stalls and bus stands, possible suspects were debated and dismissed. But there was no point carrying out an investigation. She was, to the best of our knowledge, cured. **SQ**

Nightshade

A S T O R Y

by Joyce Carol Oates

Joyce Carol Oates, one of the most eminent and prolific of contemporary literary figures, is the author of works of fiction, poetry, drama, and criticism. She received the National Book Award in 1970 for her novel, *them*. Her thirty-seven novels include *Black Water*, *Zombie*, *The Falls*, and recently, *The Gravedigger's Daughter*. Oates is professor of Humanities with the Program in Writing at Princeton and is a founder and editor of *The Ontario Review.*

SUPERSTITIOUS BELLEFLEURS spoke of Nightshade as a *troll* (as if anyone had the slightest notion of what a *troll* was!) but it is more reasonable to assume, as Leah, Hiram, Jasper, Ewan, and the other "reasonable" Bellefleurs did, that he was a *dwarf.* Not altogether an ordinary dwarf of the kind one might find elsewhere—for surely Nightshade, hunchbacked as he was, and with his wide, thin, near-lipless mouth that stretched fully across his face—was unusual. For one thing he was distressingly ugly. If you wanted to like him, or simply to "take pity" on him, his oversized but wizened face with its chip-like colorless eyes, and the queer indentation on his forehead (as if, it was observed, someone struck him long ago with the blunt edge of an ax), and that maddening unslackening, joyless wide smile, were so repulsive, you turned away in alarm, your pulses racing; and the things Nightshade carried about in his numerous leather pouches and boxes (they were rumored to be bits of dried animals but were probably only medicinal herbs, like boneset, heal-all, henbit, dogbane, and, indeed, nightshade) gave off a sickish odor that intensified in humid weather. Bromwell estimated that Nightshade would have been about five feet tall had he been capable of standing upright: but he was so badly deformed, his spine bent and his chest so caved in, that he stood no more than four-feet-nine. Isn't he sad, people said when they first saw him; isn't he pathetic, they murmured upon subsequent sightings; isn't he *hideous*, isn't he *unspeakable*, they finally said, when neither the poor thing nor Leah was within earshot. (It was to be one of the most nagging of the Bellefleur mysteries, Nightshade's appeal for Leah. For surely he came to acquire an extraordinary value in her imagination, during Germaine's third and fourth years, and a remarkable intimacy as well—an intimacy, alas, that, though it never overstepped the affectionate but formal relationship of a woman and her favored manservant, nevertheless provoked, in the ignorant, all sorts of cruel, foolish, spiteful, and obscene speculation.)

Nightshade came to dwell at Bellefleur Manor quite by accident—through, in fact, a series of accidents.

After the tragedy of the infant Cassandra's death, a number of Bellefleur men, joined, at various times, by friends and neighbors and visiting relatives (among them Dave Cinquefoil and Dabney Rush) sought, with shotguns and rifles and even a light-weight multiple-action gun of Ewan's, the Noir Vulture, which was believed to inhabit the deepest reaches of the swamp; but their expeditions were fruitless. They shot and killed, or shot and left for dead, any number of other creatures, in their understand-able disappointment—deer, bobcats, beavers, skunks, hares, rabbits, raccoons, opos-sum, muskrats, rats, porcupines, snakes (copperheads, ringnecks, water moccasins), even turtles and bats; and a great variety of birds, primarily herons, hawks, eagles, and egrets, who somewhat resembled the deadly vulture—but they came away, exhausted and bitter, without the object of their hunt. Gideon, who had shown little interest in hunting, in recent years, was especially determined to kill the Noir Vulture, and led nearly all of the expeditions into the swamp; even when feverish from snakebite, he insisted upon joining the other men. He never spoke of Cassandra, still less did he speak of Garnet, but he often spoke of the Noir Vulture and how he would hunt it down—how he wouldn't rest until it was killed. (Bromwell frequently told his father that there must be, of course, more than a single bird, though legend had it that only a single Noir Vulture existed—for how, otherwise, the primly courteous boy inquired, could the creature *reproduce* itself?) But each of the hunting expeditions ended in failure, and Gideon became increasingly bitter. He once suggested that the entire swamp—some sixty or seventy acres—be firebombed: couldn't Ewan (who had just been elected, by a narrow margin, Sheriff of Nautauga County) acquire the necessary equipment . . .? But Ewan laughed away the notion, which must have been a joke. We'll kill the thing eventually, he said. Don't worry, it won't escape *us*.

Yet the weeks passed, and the Noir Vulture was not even sighted, let alone shot.

By a happy coincidence there arrived at the manor, after an absence of many years (no one could quite remember how many, not even Cornelia), Gideon's brother Emmanuel, who had been exploring the Chautauquas in order to map them thoroughly: for even at the present time maps were crude and unreliable. Emmanuel reappeared in the kitchen one afternoon in his sheepskin jacket and hiking shoes, carrying a weathered knapsack, and asked the cook, in his soft-spoken, rather inflectionless voice, if he might have something to eat. The cook (newly hired, since the debacle of great-grandmother Elvira's birthday party) had no idea who he was but saw the Bellefleur nose (in Emmanuel it was a long straight beak of a nose, with unusually small nostrils), and was shrewd enough to serve him quietly and without fuss. He was an extremely tall man, perhaps Gideon's height, with silvery brown hair that fell to his shoulders, and tanned, leathery skin that glinted with something metallic—salt, mica— and long, narrow, impassive eyes in which the dark iris floated like a tadpole, with a tadpole's tiny curl of a tail. It was difficult to say how old he might have been: his skin had so weathered that it looked ageless, timeless; he must have been about Gideon's and Ewan's ages but looked much older, and at the same time perversely younger. A servant ran to get his mother, and soon the whole household was alerted. Though most of them crowded into the kitchen, Emmanuel continued to eat his beef stew, chewing each mouthful slowly, smiling and nodding in reply to excited questions.

It was evidently the case—much to his family's surprise—that he was *not* home for good; he planned to stay at the manor only a few weeks. The cartography project was not completed. He said, softly, in response to an exclamation of Noel's, that it was *far* from being completed, it would require years more of exploration. . . . Years more! Cornelia said, trying to take his hands in hers, as if to warm them, what on earth can you mean! Emmanuel pulled away, expressionless. If his face seemed to have an upward cast, a half-smiling air, it was because of his long, curling eyes; his lips were quite immobile. He explained quietly that the project he had set himself was a difficult, even a merciless one, and though he'd already covered many thousands of feet of parchment with his mapping and notations, he was really nowhere near finished, for, for one thing, the land was always changing, streams were rerouting themselves, even the mountains were different from year to year (and even from day to day, he told the family, solemnly, they were eroding. Mt. Blanc was now only about 9,000 feet high, and lost a fraction of an inch every hour), and a fastidious cartographer could take nothing for granted, though he had once charted, judiciously enough, all that he knew. But is that important, Noel broke in, laughing uneasily, I mean, you know, an inch here, an inch there—! Isn't it time you began to think,

Emmanuel, about marrying—settling down—making your place *here* with us. . . . (It might have been at that precise moment that Emmanuel decided not to stay at the manor as long as he'd planned, but his face was impassive as he listened to his father's remarks. He was to leave home again on the morning of the fourth day of his visit, explaining to one of the servants that the manor was too warm for him to sleep comfortably, and the closeness of the ceilings oppressed him. And a certain gully at Lake Tear-of-the-Cloud nagged him, for he was convinced, suddenly, out of nowhere, that he had charted it incorrectly.)

But before he left he was able to answer Gideon's questions about the Noir Vulture. From out of his heavy oilskin knapsack he took a roll of parchment which he opened, carefully, spreading it on a table, explaining that this crude and really quite inadequate "map" was meant to cover the desolate swamp and marshland to the south of Mt. Chattaroy, which he had first investigated as a boy (indeed, hadn't Gideon accompanied him on one of his expeditions?), and again a few years ago, but without entirely satisfying himself that he knew it. However, he said, pointing with a forefinger (the nail of which curved wickedly, like an eagle's talon), I'm reasonably sure that the bird you want inhabits this region *here*. And he indicated an area of lakes and islands some twenty miles north of Bellefleur Manor.

Gideon stood leaning over the map, careful —for his brother seemed rather nervous—not to touch it. The intricate meandering lines were dizzying; he had never seen a map *quite* like this, and the few words that were included were obviously Indian names, no longer used. But he could, he thought, make his way to the Noir Vulture's habitat without difficulty. . . . Evidently they had underestimated its distance from the lake.

He straightened, smiling. He halfway wanted to seize his brother in his arms, and embrace him; but he mastered the impulse. That bird, that thing, that devilish son of a bitch, he laughed, won't escape *us*.

While the ignominious failure of the earlier expeditions had not dampened Gideon's ardor, but seemed, rather, to have increased it, the other men—Ewan in particular, who was busy with his new responsibilities—were somewhat discouraged; and the weather was growing chillier day by day. (After the terrible heat-wave of late August a wall of cold air moved downward from the mountains, and brought a premature frost on the very first day of September.) So Gideon was able to cajole only Garth, Albert, Dave Cinquefoil, and a new friend named Benjamin (who shared Gideon's fascination with cars) into joining him on the hunt.

They took one of the trucks from the farm, and drove some fifteen miles north, along dirt roads and lanes and logging trails, until they were forced to give up and walk; at that very moment a light, chill rain began to fall though the sky appeared cloudless. Gideon passed his flask of bourbon generously about but drank very little himself. He was almost desperately anxious to press forward. At first the others tried to keep up with him, then they gradually allowed themselves to fall behind. Garth was the only person who had actually sighted the Noir Vulture: he had seen it, or something closely resembling it, while hunting white-tail deer as a boy of twelve. Albert had never seen it but believed fervently in it. Young Dave Cinquefoil and Benjamin Stone of course hadn't any idea what they were hunting—only that it had carried off and devoured an infant, and must be killed. Gideon had convinced himself that he had once seen the bird, many years ago, but the creature in his mind's eye was shimmering and indistinct, a fabulous bird composed of steaming vapors, with a glaring red eye and a dagger-like beak. It was a monster and must be killed. It had, after all, carried off a Bellefleur child. . . . It had carried off *his* child.

His long desperate strides carried Gideon away from the others. A dangerous way to hunt, but he took no notice. In the distance he heard a curious sound. At first it put him in mind of bowling (for he frequented the bars of certain roadside bowling alleys where, over the months, he had made interesting new acquaintances); then he thought it must be thunder, low and rumbling; then he wondered if it might be a waterfall. He was climbing a ridge, the marshy land to his right, and it was altogether likely that a small river or creek lay ahead. He *thought* there might be a waterfall—he believed he had once hunted this area many years ago.

The thunderous sound rose and fell, and went silent. But it had come from somewhere close by. Gideon, panting, climbed the ridge as the sun began to shine with a sudden summery warmth. The swamp to his right gave off a rich brackish odor of decay and the tall pale oat like grasses through which he plunged smelled of moisture and heat. He was suddenly very excited—he heard laughter ahead. He raised his gun and touched his trembling finger lightly against the trigger.

And then—and then, at the top of the grassy knoll, he found himself staring down in astonishment at a group of children. They were playing in a meadow. The grass was short and extremely green; it was close-cropped enough to be pastureland, but Gideon was certain that this land wasn't used for grazing. The children were playing rowdily, shouting at one another, emitting high-pitched squeaking laughter. They were lawn bowling—it must have been a schoolhouse picnic—but why were they trespassing on Bellefleur land, and who were they and where was their teacher? The sound of the wooden balls (which were about the size of croquet balls) striking the clubs was disproportionately loud, as if the noise echoed in a small room, ricocheting off a low ceiling. Gideon flinched. The children's high-pitched laughter was also extremely loud. Though ordinarily Gideon liked children and even the idea of children it struck him suddenly that he didn't like *these* children and would take pleasure in running them off his land. . . .

So he descended the slope, shouting at them. They turned in amazement, their faces screwed up in angry, belligerent expressions, and he saw that they weren't children—they were midgets—some fifteen or twenty midgets—or were they (since their heads were oversized and their bodies misshapen, some of them quite grotesquely, with humps between their shoulders and crooked, caved-in chests) dwarves?—but why were they trespassing on *his* property—and where had they come from?

Gideon recklessly approached them, and though he saw, to his mild alarm, that they weren't backing away, that they were staring at him, in fact, with queer frozen expressions—grimaces so contorted they appeared to be involuntary, as if facial muscles had locked in spasms; eyes half-shut or screwed up in malevolent mocking winks; ugly little grins in which the preternaturally wide mouths were held shut and the thin, pale lips were stretched tight against the teeth—still he continued down the hill, slipping and sliding, though the safety lock wasn't on his gun and what he was doing was extremely unwise.

The force of the first wooden ball, striking him on the shoulder, was enough to nearly fell him; and in his pain and surprise he actually dropped the shotgun—but in another instant, acting before he had time to think, he snatched it up again. By then, however, the dwarves were upon him. Shouting and jabbering and squeaking, obviously furious despite their frozen screwed-up faces, they swarmed up the hill, like a pack of wild dogs, exactly like a pack of wild dogs, and one seized Gideon by the thigh and another climbed up him and seized his hair, knocking him over by the sheer weight of his body (which, though stunted and undersized, was remarkably heavy), and before Gideon had time to cry out he felt teeth sink in the fleshy part of his hand, and there was a terrible paralyzing kick to his groin, so that he nearly lost consciousness, and the high-pitched squeaking was exactly like that of shrews devouring prey—even other shrews—and even in the midst of his wild desperate struggling (for he *wanted*, ah, how he *wanted*, to live) Gideon knew that they were going to kill him: these ugly misshapen creatures were going to kill *him*, Gideon Bellefleur!

But of course it was not to be, for Garth had come up behind Gideon, and, at that unearthly sight, simply fired into the air, and the little men, terrified, scrambled off Gideon. Even in his consternation Garth was a cautious enough hunter to aim away from his uncle—he had time for only one more shot, so he turned to fire at a dwarf who had been jumping about at the edge of the commotion, tearing at his dark coarse hair with both hands in a paroxysm of excitement. The buckshot tore into the hideous little creature's right arm and shoulder, and brought him down at once.

The other dwarves fled. Though panicked, they had prudence enough to snatch up their bowling balls and clubs, and not one was to be found afterward; but the meadow was so badly chewed up, it was not difficult to ascertain that a peculiar game of some kind had been played there. By the time Albert, Dave, and Benjamin arrived, out of breath, the other dwarves had disappeared, and only the one Garth had shot remained. He was groaning and writhing about, bleeding from innumerable little wounds, his great misshapen head flailing from side to side, his claw-like fingers plucking at the grass. In silence the men gazed down upon him. They had never seen anything *quite* like him. Not only was the creature hunchbacked, but his spine had curved so brutally that his jaw was mashed against his chest. He looked (the image flew into Gideon's mind, though he was staggering with pain and exhaustion) like a young April fern, coiled up, so tightly coiled up you would never think it might grow straight and flare out into its extraordinary beauty. . . . But, this creature, how ugly! How repulsive! His shoulders appeared to be musclebound, and his neck was as thick as a man's thigh; his hair was coarse and shaggy and without luster as a horse's mane; there was an indentation on his forehead, a mark deep in the bone itself, and the skull had grown about it asymmetrically. As he whimpered and groaned and begged for mercy (for his queer gibberish, which sounded part Indian, part German, part English, was quite intelligible), he opened his mouth wide, as if grinning, and it is not an exaggeration to say that the mouth extended almost fully across his broad face, traversing the muscular cheeks. He flopped over onto his belly and began to crawl, dragging himself toward a patch of higher grass and weeds, like a wounded turtle. The sight of his oily blood on the ground went to Albert's head. He drew out his long hunter's knife and begged permission from Gideon to cut the thing's throat. Just to put him out of his misery! Just to shut up that babbling! But Gideon said no, no, better not. But didn't he lay *hands* on you, Albert said, didn't he *touch* you! And he ran over, fairly dancing with excitement, to the patch of weeds in which the dwarf lay clutching frantically at the soil and. grass, and seized hold of the dwarfs hair and lifted his head in triumph. Gideon, please, he begged. Gideon. Gideon. Just this once. Ah, *Gideon*. . . .

No better not, Gideon said, adjusting his clothing, sucking at his wounded hand, after all the thing is *human*.

They called him Nightshade because it was a patch of purple nightshade he had dragged himself into, and they noted with what desperation, and what remarkable skill, he was crushing leaves and berries and mashing them against his wound. Within a few minutes the worst of the bleeding had stopped. And so efficacious was the nightshade juice that the creature did not afterward suffer any infection, and within a few weeks appeared to have totally forgotten his injury.

Long afterward Gideon was to regret not having allowed his nephew to slit Nightshade's throat: but, after all, how could he have foreseen the future, and how, in any case, could he take it upon himself to condemn even so repulsive a creature to death? Killing in the heat of a fight was merely killing, but killing in such a manner was murder.... No Bellefleur has ever committed murder, Gideon said.

So they brought the dwarf home, carrying him for five torturous miles from a maple limb held at either end by Garth and Albert (his ankles and wrists bound, he was unceremoniously slung from the pole, like a carcass), and then laying him in the back of the truck. He had long since lost consciousness. But each time they checked his feeble heartbeat (for, if he had died, it would be wisest just to dump him into a gully) they saw that he was alive, and would probably remain so. What a *heavy* little bastard he is, they exclaimed.

Because Gideon had saved his life, Nightshade was always craven before him, and would possibly have adored him—as he adored Leah—had he not sensed Gideon's nature, and prudently shied away from him whenever they happened to see each other. But at the very sight of Leah—Leah striding into the room, though her hair was disheveled and she looked somewhat drawn, not *quite* herself—a moan escaped from Nightshade's lips, and he flung himself to the floor, and kissed it, in honor of the woman he took to be mistress of Bellefleur Manor.

Leah stared at the hunchback, stepping back from his desperate furious kissing; she stared, her lips parted, and it was a long moment before she looked up at her husband, who was watching her with a small, calm, malicious smile. "What—what is this," Leah whispered, clearly frightened. "Who is . . .?"

Gideon gave the dwarf a little shove with his foot, pressing the heel of his boot against the hump. "Can't you see? Can't you guess?" he said. The color had flooded back into his face and he looked quite triumphant. "He's come a long distance to serve you."

"But who is . . . I don't understand," Leah said, drawing back.

"Why, it's another lover, can't you see!"

"Another lover . . ."

Leah looked at Gideon, her face furrowed and her lips puckered as if she were tasting something vile.

"Another!" she whispered. "But I have none now."

In time—in a very short time—Leah came to find Nightshade delightful, and took him on as a special servant, *her* servant, since he was so clearly infatuated with her. With his immense shaggy head and his small eyes and the ugly hump between his shoulders, he was, as she said, a piteous sight—a pitiable sight—and it would be cruel for them to turn him away. And then he was remarkably strong. He could lift things, force things, unscrew caps, scramble with enviable agility up a step ladder to make a difficult repair. He could carry, singlehandedly, a guest's entire luggage into the house, showing no indication of strain except the minute trembling of his legs. Leah outfitted him in livery, and from somewhere he acquired straps, belts, buckles, and little leather pouches and wooden boxes, which gave to his costume a quaint, gnomish look. (Though he was certainly not a troll, as Leah said repeatedly, often in amused anger; Bromwell's official definition was *dwarf*, and *dwarf* it must be.)

He spoke rarely, and always with a fussy show of deference. Leah was *Miss Leah*, uttered in a half-swooning murmur, as he bowed before her, bent nearly double, a comical and somehow—or so Leah thought—a touching sight. He could play the mouth organ and did simple magic tricks with buttons and coins, and even, when he was especially inspired, with kittens; making them disappear and re-appear out of his sleeves or the shadowy interior of his jacket. (Sometimes, the children saw to their half-frightened astonishment, he made things—even kittens—appear when other things, unmistakably other things, had disappeared! . . . and it alarmed them, and kept them awake at night, worrying about the fate of the things that *had* disappeared.) Though he was so silent as to appear nearly mute, Leah had the idea that he was uncommonly intelligent, and that she could rely upon his judgment. His subservience was of course embarrassing—silly and annoying and distracting—but, in a way, flattering, and if he became too profuse in his adoration she had only to give him a playful kick and he sobered at once. Despite his freakish appearance he was a remarkably *dignified* little man. . . . Leah liked him, she couldn't help herself. She pitied him and was amused by him, and gratified by his loyalty to her, and she liked him very much, no matter how the other Bellefleurs—and even the children, and the servants—disapproved.

How odd it was, how annoying, how selfish, Leah thought, that they didn't care for poor Nightshade. Surely they must pity him? Surely they must be impressed by his indefatigable energy and good nature, and by his willingness (and his eagerness) to work at the castle for no salary, only for room and board? She could understand Gideon's contempt, for Gideon, she had always thought, was a severely limited person, as crippled imaginatively as Nightshade was crippled physically, and the sight of something *wrong* frightened him. (She recalled what a whimpering coward he had been at Germaine's birth, and how she had had to baby them both.) But it was strange that the others disliked Nightshade, too. Germaine shied away from him, and the older children, and grandmother Cornelia avoided looking at him, and it was said that the servants (led by the silly superstitious Edna, who would have to be replaced before long) whispered that he was a *troll*. . . . A troll, imagine, at Bellefleur, in these modern times! But it was unmistakable, the others' dislike of him, and Leah resolved not to give in to it: not to Germaine's silly fears, not to her sister-in-law's vague mumbled objections (for Lily didn't dare speak aloud in opposition to Leah; she was *such* a coward), not even to Gideon's disdain. In time, Leah thought, they will like him well enough; they'll like him as much as *I* do.

The first night great-aunt Veronica saw him, however, Leah couldn't help but be struck by something not only peculiar but, it seemed, *irrevocable* in the older woman's attitude. When Veronica descended the wide circular stairs, one be-ringed hand on the railing, the other grasping her heavy dark skirts in order to lift them slightly to keep from tripping, she happened to see Nightshade (it was his first evening as Leah's "manservant"; he was wearing his handsome little livery uniform) drawing a chair close to the fire for his mistress; and in that instant she froze, froze with one high-buttoned shoe uplifted, and her hand grasping the railing tightly. How very *queerly* aunt Veronica stared at Nightshade who, on account of his stooped-over posture, did not at first see her. It was only as he withdrew, backing out of the room, bowing, that he happened to lift his eyes to her—and, for a fraction of a moment, he, too, froze—and Leah, who would ordinarily have found all this amusing, caught a sense, a near-indefinable sense, of Veronica's and Nightshade's mutual alarm. Not as if they knew each other, for it wasn't that simple, but that, instead, (and this is very difficult to explain) what they were was kin. And afterward Veronica sat leadenly at her place at dinner, pretending to sip her consommé, pushing food around on her plate as if the very sight of it nauseated her (for there was the pretense, with Veronica, that she was—despite her generous heft—a finicky eater), swallowing a few mouthfuls of claret before excusing herself and hurrying back upstairs to "retire" early.

Nor did the cats like him. Not Ginger and Tom, or Misty, or Tristram, or Princess—least of all Mahalaleel, whom Nightshade tried to court, offering him fresh catnip (he carried various herbs wrapped in waxed paper carefully tied with string in his several pouches and wooden boxes)—but Mahalaleel kept his magisterial distance and would not be tempted. Once Germaine came upon Nightshade in the dim, teakwood-lined reception room stooped over more emphatically than usual, holding something in his gloved hand and calling *Kitty-kitty-kitty, here kitty-kitty-kitty*! in his high-pitched squeaking voice—and a moment later Mahalaleel, his back and tail bristling, bounded past the little man and ran out of the room. Nightshade paused, sniffed the herb in his hand, and followed along after the cat, calling *Here kitty, here kitty, kitty-kitty-kitty* in a tireless, unoffended voice. SQ

From the book Bellefleur, *reprinted with permission of Dutton, 1980, © Joyce Carol Oates*

Put to Sleep

A STORY

by Pamela Painter

Pamela Painter is the author of two collections of short stories, *Getting to Know the Weather* and *The Long and Short of It*. Her short fiction has been published in numerous magazines and journals and included in several anthologies. She is the recipient of three Pushcart Prizes, the John Cheever Award for Fiction, and a grant from the National Endowment for the Arts. A teacher in the Writing, Literature, and Publishing Program at Emerson College, Painter is coauthor of the widely used textbook *What If? Writing Exercises for Fiction Writers.* She lives in Boston.

JACKSON'S FATHER CALLS at 5 a.m. "I'm depressed," he tells Jackson, "but that's not why I'm calling." Jackson's father, who turned ninety-two a month ago, says he just wants Jackson to know he's going to put Bucknell to sleep.

"Dad, you can't do that. Bucknell is a great dog," Jackson says. Bucknell, an Irish setter, has been a lifeline for Jackson's parents for the past eight years; he was named for the college whose football team Jackson's father's team could never beat. Jackson takes the phone from the bedroom, where his wife is sleeping soundly, to his drafting table in the next room. "What does Mom say?"

"She says she won't have to worry about me out walking Bucknell on ice or keeping track of dog food. Sending Gus out to find those special real-meat dog bones." Jackson's mother stopped driving a year ago when she turned eighty. Now Gus shows up twice a week to drive Jackson's parents on errands—the dentist, the doctor, and the butcher shop for Bucknell's bones.

"Bucknell's not sick, is he?" Jackson says. He pictures Bucknell drooping over the foot of his parents' bed, snoring noisily through dreams of hunting swift wild animals he's never seen, while Jackson's father is plotting to murder Bucknell. "Give Bucknell to Gus," Jackson says.

"Gus has us," his father counters.

"I'm coming to get Bucknell. I'm bringing Bucknell back home with me," Jackson says. "Then we'll talk about depression."

"Nothing to talk about. Depression's depression." His father hangs up.

It isn't light yet when Jackson pulls into his parents' drive. Bucknell's stuff is on the porch, ready to go, in two plastic bags. Jackson's mother is watching Bucknell lope around the dewy yard. She wrings her hands in front of her herbal apron, her eyes are red, but the story has been that Bucknell is his father's dog. Dry-eyed and resolute, Jackson's father appears and makes a gesture that could be hello or good-bye. He doesn't acknowledge Bucknell, who is prancing around, pushing a slobbery tennis ball into his crotch.

Jackson loads up the car. When he calls Bucknell's name, the setter bounds down the walk with his breed's reckless stupidity and sits in the passenger seat, happy for the unexpected ride. His wet nose makes a prism of the window. He barks at anything that moves.

Back home, as the sun begins to rise, Jackson puts Bucknell's plaid blanket in the living room near the unused fireplace, his dog dish in the kitchen, his water bowl beside it. Puzzled, Bucknell pads around behind Jackson, sniffing as he goes. Jackson tells him everything will be all right. Jackson doesn't know what to tell his wife, who is still asleep. She sleeps through everything.

An hour later over breakfast, his wife voices her displeasure with the unexpected guest. Hearing his name, Bucknell thumps his tail. He hovers carefully at a distance, well trained not to beg at the table. Jackson tells his wife about the new depths to which his father's depression has sunk.

"I'd be depressed at ninety-two," she says, his wife, the psychiatrist.

"I don't find that medically helpful," Jackson says.

"Well, we do seem to have a dog now," she says. She's already dressed for the day, her long hair pulled back from a wise, high forehead and coiled into a bun.

Jackson leaves with Bucknell, to buy Bucknell fat fake bones and a few meaty real ones. They are meant to keep Bucknell occupied while, in the office adjoining the library, his wife sees her patients. She tells Jackson there are personal details that patients shouldn't ever know. They might be freaked out if they heard a dog bark, or even knew they had a dog, never mind a child or children, which Jackson fears they will never get around to planning for. "Freaked out" are Jackson's words. "Interrupted transference" are hers.

"The world has dogs in it," Jackson tells her. "The world is full of children and dogs."

She doesn't answer. In her world, dogs do not bark.

All day Bucknell obligingly lounges by Jackson's drafting table as he sketches dazzling new kitchens, designs cunning granite countertop arrangements for upwardly mobile tract-home McMansions. While he and Bucknell take long walks in the burgeoning woods across the street, he tells Bucknell about the importance a well-designed kitchen plays in the family dynamic. Bucknell makes proper use of these walks, stopping at trees and fire hydrants, staking out new territory of his own. That night Bucknell jumps onto the bed, clearly intending to sleep with them.

"Not on the bed," Jackson's wife says, tying her silk pajama bottoms with a double knot.

So Bucknell lurks around the edges of their king-sized mattress, a solid alert presence. At 5 a.m., still on Jackson's father's schedule, the dog starts to pace around and sniff. Even with his eyes closed, Jackson feels Bucknell watching them sleep, feels the breeze from his wagging tail.

IT'S BEEN THREE WEEKS. Bucknell now wakes at 6 a.m. He and Jackson watch Jackson's wife sleep. Her hand is tucked beneath a freckled cheek, partially covered with fine, long hair. Jackson smoothes it back and tucks it behind her ear. She opens one eye. Bucknell senses their movements and quickens his pacing. From her side of the bed Jackson's wife says, "Somehow, it's like having your parents in the room. Patrolling our sleep, curtailing our sex life." And Jackson thinks, *if it's the dog, enough of that.*

The next day Jackson goes over to talk to his father about his depression. They sit around the red and chrome kitchen table, bought in the forties. Jackson's father is wearing a tie with his sweater. Jackson's mother sets the kettle to boiling. "Look at your dad moping around. He misses the dog," she says.

"Dad was depressed *before* I took the dog," Jackson reminds her. "He was going to put Bucknell to sleep."

"Your mother doesn't believe in depression," his father says. "Tell that to your wife."

"You miss Bucknell," Jackson's mother says to his father, her tone accusatory. Jackson's cue.

"Look, I can bring Bucknell back," he says.

"I told you I'll have him put to sleep," his father says. "I'm too depressed to have a dog." His bald head glows in spite of his depression.

Jackson schedules an appointment with his father's doctor, who puts his father through a variety of tests. They wait for the results, and Bucknell goes through a lot of bones. He now sleeps on the bed with Jackson and his wife, snuffles through satisfying predatory dreams, still wakes too early.

"Tell me about the dog," Jackson says to his wife one evening before she turns off the light on her side of the bed.

"It would probably take six months of sessions to unravel the dog," she says into her pillow.

"Bucknell's only eight, so we must have four or five dog years ahead of us to do it," Jackson tells her. Then it occurs to him to ask: "Sessions for whom?" But his wife is already asleep. Bucknell's tail vibrates on the mattress like a drumstick.

Electrolyte imbalance is what the doctor tells Jackson's father. "Your depression is easy to fix. Two miracle drugs will do it." A week later Jackson's father calls again at 5 a.m. As Jackson shuffles into his study, Bucknell jumps down from the bed to follow. Jackson's wife probably thinks the slight movement is Jackson. In a booming voice, his father says he's coming by for Bucknell.

"To do what?" Jackson asks, but his father hangs up. Jackson waits in the kitchen with a wide-awake Bucknell.

"I'm taking him home," Jackson's father says through the screen door, as if he had never threatened any dire alternative. Bucknell lopes around his flannel knees in ecstasy. "Gus is going to stop by PETCO and fill the trunk with dog food," Jackson's father says. He scratches Bucknell's ears in a way Jackson never thought to.

"Aren't you glad I took Bucknell in," Jackson says, handing over Bucknell's blanket, dog bones, leash, dish, and water bowl. Gus waves from the car.

Jackson is to get no credit from his father. "You two ought to get a dog," his father says as Bucknell tugs him down the walk.

"You know we don't want a dog," Jackson says.

His father shakes his head in disgust. "That wife of yours coddles her patients too much. Treats them like kids. You ought to have some kids." Bucknell barks as they all drive off.

What Jackson doesn't know yet is that a year later when his father calls at 5 a.m., Bucknell will already have been put down. His father will have told his mother he was taking Bucknell to Jackson but instead instructed Gus to take them to the pound. "Doing the hard job," his father will say.

There are things Jackson does know. It is still early. Jackson's wife is still sleeping, and the newspaper hasn't come. Jackson can avoid patients and designing kitchens for a few more hours. Dogless, he goes back to bed, turns his pillow over, and pulls up the quilt. His wife slumbers on beneath the light touch of his hand on her back. Jackson puts himself to sleep. **SQ**

Pretty Parts

A STORY

by Hannah Pittard

Hannah Pittard is a graduate of the University of Chicago and the University of Virginia. At UVA she was a Henry Hoyns Fellow in the MFA program in creative writing and received the 2006 Amanda Davis Highwire Fiction Award. Raised on the eastern shore of Maryland, she now lives in Charlottesville, Virginia, and teaches at James Madison University. Pittard has completed a collection of short stories, "There Is No Real Name for Where We Love," and is at work on a novel.

THEY WERE STANDING in front of a mirror, the two of them, not touching, side by side. She'd said, "I want to know what you think of my body" and stripped down to nothing. He had done the same silently, respectfully, aware that this was a gift, not yet frightened by what it might lead to or what it might mean. She was taller but only slightly. They didn't talk about that. She was wider also but only at the hips, and they were both rib-thin, and the skin pulled over their collarbones in a pretty way. There were muscles on his arms. He had hairy armpits. She was surprised by this every time. He was thirty but little, a boy with man features. The clerk at the desk had laughed when he'd produced his license.

He said, "My girlfriend thinks I have short legs because I have a long torso."

She said, "I have long legs. They say short torsos look bad in bikinis. But I have long legs."

He said, "I don't have short legs."

She said, "But I don't wear bikinis."

Again she said, "I want you to tell me about my body."

She closed her eyes and waited.

He said, "We can't have sex."

She said, "Stop saying that. It makes me feel cheap. I don't want to have sex with you. Tell me about this body now." She rubbed her stomach. She looked hungry. She always looked hungry.

"You don't want to have sex with me?"

They had been speaking to each other's reflections. Now she turned her face to him, her body still squared with the mirror, and said, "Yes, I want to have sex with you."

"Then don't say it that way. Say can't or won't, but not that you don't want to. Do you see?"

She bit at her knuckles. "Yes, I see." They turned back to the mirror, both of them studying her body.

He said, "You have an ingrown hair."

"The pretty parts. Tell me those. Don't embarrass me."

The mirror was the size of a small wall. It had no frame and was propped on a low cabinet so there was a full view of her body—his as well, though they weren't looking at that—but also of the room behind them and of the unused bed.

"You have long fingers."

"Yes."

"You have a high waist."

"What do you think of high waists?"

"You have moon-shaped toes."

She looked down, her chin brushing against her collarbone. She seemed earnestly to be studying her toes, hoping to see the moon at her feet. He wanted to touch her then. He wanted to show her that with her feet so close together the curve of her toes looked like the edge of the moon. He wanted to say, "Do you see? A half-moon. It's uncommon." He wanted her to know that being in a room with her was becoming as painful as not being in a room with her. He was filled with her and it made him feel close and sick and stuffed up inside. He wanted to hit her. He wanted to spit on her, kick her, ball her up, collapse her into something small. He loved her, and he hated that he loved her.

She said, "Tell me about the things you can't tell me about when I'm dressed. Tell me those things."

"You're demanding."

"Yes."

"You're small and not small. You have dark pubic hair. You have a lot of it."

"Does that bother you? Is that unattractive to you?"

"Your right nipple is larger than your left. Your face is perfectly even."

"No, it's not."

"You're perfectly even and crooked at the same time. You have moles, more moles than I have ever seen on a body. You have short hair, and your chin is well defined. When you're nervous you bite your knuckles so hard that I think they might bleed. You look Indian."

"I am Indian."

"No, you're not. You look Polish."

"I am Polish."

"No, you're not."

"Tell me her name."

"No."

"Why?"

"Because you said before you didn't want to know it."

"And before I didn't want to know it. Tell me her name."

"Paige."

"You're a liar."

"Yes."

She looked him in the eyes by way of the mirror. She balled her hands into fists to keep them from shaking.

She thought she might fall over. She was dizzy from standing so still. She wanted to shift her weight to one side, but she stayed where she was. She said, "Tell me."

He took his eyes away from her, focused them on his own reflection. He thought about punching the mirror. He thought about picking up his clothes and walking out of the room. He said, "Heather. Her name is Heather." He didn't look at her.

"Yes," she said. "That's it."

They were both quiet. It seemed she wanted him to speak. She wanted him to talk and never stop talking. She wanted to beg, but begging would ruin it. She wanted to bite the inside of her palm, her arm, her fingers. She waited until she couldn't wait anymore and said, "I know that's it because it hurts when you say it. Say it again and then never after that. But say it once more and I'll show you where."

She was rocking. The room was unsteady. He said the name again, and she brought her hand, open-palmed, to her chest. "Here. It hurts here." This would change everything. This was something from which she would never recover.

"I wonder if you'll flash in front of me when I'm eighty. The life we might have had together."

"Don't do that," she said.

"What?"

"Don't be maudlin."

She had started to cry. "It will pass," she said.

"It will pass," he said. "Look at me."

She looked at him, again through the mirror.

"Not like that," he said. "Look at me."

She turned her body, everything; she turned it toward him and felt naked for the first time.

"Listen," he said. "I want to hit you. Do you hate me? Listen. I want to tear you apart. Do you think I'm making this up? Do you think I don't mean the things I say at night in the morning? You're killing me. Tell me you don't hate me."

The skin on her chest was blotchy and hot. Her eyes were pink and there was liquid coming down her face. She was rocking and her fists were pumping, but she felt calm. She said, "I adore you."

He said, "It would ruin it if we had sex."

"Yes."

"It would disappear these things."

"Yes."

"I would hate you."

"Yes."

"We're the same person."

"Yes."

"Show me again where it hurts."

She showed him, moved her panicked hand to her breastplate once again and felt the fist inside hitting it back.

He said, "Tell me about your children."

"I don't have children."

"Tell me about them anyway."

She said, "I don't know how to do that. I don't understand."

He said, "Put your clothes on."

"What?"

He said, "Put your clothes on. I can't touch you without your clothes on."

"That's not for you to say. I don't understand."

He saw that there was no graceful way to do it. He saw that it would be best for her if he turned away or left the room or just closed his eyes, but he stayed with her reflection in the mirror, and he knew she was aware of it. She reached for her underwear and nearly lost her balance. She jumped a little to regain it and she laughed at herself but the sound she made was high and thin. "You're a fake," he said.

"No," she said. "Not yet. I'm not ready. It isn't fair for you to stop until I'm ready too."

"You're a fake," he said.

"This isn't fair."

She was crying again, but she was also moving now. She was pulling on her underpants and tripping and pulling on her pants.

He spit at her.

She looked at him then. Her hands were perfectly at her sides, her chest still bare. He had a sudden feeling like vomit that she might tire of this before he did, leaving him in some unfair prison of obsession and hatred. She looked for a very long time at him, and the longer it lasted the more panicked he felt. Her mouth opened. She shook her head once, but it seemed more an inward gesture than an outward one, as if she'd been having a conversation without him the entire time. She picked up her bra, her legs now quite steady.

"You're statuesque," he said.

"Yes," she said. "That's it." **SQ**

Bibi from Jupiter

A STORY

by Tessa Mellas

Tessa Mellas is a graduate of St. Lawrence University and holds an MFA from Bowling Green State University in Ohio, where she is currently a specialist in developmental writing and English composition. Mellas was formerly a theater director at the Northwood School in Lake Placid, New York.

WHEN I MARKED on my roommate survey sheet that I'd be interested in living with an international student, I was thinking she'd take me to Switzerland for Christmas break or to Puerto Rico for a month in the summer. I wasn't thinking about a romp around the red eye of Jupiter, which is exactly what I'd have gotten had I followed my roommate home. Apparently, American school systems have become pretty popular all over. Universities shepherd foreigners in. Anything to be able to write on the brochures, "Our student body hails from thirty-three countries and the far reaches of the solar system."

You'd think there'd have been an uproar over the matter. I mean, here we have student funding going down the toilet and everyone staging protests to show they're pissed. And she gets a full ride, all the amenities paid for. She comes in like a Cuban refugee, minus the boat, sweeps up all the scholarships. And why shouldn't she? She probably qualifies as fifteen different types of minority. Don't get me wrong. I don't have anything against her. We were friends. I just didn't expect her to be so popular. I figured I'd have to protect her from riots and reporters. But as it turns out, she was really well liked.

The first time I met her I nearly peed my pants. It's the end of August, and I've got all my stuff shoved in the family van, a bit too unorganized for my father's taste, but we live only an hour from campus. I'm hoping to get there first to pick the best side of the room, the one with the most sunlight and the least-damaged furniture. I get up early just to beat her there. But I don't.

She's sitting at her desk already, reading the student handbook. I double-check the room number. 317. I've got the right place. This is my roommate.

At first I think she's an inmate. She's wearing this light-blue jumpsuit, and she's got pale-green skin that makes her look sickly. Gangrene, I think, not quite knowing what that is. It just sounds like a disease that would turn you green. She's not an all-out green. Tinted, rather, like she got a sunless tanner that didn't work out. Her ears are inset like a whale's, and she doesn't have eyelids. She's this tiny little creature, not even five feet tall, completely flat, no breasts. It doesn't even look like she has nipples.

My parents are right behind me. My mother's carrying my lava lamp like some offering. My father's got my futon extended over his head, trying to be all macho in case my roommate's a babe. They drop my stuff on the side of the room with a broken closet door and turn to this green, earless girl. They're all excited, want to make friends with the new roommate. So they start asking questions: "How was your drive? Do you like the campus? Have your parents left already?"

Not even acknowledging the obvious. That she's green. Maybe they didn't notice. Like I said, it was a pale green, a tint really, but it was pretty obvious to me, and she had weird eyes too, beady black pinhead eyes like a hamster's.

So finally I ask, "Where are you from?"

And she says, "Jupiter."

"Jupiter, New York?" my parents ask.

Not that they know there *is* a Jupiter, New York. It just makes more sense than the other possibility.

"No," she says. "Jupiter, Jupiter. The planet."

"Oh," they say. "I didn't realize we'd found life on other planets yet. How interesting."

She says, "You didn't. We found you," and goes back to her reading.

That shuts my parents up fast. They have no response. They do an about-face and head back to the car.

"Jupiter," my father's saying. "You believe that, Cath?"

My mother's shaking her head, saying, "Jupiter" over and over. First, like it's a word she's never heard, a word she's trying to get used to. Then like a question. "Jupiter?" Not quite sure whether or not to believe it. She says it several more times, looks at my father, then me.

"I was worried about Angela living with city kids," she says. "This is a bit different." She unlocks the car, grabs a handful of pillows, and adds, "Is Jupiter the one with the rings?"

"I thought Jupiter was made out of gas," my father says. "How can she live on a gaseous planet?"

"Let's just drop it," I say. "She could be from the moon, for all I care."

As it turned out, she *was* from the moon. Well, one of them. Apparently Jupiter's got a few dozen. The one she's from is called Europa—by Americans at least. But she tells everyone she's from Jupiter, says it's easier to explain. Her name is Bibi. No last name. Just Bibi. I looked it up. It means "lady" in Arabic. Ironic, as her kind doesn't have genders, just one type, like flowers, self-germinating and everything. But she looks more like a girl than a guy, so that's how we treat her while she's here, even though her body parts serve both functions.

She tells me most of this the first night in the dorm. I'm unpacking my toiletries and makeup, and she's still reading. I say, "Your parents were cool with you coming to America? Mine wouldn't even let me go out of state."

"I don't have parents," Bibi says.

"Oh, Christ!" I say. "I'm sorry. That's shitty." What can you say in a situation like that? I mean, I'd never met an orphan.

"It's fine," she says. "Nobody has parents. I grew up like this, sort of in a dorm."

"How can nobody on Jupiter have parents?" I ask. I know I'm being nosy, but you've got to admit, it's a bit strange.

"It's kind of complicated," she says. "I don't feel like getting into it."

I'm about to insist when there's a knock at the door. Bibi jumps to get it, and these men wheel in a full-size fridge. It's brand-new, a Frigidaire, one of those side-by-side freezer-and-fridge jobs complete with ice maker. They prop it against the window, plug it in, and leave.

"What the hell is that?" I ask, knowing damn well it's a fridge, not quite sure what it's doing in our room. My parents bought us one of those mini units, just enough space for a Brita filter, pudding snacks, and string cheese. The university had exact specifications on which ones were allowed. This Frigidaire wasn't on the list. Bibi explains how she got special permission to have it in the room, says she has a medical condition.

"What kind of condition?" I ask. "Are you contagious?"

"It's not a viral condition," she says. "I need a daily supply of ice."

"Ice," I say. "For what?"

"Don't they teach you this stuff in school?" she asks. "The basics of the solar system?"

"Of course," I say. "Third grade. We memorized the planets. There was a song."

Apparently she doesn't believe me. She goes to my dresser and starts grabbing stuff. She throws my nightie in a lump in the middle of the floor and says, "That's the sun." She places a red thong beside it and calls that Mercury. Venus is a pair of toe socks. Earth a blue bra. Mars a pair of panty hose. And Jupiter and all its moons are my best sparkly panties. She lines them up, stands to the side, and says, "See?"

"Yeah, I get your point," I say, though I don't really. I'm too pissed that my underwear is on the floor. Matching bras and panties aren't cheap. "I appreciate the astronomy lesson," I say, but she cuts me off.

She points at my bra. "You're here," she says. "We're there. See how far we are from the sun? It's cold. We don't have sweat glands. Your planet is hot, so I need ice. *Capisce*?"

Capisce? Who the hell does she think she is? A Jupitarian girl trying to intimidate me with Italian. Barging in with her refrigerator. Taking the best side of the room and making my thong into a planet. I snatch her solar system off the floor and stuff it back in my drawer, say, "I don't know much about Jupiter, but here shit like that just isn't cool."

There's another knock at the door. I'm about to say, "That better not be a fucking stove," when these guys from down the hall walk in. They want Bibi to join them for a game of pool.

"I'm Angela," I say, extending my hand.

"You can come too if you want," they say. But it's clear they're just interested in Bibi.

I shrug. "I got stuff to do. Maybe next time."

And Bibi takes off. No apology. No "I'm not going without my roommate." No nothing. She just leaves me there with her big fucking fridge while she goes to shoot pool with these boys she's never even seen. I'm not sure what they see in her. She isn't at all pretty. I mean, I don't think so. We have very rigid aesthetics here, right? How can you count a green earless girl without eyelids as pretty?

I watch them head down the stairs. The dorm is quiet, empty. I thought people were supposed to congregate on their floor the first night, praise each other's bedspreads and posters and shit. The door across the hall opens, and a guy wearing pink pants and a polo shirt steps out.

"Hey," I say.

"Hey," he replies.

He's wearing his collar propped up like he's Snow White. His hair is gelled back and all goopy. I want to tell him that went out of style with the Fonz but instead say, "I'm Angela," even though it's written on the construction paper sign on my door.

"Call me Skippy," he says, even though his sign says John Ward III.

"Where'd the nickname come from?" I ask.

"I made it up. People say you can reinvent yourself in college."

"Huh," I say. "Good choice."

"So that green girl's your roommate?" he asks.

"Yeah. Afraid so."

"Do you know when she's getting back?" he asks. "I heard she's from Jupiter. You think you could introduce me? *Lloyd in Space* is my favorite cartoon."

THE FIRST WEEK wasn't at all what I expected for freshman year. Bibi followed me all over the place, dragging her leaky ice packs with her. Didn't quite understand we had different schedules. She's taking all these science and math courses. And I have this good mix. Swahili. Ballet. Psychology. Statistics. My adviser made me take that last one, said I needed a math credit. But besides statistics, I'm thinking classes will be fun.

Then in psych lab I turn around, and there she is sitting behind me. She's even got the books. I figure she must have bought them for both our schedules. How's a girl from Jupiter to know better?

Everyone wants to be her lab partner. They crowd around her desk and ask stupid questions, like, "Are you going to be a psychologist? Will you go back to Jupiter and counsel manic-depressives?"

"No," she says. "I'm a neurobiology major. Stem cell research. I'm going to learn to grow pancreases and livers on rats, then take them back to Jupiter and implant them in bodies."

"Right," I say. "You're not even supposed to be here. Don't you have chemistry?"

She doesn't answer, just prepares her rat for the maze.

Of course, hers finishes first. Mine gets stuck in a corner and falls asleep.

But what does it matter that her rat's the smartest? The girl doesn't have any common sense. She forgets her shoes all the time, puts the toothpaste in her mouth instead of on the brush, and doesn't close the stall door behind her when she goes to the bathroom. No one wants to see how Jupitarians pee. Actually, everyone was interested, but once they saw it, they didn't want to see it again.

AROUND THE THIRD WEEK I finally get a look at her schedule. It's in one of those ugly-ass Trapper Keeper things. As it turns out, Bibi *is* enrolled in my classes. Hers too. She's taking nine at once. I didn't think that was allowed. Maybe they make exceptions for Jupitarians, figuring anyone from another planet is more intelligent than we are. Bibi is pretty smart, actually, gets perfect scores on the tests, even though she says absolutely nothing in class.

And to top it all off, even the boys are into her. That guy Skippy won't stop hanging around. He's a complete dork, a grade-A loser. He stands outside our door like he's the king's guard. At night he brings Bibi ice cream and Popsicles. He follows her to dinner and leaves flowers outside our door, nasty weedy ones with ants. Bibi hangs them from the ceiling, and the flowers die because there's absolutely no light in the room. She won't let me open the blinds, not even a crack, on account of her condition. So now we've got all these ants crawling across our ceiling between brown, crusty root systems. And Skippy's become this stalker. I find him in my closet behind my shoe rack and Dustbuster.

"Just playing hide-and-seek," he says, and winks.

"Hide-and-seek, my ass," I yell. "She doesn't even have a vagina!"

I call my mother and tell her about Skippy and the ice packs and the ants. My mother tells me to be patient. She reminds me about Martin Luther King Jr. I tell her she shouldn't send Bibi presents anymore. She puts something in all my care packages for Bibi. Cookies. Statuettes from the dollar store. *Soup for the Soul* books. I tell her, "Bibi doesn't need presents. You should see this girl's checks. The government gives her plenty of money."

My mother says presents are different. Bibi doesn't have parents. She tells me to be mindful of that. I tell my mother no one on Jupiter has parents. She says that doesn't sound right, and I agree. I mean, a whole planet full of orphans. That just seems too sad to be true. She's probably lying, I think. Going for the pity-party vote. I could press the issue, but I don't. I think about Martin Luther King Jr., and when Bibi comes back I give the roommate chitchat thing another try.

"So who do you have the hots for?" I ask.

And she says, "Nobody, really."

I'm not quite sure how it works for Jupitarians since they can self-germinate. She seems pretty asexual, never mentions boys.

I say, "What about Skippy? He wants you bad."

"Oh, him," she says, as though she hadn't noticed. She gets her shower caddy and heads down the hall. I stare at the door after she's gone.

Maybe she's bisexual. Maybe she's gay. I wonder if she masturbates when I'm out of the room. It seems like genderless people don't care about anyone but themselves. They might, but Bibi could give two shits about me.

BY THE TIME Thanksgiving rolls around, I'm getting pretty sick of her. I mean, how many times do you have to tell a person, "Put on your shoes," before she gets it right? There's snow on the ground, and she's prancing in it like some leprechaun. She walks around in her bare feet, leaving these monster frog prints. Did I mention Jupitarians only have three toes? It's like she needed to show them off. You'd think she at least would have tried to fit in. I think she liked being different. Everyone was always stopping by our room to see what the alien was up to. I was happy to have a week at home without her.

But there was no place for her to go, and my mother offered our house, insisted, really, said, "Angela, if we were dead, I would hope someone would be nice enough to take you in for the holidays."

I guess she was right. Bibi couldn't very well go back to the moon. The least I could do was share my goddamn turkey with the girl. My turkey. My gravy. My family.

Bibi stayed in the guest room, and wouldn't you know it, she got along great with my mom. Better than me. The two of them bonded like bears.

My mother showed her how to cook cranberry sauce and corn bread from scratch and, of course, how to pull the guts out of a turkey. Bibi was fascinated, watched my mother tear the bird's insides out of its ass, leaving this hollow pink part in the middle. Bibi couldn't stop staring at it until finally I said, "It's only a turkey. Gobble, gobble."

Bibi didn't answer, just looked at me like I'd threatened to cut off her head.

And my mother said, "Angela, why don't you help your father clean the garage?"

Things went on like this for days, my mother acting like Bibi's her new adopted daughter and treating me like chopped meat.

Then Thanksgiving Day, we sit down for dinner, and, of course, my mother makes us hold hands. We do this every year, even though we're a family that doesn't go to church. Even though we're a family that doesn't pray. My mother insists we still believe in God.

She starts out as usual with, "Thank you, Lord, for the food before us." Then she goes off on this new part, says, "Thank you for bringing this space child into our lives. May our civilizations be as peaceful as those of the Pilgrims and Indians."

I want to say, "God, Mom, does everything have to be about Bibi?" Instead, I grab the nicest piece of turkey and dump gravy all over, a little extra in case Bibi helps herself to more than her fair share. But she doesn't. She takes some potatoes and squash, a little cranberry sauce and corn bread, really small portions. My father tries to pass her the turkey.

"Don't you like meat?" he asks.

My mother says, "Bill, maybe she's a vegetarian."

"No," Bibi says. "It's just that the turkey reminds me of my mother."

I WANT TO ASK BIBI what the hell she meant at dinner, but she goes to bed early and shuts the door. The next day my mother takes us to the mall. I'm thinking she feels bad about the turkey thing because she tells us to buy any outfit we want. But Bibi doesn't want clothes. She goes to the cooking store and buys a turkey baster and oven mitts. And now I'm really confused.

We go to the food court for lunch. We get Sbarro's, chow mein, and Arby's. My mom's sucking a slushie. She gives Bibi a sip, says, "Tell me about your mother."

Bibi says, "I never had a mother. No one does. She died before I was born."

It's been three months, and this chick still hasn't explained the no parents situation. So I say, "What's the deal? No parents. No fathers. How exactly do you make babies?"

My mother gives me this look like I'm being rude.

"What?" I say. "You started it."

Bibi swallows the rest of her egg roll, asks, "You wanna see?"

"What? Here?" my mother says.

"Just look." She lifts her shirt, and there's this hole where her belly button should be. It's the size of a nickel, but it scoops in and up like the inside of a funnel. She does this right in the middle of the food court. People turn and stare. My mother tells her to pull down her shirt.

"So it's like a vagina," I say.

"Except you put your own pollen up there, push it in real deep instead of flushing it."

"What a relief," my mother says. "I thought you couldn't have children."

"I can," Bibi says. "But I won't. Anyone who has a baby ends up dead."

"Childbirth used to be risky here," my mother says. "Thank God for modern medicine."

"No," Bibi says. "Procreation is suicide. Babies can't come out the bottom. There's no hole. To get out, they gnaw through your stomach. They eat through the other organs too."

I sit there, shocked, my fries turning to mush on my tongue. "My God," I say. "Why would anyone want to get pregnant?"

"They say it's wonderful. Like being on heroin for nine months. The best euphoria there is."

"Christ Almighty," I say, "that's some mad kind of population control." I ask her if she's heard of the one-child law in China, but she doesn't answer.

"You're in good hands now," my mother says and gives her a hug, rocks her back and forth in her arms. Right there in the middle of the food court like she's five years old. I just sit and stare at my food. As though I could eat after that.

MY MOTHER DROPS US OFF at school on Sunday, tells Bibi if she needs anything to call. We carry our laundry upstairs. Under our clothes, we find notes from my mother on matching stationery taped to bags of Hershey's kisses. Mine says, "Loved having you home. So nice to spend time with you and Bibi."

"Your mom's really cool," Bibi says. She props her turkey baster and note up on her dresser.

"Yeah," I say. "I guess."

Now that she likes my mom, she wants to be friends with me. Go figure.

I curl up on my futon with a piece of leftover corn bread. My mother sent us back with plenty of food. "So did you ever think of doing it?" I ask. "Just to see what pregnancy's like? Don't you think you will eventually?"

"Why would I do that?" she says.

"Don't you think you're missing out? You said it's like drugs. I'd try that."

"I want to live as long as possible," Bibi says. "That's why I'm here."

"How does your planet feel about stem cell research?" I ask.

"They don't understand why things should change."

"Yeah, it's kind of the same in America," I say. "Stem cell research is a sin. Better watch out. They might throw you out of the country."

She empties her chocolate kisses into this porcelain bowl my mother gave her.

"I think you'll do it," I say. "That's what the turkey baster's for, right? To stick the pollen all the way up?"

She just stares at me with her black eyes bugging out, and for a second I think she's going to throw the bowl at my head. Either that or she's going to cry. But she just turns and walks out of the room.

She didn't come back that night. I'm not quite sure where she went. And frankly, that night I didn't care.

BIBI DIDN'T SPEAK to me for weeks. We gave each other the silent treatment and slammed the door a lot. I called my mother and told her I wanted to switch rooms. She said, "Angela, that's not how we deal with our problems."

I went to the RA and asked how long it would take to get a new room. She said I could file a complaint, but room changes were rarely approved.

It looked like Bibi and I were stuck with each other, at least six months more.

I started thinking I should muster up some sort of reconciliation. I thought about apologizing. Maybe she'd apologize too for being such a bitch all the time. I had a plan, was going to do it after my last class the Monday before finals. I swear I was going to.

But then I get back to my room, and Bibi's in bed with Skippy. He's straddling her stomach. His schlong's way up in her belly, shoved up there real good. He's riding her like a madman, and Bibi's arching up so her belly keeps hitting his balls.

I slam the door behind me and sleep in the lounge.

Who did she think she was having sex with a human boy, and one from our floor? It's not that I liked him. He was too pimply for me. But she'd been lying to me all semester, pretending she didn't understand my crushes, and now this. She loses her virginity to Skippy. She loses her virginity before me. I couldn't believe a Jupitarian had beaten me to it.

Still, I figured I'd be the bigger person. I figured we should talk. The next day I get back from ballet, and she's sitting at her desk reading chemistry, taking pages of notes, pretending like nothing happened. So I sit on my futon and sigh this huge sigh, hoping she'll get the gist we need to talk. And when that doesn't work, I say, "If you're going to be one of those kinds of girls, we need a system."

She says, "Skippy told me to put a bra on the door. I don't have any. Is that what you mean?"

"Yeah, that's what I mean," I say. And then, "So what's the big idea? I thought you were genderless. Were you lying about the self-germination?"

"I can't get pregnant the human way. It's got to be my own pollen. You're not even the right species."

"A girl who can't get pregnant," I say. "The boys are going to love that."

She shrugs. She doesn't even care that she just lost her cherry. It doesn't even faze her.

"So did you orgasm all over good ole Skippy?" I ask. "Was he good? Can Jupitarians even get off?"

"You're so stupid," she says. "Would a species survive if they couldn't orgasm?"

"Screw you," I say. I grab my towel and shower caddy and slam the door behind me. Emily, our next-door neighbor, is just leaving for class.

"God," I say, "that Bibi is such a whore. I wish she'd warn me before she fucks guys in the room."

Emily says, "Really? Bibi? I didn't know she could. We were wondering about that."

"Yeah," I say. "She's a little bitch."

"Didn't she go to your house?" Emily says. "I thought you were friends."

"Not anymore."

I pound down the hall as hard as I can, though flip-flops don't make much noise. I slam the bathroom door to let the whole floor know Bibi's a skank. I let the hot water wash over my back. "Slut," I say under my breath. And then a little louder, "At least I'm not a slut." I say it as though I'm talking to someone in the opposite shower stall. "You're such a slut," I say again and imagine Bibi across from me. I say it once more, almost shout it, "You're the biggest slut in the whole galaxy, and I wish you'd go back to the moon!"

I'M NOT SURE if it was Skippy who spread the word or Emily. It might even have been me, proclaiming loudly from the shower stall that day. Whoever it was, my bra ended up on the door an awful lot the next month. I left a note on her desk that said, "Stay the hell away from my underwear drawer."

Bibi did a different guy nearly every day. I saw one of those little black books on her desk. She had all the boys on the hall penciled in. There were even some names I didn't know. She really *had* turned into a whore. I wondered if they paid her or if she did it for free. I missed the old Bibi. The Bibi who forgot her shoes. The Bibi who studied all night. The Bibi who didn't know jack shit about boys.

We stopped talking. We just came and went as though we didn't know each other. I moved my futon into Emily's room and slept there most of the time. I wondered what would become of Bibi. I figured her grades would plummet and she'd get kicked out of school. But when I got back from Christmas break, her marks were posted to the wall, nine A's. She'd completed a whole year of college in four months.

I'm not sure how she kept it up, the sex and the studies. Her second semester she upped her course load to ten. They even let her into a graduate class. Like I said, if you're not from America, they let you get away with that shit.

Then around February she starts looking greener. I wonder if she has that winter seasonal depression thing. Then one day I get back to my room, and Bibi's jumping all over her bed. She's got the music cranked as high as it goes, some god-awful Broadway crap, and she's singing, "I feel pretty. Oh, so pretty." And she's wearing this outfit that's half her clothes and half mine with my best sparkly panties around her head.

"What the hell's going on?" I say. "I thought I told you not to touch my stuff."

She jumps off her bed and dances this little jig in front of her fridge. She looks so goddamn ridiculous I have to laugh.

"Did you find some solution to Jupiter's baby problem?" I ask. "Is your research going well?"

"No," she says. "I'm pregnant."

"You're not," I say. "I thought you couldn't."

"Well, it's not like I had proof it was impossible," she says. "But I guess I can. I'm pregnant with a half-human baby." At this, she bursts into laughter. Pollen puffs out of her ears in these yellow clouds around her head.

"Who?" I say. "Whose baby is it?"

"A boy's," she says. "A human boy's." And then she's surrounded by pollen again. She swirls it around with her hands. "Can you believe that?"

"You going to keep it?" I say. "If you give birth, it'll kill you, right?"

"I'm giving birth to the first half-human, half-Jupitarian baby ever!" she screams. She rips the panties off her head and twirls them in the air.

"Can't you get an abortion? Those are common here. They'll get rid of it. You'll be fine."

"I don't want an abortion," she says. "I want to be eaten alive."

I didn't know what to say. She'd turned ten types of crazy. It must have been that euphoria she told me about. I began to wish I had a normal human roommate I could take to the clinic so things would be better. I'd never had a friend with a life-threatening illness. Only grandfathers and uncles. There was nothing I could do in this situation. Bibi had lost it. Her condition was terminal, and she didn't even care.

In the weeks that followed, Bibi stopped seeing the boys. I moved my futon back into our room, and we started talking again. I became Bibi's bodyguard, her protector, shielding her from all the male scum on the floor. Boys would stop by and say, "I'm here for some alien sex."

I'd say, "Fuck off. You're an asshole." And they'd go away.

By March Bibi had given up her studies. No more stem cell research. Instead, she starts holing herself up in our room making sculptures out of dining hall silverware. She hangs them from the ceiling where the ants used to be and opens the windows to watch the dead flowers blow in the breeze.

We start having parties in our room every weekend. Everyone brings beer and fills up our big-ass fridge. The RA doesn't give a damn because Bibi got her through chemistry first semester, and she hopes she'll get her through physics next fall.

I call my mother and tell her we're getting along great. I tell her Bibi is the best. My mother's glad we're back to being friends, says she knew we'd work it out. I don't mention that Bibi is pregnant. My mother would be disappointed. She wouldn't understand.

Finally Bibi and I do everything together like roommates should. We order pizza rolls at midnight, rate the guys on the hall, redecorate the room. We move the beds against one wall and scatter huge pillows on the floor. Bibi finds these red Christmas lights on sale at the hardware store and hangs them up. She turns them on and lies under her swaying spoons, pretends she's watching hot liquid hydrogen swirl around Jupiter from the moon. She says, "Angela, come lie with me. We can watch Jupiter together. Better enjoy me while you can. Pretty soon, this baby will eat its way out."

"Don't talk like that," I say.

"Like what?" She dangles her three-toed feet in the air, says, "It's okay. It's only death."

By April she's really showing. She's got this great green hump of a belly, draws faces on it with finger paint, and calls it Skippy Junior. Every day she plans something different. She says, "Let's take Skippy Junior to the zoo. Let's take Skippy Junior ice-skating. Let's take Skippy Junior for parachute lessons."

I say, "Bibi, I've got classes."

She says, "I'm going to be dead in a few months. You can study then."

So we go ice-skating and snorkeling and rent lots of porno and drink slushies. Bibi does this thing with her turkey baster, fills it up with slushie and lets it volcano into her mouth. Half goes in. Half gets all over, which makes the ants come back. But this is kind of great, just like before when we hated each other and Skippy was a stalker. Back when Bibi studied all the time and didn't care about parties or drinking or boys.

The new Bibi is completely different. She dances all over the room, begs me to go with her to clubs, says, "You gotta teach me that booty bounce thing." She puts on a sparkly shirt and lipstick, a short skirt and heels. She tapes a paper bow tie to her stomach and says, "Skippy Junior's ready."

So that's what we do. We go to the only dance club in town, Freaky Willy's. And I teach Bibi how to dance the American way. I show her how to grind like a skanky ho.

We run into Skippy at the club. He's there with some guys. His acne looks a bit better. He buys us both drinks, Coronas all around. You've got to give him credit. At least he got us good beer. Then he wants to dance with Bibi. He seems genuine enough. Anyhow, there's no way he can get sex with her funnel closed up. One of those really bouncy songs comes on with the flashing lights, and Bibi drags Skippy to the dance floor and rocks it out.

I sit at the bar and watch. She's picked up the booty bounce, no problem. She looks kind of sexy gyrating her tiny hips, her shoulders bopping with the music. In this light she doesn't even look green. Skippy puts his hand on her back and tries to shake his pelvis too. But you can tell he's not the dancing type. You can tell he just did it so he'd have an excuse to touch her. He walks us home, and Bibi invites him in for a drink. I go to Emily's room until he leaves.

When he's gone, I ask, "So does he want you back? Is it his baby?"

"Don't you know anything?" she says. "It's nobody's baby. On Jupiter, people don't belong to other people."

WHEN I WOKE UP, she was gone. There was a note on my desk that said, "Thanks for teaching me to dance. Thanks for sharing your family." Most of her stuff was still there. I assume she went back to Jupiter, but who's to be sure. I don't like to think of the other possibilities.

After that, there were lots of policemen and school officials who wanted to know where Bibi went. I told them I didn't know. Word got out to the papers. Skippy came by our room and put a bouquet of weedy flowers by the door.

He said, "I really loved her. I don't know why she had sex with all those other guys."

"I know," I said. "I'm sure it was your baby."

I invited him in. We sat on Bibi's bed real close, and it felt better, that warmth, being next to someone who understood. We stayed like that for hours, shoulder to shoulder, didn't even talk. When it got dark, we slid under the covers. I was wearing those sparkly panties, the ones Bibi tossed on the floor that first night, the ones that were Jupiter. Skippy slid his hand down the front, brushed his fingers against what I imagined to be Bibi's moon. I didn't even mind when he aimed his boner at my belly button. I guided it lower, and he found the right hole.

"What if she comes back?" he asked.

"She won't," I said, and kissed him hard.

He moved his hips back and forth and buried his head in my neck. My eyes locked on the turkey baster on Bibi's dresser, and I tried to imagine that she had never been there. That she had never existed. That I had gotten here all on my own. **SQ**

How to Talk to Your Mother: Notes

A STORY

by Lorrie Moore

Lorrie Moore, an accomplished storyteller, is the author of two novels and three collections of short stories and the recipient of a National Endowment for the Arts Award, fellowships from the Guggenheim and Rockefeller Foundations, the Rea Award, and a PEN/Malamud Award for Short Fiction. Elected to the American Academy of Arts and Letters in 2006, Moore is currently a professor of English at the University of Wisconsin at Madison.

1982. Without her, for years now, murmur at the defrosting refrigerator, "What?" "Huh?" "Shush now," as it creaks, aches, groans until the final ice block drops from the ceiling of the freezer like something vanquished.

Dream, and in your dreams babies with the personalities of dachshunds, fat as Macy balloons, float by the treetops.

The first permanent polyurethane heart is surgically implanted.

Someone upstairs is playing "You'll Never Walk Alone" on the recorder. Now it's "Oklahoma." They must have a Rodgers and Hammerstein book.

1981. On public transportation, mothers with soft, soapy, corduroyed seraphs glance at you, their faces dominoes of compassion. Their seraphs are small and quiet or else restlessly counting bus seat colors outloud: "Blue-blue-blue, red-red-red, lullow-lullow-lullow." The mothers see you eyeing their children. They smile sympathetically. They believe you envy them. They believe you are childless. They believe they know why. Look quickly away, out the smudge of the window.

1980. The hum, rush, clack of things in the kitchen. These are the sounds that organize your life. The clink of the silverware inside the drawer, piled like bones in a mass grave. Your similes grow grim, grow tired.

Reagan is elected president, though you distributed doughnuts and brochures for Carter.

Date an Italian. He rubs your stomach and says, "These are marks of stretch, no? Marks of stretch?" and in your dizzy mind you think: Marks of Harpo, Ideas of Marx, Ides of March, Beware. He plants kisses on the sloping ramp of your neck, and you fall asleep against him, your underpants peeled and rolled around one thigh like a bride's garter.

1979. Once in a while take evening trips past the old unsold house you grew up in, that haunted rural crossroads two hours from where you now live. It is like Halloween: the raked, moonlit lawn; the mammoth, tumid trees, arms and fingers raised into the starless wipe of sky like burns, cracks, map rivers. Their black shadows rock against the side of the east porch. There are dream shadows, other lives here. Turn the corner slowly but continue to stare from the car window. This house is embedded in you deep, something still here you know, you think you know, a voice at the top of those stairs, perhaps, a figure on the porch, an odd apron caught high in the twigs, in the warm-for-a-fall-night breeze, something not right, that turret window still you can see from here, from outside, but which can't be reached from within. The ghostly brag of your childhood: "We have a mystery room. The window shows from the front, but you can't go in, there's no door. A doctor lived there years ago and gave secret operations, and now it's blocked off." The window sits like a dead eye in the turret.

You see a ghost, something like a spinning statue by a shrub.

1978. Bury her in the cold south sideyard of that Halloween house. Your brother and his kids are there. Hug. The minister in a tweed sportscoat, the neighborless fields, the crossroads are all like some stark Kansas. There is praying, then someone shovelling. People walk toward the cars and hug again. Get inside your car with your niece. Wait. Look up through the windshield. In the November sky a wedge of wrens moves south, the lines of their formation, the very sides and vertices mysteriously choreographed, shifting, flowing, crossing like a skater's legs. "They'll descend instinctively upon a tree somewhere," you say, "but not for miles yet." You marvel, watch, until, amoeba slow, they are dark, faraway stitches in the horizon. You do not start the car. The quiet niece next to you finally speaks: "Aunt Ginnie, are we going to the restaurant with the others?" Look at her. Recognize her: nine in a pile parka. Smile and start the car.

1977. She ages, rocks in your rocker, noiseless as wind. The front strands of her white hair dangle yellow at her eyes from too many cigarettes. She smokes even now, her voice husky with phlegm. Sometimes at dinner in your tiny kitchen she will simply stare, rheumy-eyes at you, then burst into a fit of coughing that racks her small old man's body like a storm.

Stop eating your baked potato. Ask if she is alright.

She will croak: "Do you remember, Ginnie, your father used to say that one day, with these cigarettes, I was going to have to 'face the mucous?' " At this she chuckles, chokes, gasps again.

Make her stand up.

Lean her against you.

Slap her lightly on the curved mound of her back.

Ask her for chrissake to stop smoking.

She will smile and say: "For chrissake? Is that any way to talk to your mother?"

1977. At night go in and check on her. She lies there awake, her lips apart, open and drying. Bring her some juice. She murmurs, "Thank you, honey." Her mouth smells, swells like a grave.

1976. The Bicentennial. In the laundromat, you wait for the time on your coins to run out. Through the porthole of the dryer, you watch your bedeviled towels and sheets leap and fall. The radio station piped in from the ceiling plays slow, sad Motown; it encircles you with the desperate hopefulness of a boy at a dance, and it makes you cry. When you get back to your apartment, dump everything on your bed. Your mother is knitting crookedly: red, white, and blue. Kiss her hello. Say: "Sure was warm in that place." She will seem not to hear you.

1975. Attend poetry readings alone at the local library. Find you don't really listen well. Stare at your crossed thighs. Think about your mother. Sometimes you confuse her with the first man you ever loved, who ever loved you, who buried his head in the pills of your sweater and said magnificent things like, "Oh God, oh God," who loved you unconditionally, terrifically, like a mother.

The poet loses his nerve for a second, a red flush through his neck and ears, but he regains his composure. When he is finished, people clap. There is wine and cheese.

Leave alone, walk home alone. The downtown streets are corridors of light holding you, holding you, past the church, past the community center. March, like Stella Dallas, spine straight, through the melodrama of street lamps, phone posts, toward the green house past Borealis Avenue, toward the rear apartment with the tilt and the squash on the stove.

Your horoscope says: be kind, be brief.

You are pregnant again. Decide what you must do.

1974. She will have bouts with a mad sort of senility. She calls you at work. "There's no food here! Help me! I'm starving!' although you just bought forty dollars' worth of groceries yesterday. "Mom, there is too food there!"

When you get home the refrigerator is mostly empty. "Mom, where did you put all the milk and cheese and stuff?" Your mother stares at you from where she is sitting in front of the TV set. She has tears leaking out of her eyes. "There's no food here, Ginnie."

There is a rustling, scratching noise in the dishwasher. You open it up, and the eyes of a small rodent glint back at you. Shriek, as in cartoons. It scrambles out, off to the baseboards behind the refrigerator. Your mother, apparently, has put all the groceries inside the dishwasher. The milk is spilled, a white pool against blue, and things like cheese and bologna and apples have been nibbled at.

1973. At a party when a woman tells you where she bought a wonderful pair of shoes, say that you believe shopping for clothes is like masturbation, everyone does it, but it isn't very interesting and therefore should be done alone, in an embarrassed fashion, and never be the topic of party conversation. The woman will tighten in her lips and eyebrows and say, "Oh, I suppose you have something more fascinating to talk about." Grow clumsy and uneasy. Say, "No," and head for the ginger ale. Tell the person next to you that your insides feel sort of sinking and vinyl like a Claes Oldenburg toilet. They will say, "Oh?" and point out that the print on your dress is one of paisleys impregnating paisleys. Pour yourself more ginger ale.

1972. Nixon wins by a landslide.

Sometimes your mother calls you by her sister's name. Say, "No, Mom, it's me. Virginia." Learn to repeat things. Learn that you have a way of knowing one another which somehow slips out and beyond the ways you have of not knowing one another at all.

Make apple crisp for the first time.

1971. Go for long walks to get away from her. Walk through wooded areas, there is a life there you have forgotten. The smells and sounds seem sudden, unchanged, exact, the papery crunch of the leaves, the mouldering sachet of the mud. The trees are crooked as backs, the fence posts splintered, trusting and precarious in their solid grasp of arms, the asters spindly, dry, white, havishammed (Havishammed!) by frost. Find a beautiful reddish stone and bring it home for your mother. Kiss her. Say: "This is for you." She grasps it and smiles. "You were always such a sensitive child," she says.

Say: "Yeah, I know."

1970. You are pregnant again. Try to decide what you should do. Get your hair chopped, short as a boy's.

1969. Mankind leaps upon the moon.

Disposable diapers are first sold in supermarkets.

Have occasional affairs with absurd, silly men who tell you to grow your hair to your waist and who, when you are sad, tickle your ribs to cheer you up. Moonlight through the blinds stripes you like zebras. You laugh. You never marry.

1968. Do not resent her. Think about the situation, for instance, when you take the last trash bag from its box: you must throw out the box by putting it in that very trash bag. What was once contained, now must contain. The container, then, becomes the contained, the enveloped, the held. Find more and more that you like to muse over things like this.

1967. Your mother is sick and comes to live with you. There is no place else for her to go. You feel many different emptinesses.

The first successful heart transplant is performed in South Africa.

1966. You confuse lovers, mix up who had what scar, what car, what mother.

1965. Smoke marijuana. Try to figure out what has made your life go wrong. It is like trying to figure out what is stinking up the refrigerator. It could be anything. The lid off the mayonnaise, Uncle Ron's honey wine four years in the left corner. Broccoli yellowing, flowering fast. They are all metaphors. They are all problems. Your horoscope says: speak gently to a loved one.

1964. Your mother calls you long-distance and asks you whether you are coming home for Thanksgiving, your brother and the baby will be there. Make excuses.

"As a mother gets older," your mother says, "these sorts of holidays become increasingly important."

Say: "I'm sorry, Mom."

1963. Wake up one morning with a man you had thought you'd spend your life with, and realize, like a rock in your gut, that you don't even like him. Spend a weepy afternoon in his bathroom, not coming out when he knocks. You can no longer trust your affections. People and places you think you love may be people and places you hate.

Kennedy is shot.

Someone invents a temporary artificial heart, for use during operations.

1962. Eat Chinese food for the first time, with a lawyer from California. He will show you how to hold the chopsticks. He will pat your leg. Attack his profession. Ask him if he feels the law makes large spokes out of the short stakes of men.

1961. Grandma Moses dies.

You are a zoo of insecurities, a Las Vegas of neurosis. You take to putting brandy in your morning coffee and to falling in love too easily. You have an abortion.

1960. There is money from your father's will and his life insurance. You buy a car and a green velvet dress you don't need. You drive two hours to meet your mother for lunch on Saturdays. She suggests things for you to write about, things she's heard on the radio: a woman with telepathic twins, a woman with no feet.

1959. At the funeral she says, "He had his problems, but he was a generous man," though you know he was tight as a scout knot, couldn't listen to anyone, the only time you remember loving him being that once when he got the punchline of one of your jokes before your mom did and looked up from his science journal and guffawed loud as a giant, the two of you, for one split moment, communing like angels in that warm, shared light of mind.

Say: "He was O.K."

"You shouldn't be bitter," your mother snaps. "He's financed you and your brother's college educations." She buttons her coat. "He was also the first man to isolate a particular isotope of helium, I forget the name, but he should have won the

Nobel Prize." She dabs at her nose.

Say: "Yeah, Mom."

1 9 5 8 . At your brother's wedding, your father is taken away in an ambulance.
A tiny cousin whispers loudly to her mother, "Did Uncle Will have a hard attack?"
For seven straight days say things to your mother, like: "I'm sure it'll be O.K." and
"I'll stay here, why don't you go home and get some sleep."

1 9 5 7 . Dance the calypso with boys from a different college. Get looped on New
York State burgundy, lose your virginity, and buy one of the first portable electric
typewriters.

1 9 5 6 . Tell your mother about all the books you are reading at college. This will
please her.

1 9 5 5 . Shoplift a cashmere sweater.

1 9 5 4 . Do a paint-by-numbers of Elvis Presley. Tell your mother you are in love
with him. She will shake her head.

1 9 5 3 . Smoke a cigarette with Hillary Swedelson. Tell each other your crushes.
Become blood sisters.

1 9 5 2 . When your mother asks you if there are any nice boys in junior high, ask
her how on earth would you ever know, having to come in at stupid nine-thirty
every night.

1 9 5 1 . Your mother tells you about menstruation. The following day you promptly
menstruate, your body only waiting for permission, for a signal. You wake up in the
morning and feel embarrassed.

1 9 4 9 . You learn how to blow gum bubbles and to add negative numbers.

1 9 4 7 . The Dead Sea Scrolls are discovered.

You have seen too many Hollywood musicals. You have seen too many people
singing in public places and you assume you can do it, too. Practice. Your teacher
asks you a question. You warble back: the answer to number two is twelve. Most of

the class laughs at you, though some stare, eyes jewel-still, fascinated. At home your mother asks you to dust your dresser. Work up a vibrato you could drive a truck through. Sing: "Why do I/ Have to do it now?" and tap your way through the dining room. Your mother requests that you calm down and go take a nap. Shout: "You don't care about me! You don't care about me at all!"

1946. Your brother plays "Shoofly Pie" all day long on the Victrola.

Ask your mother if you can go to Ellen's for supper. She will say, "Go ask your father," and you, pulling at your fingers, walk out to the living room and whimper by his chair. He is reading. Tap his arm. "Dad? Daddy? Dad?" He continues reading his science journal. Pull harder on your fingers and run back to the kitchen to tell your mother, who storms into the living room, saying, "Why don't you ever listen to your children when they try to talk to you?" You hear them arguing. Press your face into a kitchen towel, ashamed, the hum of the refrigerator motor, the drip in the sink scaring you.

1945. Your father comes home from his war work. He gives you a piggyback ride around the broad yellow thatch of your yard, the dead window in the turret, dark as a wound, watching you. He gives you wordless pushes on the swing.

Your brother has new friends, acts older and distant, even while you wait for the school bus together.

You spend too much time alone. You tell your mother that when you grow up you will bring your babies to Australia to see the kangaroos.

Forty-thousand people are killed in Nagasaki.

1944. Dress and cuddle a tiny babydoll you have named "the Sue." Bring her everywhere. Get lost in the Wilson Creek fruit market, and call softly, "Mom, where are you?" Watch other children picking grapes, but never dare yourself. Your eyes are small dark throats, your hand clutches the Sue.

1943. Ask your mother about babies. Have her read to you only the stories about babies. Ask her if she is going to have a baby. Ask her about the baby that died. Cry into her arm.

1940. Clutch her hair in your fist. Rub it against your cheek.

1939. As through a helix, as through an ear, it is here you are nearer the dream flashes, the other lives.

There is a tent of legs, a sundering of selves, as you both gasp blindly for breath. Across the bright and cold, she knows it when you try to talk to her, though this is something you never really manage to understand.

Germany invades Poland. The year's big song is "Three Little Fishies" and someone, somewhere, is playing it. SQ

Visit from the Gods

A STORY

by Lore Segal

Lore Segal's work includes essays, translations, and children's fiction and novels, most notably, *Her First American*, which received an award from the American Academy and Institute of Arts and Letters. The recipient of a Guggenheim Fellowship and grants from the National Endowments for the Arts and Humanities, Segal has taught writing at Columbia University, Princeton, Bennington, Sarah Lawrence, the University of Illinois, and Ohio State, from which she retired in 1996.

IN THE HALLWAY there's Zeus leaning by the bannisters, having a quiet smoke. The party has got too hot and noisy for him, he says.

"Me too," I say. "I'm going up to bed." I lift my cheek for a goodnight kiss but his tongue thrusts straight and deep between my lips and the world suspends its rotation. His hand inside my blouse touches, his mouth lifts out of mine, pronounces my name as if it were a foreign language: "Lucinella."

I'm looking into the same astonished roundness of eye that Europa saw the moment of her rape, for whether disguised as bull, swan, golden shower activity (as they say on television and which requires a great imaginative effort) or as my aging politician, your true lover has the grace to be dazzled by each new passion. His veteran's confidence needs no double entendre to leave loopholes for a misunderstanding. He says, "Let's make love."

Now I know Zeus and I are going to be lovers—I've frozen. I want my mother. "Let's not!" I say.

"Let's," he says, waits. No rape, no suasion. There's no need:

"All right," I say, and his immense arms take me up and lift me through the front door down the porch steps.

"But you're married," I say, ashamed to be so vulgar but it is Hera who's my sister. I have been jealous in my day. What does Zeus know!

"We won't tell her," says Zeus on the faintest rising pitch of irritation. "Hera and I've been married these eons and have eternity to go." He carries me over the midnight fields, tree and stone, into his bed. And when the earth resumes its motion, the direction has been radically altered. I've slipped away and run back to New York. I'm not ready yet to meet him with my morning face.

At home his letter awaits me: A quick page of astonished jubilation. Happiness is its keynote.

Puzzlement is mine. Elation must learn to co-exist with my guilty treachery and that's not hard—oh shabby guilt! But as for happiness, there's a word! I smile and I smile, but how shall I recognize what I can't exactly remember ever meeting face to face? And I don't know the rules: Is it okay to dispatch my prickly perplexity into Arcadia? If I could talk with him for half an hour, I would understand everything and so I write him what I meant never to say: Come!

He writes back to say he will be here at 8:15 but must leave at 7:20 the next morning. He arrives on the dot.

I DOUBT IF I'd have given Zeus a second look in his hey-day when he was gaudy with health, with his dark red locks, his bristling beard, eyes like oxidized copper sparking pink and gold and purple lights, and his immense size. I prefer my gods in their twilight. I lean into the voluptuous laxness of Zeus's elderly flesh. His divine cock has lost none of its potence and his hand is omniscient.

It was simpleminded of me, but I used to feel superior to kings: I imagined Zeus muscle-bound and stupid with power, rattling his enormous thunder, unable to control the whims and spectacular tempers of his oversized relations, but in my bed his mind moves feelingly. It's just that mine, being human, leaps more nimbly, like a street arab, which he enjoys. I sense his smiling in the darkness. When I get silly he reaches out laughingly to fetch me home to good sense. We make love again, sleep awhile and make more love, go to the kitchen for drinks and come back to bed and more love and more talking.

I ask Zeus to visit inside my head. (You are also invited. Though the style of the interior may differ, I assume we have the same amenities so that in here he and I, and you, may become intimate. Of course, like every hostess, I am a little nervous. Notice how I elide my sentences and keep my books short. I'm looking round for signs of a yawn burgeoning behind your compressed lips. You don't want to hurt my feelings, I know, but feel free to leave any time. Though your departing back will make a permanent dent in my confidence, it's minimal and I prefer it to your sufferance behind my back.)

MORNING. I'm chilled by the expanse of air that separates me from Zeus. He's sitting on the edge of my bed. Once he's put his socks back on there's no seduction of mine that can keep him a minute after 7:20.

"Hey, what did I do wrong?" I ask in my letter. I thought I was joking but Zeus is like me, used to dealing in words, and hears the faint trouble in my tone and finds me troublesome and I hear a faint rising pitch in his tone when, to avoid trouble in the future, he gently and deliberately maps the boundaries of our permitted pleasures which have the circumference of points reiterated on a razor's edge. Enthusiastically I entrust myself to his experience, which will maneuver us both over this difficult terrain, because I can see the two-hundred and fifty-fifth, -sixth, and -seventh word of his letter out of focus with passion and my left nipple rises to meet the lack of Zeus's hand.

I write him back a poem and all's well so long as I keep typing, but in the interval between the extraction of one page, before I can insert the next, desire creates the phantom of his tongue. I look down: No one there—though even the reality is always so palpably unlikely I never believe it.

In bed, nights, I thrust my hand into his massive absence.

AND THEN HE'S HERE: I had forgotten the fit of his enormous chest into my arms.

I invite myself for a tour of the inside of Zeus's head, but keep peering at him to make sure I'm welcome, I'll retreat at a moment's notice. He's looking all around, surprised. He stumbles. I take his hand. He's used to freer movements in a larger landscape with a fresher circulation of the air while I am most at home playing indoors, though I love to look out through his eyes to see what the world's like when one is male, beautiful, immortal. I've never been to Greece. (Once I dreamed I sat on a sunny rock the size and shape of the map of Naxos; my footbath was the Aegean as blue as the temperature of my own blood.) I ask him what's under foot when you stand on Olympus, and how do you throw lightening? I've never been that angry. Look down there: An aerial view of history! To have a will capable of intervention and refrain—though he might have sent his heroes sooner when monsters were devouring that lovely young flesh, but then you have to look at things in their historical perspective; you have to remember how problematical problems are compared with hindsight, and Hera no help. Delicacy forbids speculation. I will not wonder what she's like to lie with (what I want to know is what it feels like to desire me) but I question Zeus about Leda, Europa, and Jason's mother—what was her name?— I am in love with the delicacy of his reserve (how civilized he's grown!) though all I wanted was to know how his affairs ended so I can prepare.

I cry with loneliness for that day when he will not be holding me like this, or will be holding me like this while I scheme how to disengage myself; he doesn't ask me what's the matter. Think of all the women mortal and other, who've wept like this in Zeus's arms and he perhaps, when he was young, in theirs. He knows how it will all come out. He strokes my hair and keeps holding me. My tears grow cosy: for sophistication's sake I'd swear it is the nature of ardor to cool but I can't believe it.

HE'S PUTTING ON his socks again, shaking each one methodically before he inserts his toes. Watching him, I begin to understand: from the minute he rises out of the sheets until he leaves by the front door at 7:20 he keeps his attention sideways to me, and this enables him to walk out of my room while I, still sensually attached, follow behind him. I stand in the doorway and watch him profiled over the kitchen sink: he's letting the water run cold. He, whom within the half hour I held where a woman wears her baby, is standing upright over there; by himself, he turns, opens the cupboard door. What's he looking for? He's choosing himself a glass, fills it, lifts it, tips it at the lip: I can see the water pour through his lips, watch it hurdle the adam's apple; now it's flowing down his insides where I can't follow.

So that's how it's done! I can learn: I'll go drink a glass of cold water too. It doesn't hurt. He's gone. On my way out I meet the super in the hallway and embrace him. "Sorry, my mistake!" I say laughing. He hugs me and says he will have my dripping kitchen faucet fixed this morning. "Thank you, you good man, you excellent super!" In the lobby I catch the doorman's hand and press my cheek into its palm. The doorman and I sit together on the sunny front steps. He tells me about his boy back from Vietnam doing nothing all day except sit and watch TV and cut his toenails. I say you can't tell with people, you think this one's flipped out and next year you meet him and he's married, with a Plymouth, and three years later he's in Bellevue! You never know with young people these days.

A LETTER FROM ZEUS. I get my magnifying glass to check this word here that looks like "love", and is. Don't look now: I think this is happiness. And Zeus, as I said, knows the weight of words. When he writes "love" he knows what he means, what kind and how much, depending on the word that precedes and follows it, the nearest mark of punctuation and its place in the body of the letter (sixth word of the second line in the second paragraph).

I run to the mirror, the way you might run to the corner of the street to see the passing astronaut or what visiting royalty looks like, and it's me and it seems to me perfectly reasonable that I am Zeus's beloved.

I write him back stories, whole novels, juggling words for his entertainment, elated by my mastery for these days I can keep three, six, twelve perceptions and two mutually exclusive feelings in the air at one time, as well as a secondhand thought and a half, and a joke about juggling. "Oh Love," I write him back and we both know I mean the kind unfreighted by work-a-day life. Never will he scrumple up his bathroom towel; nor will I be angry when he falls asleep after every party though he promised to help with the cleaning up: these are the things that scuttle love when it is anchored in reality. Not Zeus and Lucinella! We two accomplished lovers meet from time to time without rancor and in mutual joy sail our toy loves.

HE ARRIVES TODAY. It is our anniversary. He asks, "What shall I give you, Lucinella?"

Dumbfounded I wonder: What does one ask of a retired god?

"Shall I show myself to you in my glory?" he offers.

"Good heavens, no!" I cry. (Just now I peeked and saw his enormous face in mid-passion suspended over mine and quickly closed my eyes.)

"Would you like me to translate you among the stars?" he asks, and I'm tempted: the constellation of Lucinella, poet, in the heavens for eternity. "That's not what I want!" I say surprised. I'd rather thought it was.

"Ask me for something," he says, rises, walks toward me, embraces me, though it's already 7:15. Still I hesitate.

"What, what!" he asks. I am afraid. He kisses me. "What, Love?"

"Become human for me," I whisper rapidly so he won't hear what I'm saying, but he throws his head back and laughs and kisses me delightedly as if I'd said something superlatively witty. We're both laughing. Still he holds me. This is our anniversary. It is 7:20. SQ

The Chief Inspector's Daughter

A STORY

by Hasanthika Sirisena

Hasanthika Sirisena was born in Kandy, Sri Lanka, and grew up in Rocky Mount, North Carolina. Her work has appeared in several literary reviews. She has been nominated for the Pushcart Prize and this year attended the Sewanee Writers Conference as a Georges and Anne Borchardt Scholarship recipient. Sirisena teaches creative writing at the City College of New York and at the Gotham Writers' Workshop.

A BEGGAR recently discovered the bodies of four men and one woman in an SUV abandoned on the border of Colombo 8. The corpses' heads and hands were missing so that the victims could not be quickly identified. *Sri Lanka Daily* added, disapprovingly, that the woman had been posed in a provocative way, as if the body of a headless, handless woman could lure a man to sexual misdeeds. A rumor quickly spread: the victims were Tamils executed by the Sri Lankan army. We know, though few of us admit, our soldiers do such things. But I know, this time, we are all of us wrong.

I am drawn to these victims because I was there the night they were killed. Forsythia Lane where the SUV was found is one of the safer parts of the city. The lane is off the main street and is unpaved, nothing more then a pitted and potholed dirt road. With the recent bombings, it is one of the few places a seemingly empty parked car can remain unnoticed. And this is where my boyfriend and I drive when we want to make love.

We are both medical students at the University of Colombo and are still young, only nineteen. We both live at home. My father's servant, Saroja, lives in a small room beside our kitchen; she sees and hears everything. There is no way for me to arrange for Siva to come to my house. But even if I were able to arrange it, I love my father and do not want to disrespect him in his home.

Instead, we pull the car to a stop under a large nag champa tree, the most romantic place on the lane. The yellow flowers shimmer and quiver in the night. Occasionally the breeze shears the blossoms from their stems, and a tumult of petals surrounds us. In those moments I'm reminded of a gift my American-born cousin gave me. A snow globe, she called it.

Siva and I were there under that tree the night of the murders. We were in the backseat of his father's car when Siva noticed headlights approaching. As the blades of light swept over Siva's back, the air went out of him, and his body rested heavy on top of mine. I nudged him away, propped myself on my elbows, and peered out the window in time to see an SUV and another smaller car pass.

After the cars were gone, Siva became reanimated, as if a switch had flipped, and scrambled into the driver's seat. He backed down the lane without waiting for me to crawl into the passenger seat.

These victims, they cannot be completely innocent, no? If the killers were out solely to cause trouble and hurt Tamils, why had they not come to our car? Siva is a Tamil. They would have hurt him also, and me for being with him. But I do not say any of this. Since that night, Siva's behavior toward me has changed, and I know what he thinks: I am Sinhalese and I cannot be completely trusted.

THE AUTOPSY ROOM at the university medical school has little more than a sputtering air conditioner to cool it. With the ten students that make up my class, as well as our lecturer, the room has become unbearably hot. I arrive a little late so that I don't have to go too far inside and can face the window. When the heat and the smell of the corpse become too much, I stare out over the tops of the king coconut palms and imagine the ocean somewhere in the distance.

The room is tiled from floor to ceiling. The tiles are aged and cracked; the grout is covered by a rust-colored mold. On an especially humid day condensation forms, and the walls appear to bleed. Reddish brown stains spread across the tiles. The room frightens some of the hospital workers, who make quite a racket whenever they are told to go inside. They say the stains are the blood of the dead. Others say the room is possessed by the *yakka*.

Today we are autopsying a young woman. I look over at Siva. He is standing at the other end of the room, concentrating on what our lecturer is saying. I try to smile, but he pretends to be concerned about a fly buzzing near his face. He refuses to look in my direction. This is not unusual for him. He is a very good student, grateful for the opportunity to go to school and very serious about his studies. After lecture I try to make my way to him, but he is walking too far ahead.

It's only later that afternoon, as I'm waiting for the bus, that I see him studying with another student at the corner Barista. Siva has his laptop out and is typing; his friend Ibrahim is reading the newspaper. We don't sit for our exams for another month, but Siva began studying at the start of the term; he studies every moment he can. I go in and slide into the booth next to him. Siva puts his arm around me and pulls me to him. His friend smirks as he watches us.

"Shouldn't you be studying also?" I ask Ibrahim.

He points to an article in the papers about the murders on Forsythia Lane. "My uncle and brother have a theory," he says to Siva. "This is a police killing." He brings his hand to his throat and makes a slicing motion. "My uncle says this is what the police do to you when you cross them." He looks at me slyly.

Siva purses his lips. "Your uncle talks nonsense, men." Ibrahim starts to protest, but Siva waves dismissively. "Go get another cup of coffee." Ibrahim seems reluctant at first but finally gets up and leaves.

I nestle into Siva. He is big, built thick and muscular. I am tall and strong, not one of the petite, slender girls—the pretty girls, they are called—so revered by Sri Lankans. But when I am next to Siva I feel fragile. He could crush my ribs with one firm squeeze.

The talk of the murders has reminded Siva of something. He tells me a white Peugeot had driven slowly by his parents' house yesterday. The same car returned and parked across the street for half the day.

Sri Lanka is a paranoid country. Twenty years of civil war makes us jump at our own shadows. Everyone has stories like Siva's. Stories of cars and vans that come in the day or in the middle of the night. He sees the disbelief in my expression.

"Sonali, we were there, at the place where they found the SUV. My father's car was there." I nod, but I do not want to urge him to think of that night. I do not want him to focus on the deaths of those people. "When those cars passed, maybe they could have belonged to the killers, no? Maybe they took down my father's license plate number."

I pull away from Siva and study the side of his face. "Those cars could have belonged to anyone. Maybe others have caught on, and they drive there for the same reasons we do." I try to give him a coy look, but he is staring into the screen of his laptop. "I will put a conversation to my father."

"No." Siva responds too quickly. "Tell your father nothing. He is unable to do anything."

"Of course he will do something. You do not have to worry about him finding out why we were there. I'll tell him a good story." Siva has pulled me tighter to him, but he is still not looking at me. Instead, he is hitting the escape key of his laptop, as if there is something wrong. "He will help anyone I ask him to help." I am sure of this, and I will Siva to have confidence in my ability with my father.

But he has gone pale, and I realize he is truly frightened. "Say nothing," he begs. "I am probably wrong about the car. It's nothing."

We speak English to each other because I do not know Tamil, and he does not speak Sinhala unless he must. There are other things that divide us—different gods, different history—but Siva and I also have at least one thing in common. I want to urge him to find somewhere else we can drive to. I want nothing more than to ease the burning I feel whenever I am near him. The pure physical need that overcomes me too often these days. But Siva slams his laptop shut and lets go of me. Unsure of what else to do, I straighten my shirt and run the palm of my hand over my hair. Siva packs away his computer.

WHEN I RETURN HOME, I open the front door and nearly step on a dead koi. There is a small fishpond near the veranda. The fish occasionally leap from the pond onto the porch. One of my father's dogs must have nudged it over to the entryway. I know there is a reasonable explanation, but after my conversation with Siva, I am disconcerted by what seems to me an omen.

I call the servant, Saroja. "*Mokuda, annay?*" I ask. I try too hard to keep my voice from trembling. When Saroja sees the fish, she brings her hand up to the side of her face; her mouth forms an *O*. Her expression makes her look not unlike the dead fish. But as soon as this image comes to me, I feel sorry for conjuring it. Saroja is Tamil, and I have tried of late, since falling in love with Siva, to be careful how I think of Tamils. I tell her to bring a broom and a page of an old newspaper. She must hurry. My father will be back soon, and if he sees this he will be angry.

When my father returns from work, he is in a foul mood. He is the chief inspector at the Colombo 13, Kotahena, police station. He comes from a family of police officers. His grandfather was a constable in Panadura; his father was part of the team who investigated the assassination of Bandaranaike. My father is proud of his job, though it is at times dangerous. He has received death threats and even thought of retiring when my mother was ill, for her sake. But since her death he has only worked harder.

My father is tall and slim with dark skin the color of treacle. He is handsome; there are many women who come to the house with presents for him. Relatives have mentioned to him he should remarry. But even when my mother was alive, he kept to himself, talking little. He does not seem to miss her now. I have replaced her, and I am all that he needs.

He knows, since I am his only child, that I will take care of him as he grows old. This is why he tolerates my relationship with Siva. He does not hate the Tamils and even argues they should keep Jaffna. But he also voted for the JHU and believes in the need to preserve the Sinhalese race. Because of me, he is friendly to Siva and his family. He sends Saroja to their house in a rickshaw carrying king coconuts or durian or *rambato*, if the fruit is in season.

My father is sitting on the veranda nursing his arrack and reading this morning's *Sri Lanka Daily*. He is so engrossed he barely notices when I offer him a plate of short eats. I look over his shoulder. I see he is reading an article about what the press has now dubbed the "SUV murders." The woman has been identified; it turns out she lived in Kotahena. I ask my father if he knows her. He shakes his head. Then I ask him if he has heard anything about the crime, anything particular about the bodies.

He talks to me often about his work, especially now that my mother is gone. But he peers into his tumbler as if he has spotted a bug. He asks me why I'm curious.

I try to laugh and make light of my inquiry. "I have an interest in dead bodies. I'm interested in pathology."

"Pathology," he scoffs. "This is not a job for women."

"I don't want to be any old lady doctor, patching scraped knees and easing stomach upsets. Pathology interests me. There are so many things that happen to the body after death. So many things you can tell about how someone lived." I know better than to speak with him when he is in one of his moods, but I'm carried away. "And also the possibility of helping to solve mysteries." I realize as soon as I say this that I have misspoken.

He laughs. "You are very young, no? Not even twenty." He picks out a meat patty from the plate of pastries. "Last week a man died after someone threw lye in his face. It is the boss of the restaurant he works at. No mystery. Three days ago a mother arrived at the station claiming her three-year-old son is being buggered. It is the stepfather. No mystery. When a husband is murdered, we arrest the wife. When a son is murdered, we arrest the father. There are no mysteries. There is nothing to solve." He finishes the patty and wipes his hand on a serviette. "You, *duva*, do not have the stomach for these things. Some women, yes. A woman who has lived a hard life. But not you."

He thrusts his tumbler toward me and asks me to refill it. When I lean forward to take the empty glass, he touches my forearm and looks up at me. He slurs a little as he speaks. "You are all that I have. You must do as I say." He pauses. "A girl like you should aspire to something noble. Working with children. Children will love you," he persists gently.

After dinner, after my father has gone to bed, I take the newspaper and find the article. The woman, the paper claims, was a known prostitute and petty criminal, frequently arrested. I wonder if my father is telling the truth when he says he doesn't know her.

Siva calls in the morning. He is crying. His brother was copped the night before and is still being held at the police station. He wants me to ask my father for help. But before I can ring the Kotahena station, Siva phones and tells me his brother was released and is back home.

I try to call him later, but nobody, not even a servant, answers. Siva's family is rich, and they have a house in the Cinnamon Gardens, the wealthiest part of town. Even though it is hard now to find servants, his family has enough money to pay well. They have a cook and a gardener and even an ayah for Siva's youngest brother. There is always someone at his home, and I begin to worry. Why will no one pick up?

I don't see Siva again until the next morning. He is in a far corner of the university library. When I express my concern for him, he tells me what happened.

The family's cook had gone to the market in the late afternoon. As he made his way back home, two men on a motorbike tried to kill him. One of the men had held a cricket bat out as they passed, coming up from behind, riding at a high speed. The cook's legs were shattered, and he might never walk again.

"Someone wants to destroy my family," Siva whispers. The white Peugeot, his brother's arrest, and now this. I want to remind him this is how things are here. If we hadn't been on Forsythia Lane, all these things could have happened anyway. Then Siva would have searched for any omen or any superstition. Now Forsythia Lane is the most convenient explanation for something that has no reason.

But I don't say any of this. I do the only thing I can. I tell Siva that I will ask my father to place a call to the Colombo 7 police station. He will talk to the chief inspector there.

Siva scowls. I can see the muscles in his jaw clench. I try to hold his hand, but he shrugs me off. "How is it you do not know?" He asks this question again and again without blinking or looking away.

I stare through the stacks of old books, mildewed and rotting in the heat. "Know what?"

Siva flips open his laptop and types my father's name. He begins to read from a website.

Abdul Azeez lost use of his hands and arms after being hung by his wrists for forty-eight hours. Nihal Jayewardene disappeared. Last seen at the Kotahena station. Lakshmi Fernando gang-raped by three policemen at the Kotahena station house. Priya Jeganathan burned with a cigarette on her face, arms, and genitals.

Siva is about to go on, but I reach over and close the laptop. As I walk away, I teeter like I'm drunk. He does not call to me or come after me. I step out into the sun and am grateful for the scorching heat, so strong it makes me forget, for a moment.

MUSLIM/SINHALA/TAMIL/BURGHER. UNP/LTTE/JVP/JHU/TNA. Royal/Thomian. There are too many choices. But, still, they demand that I choose.

I am not a fool. I have heard the rumors about my father. It is impossible not to. But I know without asking how he explains what he has done. The rumors are all half-truths and exaggerations by people who do not know how it is here. These people lead hard, desperate lives. They are brutal, and my father must talk and act using that same brutal language. This is the only way we can all be protected.

But I have never needed any explanations. I have never spent any time, until now, wondering what my father is capable of.

I DO NOT GO HOME. Instead, I wander the streets and then take a bus to Forsythia Lane. It is early evening and still light by the time I reach it, about seven o'clock.

I do not know what it is like for Siva, though I've tried to imagine. He told me once that swinging his legs out of bed, planting his feet on the clay floor beneath him, was not simply a physical act. It was a mental act, one propelled by urgency and single-mindedness. If he thought too hard, he would never leave his room. And every day something, sometimes something very small, nothing more than a loose word, made getting up the next day another nearly insurmountable obstacle.

No, I do not know what it is like to be that afraid.

From above me comes a piercing shriek, and the trees explode in a flurry of ripped leaves and broken branches: two mongooses fighting. Ahead of me a polecat noses through garbage left in the bushes. I consider turning around, but suddenly it seems important to move forward, to find what I've come here to see.

I approach the nag champa where Siva and I come. As I stand underneath, remembering our times here together, a man steps out from behind. In the remaining light, I can see he is old and stooped, with nothing but a tattered sarong to cover his body. Thick white hair, coiled like tiny watch springs, extends from his chest across his stomach. "*Machee*, my children are dying," he hisses as he moves toward me, his palm extended. "My wife is dying." He smells of *kassippu*, the moonshine only the poor drink, and he speaks in heavily accented Sinhala, the way a Tamil might. His next words are all in Tamil, and I do not understand what he is saying.

Has he been living here all the time? Did he see Siva's car when we came here together? Did he watch us? Even though he smells as if he is drunk, his eyes are bright and alert, and he is studying me. He leans his weight on an old broom handle when he walks, but he can't mask his natural agility. It occurs to me he isn't really a beggar, but I still give him something.

I should turn back now. If I am hurt, people will have no sympathy for me. They will say I deserve it for coming here alone. They will say that because I am a chief inspector's daughter I believe I am untouchable, invincible. But this is not how I am. I am here only because I love Siva and my father, and I feel that there is something here, some proof that we are, all of us, innocent.

I walk down the lane without looking back. If I turn I will see the beggar standing straight, peering at me as I walk away. He will suddenly look younger and stronger. Once I've seen his true self, he will not allow me to leave. I walk on, aware now only of pushing my body forward, even as the lane grows dark.

I reach the cul-de-sac where the SUV was found. I expect something—markers, colored tape—but I see nothing to indicate a crime has taken place. Only a long wall that protects a derelict building and a cluster of aging forsythia bushes. It is dark now, but my eyes have grown accustomed. I can make out the form of things, but the ground around me is vast and regular and black. There is the warm breeze and the scent of jasmine. In the distance I hear the steady hum of motors and look behind me to see the headlights of two motorbikes approaching.

The bikes stop, and two men dismount. Though it is dusk, there is still enough light that I can make out their uniforms. One holds a torch, and they both have their hands to their waists. They are both gripping their batons; I know this without having to see. "Madame, what are you doing here?"

One of the constables moves quickly; he grips me by the arm. He digs his fingers into my flesh and pulls me close enough to him that I can smell the betel on his breath. I glimpse, for a moment, his stained, rotting teeth. The other holds the torch in my face so I am blinded.

But when I try to put my hand up to block the light, he exhales rapidly, a sound like air being let out of a tire. The man who is holding me moves away. He is being pushed back.

"Sonali," the man with the torch whispers. "Sonali, what is this?" He lowers the beam enough so that I can see his face. "Do you recognize me? Preshan." I nod. I have seen him before; he works for my father. Since I was a little girl, he has helped me find my father whenever I stopped by the station. He has even come to my house when my mother was sick.

The other constable is staring at his partner. "You know this person?"

"It's Sonali Gajaweera. Chief Inspector Gajaweera's daughter." The other constable looks at me, his mouth open. "What are you doing here?" he asks. This is not a demand but more a question of wonder.

I am emboldened by his meekness. "What are *you* doing here?" I ask him. "You are far from Kotahena." Anger flashes across his face, and he steps toward me. But Preshan is faster; he puts a protective arm around my shoulders and guides me toward the bikes. When I look back at Preshan's partner, he has his hands on his hips, and he is staring at the sky. When he approaches us, I can tell he wants to speak with Preshan, alone, but Preshan refuses to acknowledge him. "Leave us. I will take her home," he says.

Preshan watches as his partner's bike disappears down the lane. He turns to me. "What are you doing here, Sonali? It is not good for a girl to be out at night alone." Preshan's tone is soft, almost conciliatory. "Some people were murdered here."

"I know," I reply.

"Why are you here?" he presses.

I want to tell him about Siva, about how his family is being harassed. How Siva believes, how I believe, it is because of what we saw that night. How my father avoided speaking to me of the murders. Why would Preshan be here unless my father were involved? And if his men are involved, why would he not just tell me this when I had asked earlier? "Why are you here?" I whisper.

"We saw you walking up the lane alone."

I imagine the people in that report. Was it Preshan who burned that woman with the cigarette? Was it his colleagues who raped that woman? Where was my father for all of this? Or is it all lies? I cannot tell anymore. "They say those men were murdered by the police."

"'They'?" Preshan scoffs. "They also say it is a military murder. They say it is a gang murder. Or schoolboys on drugs. They will soon say it is you, Sonali, if I do not take you home." He is about to walk to his bike when, suddenly, he swings the beam of light onto my face. I wince and try to look away. "What *are* you asking?" he demands.

I stand there, quietly. He sighs. "I will let your father know about your theories. Perhaps if he's in a good mood, he will share with you the truth."

He tells me to get on the back of his bike. I put my arms around his waist. As he starts slowly down the lane, I grip him tightly, pressing my body to his.

MY FATHER OPENS his wallet and gives Saroja a few rupee notes. I am standing to the side, next to the dining room table; he has refused to look at me since he and Preshan talked in the kitchen. Go to the market, he tells Saroja. Stay away for a little while, he adds. Saroja is reluctant to leave, but she is also afraid. My father and I stand quietly, both of us waiting until we hear Saroja dragging closed the metal gate that leads to the street.

When she is gone, my father slaps me. I have to brace myself against the table to keep from stumbling.

But he doesn't appear angry, only concerned. "Are you mad?" he asks. "Are you ill? You are walking in the street at night like a whore? Talking nonsense."

My cheek stings, and the pain makes me giddy. "I was there the night those men were murdered, *thatha*. You need to tell your men that."

My father's lips tremble; his eyes narrow. Then his expression quickly returns to that of concern. "You're ill, *duva*," he coos and makes as if to check my forehead for a temperature. "Let me help you, darling."

"Siva and I were there the night of the murders." My father looks confused. "You have heard his father's car was seen there, no? You were told the car was parked on the lane."

"What are you babbling?"

"But did you know *both* of us were there? Did your spies tell you that?"

"You are not feeling well. Come upstairs—"

"That was why his father's car was there. We were there so we could be together, *thatha*." I take a deep breath. "You can leave his family alone now. You do not have to hurt them because they know nothing. We saw nothing."

My father is looking from my face to the floor and back again; his mouth is moving but no sound comes. "All rubbish," he finally mutters.

"The murdered woman was from Kotahena. A known prostitute, the papers call her. Arrested frequently. How could you not have heard of her?"

"How is it that you think I've met every prostitute in Kotahena?"

"A known prostitute? Your men are investigating? Why, *thatha*? Colombo 8 cannot handle this case on their own?"

My father shakes his head. "I do not know what you mean. Who are *my* men?"

"Don't lie," I say this as calmly as I can manage. My father steps back, startled. "Why do you continue to lie? I recognized him. I recognized Preshan. I know he works for you." I pause long enough to catch my breath. "All the time you have lied, about everything."

He pushes me but not hard. It is a feeble attempt by someone who is angry but cannot do any harm, a schoolboy reacting to a taunt. I grip the edge of the table.

My father is standing, breathing hard, his head bowed. He is a guilty man. Or perhaps it is I who am the guilty one. "I know what you do," I say. My voice wavers and sticks to the back of my throat. "I've known for a long time," I croak, "all you have done to people." I let go of the table. I'm breathing hard, and I need a few seconds to catch my breath. "Siva says the police are harassing his family. If you are hurting him, if you are hurting Siva or his family, I will leave you." My father's eyes widen; he blanches. He is not angry now or concerned but scared. "You can die here alone. As you should."

This time he pushes me hard enough that I lose my balance. I do not black out when my head strikes the floor. I hear the impact of my skull, but it does not sound as if it is coming from me. It is instead as if a bomb has ripped through my house. I curl up, tight, more from the pain than because I am afraid my father will hurt me. He leans over and whispers my name; he nudges me. I cannot respond or think because of the pain. After a little while, I hear him walk away.

I AM STILL on the floor, my arms over my head, when Saroja and Siva arrive. Saroja cradles my head in her lap.

I ask them where my father is, but Siva ignores my question. Instead he tells me, if I can move we need to go to the hospital. I try to stand on my own but feel dizzy as soon as I take my first step. I have to lean against Siva. We walk slowly to the street, and Saroja hails a three-wheeler.

Again, I ask about my father. Siva explains that neither he nor Saroja has seen or spoken to him. After my father told her to go, Saroja had taken a three-wheeler to Siva's. When they arrived at my house, my father's car was gone. They found me on the floor, unconscious.

At the emergency room, a lady doctor tends to me. She tells me I should stay the night. I have a concussion, and they want to make sure there is no more serious injury.

After she's left, Siva stays at my bedside. He brushes my hair from my face and mops at my bruised face with a damp towel. Next to me a woman is screaming in Tamil, and I ask what she is saying. But he says not to worry.

As I look up at Siva, I wonder how long he has harbored this knowledge of my father. Has he always looked at me and wondered? Does he ask himself what I am capable of? I whisper to him that he should leave. He doesn't understand at first. He tells me Saroja called my aunt, and she will be here soon. I repeat myself, louder. I want him to go.

The pain is a screeching inside my head. The sound obliterates all my emotions and thoughts, and I can only close my eyes against it.

When I open my eyes again, I want you, Siva, not to be here.

When I awake, it is morning. My aunt is standing over me. The lady doctor is next to her. My aunt smiles and strokes the side of my cheek while the doctor explains how well I'm doing. But I'm not listening. Instead I'm searching the room, but Siva is gone.

TWO WEEKS AGO the inspector general released the identities of the murdered men: four Muslims who worked in the tea trade. A new rumor started to circulate: corrupt government officials had them executed. A few days later *Sri Lanka Daily* reported that two customs agents had been arrested. The murders were retaliation against a planter who refused to be extorted. The prostitute from Kotahena was, most likely, only a lure. An innocent bystander.

Next to the article were three photographs of the inspectors who worked on the case. I recognized all three: the Forsythia Lane beggar, Preshan, and Preshan's partner. The article also explained that Preshan had recently been promoted to his new post from the Kotahena department. This was his first major case.

I have not seen my father since that night. I live with my aunt now, my mother's sister, in Panadura, and I take the bus to school. My father does not speak to me, and I do not ask. I am aware that he sends money for me through Saroja.

I see Siva in the halls at university, but I always duck away before he can stop me. Finally he waits for me outside my classroom. He tries to explain how sorry he is. What to do, I tell him. I will never know what it is like to be afraid the way he is afraid, and he will never understand why I lived as long as I did with my father. He seems shocked at first that I would be so direct with him, and then he looks at me helplessly. I think of what the Lord Buddha has told us: when you see a drowning man, you should not help him. I have never understood this until now. It is too hard, in this moment, to reach for Siva and pull him to me. I am not strong, and it is better, much easier, to let him go. So I say the truth.

There is nothing we can do for each other; there is nothing more to say. SQ

The Bulls at San Luis

A STORY

by Don Waters

Don Waters's debut story collection, *Desert Gothic*, won the 2007 Iowa Short Fiction Award and was published by the University of Iowa the same year. His fiction can be found in several fine literary magazines. Waters lives in Santa Fe with his partner, the writer Robin Romm.

THE PRICE TAG on the Night Owl Infrared Specs was steep, but the binoculars do the job. Amplify starlight. Invert darkness. Organize the desert into Cye's X-ray.

A green-tinted figure roams into Cye's lens. "*Uno.*" He sees another. He starts the math. "Two."

This is Cye's second run in a month. He's nicknamed the rendezvous El Cementerio because several large, wind-chiseled boulders have eroded into the shape of headstones. Rumor has it, beneath every other rock near the border is a grave. Out here, along the line, Cye believes it.

He counts nine men a half mile away. They're kicking up a hell of a dust cloud, and they're late but on target. Cye flips a lever under his dash. A strobe attached to his front grill begins to pulse. His Suburban becomes a beacon. When the group spots him, they turn.

In the three years he's been running illegals, Cye's seen his share. When he's not playing hide-and-seek with Bronco-patrolling border cops, he's watching missile-heavy jets lay fume trails across the sky. Even when his passengers avoid the bombs, the sunlight inflicts its varying punishments. Heat exhaustion, dehydration, hyperthermia, or some combination of.

Night is the time to hustle. At night, when darkness cools the badlands, the border stirs.

El Cementerio is outside *la migra's* reach. Cye picked the place because it rests inside the Barry M. Goldwater Air Force Range, a great chunk of hot Arizona desert that cuddles the Mexico line. Kicker is, illegals must haul ass twenty miles or so across an active bombing range to make it.

Before the big walk, they're lined up and pep-talked.

"*Eviten los tanques.*" The U.S. Army retires tanks out there. And the Air Force bombs those tanks, *entienden?*

Some people don't listen, of course. Folks climb into abandoned Bradleys to find shade, *tener sexo*, whatever. A bunker buster once honed in on some poor *pendejo* as he was pinching a loaf inside a WWII Sherman. Cye was later given the replay: the blast turned the guy's ass into a crater.

Immigrant trails demand sacrifice. Cye understands this, but lately the stories have begun to eat at him. Every sad report forces introspection, which he hates. Worst-case scenario, he could always take matters into his own. If the time comes, when the time comes, he could always wander into the scorched flats, walk until he couldn't anymore, and sit beside a rock with his name on it. Sure, something like that.

Hints of creosote waft through the window and settle on Cye's tongue. He flips on a light, and the side-view mirror captures his profile. The sun has deepened the lines beside both eyes. He's also going prematurely gray. White wires jut from his temples.

It's been almost a year since the asshole in Phoenix handed Cye a leaflet, "Preparing for Your Illness." Cye shredded it. For days afterward, he wondered if the physician predicted that kind of response. Bloating, an occasional lightning rod of pain. Cye tries not to acknowledge his terminal disease. He tries not to lend it authority over his remaining time.

From out of the darkness, the illegals emerge, one by one. Aglow in his head-lights, the nine men look exhausted. Arms hang heavily from shoulders. *El desierto* has left them speechless.

Often, Cye wonders what his passengers think of his blue eyes, a trait inherited from his *gringo* dad. He wonders if the color elicits quiet judgments. Cye's always thought the rest of him—his dark complexion, his thick hair and sloping cheek-bones—belong to his *madre*, to *Sinaloa*, to *México*.

LA MIGRA HAVE their job: tracking, spotting, chasing. And Cye's got his.

In the dry Arizona lowlands, Cye plays Moses. On drop-offs, when he nails the destination, dudes wrap him in hugs. *Señoritas* pinch his ass. Old women drape rosaries around his neck.

"Mi mejor conductor," El Jefe likes to say about Cye. *"Un fabricante del dinero."* His best driver, a real moneymaker.

Border crossing is an act of faith. Cye believes in the principle. He believes in salvation and exodus, that big march into the Promised Land. Most places, the border's nothing more than a useless strand of barbed wire, a total joke.

Cye's boss, El Jefe, the people-broker, runs operations out of Ciudad Juárez, just over the bridge from El Paso. Cye met Jefe in Phoenix years ago, in English 1A, day one of community college. Back then, Jefe was a buck-toothed *cholo* wannabe, and Cye was rearranging his late twenties, drying out, deluding himself into believing he wanted to repair air conditioners. The first day of class, Jefe sat next to Cye, accidentally bumped his foot, and confessed that he was there to polish the more important verbs: buy, sell, own.

Inside Jefe's cramped cinderblock office, he's now got satellite phones and a Rolodex full of business. Excel spreadsheets radiate from laptops. Stacks of new Blackberries are piled in the corner, waiting to be used, each gadget registered to a nonexistent person. El Jefe arranges the loads. He faxes Cye quantities, times, and dates.

"Pinche gringos need us," El Jefe likes to say. Jefe has a crazy set of long teeth that overlap a fat bottom lip.

Dry-erase boards sit propped on easels. Jefe draws contour maps on them, marking flow points. He likes embellishing his sketches of desert peaks, turning burnt mountain ranges into columns of too-perfect breasts. Jefe also has the habit of signing the boards with looping *J*'s, which look like snakes, as though the synchronized machinery of his operation were a work of art.

When certain corridors of the border become overcrowded, Jefe simply erases the paths and repositions them. The paths always lead north.

"Two thousand miles of invisible highway," El Jefe also likes to say, his teeth clomping down on his lip. "And the flow is strong, *cabrón*. The flow is relentless."

Stopping it, Cye knows, is like stopping a tsunami with a tennis racket. During election years, sure, the Feds always put on a show. They hoist stadium lights, concoct new strategies, rally Congress for more funds, for more symbolic fence line. Traffic only gets redirected, to the most desolate regions, to rural hick-spots, to the desert.

Cye memorizes old dirt roads and alternate shortcuts. He counts the faces. He moves the people. Totaling up his cut, he has one hundred and eighty grand saved. The money's stuffed inside hollowed-out aerosol cans, a pantry's worth, in his rarely used apartment in Mesa.

Cye's a simple man. He likes his apartments spotless, unfurnished, and easy to maintain. He considered buying a house once, in Vegas, on the links. He even squirreled away a down payment, more than enough. But after the diagnosis, he reneged at the last minute, disappointing the attractive real estate broker and, not surprisingly, any shot at a date.

CYE POPS THE LOCKS. The men pile in, wrestling for room. They argue with their elbows. Mostly, the damage is to their cheeks, arms, and necks, which are burned, tender. Cye distributes water bottles. Five of the men are dressed in blue tracksuits, like a team. Except for a fine coating of dust, the suits look new, as though the quintet saved up for their Arizona debut.

Cye says, "If you're near one, a seat belt, use it."

The youngest, a teenager, decides to take the front passenger seat. The kid's upper lip is latticed with cracks and his eyes nictitate, a trace of buzz melting from them. Cye knows he's been chewing Metabothin diet pills, a favorite among border jumpers. Ephedrine helps pick up the clip on the long walk.

Cye tosses a gallon jug in the kid's lap, nailing him matter-of-factly. "Seat belt, *por favor*," he says.

The kid's wounded gaze drifts to Cye's earlobe, pausing on his turquoise stud.

Cye stays quiet during the drive. He likes fiddling with the stereo, listening to AM sports talk. Mostly, he eavesdrops. He enjoys the men's stories. Cye's mom is *mestiza*. She crossed under the radar in the sixties. Growing up, she nagged his dad in English but rattled off Spanish when talking to her son. So when there's talk, he understands.

It's a short, bouncy ride to I-8. Cye hits pavement, leaving the dirt road behind. He races toward northbound 95, which will shuttle them to Nevada.

Discussion arises among the five men in tracksuits. Three of them are stacked like tuna cans in the rear cargo area. Turns out they're brothers, from Oaxaca. Manny, the ringleader, does all the talking. Apparently the brothers worked for a time at a *maquiladora* in Nogales. They had fifty-cent-an-hour, ten-hour-a-day shit jobs, folding cardboard boxes, then packing tennis shoes into them. The pay sucked, workers were mistreated, etc.

Manny made the call. They hadn't tried *los Estados Unidos*. Yeah, he says, decorating his sentences with his hands, he figured they should try Vegas. When Manny says Vegas, he means it. He forms a fist and punches one hand with the other: *Vegas*.

El Jefe advanced the brothers the fare: sixteen thousand pesos per person.

So, yeah, Manny says, the deal is they'll crash at one of Jefe's houses. They'll work and repay the loan—meaning, Cye knows, plus ten interest points.

CYE COUNTS SHRINES along northbound 95. Periodically his high beams light up a new roadside memorial. By his estimate, he's spotted thirteen, one more than on his previous run. Cye floats scenarios at each sighting: a blowout, resulting in loss of control. Or some drunken old fart, asleep at the wheel, wrapping it around a guardrail.

South of Parker, Arizona, Cye trolls the roadside, looking for number fifteen. His passengers are completely wiped out. Every hard shoulder has become a pillow. The journey for them is twelve hours under hot sun plus seven more on the road.

Thinking he missed it, Cye considers doubling back. At last, he pulls up alongside a rickety white cross. Propped against the cross is a cheap drugstore wreath, its plastic petals shriveled into kernels.

He began caretaking not long after his diagnosis. He found the spot by accident during a midnight shuttle ride. A piss break, dropped trou, cold air nipping his crack. He was aiming his stream at a large saguaro when he realized he was standing on a dirt-covered cross. Duct-taped to it was a smudged Kodak snapshot of a young couple, decked out in tuxedo and wedding dress. The young white man in the picture sported an Oakland Raiders cap. Next to him stood a pretty Latina, her forehead covered with pimples.

Cye was struck. This was where the couple died. The thought electrified him in shivers. He ran a finger over the girl's face, over her pimply brow, imagining he could feel the bumps, that he could read her like Braille.

That night, he began to dig. A hole opened, and he resurrected the cross and reinforced it with rocks. He gave them names: Richard and Eva, after his parents, another mixed pair.

For so many years Cye never paid attention—this, that, whatever. He was always consumed by bars and the women in them, followed later by gas stations and cash drops and *hola, adiós.* Nowadays, Cye's been growing more aware of tributes in all their forms. Streets, names of towns, rivers. Denver is named in honor of James Denver, and so on.

Cye grabs a plastic grocery bag from under his seat. It's filled with candles, little white numbers he bought at the Dollar Depot in Tempe. The candles are small, white wax, encased in clear glass.

Chilled nighttime air opens his sinuses. Affixed to the cross's left arm with fishing wire is a new Raiders ball cap. Cye left it his last visit. He's an Arizona Cardinals fan. He despises the Raiders. But the gesture felt important.

The couple's memorial isn't the great pyramid, but it's something. In a year, maybe less, it'll be gone, who knows. And it's impossible not to wonder. How was their last second? Terrifying? How much blood and pain?

Cye lights two candles, one for her, one for him. He shields them with rocks, protecting the flames from a breeze. Stapled to the couple's photo is a note. Blue paper, folded, and until now Cye hasn't dared to touch it. He figures it's probably some pathetic poem, some sister's hysterical letter. On the one hand, learning about Richard and Eva could ruin them for him. That's the deal with getting to know people. Then there's the other hand. The note could teach him something. Maybe tell him how not to worry. Maybe give him guidance.

Cye doesn't sit well with indecision. He removes the staple and shoves the note into his pocket.

When he opens the driver-side door, the kid's eyes slam shut. He's pretending to be asleep. The kid has been watching, which makes Cye feel responsible. A shiny glaze of saliva rings the kid's mouth. Over the past few hours, Cye's monitored the boy's dirty little habit.

Cye says to him, "You're making love to that thumb. Maybe your mouth should find a better target."

LONG DRIVES EXACERBATE Cye's symptoms—nausea, no appetite, heartburn. It's as though an animal is hibernating in his gut, distending his intestines.

Cye shuts down the air. Without it, the cabin fills with the cruel stink of men and sweat. The sun crowns between two mountains and floods the cabin with light. Soon the murmuring begins. Distances close between highway Mini-Mart sightings. The men know they are drawing close. Already it's pushing ninety degrees.

In the daytime, Vegas shines. All that sun, all those hotel windows. *El Norte*, especially Vegas, means payday. Vegas is industry. Expansion demands cheap, capable hands needed for landscaping, laundry, and drywall. Twice a month, Cye makes a drop, and the drop pays well. El Jefe's got contracts with several outfits.

In an industrial district near the airport, Cye pulls into a lot encircled by chain-link. The lot sits under an overpass. Above, bikini-clad breasts painted on a billboard publicize a strip-club chain. At night, Cye's seen them; neon nipples shaped like arrows point at the off-ramp.

Hernan is waiting, as usual, leaning against a teal-colored Chevy. He's El Jefe's go-to in Vegas. Cye's never been bothered by Hernan. He's a business type, an aficionado of silk shirts, gold chains, and pilot glasses that hide bulging eyes.

"That billboard makes me want to play grab-ass," Cye says to Hernan, stepping down from his rig.

Hernan holds a clipboard. As each man climbs out, Hernan ticks a box on a form.

"The Grand Admiral," Hernan says. He never stops talking business. "You know, that new three-billion-dollar casino? They're excavating a lake. Preparing for yachts. Races. We need hands," he goes on.

Cye says, "Yachts?"

"For the marina," Hernan says.

Cye says, "Marina?"

The young kid walks over with his hand extended. His smile opens a thin wound on his damaged lip. When Cye takes the kid's grip, it feels as though a sword enters through his belly button. It twists.

Cye doubles over, desperate for a breath. It's difficult to swallow. And the afterpain is warm, sharp, like he's been brass-knuckled. The first time this happened, he thought of coyote traps snapping around his midsection. That pain was particularly toothy.

"*¿Qué te pasa?*" Hernan says.

Cye says, "Too much driving, man." He pinches a roll of love-handle fat. "Gas, I think. I don't know. Haven't eaten." He's prerehearsed his lies.

As he crouches (crouching curbs the throbs), he scrutinizes the men he delivered, measuring their anxious shifts. For a moment, he's frightened by a vision of their skin peeling away, unfurling like old wallpaper, and their skeletons peeking through.

That horrible afternoon in Phoenix—in fact, the worst afternoon of Cye's fucking life—he nearly tossed up the chalky barium concoction in the doctor's face. Six, the specialist said—what, seven months? Cye's standing on month eight, without treatment, so what's the guy know? *Está loco*, Cye thinks. He refuses to buy into some countdown.

"Listen," Hernan says. He distributes paperwork to the illegals, fake work documents. "We got this *puñeta* over there," Hernan says. He directs Cye toward the gate with his pen. "Guy told me, in so many words, he wants to be dropped. He wants to go back."

Cye looks over. A middle-aged man is standing next to a suitcase. He's *mestizo*: squat, black hair, the standard. But this guy is dressed in a brown suit, as though he's ready for something special. Indeed.

"Back?" Cye says to Hernan.

"Over the line," Hernan says.

Cye says, "Who goes back?"

The stranger also wears a cinnamon-colored Stetson. A crisp white button-up accentuates his dark skin.

"So, where's your guitar?" Cye says to the stranger when he walks over.

The man says, "*¿Qué?*"

"You miss the traveling ranchero bus or something?"

The man draws down his eyelids, indicating his annoyance. "I need to get to Interstate 8," the man says. Traces of Mexican shrapnel scar his English. "There's a rest area outside Yuma," he goes on.

Another thing, the man's left front tooth is gold-capped. There's a cutout in the center. A tiny white heart in the middle flashes when the man speaks. Distracting.

Cye says, "This ride is usually one-way."

"You live in Arizona, I hear," the man says. "Hernan tells me you're driving back this afternoon."

Cye breathes deeply. His airways open. The pain is fading. He's seen this sort of thing before. He knows the man can't just skate over like everyone else because he lacks paperwork. Without paperwork, he could be hassled or arrested. Without papers you're as good as invisible, as though papers prove a beating heart. Typical bullshit. Life limited by government formalities and imaginary lines.

Cye says, "*Migra* set up checkpoints around there. That area spoons the border. So you know," he says, "what I'm saying is, I'd be taking a risk dropping you."

From his suit pocket, the man pulls out a wad of green. He peels off five bills.

Lately, Cye's been searching for excuses, reasons to give it up, remain in bed, say to hell with everything. Somehow he finds the muscles required to scrape a toothbrush across his gums. One foot in front of the other, in front of the other.

MIDAFTERNOON, the drive south is two walls of brown and straight, white highway lines. Cye's passenger, turns out, is named Nunez, but that's about as much info as Cye's able to extract after fifty-something miles. Nunez, apparently, enjoys the quiet. But quiet makes road trips unpleasant. Quiet tends to hum like a busted refrigerator. Cye's usually got a cab full of yammering illegals. Arguments, debates. Cye doesn't trust the quiet. Silence has a way of turning his thoughts into bombs.

Cye shoves in a cassette tape, tinkering with the volume. He says, "I've seen a few accidents on this stretch of road."

Nunez ignores the bait. He chooses to stare out the window, as though he's communing with the landscape, its monotonous browns and crimsons. Those hands of his are restless, though. Nunez twirls a gold band around his marriage finger. At least the guy shrugged off his suit jacket. Thing was making Cye sweat.

Cye says, "Six months ago, this guy in front of me, driving a Jeep, his heart exploded. I watched the crash through the windshield like a movie." He says, "Dude swerved to the right, hit the shoulder, overcompensated the wheel, and took out a Pontiac in the on-coming lane."

This is high-quality material, topical. Everyone enjoys firsthand tragedy stories. But not Nunez. Nunez continues his ridiculousness, saying nothing. A distant look clouds his eyes as he fingers his goddamn ring. Cye moves up Nunez's wrists, noticing a pair of cuff links ornamented with miniature black bulls. Not only that, an elaborate, embroidered *N* adorns his shirt pocket.

Cye wonders what the big production is all about, especially the gold tooth with the heart. What business does Nunez have traipsing through the desert looking like Ramon Novarro? Nunez wants to be taxied into bomb country, near El Cementerio, right inside *migra* cutting lanes and migrant footpaths. Sure, Nunez could nosedive south and walk twelve desperate hours. If he hustled, he could make it. In fact, he'd likely pass crews moving north.

Cye says, after a while, "Be nice if there was somewhere to go with my words." He says, "Be nice if you spoke."

Nunez pinches his chin, and he says, "Road signs look venomous." At last, a sentence. It's like pulling molars. "Blacks and yellows, the striped kind," Nunez says. "Reminds me of snakes and spiders. Maybe they do that to help people avoid accidents. Scare them. So people pay attention to the road."

Cye shoots Nunez a hard sideways glance. He imagines pulling over, smashing that little gold trinket out of Nunez's grin. Instead, he pops the cassette tape out, scanning the AM dial. The only station with reasonable reception is public radio, the BBC. Cye listens resentfully: soccer scores of European teams he doesn't know, delivered via some effete-sounding dickhead. Cye's never traveled outside the lower forty-eight.

A pathetic stream parallels the highway, dipping under sage, appearing again. Eventually the land drinks it away. On these long round-trips, Cye stops midway, in Quartzsite, a former mining town. A highway sign points out that Quartzsite is twenty miles up-road. Cye's never liked the place, with its gas stations, countless mobile homes, and nothing to do, but dried sweat granules are caked on his back. And his palms and knuckles ache. A hot shower, he thinks, sleep.

Before they pull off, Cye gestures to Nunez's ring, and he says, "All right, you got me. Who's behind the hot property?"

Nunez shows that little heart of his, wet with saliva.

"Eloisa," Nunez says. He says the ring connects him to her, his children, everyone important in Mexico. He says, "People never ask."

CYE DRIVES TO THE ARROYO. The motel is on a dead-end street, rimmed on either side by crumbling, pink adobe walls. It's an unremarkable building. A frayed Mexican flag billows from a rust-covered pole. Cye uses the motel for overnights, midrun logistics, and so on. Over the past six months, he's clocked more than twenty-thou on his odometer. At the Arroyo, the beds are free.

As usual, Fausto's in the office watching TV, couch-lounging, his hand buried inside a box of kid's cereal.

Cye says, stepping inside, "Ding dong."

"Oh," Fausto says, looking up. "Jefe mentioned something about you."

At six-foot-five, Fausto's the tallest Mexican that Cye's ever met. Fausto was once a star JC ballplayer in Phoenix. But he tore his ACL before graduating to Division I. His wide skull makes his face look stretched, his cheekbones polished.

Cye says, "Caught a sliver of the Bruins game on the radio."

"I don't want to hear it," Fausto says. His exhale signals disappointment. He picks through a pile of green, saguaro-shaped key chains inside an old coffee can. He says, "Poor season for State."

"That UCLA point guard shot the lights out," Cye says.

Fausto changes direction. "Anyway, look at you. Start hitting the weight bench or something?" He says, "You're getting lean."

It's hard for Cye to admit, but he has shed body weight, poundage. Cye says, "Funny." He changes direction, too. "We have a guest, so I need another key."

The Arroyo's No Vacancy sign is always lit. El Jefe owns the place. It's a shelter company he uses to launder money, store illegals, etc. Fausto's only responsibility is to report a full house nightly. This way, a portion of Jefe's dirty bills hop onto the books, cleaned.

Cye settles into Room 18. Before he can get comfortable, Nunez raps loudly on his window. Nunez tells him some funny news about a two-foot-long Gila monster inside his bathroom. Cye follows Nunez, and sure enough, the thing is hiding behind the toilet, its skinny forked tongue darting in and out. Lumps of gray shit are caked to the tiles.

Cye finds Fausto in the office. "Can Nunez get a room without reptiles, please?" he says.

Cye slashes his drapes shut. Prior to stepping into the shower, he washes a large brown spider down the drain. Steam blooms, warming the cold bathroom, and for a moment Cye stands completely still, liberated from his jeans and socks. Naked suits him. He tries to avoid the thought, but he can't escape it. He will miss the feeling.

And has he been working out, asks Fausto. That smart-ass. Still, Cye has begun cinching his belt tighter. His jeans hang looser.

About Cye's rotting stomach, El Jefe knows nothing. Neither does his mom or dad. Fact is, Cye hasn't shared the test results with anyone. When worries about his condition arise, fear nukes them into oblivion. He focuses instead on errands, sports, anything, whatever.

Nothing can be done, however, about constant reminders. Lately, deep red blood-strings streak his morning toilet bowl.

LATER, CYE STARES at a spiderweb clinging for its life. It sways in the corner from the fan's airstream. A knock comes at the door. He shuffles over, towel around his waist.

"Look what I found," Nunez says. He lifts two sixers of Tecate, cans. "I also found two folding chairs behind that dumpster," he says.

Cye peers outside. Nunez has assembled a little outdoor lounge, complete with buckets of ice from the machine. Cye wonders how Nunez suddenly found nice. His Stetson is gone, same with his jacket and dress shirt. He's whittled himself down to a white T-shirt and shorts.

"Fifteen minutes of remaining daylight," Nunez says. "So I thought, why not?"

Cye jumps into jeans. Gusts of warm air tangle his hair, breeze-drying it. Nunez hands him a can, and Cye says, popping the beer, "You never said. People usually can't stop talking about their experience. Blah blah. Biggest decision of their lives. The border cross."

Nunez pours rim foam onto the cement. "I'm following the money I made home," he says. "That's all."

Cye nods. "Makes sense."

"I worked. I sent back what I earned," Nunez says. "And I learned to forget that night we came over. I'm right here, next to you. But I am always in Veracruz."

"Sounds a bit like living in the middle."

"For six years," Nunez says.

The beer tastes like aluminum, liquid nickels, how Cye likes it. A television drones in the office. Except for Fausto, who's busy flipping through TV channels, the motel is empty. Poor Fausto. First that knee of his, and now he's serving time at the Arroyo. El Jefe got word Fausto was dealing rare lizards at swap meets, earning side cash. Selling lizards isn't a big deal, but it is a crime. And extracurricular pursuits that could bring sideways heat on Jefe is a no-no. Rule number one, *cabrón*.

Quartzsite isn't much of a town, and there isn't much ambient light. Soon Nunez's face disappears under a curtain of shadows. The outdoor bulbs don't light up. Cye notices that there aren't any bulbs, just a row of empty sockets. Damn Fausto.

Cye returns from the Suburban with three candles.

"We're full of surprises tonight," Nunez says.

The soft, flickering glow dyes the red Tecate cans, making them appear warm, like coals. He was up all night, and his stomach registers it. All this back-and-forth is exhausting. The demand never stops. He hasn't had a full night for what feels like weeks, so when he pops another beer, he considers it a sleep aid.

"You know, we're not far from a crossing station," Cye says. He tumbles into his chair. The beer has already made his eardrums buzz. He says, "There's a small border shack a few hours south. I could drive you there. Sure as hell beats the desert."

Nunez shakes his head. "I want to walk it."

"People die on that walk," Cye says. He wants Nunez to understand. "I mean, it happens. It's a full day of walking through nowhere."

"I've heard," Nunez says.

So. Nunez owns that particular brand of confidence. Just like Cye's mom, foolish and proud. It makes Cye feel reduced.

He holds his beer can over a candle. He considers extinguishing it. A strand of heat rises from its rolling flame. Cye warms his fingernail on the flame instead, watching how a delicate, invisible heat stream displaces the air around it. He's unable to distinguish, near its hot tip, where the flame tapers and where the air begins. It is flame, and then, simply, it is nothing, a disappearance.

"Still," Cye says, considering Nunez's wish, "that hike is a hell of a thing."

"*Deseo ir a mi país*," Nunez says. He wants to go home. Cye senses the weight of Nunez's eyes. He dislikes the feeling of someone trying to read him.

"Foolish," Cye says. This man has a choice. And that choice is reckless. Ending the conversation, Cye says, "Goddamn stubborn."

When the evening turns chilly, Nunez excuses himself, leaving Cye alone. Cye stacks his empties—three, five, seven. Every so often, he lowers a finger into the dying flame. After tempting it one too many times, he manages to singe himself, curling a few small hairs. He burns his skin too, just when he thought, stupidly, he was beginning to master the distance.

IN THE MORNING, Cye wakes early. He tosses in bed, bargaining with his pillow. He pinches it between his kneecaps. Sheets spool around his legs. He'll give everything back, his money, his Suburban, especially all his crap decisions. He will do better. During early-morning hours he can sense the end rushing toward him. It feels like cold fingers pinching his throat, a slight shift in his chest cavity.

Cye stares at the note he stole off the highway cross. It sits on the end table. After a one-rinse shower, he pockets it.

Cye pounds on Nunez's door, and when Nunez answers, his eyelids are struggling. It's before dawn. They should head out, grab a bite, Cye says, bouncing on his heels. "I should drop you before the sun turns radioactive."

Daytime crosses are easier, Cye explains to Nunez as they drive south. He taps the wheel with both thumbs. "*Migra* aren't out en masse, like at night." But daytime crosses are dangerous, when the sun's highest, hottest, when the flats are stunning but at their absolute worst. Cye recites the horrors he's seen: grown men crying, tottering on their heels, as though they'd day-tripped through hell. Delirious eyes staring out from behind cracked, Gucci-imitation sunglasses. And then their minds, fully sun-drugged, their discombobulated words hitting the air diagonally.

"Not too late to just drive over," Cye says. He awaits a response from Nunez, but it doesn't come.

A diamondback basks in the middle of Interstate 8, west out of Yuma. Cye pit-stops at a pancake joint and orders six-deep flapjacks. He smothers the load in syrup. Nunez picks blueberries off the lid of a muffin. Lukewarm coffee slices through Cye's seven-beer hangover, while a bonfire builds in the pit of his stomach. He envisions a scalpel peeling off stomach lining. The fuckhead in Phoenix instructed Cye to eliminate alcohol, coffee, sugar—shit, everything he likes.

"Truly a man of few words," Cye says to Nunez, who's sitting quietly opposite. Nunez offers a small smile. Like the day before, he's dressed to the nines. They hop in the Suburban and drive on.

Desert is the perfect liar. Distances deceive. Everything appears closer-than. You have to respect and understand the land, or else.

Nunez tips the visor, denying a rising sun. Again, his attention wanders off into the view. He follows the landscape's rigid lines, its shadows produced by cliffs. Mesquite trees bathe in an endless amber sea.

Nunez says, quite suddenly, "I crossed with my friend Enrique." His Stetson bounces on his knee. "We came over at San Luis. That area was just abandoned ranches. And big sandlots."

Cye wants to draw him out, open him up. He says, "Right. Still lots of both."

"There was a larger ranch," Nunez says. "Mexican owned. It bled over the line."

"That so?" Cye says. Every border brother has a story. "You came over at night?"

Nunez nods. "We were a group. The guide we paid drove us to a field. He told us, crawl. And when we see horns, he said, go low, and crawl. That land was shredded. Bulls roamed it. Thousand-pound Brahmans with those long *burro* ears. Ever seen those?"

Cye says, "I don't believe so."

"The guide told us that *migra* didn't patrol private land. Enrique counted for hours. One hundred bulls. Two hundred. We crept around them. It was what we had to do. Through dried up piss clods and *mierda*. When some of the others stood to walk, *los toros* panicked. Two boys were trampled." Nunez traces the brim of his Stetson. "But Enrique and I crawled," he says. "And we moved low, in shit, and the beasts didn't mind us."

A quick, uncomfortable sadness overcomes Cye. He imagines a dark field sprinkled with easily spooked bulls and desperate men.

In the northbound lane, they both spot a checkpoint, two *migra* Broncos and a long white passenger van.

"See what I said," Cye says.

A row of heads, obviously illegals, decorates the van's windows like stilled *muñecas*.

Cye says, "They'll be fingerprinted, escorted back. Same old."

"Until next try," Nunez says.

"Right," Cye says.

Cye decides to dirt-road it. An inlet in the brush leads them south. At a crossroads, where Cye usually turns for El Cementerio, he drives straight. After a few miles, he knows he can stop at any time, drop Nunez, earn the five bills. But he keeps going. He wants to give Nunez a better-than-usual shot.

Cye knows of a dry floodwash. They drop downslope into it, tearing along the dusty playa. Soon they enter the Barry Goldwater Range, marked with yellow government signs, their stern military warnings long since defaced.

Nunez says, "Anywhere is good. Anywhere."

Cye doesn't stop. They pass a gigantic B-52 warplane embedded sideways into the earth. One wing points skyward and throws a long westward shadow, like a sundial. Across its side are gaping holes. Clearly it's been shelled. When the floodplain vanishes, Cye drives into a rocky open bowl. Brush scrapes his chassis.

It's the closest Cye's been to the border. There's no evidence of any line or boundary whatsoever. It's just rocks and cacti. In the distance, the bald peaks of the Tinajas Atlas Mountains smolder. Heat has already begun seeping through the windows. The air-conditioning can't contain it.

"Okay," Cye says, stopping. He stares ahead, gripping the wheel. "Okay," he says again.

A small bird pops from a pared hole in a nearby saguaro. Cye asks himself how that thing survives with all this constant pressure.

Nunez stuffs water bottles into his suitcase, adding more weight.

"Sure that outfit is the smartest idea?" Cye says to him. Even imagining walking through this baked desert in a suit makes him feel miserable.

Nunez dons his Stetson, crowning it all off. It's that toothy heart again, twinkling inside Nunez's mouth. And he says, "Think of the bulls." He says, "That night, and the men and the bulls. I crawled over in shit, *compadre*. I owe it to myself to walk back. My own two feet." Nunez struggles with the suitcase, counterbalancing to his left. Without a handshake, not even *adiós*, he turns and walks away.

He'll make it, Cye thinks. Nunez is like Cye's mom. He's that type. He has to make it.

Querida Rosa, reads the first line. Behind the wheel, Cye unfolds the crumpled note. It's a short paragraph, chicken-scratched in red ink. Turns out, it's a letter from the dead girl's mother. So. The girl's name is Rosa. Nineteen-year-old Rosa. *Querida Rosa . . .*

Third line in, Rosa's mother misspells the word *children*. *Childen*. She forgot her goddamn r. The mistake bothers Cye. How careless. Again he reads the lines, seven in all, which skip between English and Spanish, and he waits for the mother's sad, angry words to hook him in the throat and crush his lungs.

But nothing happens. Nothing happens, he realizes, because these words don't belong to him. They belong to a girl once named Rosa, a teenager who haunts the side of a lonely highway, who now lives inside others and on this lost piece of creased blue paper.

Cye idles along the border, left to wonder. There was blood again this morning in the toilet bowl.

He shreds the note and scatters the pieces on the dirt. Thin sheets of clouds, outlined in pink, shade Nunez from the sun as he walks. The farther he goes, through a meadow of stones, the more he shrinks.

Cye says, *"De nada."*

He jams the Suburban in drive and turns around. Cye rolls slowly over patches of cholla and scrub. There are few signs of anything in the desert. This comforts him for now. Cye knows the route. He's not certain of much. But he knows the direction home. SQ

NONFICTION:
ON WRITING

Dangers

AN ESSAY

by Rick Bass

Rick Bass, writer and environmental activist, is the author of more than twenty books of fiction, nonfiction, essays, and short stories. His most recent novel, *The Diezmo,* **published in hardcover by Houghton Mifflin in 2005, was first serialized online in** *Narrative.* **"Dangers" is adapted from a talk he gave at the Park City Writers Conference in the late 1980s at the beginning of his distin-guished career. Rick lives in Montana's Yaak Valley with his wife and daughters.**

BEGINNING WRITERS look for rules, guidelines, clever sayings that can be posted on a mirror, and these things are important, or at least they were for me. My apartment used to be cluttered with sayings such as Flaubert's "Live like a bourgeois and think like a demigod." I also had on my walls crazy sentences, lines I'd typed out of novels, lines that I liked for their rhythm or their content. I had hundreds of these snippets Scotch-taped all over my walls, so that anyone who might have happened into my apartment without knowing that writing was what I was up to in my spare time might have thought I was a madman, without sense or order or reason—which I might well have been.

I am no longer quite so loony with energy. Work is harder. You're never going to have it so good as you do when all your stories are new, when you've hardly ever told a story before, not a full one, not one that rings bells in your head and in all your readers' heads. What I am getting at is how lucky a young writer is to be pushing forward, learning, and developing—and though only halfway developed, good enough to know only that writing stories is what you want to do.

Later, once your stories are accepted with regularity, and the mechanical rabbit you've been chasing suddenly disappears—the rabbit of Being Published Often—you'll find that writing stories is not so much of a game or a goal anymore, but something riskier, a duty to yourself and your readers—something to be careful with. You move more slowly, more deliberately—cautiously—trying to guard your success. You're less reckless, and that's no fun, nor is it such a good thing for your writing. I don't know much of a theory about writing. My theory is more the theory of feeling, which is no theory at all.

All I know for sure is that art makes you feel things more strongly than you did before you looked at the art: happier, or sadder, or more frantic, or calmer. It makes you feel something better and bigger than your own life, whether your life's dull and boring or violent and original.

Art makes you forget your troubles; it's an escape, a suspension of reality.

But let's forget the theory of writing or feeling and talk instead about the theory of success—the success of feeling good about yourself and about your stories and characters.

Let's say you're able to smell the bacon frying, the coffee burning: you've seen you can live a full life, or be a writer. I can count on the fingers of maybe two hands the men and women I know who are great writers and who have also lived the fullest lives possible: people who have lived just as fully as if they hadn't been writers. I suspect there aren't many of these kinds of writers. But it's not too much to shoot for, is it—to enjoy life, and write well?

The odds, however, are against you; it's almost certain that you have to give up some aspect, some area of your life, regularly, in exchange for your writing. All too often, it seems, there will be a direct correlation between the degree of success in your writing and the loss of freedom.

A LUST TO CREATE ART can be good. Lust as if for bodily love, so that once the desire's been fulfilled—you've written a good story—there's only a brief flagging of the desire, and then it's time to begin another story, because the next one is the only important one.

This kind of lust is good for a writer, in part because it keeps you moving forward rather than looking fondly back.

I guess I'll give you some rules or theories after all.

These suggestions are drawn in response to weaknesses I've observed in students' work—mistakes that can be corrected.

Do not, after writing a scene in which your characters remain seated at a table after the only other people in a restaurant have gotten up and left, say, "They were alone now." Instead, for instance, after writing, "The man had his hand on the back of the woman's white satin dress. They followed the waitress into the next room," go on to say, "The cigarettes they left in the ashtray were still smoldering."

Now your remaining characters truly are alone, and we, the readers, are alone, too, whereas if the author had said, "They were alone now"—well, they would have been alone, but at the readers' expense: we wouldn't have felt like we were in the story, with whatever was going on at that lonely table, and that's no good.

Another common failing—and you'll notice that I'm talking about negatives, rather than positives (but writing's that simple: all you have to do is avoid the pitfalls, and you're home free)—is what I call the Old One-Two. I've sprained my wrist sometimes, marking so hard through the second trailing sentence on a student's paper, or on one of mine—the Echo Sentence, I call it—when the same thought, or concept, has been said better—often brilliantly—in the previous sentence, Sentence Number One of the Old One-Two. With a good enough first line, there needn't be a follow-up.

An example: in the following student's scene, a young boy is upset, having been given some bad news by his father. The passage is as follows: "I rushed from the house, oblivious to the cold air that hit me when I opened the door. I crossed the yard and started to circle the barn, my hands in my pockets, the frozen grass crunching under my boots, anger clawing inside me."

This is okay. But listen to the next sentence—listen to the buzz go off, the Echo Sentence: "I felt helpless, then, and upset."

Writing a story is like crossing a minefield. You cross the field, with the story loosely in your arms, and you try not to step on any of the mines.

OTHER MINES TO AVOID are using the wrong word—a verb, usually—or intruding and giving the reader a homily: "There's too much hate in the world," or "You can't count on anything." Sometimes the most dangerous intrusions are the innocent ones—descriptions, usually—that swing the reader's view away from the flow of the story, shifting the view to the wrong place at the wrong time.

Similes and metaphors, used improperly, create an effect of intrusion. Mastery in the use of metaphor comes with practice. Two all-time great metaphors are Eudora Welty's: "The faded red roses were the color of a bird dog's panting tongue" and "The buzz of the cicadas was like the sound of grain being poured into a metal bucket."

Don't compare bodies to car parts. This is a common affliction among beginning writers. "The blood in my veins felt like crankcase oil on a cold morning." No. A person is not a machine, and don't you forget it.

THE MATTER OF INTEGRITY in a story is also crucial. Choose the elements in your stories—characters, events, objects—carefully. What you put into a story from the beginning must be there at the end. Don't put too many elements into a story. It's more important to work thoroughly with the right elements than to have many elements.

STUDENTS OFTEN SAY, "But this really happened; I knew someone who did this," or, "I want to write about something that happened to me when I was fourteen."

Everyone writes about things that have actually happened. But it's all too easy to be impeded by a sense of the sanctity or literalness of the death of a friend, a bitter love story, a moment of initiation.

There's an enormous difference between being a story writer and being a regular person. As a person, it's your duty to stay on a straight and even keel, not to break down blubbering in the streets, not to pull rude drivers from their cars, not to swing from the branches of trees. But as a writer it's your duty to lie and to view everything in life, however outrageous, as an interesting possibility. You may need to be ruthless or amoral in your writing to be original. Telling a story straight from real life is only being a reporter, not a creator. You have to make your story bigger, better, more magical, more meaningful than life is, no matter how special or wonderful in real life the moment may have been.

Reality—if we use that word to indicate real life, and the way things really are— should always be viewed as a sheet of ice beneath which we, the writers (with our readers in tow) are swimming, trying constantly to punch through, so that we can breathe. With every sentence we write, we must be poised and alert to punch through and make the story better.

ANOTHER THING TO DO while working the minefields: Read poetry. Poets can teach us about words, phrases, lines, sentences, and the concentrated efforts of language.

IN A DAY'S WORK, quit when you start to feel tired—not after. Quit while you still know the direction of the story, or at least the next thought or even sentence, so that when you pick up the next day, you'll have that necessary momentum right from the beginning. Each day, get a full rest. While writing, concentrate: Don't have any distractions nearby, don't write in a room full of books if you can help it. Don't browse through anything else when the going gets slow.

THERE ARE DANGERS of writing, and there are also dangers of being a writer. Here's some advice: Take care of each other. Don't cross other writers. Don't get caught up in envy or passionate personal attacks or defenses.

Pettiness is always out there. Avoid it. Be willing to learn from other writers, as well as critics.

Write every day. Don't ever stop. If you are unpublished, enjoy the act of writing—and if you are published, keep enjoying the act of writing. Don't become self-satisfied, don't stop moving ahead, growing, making it new. The stakes are high. Why else would we write? **SQ**

A Short Short Theory

AN ESSAY

by Robert Olen Butler

Robert Olen Butler was born in Illinois, and his experiences in Vietnam inform much of his fiction. He is the author of ten novels and five short story collections, including *A Good Scent from a Strange Mountain*, which won the 1993 Pulitzer Prize. Butler's stories have appeared in *Best American Short Stories*, and he is the recipient of several literary prizes. He currently holds the Michael Shaara Chair in Creative Writing at Florida State University.

TO BE BRIEF, it is a short short story and not a prose poem because it has at its center a character who yearns.

Fiction is a temporal art form. Poetry can choose to ignore the passage of time, for there is a clear sense of a poem being an *object*, composed densely of words, existing in space. This is true even when the length of the line is not an objectifying part of the form, as in a prose poem. And a poem need not overtly concern itself with a human subject. But when you have a human being centrally present in a literary work and you let the line length run on and you turn the page, you are, as they say in a long storytelling tradition, "upon a time." And as any Buddhist will tell you, a human being (or a "character") cannot exist for even a few seconds of time on planet Earth without desiring something. *Yearning* for something, a word I prefer because it suggests the deepest level of desire, where literature strives to go. Fiction is the art form of human yearning, no matter how long or short that work of fiction is.

James Joyce spoke of a crucial characteristic of the literary art form, something he called the *epiphany*, a term he appropriated from the Catholic Church meaning, literally, a "shining forth." The Church uses it to describe the shining forth of the divinity of the baby Jesus. The word made flesh. In literary art, the flesh is made word. And Joyce suggests that a work of fiction moves to a moment at the end where something about the human condition shines forth in its essence.

I agree. But I also believe that all good fiction has two epiphanies. There is the one Joyce describes, and there is an earlier epiphany, very near the beginning of a story (or a novel), when the yearning of the character shines forth. This does not happen in explanatory terms but rather is a result of the presence of that yearning in all the tiny, sense-driven, organically resonant moments in the fiction, the accumulation of which reaches a critical mass which then produces that shining forth.

And because of the extreme brevity of the short short story, these two epiphanies often—even typically—occur at the same moment. The final epiphany of a literary short short is also the shining forth of the character's yearning.

It has been traditional to think that a story has to have a "plot," while a poem does not. Plot, in fact, is yearning challenged and thwarted. A short short story, in its brevity, may not have a fully developed plot, but it must have the essence of a plot: yearning. SQ

Solo Notes

A JOURNAL

by Gail Godwin

Gail Godwin has earned three National Book Award nominations for work that includes five *New York Times* best sellers. In 2006 *The Making of a Writer: Journals, 1961–1963* was published, and in 2008 the concluding volume covering 1963–1970 is due out, along with *The Red Nun: A Tale of Unfinished Desires. Solo Notes,* a work in progress excerpted here, distills Godwin's journals and is meant to be a companion to *The Making of a Writer.*

Solo Notes: January–May 2007

Monday, January 14, 2007

34–40°

REACHED PAGE 300 today. About five more pages to go on chapter 14, "Tildy's Struggles." Then I will make a new file and begin part 2 of *The Red Nun*, chapter 15, with some 2007 emails between former classmates Maud Norton Martinez in Palm Beach and Rebecca Meyer Birnbaum in NYC.

I washed and dried my sheets and put them back on the bed. Went to Sunfrost and bought a roasted chicken, roasted vegetables, and a vegetarian shepherd's pie, all made today for the Martin Luther King weekenders who'd rather spend the money than make the dishes themselves. Got home, read the paper, gave each cat a chicken wing. Now they are both on the clean sheets, the chicken wings with them in various states of diminishment.

This has been a good day. First the milestone of getting to page 300. That's over half the book or more. And I know so much more about the shape than I did a year ago.

Thursday, January 18, 2007

DIALOGUE #1 with My Heart

GG: Heart? How am I weighing you down? Clogging you up? Stressing you out? How can I live to make you sing? Heart, it's hard to find the right tone toward you. I feel our pulse. Not slow. Not fast. Steady. A steady march. Do you like marching? Would you like to go slower when we're at rest?

Heart: Oh, you and I are alike. We're very close. It's more than pump and march. It's *when do you feel at home and when do you feel in alien territory?* You've had some experience of this today and it wearied us. You know that ___ doesn't have the space for humor. She protects herself, she has to. A person—and a heart—has to have the space and the leisure to see what's funny and to take solace from the funny. Let's explore this further, and then you may want to rest. Who do you know who has the space for humor? You know more people who don't. Did M? No. Did C? No. Did Tom? Yes, big time. Did Robert? Big time. Why is it so important? Because it's open, generous, exploring, not tight and protective and closed off.

Friday, January 19, 2007

DIALOGUE #2 with My Heart

GG: It's been a while now, since late December, since I've felt that worrisome twinge on the left side. You taught me about a sense of humor in our last talk. That was a real surprise. What else can I do to free you from clogs and to streamline our time together?

Heart: Streamline. Siphon. Sift. Keep the lumps out. You and I have developed a skill for recognizing *blockage*. You know what blockage is and where it comes from. It is what says, Stop! No! on our sauntering sojourn. It is hectic, desperate, and, most of all, untrue. It is what you *are not* and what you *don't need*. Go quickly, the shortest route: keep the dirt clouds and miasmas *out*.

GG: Where are the exciting projects that will call out new parts of myself?

Heart: Stimulus is fine. Clots and clutter aren't. Take chances as long as the air stays clean and brisk. If it clouds up, drop your project in the dust of the road and *move on*.

Saturday, January 20, 2007

28° TODAY, biting wind

Monie [Gail's maternal grandmother] died thirty-five years ago today. Gingie [Gail's and Robert's orange tiger tomcat] also died in 1987 on this day.

My Waldo [Siamese brother of Zeb] has arranged himself on my arm and chest as I write. He is being very blue-eyed and fetching.

DIALOGUE #3 with My Heart

GG: Heart, I've been reading a novel (*Author, Author*, by David Lodge) about Henry James.

He died at seventy-two. He never exercised. Was overweight. Went to 107 dinner parties in a single year.

I will be seventy in June. Go faithfully and grudgingly to Breathe Fitness twice a week and work out with Kenny. Am ten pounds overweight. Went to (ten?) dinner parties last year.

Robert, the last night in the ICU, told his nurse, Ed: "Each year I could do less and less." Robert was seventy-seven and in horrible shape. Yet he wrote music and finished a song, "The Lake," his last day in this house.

Today I had all day to write. I didn't write. It's still afternoon, and the wind is blowing, and soon I'll go to bed. Am I losing strength, or is this just my winter mode? How can I *absolutely honor* what strength you are pumping into me?

Heart: Don't fret anymore about that. Fretting is, as they say, contraindicated. Just feel your way along and do what you can. You are beginning part 2. You have to know who these women are *now*. You have a chance to come at "unfinished desires" from their adult points of view. Maud Norton Martinez and Rebecca Birnbaum, former classmates, have both done work with young people fighting their social systems. The wind whistles. A lovely sound we won't hear when we've stopped.

And remember to *feel* as you write. Just that. Get the feel of "living with all my heart" even if it hurts.

Wednesday, January 24, 2007

I HAVE TO REDO what I've done so far on "Correspondence." Rebecca wouldn't have said so much in her first letter.

Wednesday, January 31, 2007

2:13 A.M.

I no longer think "insomnia." I sleep when I sleep. Other people sleep when they sleep. Lately I have read a lot of accounts of people wanting to be more famous, better known, better at something other than what they are good at. Poor H. James wanting to be a playwright and getting booed off the stage. Wanting and envying Du Maurier's *Trilby* readership. And tonight, reading the introduction to Dodie Smith's *I Capture the Castle*: how she hungered for a lasting reputation, how she worked, how she insisted on writing four volumes of her memoirs.

7ISH P.M.

Worked for two hours on *The Red Nun*. Sailed through 2.5 pages. Chapter 16, "The Christmas Critic," is one of those bonus chapters. Meant to spring everything forward. I love Madeline. Where did she come from?

The Sears vacuum cleaner broke again yesterday, and Yolanta says it is junk and can't be fixed. I called the Electrolux store in Kingston, and the man said, "Oh, please come in, I'm here all by myself." I drove to Kingston. It turned out he was the owner of three Electrolux franchises and had given the local employees the day off. He demonstrated everything I asked for and showed me the proper way to drag the cord behind me without getting tangled up in it. He's been with Electrolux twenty-seven years. Was/is a drummer. I asked him if he was wearing Allen Edmonds shoes. He looked pleased. No, he had a pair of Allen Edmonds shoes, but these were Bostonians. What a great little creature this vacuum is. He assembled one for me and carried the whole thing (extra bags, filters, potions to kill dust mites and odors) to the Jeep and said: "We will always provide this kind of service to you."

Wednesday, February 7, 2007

LISTENING TO ROBERT'S Clarinet Quintet (1992). So proud and grateful that both of us—and together—got to do so much of what we were compelled to do. It's hard to exactly describe, but I do feel like a living ghost. Robert is so present in my inner life and dreams. Last night I dreamed he was lying outside in the rain, on a chair, covered by a blue tarpaulin. He was being rained on, his legs were splayed, at first I thought he was dead. His mouth was just that thin double line. But then he woke up, and I said, "Stay very still, and I will fix everything." How I love my Robert, dead, in dreams, in my writing, in my conversations with others. Yet how we *combatted.* But he was grateful for me, too. ("I am never bored by you.") And also, I was thinking today, as I slouched . . . alone . . . toward the new cardiology suite at Benedictine Hospital to have my pacemaker read: he must have taken comfort in knowing I was there with him, that I was younger—thirteen years younger for half the year; twelve years for the other half—and that I could drive him to the doctors, drive him through the dark!

8:39 P.M.

Called Suzette Hayes on her deathbed. She's eighty-three. They expect her to die any day, but she was totally lucid. ("Do I hear a Southern accent?") She described her assisted-living quarters to me: her furniture, the fireplace, the color of the walls, the view from the window. I told her how much she meant to Robert and me when we moved to Stone Ridge in 1973 and knew nobody. How I admired her daughter, Carrie, and that she, Suzette, was a heroine.

Wednesday, March 14, 2007

STRAINED MYSELF TODAY, starting a new character, Mother Frances Galyon, in the chapter "Two Nuns on a Walk." Felt insufficient about everything, longitude and latitude and airport terminology. Just kept going on for one, one and a half pages, for three hours. Then, wiped out, I drove to the Ashokan Reservoir and walked the old walk. It was a balmy 72° with warm, wanton winds, and I walked down and back along the causeway with a number of others looking dazed by the weather. Two older men. Two women gesturing and exchanging confidences—"I've decided to accept it. He has two dogs, bigger than we are, but . . ." When I got home Anne was leaving, and Carl had just finished grouting the shower. He had brought me a copy of the photo he took of the eagle on the ground, eating its fish in the snow.

Monday, March 19, 2007

EVENING

Just listening to the Dean of Nashville Cathedral, on a CD, talk about C. S. Lewis's *The Great Divorce* made me want to write a short ontological fantasy, maybe after *The Red Nun*. Myself, or a female protagonist, between heaven and hell.

Tuesday, March 20, 2007

MORNING

Woke with a positive take on things. I have a book to reread. *Our Mutual Friend*. I recall a bare minimum of a dream in which I hear myself talking (a recording?) and am impressed by the playfulness. The engaging voice. Definitely worth listening to.

The feeling that if I could locate a certain lock-click, a release, my stories and writing would be immense and free and a delight. Almost as if I tilted to a different angle. Something as simple as the equinox?

Thursday, March 22, 2007

MORNING

A nurse from Dr. Lader's office called. Results of my nuclear stress test were "completely normal."

EVENING

Continued with "Two Nuns on a Walk." Got to page 374.

The Episcopalians are at last realizing themselves. Turned down the ultimatum from "The Anglican Communion" that a committee of bishops from abroad must come to the U.S. and "administer" on behalf of the antigay conservatives. I hope we split off from these fossils. We parted from England in the 1770s.

Sunday, March 25, 2007

EVENING

John Irving called about 7:00, and we talked for an hour. He goes into Dartmouth Hospital for major surgery a week from Monday, and he told me Vonnegut has been in a coma for several days. He was sitting on the steps of his brownstone, smoking a cigarette, and fell to the pavement on his head. John's voice, not as gruff as in the old days, was kind and full of love. He has about 134 pages of *Last Night at Twisted River* and has started keeping a journal. He said it was after reading my *Making of a Writer, Volume One* with Rob Neufeld's footnotes. "I was mad I hadn't kept journals. Now I have to write the journal *and* my own footnotes."

Thinking of the workshop at Iowa in 1967. Of Vonnegut, our guru teacher. Of John the young father. I really got to know John when we both came back to teach in 1972–73. He brought Brendan by in a stroller to my Walnut Street house and we sat in the kitchen and talked about our books in progress. My *Odd Woman*. His *158-Pound Marriage*. Our closeness has always been through our passion for our work. I used to resent him for promoting himself better than I could. He could rattle off his prospects. That awful man from the NEA, a would-be poet—to whom I said all the wrong things out of sheer nervousness. Then John drove me home, and I wept in the car because I had been so stupid and the man had snapped at me. "How do you always present yourself so well!" I accused John. That was thirty-five years ago.

Wednesday, March 28, 2007

EVENING

Well, back and forth, to and from NYC, to Suzette Hayes's memorial service at St. John the Divine. Most of six hours sitting still. The driver, a retired army sergeant, taught soldiers to shoot, and then he worked for UPS, teaching drivers how to manage the UPS tractor-trailers. Now he does all the contract work he can get for Sutton Transportation. But he has also bought a Cadillac and will now be a self-employed driver. He has four children, three at home, the youngest nine. He parked the car at the cathedral and walked to a nearby park and ate his packed lunch in the sun "and watched people" while I was in St. James Chapel at the service.

Friday, March 30, 2007

MORNING

Time for a *reculer pour mieux sauter*. When I started this novel in 2004, I had a title, *The Red Nun: A Tale of Unfinished Desires*, and a school (unnamed) and some nuns (unnamed) and a cluster of girls (unnamed and uncharacterized, except I knew that as a group they were catalytic and that there was something in their combined backgrounds that would raise psychological ghosts, the kind I'm most wary of). At first I didn't know that the frame would be eighty-five-year-old Mother Ravenel's school memoir, published in 2006 and covering incidents as long ago as 1893. And it was a year more before I knew that there was going to be a frame *beyond hers*: the frame of what all of them would tell if we could put it in one book.

Palm Sunday, April 1, 2007

NEXT WILL BE Maud's chapter, 21, "Unmerited Degradation." In which I can face fully the horror of a young girl experiencing the social consequences of her lust.

Monday, April 2, 2007

EVENING

John came out as fine as possible. The surgeon cut no muscle. He can go home tomorrow and write his screenplays and novels and go on with his life.

Good Friday, April 6, 2007

MORNING

Six years ago Mother Winters died at the nuns' retirement residence in Boston. She had always wanted to die on Good Friday, as her brother Patrick, the bishop, had managed to do. And then ten days later, six years ago, Robert died in Kingston Hospital.

EVENING

I still need my Good Friday. So today I did not write but went an hour early to Kingston to get three thirty-pound bags of PA-PURR, the biodegradable cat litter. I also stopped at Adams and got grouper stuffed with crabmeat and had them pack it in ice. Then set off to Christ the King in Stone Ridge. I guess no Holy Week service will ever come up to those of Fr. Edward Meeks at St. Mary's, Asheville, but the short homily of Fr. Allan Ford was the most basic, heartfelt, and heartbroken commentary on Good Friday that I have ever heard. There he stood. In the aisle. That black, black, tall, elegant, slightly stooped priest, exactly my age, and he spoke of the indignities, the insults, the floggings, the crucifixion. Tears sprang into his eyes. And I thought, He believes this. At what level do I believe, compared to his level? Then I went to David's, gave him his share of the fish, and cut his hair for Easter. His friend Sandy stopped by, to advise him about the color of his house. She was beautifully dressed: rich real-estate lady in her late '60s. Thin. White-gold hair. Dark glasses perched on top of coif. Layers: purple turtleneck, black scarf, black hacking jacket with turned-up light brown suede cuffs. Loose, cuffed gray slacks, belted, with the turtleneck tucked *in*. Dark socks and dark blue Italian suede loafers. She was at first a little taken aback, then fascinated by, the haircutting scene. I said, "I don't have a license." I snipped toward D's Julius Caesar look while they gabbed about people, houses, furniture, more furniture, and then she tootled off in her little Mercedes to sell more real estate.

Wednesday, April 11, 2007

EVENING

I did over six hundred words today. I'm drained when I finish. Carl came and carried the three bags of cat litter up to the bathroom and put the potting soil in the garage. He brought in some firewood, and then I asked him to take a look at the yellow mailbox at the foot of the hill. It wobbles, I think someone rammed into it. Tomorrow I will hit page 400. Oh, and I listened to that Minnesota Public Radio program I thought I did so badly on. But I was charming, amused, said some relatively memorable things.

Sunday, April 15, 2007

2:30 A.M.

Rain, wet snow, sleet—now at 40° it's ploppy rain again. Read *What Maisie Knew* for the first time. And felt sorry for poor dead Linda Gray, my former publisher at Ballantine, who told me of her summer school at Harvard when she simply could not read *The Wings of the Dove* and she dropped out and her father refused to speak to her for the rest of the summer because she had not seized her chance. I also wondered what a novel would be like if it were as subtle as *Maisie* without all the Jamesian syntax. In which a young woman keeps putting together glimmers of her moral self and emerges unscathed.

Monday, April 16, 2007

MORNING

Wild screeching winds, heavy rain, full pond, forsythia almost in bloom. I spent all yesterday in pajamas reading *What Maisie Knew* and then *Ravelstein* again. Mentally lowered myself, again and again, into Maud's dance at the Everglades Club. Thought up Troy Veech!

AFTERNOON

Worked from 11 to 1-something. Only half a page, written over and over. Decided to approach the next scene from Maud's (limited) experience of country clubs. Then got into Googling the Everglades Club, which led to possible metaphors for layers of involvement/getting lost in the labyrinth of social desires. This chapter, "Unmerited Degradation," certainly seems to call to me.

Tuesday, April 17, 2007

EVENING

crawled from page 406 to 407. I'll get there. Went to Kenny and worked out. Anne started filing my bills for next year's deductibles. She is light-years more organized and responsive than most.

Thursday, April 19, 2007

MORNING

Decided, just this minute, to call my country club for Maud's humiliation "the Palm City Club." That way I can design it and landscape it the way I need, make it as sinister and labyrinthine as I like: "deteriorated magnificence." A perfect murky archetypal place for the perils of social climbing. And Palm City was the first name for Palm Beach.

David took me for a splendid dinner at Gigi's in Rhinebeck. Red snapper with mussels on a bed of artichokes, and we even had desserts. Afterward, to the performance at Bard of *Jane Eyre* by the Acting Company. Big auditorium of the Fisher Center almost filled. Too big a space for this sort of production. I found myself impatient of theater, stage, strained voices. The actress who played Jane had a rasping, antagonizing voice. The gist behind the production was that Jane/Bertha Rochester were two halves of the same psyche. This also felt strained. But I like HAVING GONE OUT FOR THE EVENING. Was also elated to get home and sit on the cat-clawed sofa with Waldo and Zeb on my legs and drink a glass of sauvignon blanc.

Friday, April 20, 2007

WELL, TOMORROW is the "private gathering" for Kurt V. at the Algonquin. David Plimpton is going, and John Casey is coming up from Virginia. John isn't going because of his surgery, and neither am I. John has been in frequent touch with Kurt's daughter Nanny. Kurt's son and daughters were required by the widow to submit "guest lists" of the people they invited to the gathering so she could vet them. The widow's list, however, remains unshared.

Saturday, April 21, 2007

MORNING

first curly red leaf buds unfurling on the big tulip poplar to the north. Torn between wanting to go up to Maud, but thinking I ought to empty the dishwasher and get rid of the pans in the sink—and totally clean the refrigerator—and go to the dump—and sweep the deck—and prepare the pots for planting—and swim. Which will I do?

EVENING

Report on day's progress. Well, I imagined Robert shouting, "You make so much FUSS over little things! Why not just empty the dishwasher and . . ." So in less than thirty minutes I emptied the dishwasher, washed the dirty pans, totally cleaned the refrigerator, went upstairs, and Googled "dance cards" for Maud and found twenty million entries, some accompanied by waltzes. Then wrote some more on my dance scene. Then went to P.O. and had a late lunch (turkey club) in an empty dining room at the Dragon Fly and watched the rushing stream. When I got home Loren Shultis and his landscaping crew had come to rake the gravel and clean the beds, and I was so relieved I didn't have to "go garden." Now, six years later to the date, we're reaching the time of evening when, at Kingston Hospital, I'm saying good-night to Robert, never to see him alive again, and he's sitting on the side of his bed and rumbling, "We still have some time together." For some reason this year seems worse than usual. Why couldn't I have had a bigger heart? Yet he loved me despite the paltry one I had.

Sunday, April 22, 2007

SUNRISE WAS AT 6:06

At 7:30 a.m., six years ago, which was also a Sunday, the phone rang, and a man said: "Is this Gail Godwin? This is Doctor Brown. I have bad news. Robert didn't make it."

It is over again for another year.

EVENING

Went to Christ the King in Stone Ridge and enjoyed the choir, the Anglican chant, the warmth of people who like me, and Fr. Allan's excellent sermon on Being Called. And why Jesus had to ask Peter three times: "Do you love me? Do you love me? Do you love me?" Jim Dinsmore and Father Bill Benson also came, playing hookey from St. Gregory's. They were much fussed over. David and I had lunch with them and then, on Jim's recommendation, I went off to Augustine Nursery to order eight mature boxwoods to replace the laurel and rhododendrons the deer ravaged. David said, "I prayed for Robert. Today was his anniversary." Yes, I know.

Monday, April 23, 2007

EVENING

Continued on with the reception line at the Palm City Club. I go so slowly but no longer flog myself. This is all I can do. Page. Page. Page. Just as Troy Veech is complimenting Mrs. Weatherby, I suddenly realized they'd slept together. And who clued me in on this level of knowingness but old Henry James himself. On I go tomorrow. Toward Maud's great blunder. But it brings her such knowledge—at quite a price. Went out in 80° weather to Gallo's and bought four flats of pansies, two orange and two yellow. Came home and planted. Very calming. You think thoughts. Your fingernails get dirty. Talked to Bud from 4:00 to 4:45 about the devil dream. I have work to do. I didn't want to have a written dialogue with this devil, so instead I will just write about why he was so awful and see where that brings me. "Dreams come not to destroy us, but to guide and heal us."

Wednesday, April 25, 2007

EVENING

Went on with Maud at the dance, to page 415. Anne and I were going to garden, but it started raining. So she worked on my archive files for Chapel Hill and I built a great fire, using as kindling the stalks of the one butterfly bush I got cut down before the rain. Carl came, and together we (mostly he) turned my mattress and he replaced a light in the bathroom. I have been happy today because I mostly get to live as I want. I have a project that expands me. My heart seems to be okay, till further notice. And somehow I have fixed it so I don't have to spend time with people I hate or even those who irritate me. This is fortunate indeed.

Thursday, April 26, 2007

I NEVER HAD a Troy Veech. A true snake in the garden. What did I have? Let's see. Frank W., when he was twenty-four, an officer at Ft. Bragg, and I was nineteen at Peace College. I found some of his old letters as a result of Anne's reorganizing my files. And maybe a little of B., before he found marriage and Jesus.

Troy Veech is an odd combination: disenchanted, cynical, dissolute, self-pampering, a little mean, he's not above spoiling a party or spoiling a girl or sleeping with an older married woman. But enough elegance and complexity and empathy to keep Maud out for the second half of the dance. He's also a romantic and a failed idealist. Could he end up a suicide?

Monday, April 30, 2007

EVENING

What happens after Troy Veech says: "Oh, we've got plenty of time"? How does a storyteller face/ace THAT one? I wrote from 10 to 2 and did 670 words (three complete pages) and then went limp for the rest of the day. I had planned to finish planting those pansies but lost all desire and simply watered the flats. Went to Hurley Ridge and bought milk, no-fat half-and-half, three-way lightbulbs, hot mustard, more Splenda, two boneless pork chops, a hydroponic Boston lettuce, a cuke, six-grain bread, two bottles of Newhaven Sauvignon Blanc from New Zealand, which, very cold, has become my favorite. At $13.

A dreadful thought: this novel will engage nobody but myself. It is a spread-out, multicharactered, multigenerational nothing. Well, to quote myself preaching to Anne, who has begun her novel: "Don't be afraid to FAIL." I am compelled to see it to the end just to see how it turns out, and also because I am dying to see the pattern made when all the parts are present and accounted for. At first I had thought it would be a "solo voices" kind of novel, one solo after another, but now it has evolved into, not a symphony, but more of a concerto for a community chamber orchestra. All the individual parts are needed, but in concert with one another they add up to something more. Read a horrible piece in *The New Yorker*. How one ages. The tooth enamel breaks down. The mouth dries. The balance goes. Old people neglect their feet. They fall. Twenty percent never walk again. Zebbie on my knees. Waldo neatly folded on top of the sofa, looking over my right shoulder. Soon they will have been here two years. Late sun on the white birch trunks.

Tuesday, May 1, 2007

MORNING

"Mayday!" Robert's *Pantagleize* opera based on Michel de Ghelderode's play in which the innocent Pantagleize decides to greet everyone with "What a lovely day!" which, unknown to him, is a signal for a revolution to begin. Just the sort of thing that R. loved. He got the widow's permission and went to work. "A farce to make you sad."

Outside the bedroom window, the Japanese maple leaves are just uncurling, and behind them the cherry tree in full blossom. I've been thinking about death a lot. Not morbidly, but musingly and curiously. There are apertures through which one almost glimpses . . . what? A kind of swirling ether in which death and life coexist. Death is present in my musings on it. And there's an almost touching of something, or toward something. I could not muse so steadily on death if I didn't love life so much. Robert has taught me a lot about death. He was always so aware of it. He carried it everywhere he went and—paradox—maybe that's why he lives so much for me now. He was always, daily, crossing over. Visiting death. Going back and forth. As he continues to go back and forth now. Soon, within days, the new leaves will block out the winter view of the Berkshires. Then I'll be inside the green wall of summer. Waldo in the open window is miffed and then downright horrified as the obscene noise of the power mower and weed whackers grows louder. Finally he loses it and dives under the bed. But they, too, will go away—and come back.

Up soon to finish (I hope) Maud's chapter, "Unmerited Degradation." Then what? Possibly time for another "everybody" chapter. But with something startling. Some switch of perspective. Some "Oh, NO!" from an unexpected point of view. I think I know what. SQ

1171250

Made in the USA